The Sea of Silence

The Sea of Silence

Seth Hunter

MᴄBᴏᴏᴋs Pʀᴇss
Guilford, Connecticut

McBooks Press
An imprint of The Rowman & Littlefield Publishing Group, Inc.
4501 Forbes Blvd., Ste. 200
Lanham, MD 20706
www.rowman.com

Distributed by NATIONAL BOOK NETWORK

British Library Cataloguing in Publication Information available

Library of Congress Cataloging-in-Publication Data available

ISBN 978-1-4930-5919-5 (hardcover: alk. paper)
ISBN 978-1-4930-5920-1 (e-book)

♾™ The paper used in this publication meets the minimum requirements of American
National Standard for Information Sciences – Permanence of Paper for Printed Library
Materials, ANSI/NISO Z39.48–1992.

Prologue

A Tale of Two Cities

Washington, November 1801. There had been a blizzard for the last two days and nights and though the wind had dropped, the city, which was still mostly fields and woodland, was covered by a thick fall of snow. The few buildings that had been completed, which normally rose out of a sea of mud and debris, looked very fine in this new setting, particularly the Capitol and the Executive Mansion, but it was bitterly cold and most citizens chose to stay indoors. A parade had been organised to welcome those arriving for the new session of Congress, but it had been called off because of the weather – and because most of the Congressmen had either frozen to death in their carriages on the way here or were making themselves as comfortable as possible in whatever inns and private homes they could find to accommodate them until the roads were cleared.

In the capital itself this process was already underway, hindered by a few bands of hardy urchins who were doing what urchins normally do at the first serious fall of snow. Two such war parties were thus engaged on the road designated M street which bordered the river, but they broke off pelting each other as a coach-and-four bore down on them and pelted it instead, much to the annoyance of the coachman who was having enough trouble keeping the horses steady without a hail of missiles. They could not have known that inside the coach was the President of the

United States and the Secretary of the Navy, but had they done so they would doubtless have pelted it anyway.

The carriage continued down to the river where it drew to a halt and the two dignitaries availed themselves of the steps pulled out by the footman, followed by a third gentleman who maintained a discreet distance.

The three stood for a moment in their fur coats and hats, stamping their feet a little and surveying the untamed wilderness that lay before them. Here, as in most of the city, there were a few skeletal frames of buildings taking shape, but they looked as if they still had a long way to go. One of the new senators, presently stranded on the road, had remarked that it was not such a bad city, and that 'to make it perfect, it needed only houses, inns, cellars, kitchens, well-informed men, amiable women and other little trifles of this kind'. But he was from New York where sarcasm was widely regarded as wit.

'So, this is the Washington Navy Yard,' said the president, whose name was Jefferson.

'It will be,' said the secretary, whose name was Smith. He may have sighed.

'So where are all the ships?' said Jefferson.

Mr Smith tilted his head in polite enquiry. There being no clarification of the president's remark he put a question of his own.

'What ships?'

'*Our* ships,' said the president dryly. 'Our *Navy*.'

He smiled at the expression on the secretary's face, and Mr Smith perceived that this was an example of presidential humour. Thus provoked, he reminded the president that he had sent the navy to the Coast of Barbary, some 5,000 miles to the east, with orders to remain there, delivering whatever retribution was necessary until the beys and emirs of that region had agreed to stop pirating American ships and selling their passengers and crews into slavery.

The president frowned.

'I understood that we sent but four ships to Barbary.'

'Three ships and a schooner,' the secretary informed him. The president, not being a seafaring man, might not know the difference, but the secretary did. He was not a seafaring man himself – he had served the war in the Continental Army and fought at the Battle of Brandywine – but he had been a lawyer for many years and prided himself on mastering his brief. A schooner was not a ship.

'Then what of the others?'

'There are no others,' said Mr Smith. He tried to look amused, but the joke was wearing a bit thin. November was no time to be standing around on the banks of the Potomac in a fur coat cracking jokes, and if there was a better reason to be here, Mr Smith had yet to be informed of it. It was not as if there was much to see. Building on the yard had commenced almost two years since, but Congress had been unproductive with the funding and it did not seem to have advanced very much.

'I understood that six ships had been commissioned,' the president said.

'This is true,' his companion agreed. 'We have three more on the stocks in Baltimore and Philadelphia, but they will not be ready for service until next year – at the earliest,' he added, to be on the safe side.

'So, we are without any means of defence?'

This conversation was taking a very strange turn in Mr Smith's view. It was not a subject that had overly concerned the president in the past.

'Well, there is the army, of course,' he said.

'Do you know the size of the army?'

'A little over four thousand officers and men,' replied Mr Smith, who took a lively interest in the other departments of state, having little to distract him in his own.

'Quite,' said Mr Jefferson, 'and most of them are on the western frontier fighting the Indians.'

Where else should they be, thought the secretary, but he asked a different question.

'Is this of particular concern to you, sir?'

'It could be,' the president replied. 'If there were to be a war.'

The secretary nodded wisely as if in consideration of this eventuality, but mainly to hide his rising irritation and his sense that the president was possibly becoming senile.

'And does that appear likely?' he enquired.

'Mr Imlay seems to think so,' said the president. He turned to their companion who had wandered off a few paces and raised his voice slightly. 'Do you not, Mr Imlay?'

'Sir?' The third man came back to join them. He was a tall, well-built man of middling years with what might flatteringly be called patrician features, if that was a compliment in a Republic. Mr Smith had not met him before today, but he had heard tell of him and what he had heard he did not like. He had heard that he was a spy, though America did not have spies, officially. He had also heard that he had interests in the shipping business and had made his money smuggling soap into France in the years after the Revolution when it was in short supply. He was also a writer, though the secretary had not read any of his books. One of them was a novel, he had heard.

'Mr Imlay thinks we should be prepared for war,' the president informed him in a tone that was difficult to judge. It might have been serious; it might have been jesting. 'So, I thought he should see what preparations have been made.'

The secretary gazed once more about the empty building site. They really were a long way behind schedule. He thought he should probably put some pressure on the contractors; Congress, too, so that they might be paid at some point. It occurred to him that this might be the chief reason the president had brought them down here. He asked the question that had been on his mind for some few minutes now.

'War with who – precisely? If it is not to betray a confidence? The British, the French . . . the Emperor of China?'

Brest, November 1801. The most westerly port in France, at the very end of the province called Finisterre, which is to say in English the End of the World, having been named long before Columbus found another one across the ocean. The harbour and the roadstead were filled with ships, but most were discernible only as dim, dark outlines, phantoms in the mist. They included fifteen ships of the line which the French called *vaisseaux*, five more known as *flûtes* whose guns had been stripped from the lower decks to accommodate passengers or troops, and three frigates. The numbers were not unusual, for the French Atlantic fleet had been locked in Brest by the blockade imposed by the British for almost a decade now, and the one time it had escaped it had been so badly misused it had been obliged to come hurrying back. What was unusual was the level of activity. For the waters of the harbour and the Brest Roads were heaving with smaller vessels of many kinds, scurrying like water beetles between ships and shore, laden with troops and munitions, water and provisions and whatever else was necessary to sustain them on a long voyage, while the streets leading down to the harbour were crammed with marching troops and horses and wagons and gun limbers.

Among the troops waiting to embark were a number of Poles who had enlisted in the armies of Revolutionary France for love of liberty, equality and fraternity, and in hopes of bringing some of it back to their benighted homeland which had been occupied for many years by the loathsome Russians. In the meantime, they had been fighting for the French in many other parts of Europe and had been recalled from the borders of Austria to join in this new venture, though no one had yet told them what it was or where they were going. There was speculation that it was England or Ireland, which made sense as they were in Brest, and they were not sanguine about this. It was not for fear of the British army, which was known to be negligible and incompetent, but for fear of the British ships which they knew were waiting for them somewhere out of sight of land. But now a new rumour spread that they were headed for the Americas. This seemed unlikely but they had been in the French army long enough to know that anything was possible. Some of their comrades had been sent to fight in Egypt and were still there by all accounts, trapped there by those formidable British ships.

Another rumour spread that General Bonaparte himself was to lead them, which was excellent news if it was true, for he had yet to lose a battle, though he had left his army in Egypt to do the best they could without him. This rumour gathered substance when a closed carriage with six fine horses turned up at the harbour with an escort of cavalry and a coat of arms on the door consisting of two diagonal stripes and two gold stars on a red shield. These were the arms of the Bonaparte family, one of the corporals announced. His name was Florjan Bruski and he was a former student of the University of Paris, which gave his opinions some weight – at least on the subject of heraldry. Besides, his comrades had been waiting for transport for several hours now and were bored enough to consider any rumour, however unlikely. But when the carriage just stood there with the drapes pulled down and no Bonaparte stepped out, and the escort dismounted and lounged about looking as bored as they were, they moved on to other subjects.

In fact, Corporal Bruski was right about the coat of arms, and the occupant of the carriage was indeed a Bonaparte, though not the one the soldiers had hoped for. It contained the lesser figure of his sister, Pauline, a spirited young woman of twenty-one, who was accounted a famous beauty and was about to embark on the greatest adventure of her life, though owing to the unsettled nature of the times and her own impetuous nature, she had already had more adventures than her years might propose. And the reason she was sitting in a carriage in Brest in November 1801, with an escort of cavalry, was because she had been married, at her brother's insistence, to General Charles-Victor-Emmanuel Leclerc, who had just been appointed captain general of the largest armada ever to leave the shores of France.

As well as the ships lost in the mist of the *Rade de Brest*, lesser squadrons were being made ready in six other ports, along with 20,000 soldiers of the French army, and though it was known to only a few of those about to embark, their mission – their glorious destiny, as Bonaparte had put it – was to forge a new French empire across the Atlantic.

For the young captain general – known to his intimates not without irony as 'the blond Bonaparte' – it was an opportunity to win the fame and riches that had thus far escaped him. For Pauline, who had been wrenched from her beloved Paris, it was a personal tragedy and a victory for her hag of a sister-in-law, Josephine, who had doubtless contrived the whole operation to banish her most dangerous rival to the far ends of the earth and thereby retain her leadership of fashionable society.

But she was a brave soul, with an irrepressible spirit and an optimistic nature. Her younger brother, Jérôme, was to accompany her as an officer-cadet in the navy, and she was persuaded that Napoleon would not have risked the lives of his favourite brother and sister, and so much of his own prestige on the venture unless he was assured of its success. Cap-Francais, the old capital of Saint-Domingue, was known in France as the Paris of the Antilles, and while that did not inspire Pauline as much as it might, there were other inducements that her esteemed brother had not failed to tempt her with. 'You will be the Queen of the Americas' were his parting words when she had left him at Malmaison.

So, either she would return to Paris a heroine, radiant with glory, or create such a brilliant court in the New World, the Witch Josephine would be left gnashing her rotting teeth in an extremity of rage and envy in the third-rate knocking shop she had made of the Old.

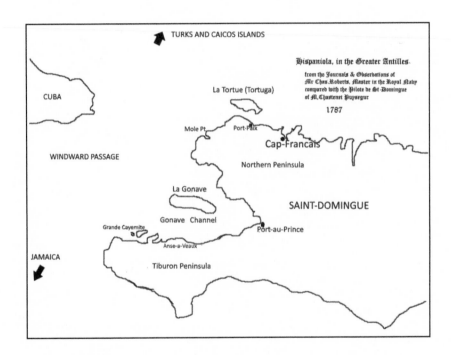

TURKS AND CAICOS ISLANDS

Hispaniola, in the Greater Antilles.

from the Journals & Observations of
Mr Chas. Roberts, Master in the Royal Navy
compared with the Pilote de St-Domingue
of M. Chastenet Puysegur

1787

La Tortue (Tortuga)

CUBA

Mole Pt.   Port-Paix

Cap-Francais

WINDWARD PASSAGE

Northern Peninsula

La Gonave

SAINT-DOMINGUE

Gonave Channel

Grande Cayemite

Port-au-Prince

Anse-a-Veaux

JAMAICA

Tiburon Peninsula

1

Between a Rock and a Hard Place

The Falmouth packet under a full press of sail in the chops of the Channel, the wind in the north-east with a hint of steel to it, the sea running high, and the light fading . . . Somewhere in that foul murk off the starboard bow is the coast of England, or to be more exact, Cornwall, whose natives preserve a stubborn distinction. To the south lies Ushant and the coast of Brittany. To the west, the Isles of Scilly. Beyond them – 3,000 miles of Atlantic Ocean. And then America.

More to the point, and a great deal closer to hand, there is a rock.

It was the proximity of this rock and the speed at which they were approaching it that presently occupied the thoughts of the two gentlemen standing at the weather rail of the Falmouth packet. They shared a wealth of experience of rocks and high seas for they were naval officers in the service of King George and had commanded a number of fine ships in their time, though this would not have been apparent to the ill-informed observer. They had been obliged to come aboard in haste at Gibraltar, leaving their sea chests to be sent on from their lodgings, and their faded uniform coats were hidden under borrowed smocks of sailcloth, crudely daubed with oil paint against the weather, and though their hats were set fore and aft in the approved manner, they were affixed to their chins with strips of canvas which gave them the appearance, as the more senior of the two had recently put it, of a pair of old gossips at a pig fayre. They were not even wholly English, the one being half-American on his mother's side and the other mostly French, having been born and raised in the Channel Isles. Besides, as mere passengers, they had no more authority aboard a Falmouth packet than the lowest cabin boy. In fact, less.

This has not blunted their capacity for carping.

'Do you think he knows it is there?' said one. His tone was flippant, in as much as the wind and the circumstances would allow.

'He must know it is there,' said the other, though his own voice betrayed a nervous concern. 'He must know this part of the Cornish coast as well as any man alive.'

Even so . . . He shifted his gaze to the individual in question: a stocky figure of a man, almost as wide as he was tall, wrapped in several yards of tarpaulin and muffler, who was standing at the con with his stout calves braced upon the deck, and a bulldog, which he somewhat resembled in appearance and manner, similarly braced at his feet. His back was firmly turned to the object of their disquiet and his face firmly set in a southerly direction, apparently in prolonged study of the two vessels that had been following them for the past three hours or more and were now about a half mile astern, and closing.

They were three-masted luggers of a type known to the French as a *chasse-marée*, which loosely translated into English as 'tide-chaser' after their propensity for racing the tide to harbour. In more peaceful times they had been employed by the wholesale fishmongers of Brittany to rendezvous with the fishing fleets off the Atlantic coast and bring back the catch to the markets of Nantes and Bordeaux and other ports along the French Atlantic coast as fresh as when it was hauled from the deep, but clearly their owners had sought to profit from a more violent trade, for each of them had been fitted out with a long eight-pounder at the bow and four smaller guns on both sides, and now they sought to use their speed in pursuit of a livelier catch. But the sea was running too heavy for a steady shot, even at a few cables' length, and being assured of this, the two men returned their gaze to the more immediate peril.

It was named on the charts as Wolf Rock. Not from any physical resemblance to this feared if much-maligned beast, but because the wind in a certain quarter was known to rush into its many cracks and fissures and produce a kind of howling noise.

Very like to that of a wolf.

It was doing it now.

'If he cannot see it, he must surely hear it,' observed the younger of the two. He was a post-captain of six years' standing and his name was Peake. 'Will he luff up or what?'

'Against wind and tide?' queried the other, whose name was Tully and a mere commander, though having served as a sailing master *en route* to this eminence, he presumed to a superior knowledge of such matters. 'We'd be laid in irons before you know it.'

'Well, he must go about one way or t'other,' insisted Peake, who occasionally challenged this presumption.

'He must wear ship,' declared Tully firmly, 'and quick about it or we're' – 'He used a term not listed in Hutchinson's Treatise on Practical Seamanship, though it was certainly nautical.

'Then they will come up with us,' declared his companion flatly, 'and we shall have to fight.'

'We shall have to fight anyway,' said Tully, 'for at the present rate they will be up with us inside the hour.'

There was no disagreement between them on this score, for though the *Antelope* was built for speed like all vessels in the service of the Royal Mail, she was clearly no match for the *chasse marée* over a distance, and they had been gaining steadily on her since they had emerged from the direction of Finisterre midday through the afternoon watch. Being rigged fore and aft, they could sail a good two points closer to the wind than the packet, and if she carried on her present course, even if she did not run upon the Rock, they would soon be off her starboard stern pounding her with their bow chasers and what other guns they could bring to bear. And if she were to go about to run up the Channel, they would turn at once to cut her off. Even at this distance, Peake could see their decks and yards were crowded with men; there must have 200 between them, all doubtless armed to the teeth. They would far prefer boarding to battering her, of course, and so carry her intact to Brest.

He watched them with a growing resentment. The triangular sails seemed to cleave the air, the sharp keels cutting through the water, they were like greyhounds closing in on the frightened hare, and yet one half-decent broadside would tear them apart. After all the ships he had fought, to be taken by a pair of fishing boats in the English Channel . . . It did not bear thinking about; maybe it was better to run upon the rock and end his life by drowning, listening to the howling of a wolf.

'He should have the guns run out already,' he grumbled, 'or at least the stern-chaser.'

For the *Antelope*, too, was armed. She carried a six-pounder at bow and stern and 2 four-pounders in the waist – popguns compared to the ordnance he had once had at his disposal, but they could still do some damage if handled right. If they could only carry away a spar, he pointed out to his companion, it would do much to hinder the pursuit. His companion said nothing. They both knew it was the handling of them that was the problem, for there were only twenty-eight men and boys to work the ship, let alone fight the guns. Peake doubted if they had ever been fired in anger, or even in practice. For sure, there had been no attempt to exercise them during their present run from Gibraltar. The captain probably thought it was a waste of time, and certainly of powder.

Peake eyed this gentleman with almost as much resentment as he had the French. It would be fair to say he had not taken to Captain Spargo during their short acquaintance. The master and joint owner of the *Antelope* was a man of some fifty-odd years, the last ten of which had been spent in his current role, mostly on the Falmouth to Gibraltar run. Doubtless he knew his business, but sadly it was all business with him, at least to judge from his table talk. Perhaps he thought they would come over all superior with him as King's officers, but whatever the reason he had been at pains to impress upon them that he was a man of considerable status and no little substance, for while the Royal Mail paid their captains a standard eight pounds a month – which was somewhat lower than the captain of a navy frigate – an enterprising fellow such as himself could make above a thousand pounds a year, he had informed them, from the agreed perk of charging for passengers and cargo.

As his present company had paid an exorbitant forty-five guineas each for the passage from Gibraltar, they considered this a little insensitive in him, particularly as he had proved rather more abstemious with the wine than either of them would have wished. They were further discomforted by the presence of the bulldog under the table and its propensity to slobber over their boots if they did not keep it fed with a steady supply of titbits, or even if they did. For Peake, who like most seafarers was somewhat given to superstition, Captain Spargo and his bulldog – which went by the name of Jowik – 'little Devil' in Cornish, apparently – had assumed an almost demonic status and he cursed the sudden impulse that had made him rush to take up a berth on the vessel only minutes before she was due to sail.

Chilled to the bone, half-blinded by sleet and salt spray, with Wolf Rock dead ahead and a pair of French gunboats at the stern (or up the jacksie, as he put it more crudely to his companion), it was not quite the hero's return he might have hoped for, had he contemplated such an occasion. But there it was, and there were they – the Rock, the gunboats and himself, arranged in a perplexing dance of death.

It was perplexing because to Peake's mind the packet should have been nowhere near Wolf Rock, and the *chasse-marée*, though highly esteemed by their fishmonger owners, had no business trying their hand at piracy, call it what you will. The worst of it was that for the first time in many years he did not even have the illusion of being able to do a darn thing about it. He had offered to command the guns, even to load and fire the stern chaser with Tully's assistance, but been curtly refused. His only hope now was the mate, who was presently standing beside the two helmsmen, trying to appear unconcerned. Although he was Spargo's nephew and apparently in some awe of him, he seemed to have his wits about him and might be presumed to have as urgent a wish for survival as those more fortunate in their kin. Peake caught his eye and spread his arms in an expression of bewildered apprehension. The mate gave a resigned shrug.

Peake was now obliged to lean far out over the rail to keep the rock in view. He could hear it howling quite clearly now, as if it sensed the nearness of its prey. The last time he had been this way there had been a marker set upon it as an aid to navigation, twenty-feet high with the metal effigy of wolf's head placed on top in a fanciful gesture he had much admired at the time. But it must have been swept away by the sea, or removed by some more officious body, less inclined to whimsy, for there was no sign of it now. The waves were breaking clear over the rock and he could see the spray hurled high into the air. He shot an anguished glance at Tully. Tully looked thoughtful.

Despite the prospect of his imminent extinction, Peake was considerably loath to alert Captain Spargo to the danger. It broke every rule that had been drilled into him since he was a thirteen-year old midshipman, and even before that, for his father, who had spent most of his own life in the King's navy, had applied much the same rigid sense of discipline in his own house. On the other hand, it was exasperating to have survived so many dangers in so many parts of the world only to be wrecked on a rock within a few miles of home, or at least Cornwall, when it might so easily be avoided. He frowned in the direction of his nemesis and cleared his throat, but it would take a lot more than that. He opened his mouth to call out the captain's name – and in that same instant Spargo turned his head and caught his eye. Peake perceived a glint of triumph, certainly of devilment. Then the captain issued the blessed words of command, *Let her go off!*

The helm hard up, the bows slowly, slowly coming round, the hands running to trim the sails as the packet fell off the wind . . . And Peake leaned upon the rail, curiously deflated, as he watched the rock slide slowly by, close enough to spit upon, if his mouth had not been so dry, and the wind not so set against it.

He shook his head in silent rebuke for there could have been no more reason for the captain's ploy than braggadocio, and a childish whim to unnerve his distinguished passengers. But he wished he had held his peace a moment longer and deprived him of the satisfaction.

'Perhaps he means to lure them upon it,' said Tully.

They both knew there was as much chance of this as that the Wolf would come alive and spring upon their pursuers in an excess of patriotic zeal. All that had been achieved by Spargo's ruse, if it could be called that, was to oblige one to fall behind the other as they approached the obstruction. All three ships were now on a course that would take them a little to the west of Gwennap Head – the true Land's End – and on into the Atlantic, though it was likely the chase would be over long before they left the English Channel. Their only chance was that one of their tormentors would carry away a spar, for they spread a great deal of canvas for such small fry, or that His Britannic Majesty's Navy would put in a belated appearance, the absence of this article thus far being something of a mystery. England and France had been at war for over eight years, and for most of that time the main British battle fleet had been stationed off Ushant, blockading the French naval base at Brest, with a smaller squadron at the mouth of the Channel to protect the great bulk of commerce that passed to and from the Atlantic. However, they had not sighted a single sail on their journey north until the appearance of the two privateers. Peake could only suppose this was due to the poor visibility, for though he had been absent in the Far East for the best part of three years he would surely have learned of any major mishap while he was in Gibraltar. Besides, it was inconceivable that the entire fleet had been lost, either in battle or in storm.

The lead pursuer was now approaching the Rock but appeared to be in no danger of running upon it, or even finding it a distraction. Even as Peake looked, the long gun at the bow opened fire. Where the shot fell he could not tell, but it prompted the captain of the *Antelope* to speak another word of command. It did not carry to the two men at the weather rail but it was picked up by his nephew, the mate, who relayed a string of orders, the purpose of which was apparent to them, and by no means reassuring.

'Ready about! Stations for stays!'

This was the manoeuvre Tully had advised against, and the two men held their breath as the bows came across the wind and the sails were promptly laid aback. But Captain Spargo clearly knew his ship – or the wind or both – a deal better than they, for she had just enough way to carry her round.

'Haul taut! Mainsail haul!'

'By God, he's foxed them!' exclaimed Tully as the sails filled on the opposite tack, for it would be some minutes before their pursuers had weathered the Rock and while it was off their beam they could not come about. The packet was now running for Mount's Bay with the wind on her larboard quarter and she had managed the manoeuvre without letting them close on her. Indeed, she had widened the distance between them by at least two cables' lengths. If she could hold them off until dusk or shelter under the guns on Saint Michael's Mount, Peake began to hope she might cheat them yet.

'Look!' Tully was pointing to the north-east. Out of the murk off their larboard bow a ship had emerged. She was three-masted and square-rigged and even in the poor light and at this distance they could see from her royals that she was a ship of war, most likely a large frigate. Their first exultant response was that she was one of theirs and they almost let out a cheer. But then, as the two ships swiftly closed, they saw the tricolour of Republican France streaming in the wind.

More orders and a pounding of feet upon the deck. But these were not sailing orders. The *Antelope* had nowhere else to run, but before Spargo lowered his colours he had one last duty to perform. The mail included a number of official documents and confidential reports, dispatches from diplomatic envoys, even spies, and it was reckoned the most heinous offence by his fellows for the captain of a Falmouth packet to let a single one fall into the hands of the enemy. For this reason, at time of war, the mail was always kept on deck in weighted, weather-proofed bags, ready to be ditched overboard if there was any danger of boarding. Since the beginning of the chase these bags had been slung over the side ready to be cut away at a moment's notice. Now, as they began to splash down into the sea, Peake became aware of his own duty in this regard. With a single oath by way of an explanation to Tully, he made his way down to his tiny cabin in the sternage. Beneath the pillow of his cot was a bulging leather portfolio containing letters and reports from his service in the Indian Ocean and before, many of which he flattered himself would have been of considerable interest to the enemy. Seizing a canvas bag that contained the rest of his possessions, he tipped them upon the cot and replaced them with the documents. Then he hurried back on deck where a quick glance assured him that the Frenchman was coming up on their larboard bow. He seized a four-pound shot from the rack beside one of the guns and crammed it into the bag. Then he stepped to the rail, paused for a moment, holding a large portion of his past, and possibly his future in his hands, and cast it overboard.

'Nathan! Come look at this.'

Tully had crossed to the weather rail and when Peake joined him there, he saw that another vessel had appeared from behind the stern of the frigate and was rapidly overhauling her. But it was apparent that this vessel was neither French nor a ship of war. She was a medium-sized brig, hung with a great many flags and pennants, among which the Union Jack was prominent, as if in celebration of some great event, like the King's birthday or a penny off the tax on beer. Her upper deck was lined with cheering figures, including a quantity of women and children, and unless Peake's ears mistook him, a brass band was playing Rule Britannia. He looked at Tully, who appeared as perplexed as he. He looked back at the Frenchman. She, too, was hung with bunting. And at that moment she fired a single round from one of her bowchasers. But not at them. Peake turned his head to observe the fall of shot about a cable's length short of the leading *chasse-marée*. At once both vessels fell off the wind and turned in the direction whence they came.

The brig was now just a few cables' lengths away.

'She is the *Princess Amelia*, the Penzance to Saint Mary's ferry.'

Captain Spargo had joined them at the rail, but aside from this scrap of information he appeared no more enlightened than they.

The ferry came closer. The people lining the rail were all shouting at once and no sense could be made of it. Peake heard the words 'war' and 'peace' and for one wild moment thought they must have come across a boatload of religious ranters on a pilgrimage to Saint Mary's.

Then a single sentence in a commanding voice carried across the strip of choppy water between them:

'The war is over – we are at peace!'

A moment more of stunned incomprehension, then mayhem. The captain prancing and waving his hat, the dog barking, the mate capering at the con and the crew whooping and cheering from the rigging or dancing a reel about the desks like the drunken sailors they were shortly to become.

'Peace?' said Tully, turning to his companion as if for some explanation of so unfamiliar a word.

But Peake had other things on his mind.

'I have just thrown my life overboard,' he said in a slightly bemused tone.

The devil dog came bounding towards him in an excess of indiscriminate affection and he stooped to embrace it in treacherous arms.

'Now for you, you Cornish son of a whore.'

2

Peace

'Most regrettable,' observed Captain Peake's lawyer raising his wig above one ear to scratch his bald pate. It was a habitual gesture. It showed that he was worrying on his clients' behalf, and therefore giving value for money. 'A minute or two later . . . '

'Quite. Unfortunately, I was not to know that.' Nathan tried to keep the irritation out of his voice. 'So, what are they saying precisely?'

'Well, there is nothing "precise" about it,' replied Mr Jennings. 'That is the root of the problem.'

Watching him the captain felt a compelling urge to scratch his own head which, having much the advantage in hair, felt as if it was more in need of the attention. The legal chambers were as overheated and stuffy as all London chambers in winter, with windows that were never opened between September and May on pain of instant dismissal, and a fire that was kept banked up with coal from dawn to dusk. A shaft of wintry sunlight highlighted a galaxy of dust which orbited endlessly in the space between the shelves of books and legal documents, the bulging case files growing fatter as the years went by. There was a wych elm outside the window, leafless and drab at this time of the year, but in spring it would be a mass of flowers, a purplish blue to begin with and then turning pink to dark red. Captain Peake wondered if the lawyer ever noticed them. He thought not.

He was in one of his customary moods of pessimism and misanthropy. Along with this went a detestation of whatever place he found himself at any particular moment in time – and himself for being there. This was probably a major reason for being a seaman. But it had been three months now since he was last at sea and the strain was beginning to show. Presently, he was in London, that den of thieves and chancers, politicians, bankers and, of course, lawyers. It always had been, of course, but recent events had not improved matters. Peace had doubtless enhanced the prospects for all these scoundrels, but not for the hordes of seamen laid off from the fleet, and officers on half pay like himself, searching for employment or diversion. He would have fled to his father's home in Sussex, but there were reasons why he did not wish to be there, either. So, for the time being he was stuck with his mother in London. And his lawyer.

'What they are *saying*,' began Mr Jennings in ponderous tones that were presumably meant to emphasise the complexity of the case, 'is that you had no *official* capacity at the time of the action, that the ships involved were, with one exception, the property of the Honourable East India Company, and that any prize money that might be accruing as a result is due to those in the employment of that company. Which does not, unfortunately, include you.'

'That is a nonsense,' declared Peake wearily. 'I may not have been in the employment of the Company, but I was appointed commander of the squadron by the Governor of Bombay on the recommendations of Admiral Lord Nelson.'

'Be that as it may . . . It is proving to be a most complicated case . . .'

Peake tried to concentrate as Mr Jennings went off on one of his long, rambling explanations, but he had never been good with legal problems. The facts of the case were indisputable, at least to him, but then he was not a lawyer. He had been sent to India by Admiral Nelson after his victory at the Nile to warn the governor of Bombay that the French were very likely coming his way and to assist in stopping them. The governor had given him command of a squadron of vessels, of varying size and effectiveness, known as the Bombay Marine, which had unexpectedly taken a number of French prizes at Port Blair, in the Andaman Isles. However, Nathan had always been aware that Jonathan Duncan was widely regarded as one of the most notorious of the 'pirates and brigands' the playwright Sheridan had condemned in the House of Commons, and that his authority to grant commissions was considerably less than that of the King of England. More to the point, both Nelson's letter of recommendation and the governor's letter appointing him to the command had been in the bag he had thrown into the sea.

These were the circumstance Mr Jennings found so regrettable.

He tried to focus on what the lawyer was saying.

'. . . besides which, they are claiming that a considerable loss was incurred during your – as they say, *unauthorised* – command in Port Blair when you ordered a warehouse to be burned down, with all the goods it contained. This surprises you?' he added, for Nathan was showing signs of life.

It did – but not because it was untrue. He had ordered the destruction of the warehouse because it contained a considerable stock of opium destined for the Chinese market. What surprised him was that the Company had the gall to raise the issue.

'The East India Company claims that it does not trade in opium,' he pointed out. 'As they have many times assured the British Parliament and the Emperor of China.'

Another long sigh. 'That may be the case, but we all know the truth of the matter and it might explain a certain level of obduracy on their part.'

Nathan raised his eyes to the carriage clock on the mantelpiece. In half an hour he was pledged to join his mother for one of her cultural evenings, and he was not much looking forward to it, but it was probably better than dying of boredom and hot air in a lawyer's office.

'Well, I am afraid I will have to be on my way,' he said. 'If I have no legal case there appears to be no point in pursuing the matter.'

'Well, I would not go so far as to say *that*,' Mr Jennings protested as he saw his fees going out the window, or in this case, the door. With skill, a case like this might be prolonged for many years. 'There are still certain representations we can make. At the very least they may be prepared to make an ex gratia payment. I have written to the Governor of Bombay and if it is your wish, I will write to Lord Nelson who is, I believe, presently in London . . .'

But Nathan was shaking his head . . . 'Do not write to Lord Nelson,' he said. 'I do not wish to embarrass him. Do what you can to embarrass the Governors of the East India Company and let us see what they will come up with.'

They were both aware that if it was possible to embarrass the governors of the East India Company, the Indians would not be selling their birthright, the Chinese would not be trading tea for opium and Richard Sheridan would not be wasting his best lines on the Members of Parliament, many of whom were in their pocket. But it was a satisfactory conclusion from the lawyer's point of view. He saw his client to the door.

'Let us no more talk of the sheeps and the horses,' the Frenchman assured his bemused audience. 'In this new century, the wise men they put the money in the balloons.'

'Oh dear,' murmured Lady Catherine Peake to Nathan from behind her fan, 'your poor father will be distraught. Think of the money he has put into all those rams.'

'I rather think he means ships, Mother,' said Nathan, who knew that his mother was perfectly aware of this but could never resist an opportunity to quiz his father even at a distance. He tried not to encourage her. 'And it is I who will be distraught if he is to be believed.'

The Frenchman was called Monsieur Garnerin and he was an aeronaut – the Official Aeronaut of France, no less – and a great authority on the subject of balloons: large balloons made of rubberised silk and filled with hot air or noxious gases which could carry heavy objects and people for great distances to great heights and at exceptional speeds. He had been up in them himself many times. He had even jumped out of them from hundreds of feet and landed quite safely by means of an invention of his which he called a parachute and somewhat resembled an umbrella. He had done so the previous week in London and landed in Grosvenor Square to great acclaim and now everyone wanted him at their salons. It had even inspired a popular ballad, a verse of which had unfortunately taken up lodgings in Nathan's head as a result of his mother singing it to him on the way here in a spirit of satire.

'*Bold Garnerin went up, which increased his repute,*
And came down to Earth in his grand parachute.'

Lady Catherine found the idea of men going up in balloons more hilarious than inspiring.

'Oh, but it is so ridiculous,' she had insisted when Nathan had voiced a mild rebuke. 'Such male vanity, and you all take it so seriously. Imagine if a woman went up in a balloon and jumped out with an umbrella. As soon as she landed, you'd have her locked her up in Bedlam and charge people to come and poke sticks at her.'

Yet conversely she appeared to have great respect for Madame Garnerin who had ascended with her husband on several occasions and once alone, earning the distinction of being the first woman in the world to have gone up in a balloon 'unaided', which is to say without a male pilot. Lady Catherine considered this to show spirit. Madame Garnerin had accompanied her husband to London but was said to be indisposed.

'He probably doesn't want her to steal his thunder,' Lady Catherine had informed her son scornfully.

Monsieur Garnerin was presently telling his audience about the potential for very large balloons to carry goods and passengers across seas and oceans, using the same trade winds available to 'sheeps', but at much greater speeds. This was greeted with some reserve, for though the talk was being held at the American legation, and at the invitation of the American minister, most of those present were subjects of King George and of a more sombre disposition than those who had cheered Monsieur Garnerin's 'aeronautics' over Grosvenor Square. Those ships of which he spoke had kept Britain safe from invasion for many years and there was understandable concern at the prospect of French troops being able to fly over them in balloons.

This sentiment was expressed forcibly when the audience was invited to put questions at the end of the discourse.

'But our two countries are now at peace,' the aeronaut protested. 'And the balloon is not a weapon of war.'

'Then why did Bonaparte take them to Egypt, if it was not to make war?' a man on Nathan's right wanted to know. Nathan looked upon him with interest – he had not known Bonaparte had taken balloons to Egypt – and he had been there. 'And why has he sent you to England, now?'

M. Garnerin expressed bewilderment. Their host, Mr King, appealed for calm and courtesy.

'Monsieur Garnerin is here for the advancement of science and of learning,' he insisted. 'To the advantage, I would hope, of both countries and others besides.'

'What is scientific about balloons?' came the response from another member of the audience, who clearly shared a similar view to Nathan's mother. 'You blow 'em up, little children go Oooh, the balloons go pop. Would you not agree, Monsewer, that ballooning is a purely frivolous pursuit that may provide a degree of entertainment for a populace hungry for spectacle, but is hardly in the category of science and learning?'

'What is "frivolous"?' the balloonist enquired of his host.

'A bit of fun?' the minister proposed.

'Ah, but of course it is a bit of fun,' M. Garnerin exclaimed. 'And what is wrong with the bit of fun? What is the purpose of life if it is not to have the bit of fun? Eat, drink, and make the love, n'est ce pas?'

'Typical Frenchie,' said the man on Nathan's right in a tone of disgust.

Lady Catherine was one of the few members of the audience to applaud unrestrainedly when the event came to an end. In fact, her enthusiasm drew some critical looks from her neighbours, and Nathan was anxious for them to be on their way before she was drawn into a conversation which past experience suggested might become acrimonious. His mother laid a hand on his arm, however, and begged him to stay a moment while she paid her respects to the American minister and thanked him for inviting her to attend the lecture.

Nathan watched warily from the back of the room. He was always more than a little guarded when his mother put herself forward in company. The American minister was supposedly an acquaintance of her brother, Nathan's Uncle Robert, who was a wealthy New York merchant and shipowner, but Lady Catherine's own position in society was far less assured. She and his father had been estranged for many years and while he tended to his sheep in Sussex, she kept her own household in London which had led to a certain amount of censure among respectable society. It would not have been so bad if she had led a quiet life under the public gaze, but Lady Catherine was by no means attached to the quiet life and had as much respect for the public gaze as that of a tigress in a zoo. Not only had she indulged in several scandalous liaisons over the years – all liaisons by a married woman being accounted scandalous – but she had made her house in Soho Square a haven for radicals and freethinkers who proclaimed the virtues of the French Revolution even while its more extreme adherents were chopping heads off. Although the United States was presently governed by a man who appeared to share much the same view, and even to admire General Bonaparte, his representative at the Court of St James was known to be of a more conservative disposition and Nathan was braced for a snub. He did not care to see his mother snubbed, even if she was indifferent to the possibility.

On this occasion, however, Nathan was relieved to see her readily admitted to the minister's inner circle and greeted by him with respect, even a degree of enthusiasm. He recalled that though Mr King was an adherent of the Federalist faction in Congress and had been a supporter of the late Mr Hamilton, he was a staunch opponent of slavery which would have done much to raise him in Lady Catherine's estimation. It was also possible, of course, that he was one of her admirers, for she had been accounted a great beauty in her day and still commanded a following in male society. He watched with cautious approval as the minister introduced her to Monsieur Garnerin and his associates, for although his initial concerns were assuaged, he remained uneasy that she would draw attention to herself in some way, either by offending the Frenchman with her views on ballooning or, even worse, by accepting an invitation to join him on his next ascent. There was a part of him that applauded his mother's audacity, another that shared his father's inclination to hide among the sheep in Sussex.

He saw that she was waving for him to join her.

'This is my son, Captain Peake,' she announced, 'who is lately returned from service in the East Indies.'

In fact, he had more lately returned from Sussex where he had been staying with his father, but his mother obviously thought this would be a dampener on the conversation.

'I have read a great deal of Captain Peake's adventures in the *Gazette*,' the minister declared. 'I am honoured to make your acquaintance, sir.'

Any gratification Peake might have felt at this announcement was tempered by Monsieur Garnerin's response, for the astronaut was regarding him with a curious frown. 'But I think we have met before,' he proposed when they were introduced. 'Was you ever in Paris, Monsieur le Capitaine?'

Peake regretted that he was not, though he expressed the earnest desire to travel there now that peace had been restored. In hopes of creating a distraction he enthused about French food and culture rather more than

he might otherwise, while his mother stared at him in frank astonishment. He tried to recall the circumstances in which he might have run
into Garnerin during one of his clandestine visits to the French capital
during the war, but it eluded him and probably would not have helped
much. A greater part of his reluctance to join his mother on her not
infrequent forays into society was the fear of just such an encounter. He
probably should have stayed in Sussex, but there was a limit to the time
he was prepared to spend discussing the fecundity of the Southdown ewe
with his father. It was one of the ironies of Nathan's relations with his
estranged parents that he was never more drawn to the one than when
he was with the other.

He was fortunate that the minister expressed an interest in India and
Nathan was able to divert M. Garnerin into a discussion on the possibilities of a balloon route to Bombay by way of Egypt and Arabia. He was
considerably relieved, however, when the company began to disperse
before the astronaut had managed to recall where and in what precise circumstances they had last met, though he looked like he was still thinking
about it. He failed to notice the other man who was observing him with
an even greater intensity from an upper landing as they took their leave.

'Well, I am glad to hear you are so eager to visit Paris,' declared his
mother wickedly when they had settled into their hired carriage. 'I hope
you will consider taking me with you.'

'I was making conversation,' Nathan told her. 'I have no intention of
visiting Paris. Any more than you have of going up in a balloon.' For he
had overheard her hinting at the possibility.

'And *did* you meet him before this evening?' she enquired shrewdly.

'Not that I recall.'

Lady Catherine did not press him. She would have known it was a
sensitive subject, though that did not normally deter her. He sometimes
wondered how much of his mother knew of his activities in Paris. She
had been a good friend of the journalist and author Mary Wollstonecraft
who had been in the French capital at the same time and was more informed of his dealings there than he would have wished. He turned his
face to the window as the carriage jolted eastward along Oxford Street,
but he did not see much of it, and not just because of the dark. His mind
was off on a different track, through different streets, in a different city,
and if he did not see Garnerin there he saw plenty of other faces he had

known. Danton and Desmoulins in the tumbrel on their way to the guillotine in the Place de la Revolution. Robespierre with his shattered jaw tied up in a bloody piece of rag, like a corpse already, on his way to the same grim destination. And Sara, of course. Sara most of all.

She was back there now, he had heard, with her young son, along with all those other exiles who had gone flocking back to France, now that peace was restored and the guillotine no longer as feared as it was. And Paris the capital of the new Europe, a magnet for tourists from England and Italy – and every other country that had tried to turn back the tide of Revolution. They'd gone down like so many wooden skittles, those professional soldiers of Prussia and Austria and Spain, bowled over by the citizen soldiers of Republican France, and the little Corsican general who led them.

Bonaparte. Another face from Nathan's past. A very gaunt face as he remembered it during those early days in Paris, with those hungry spaniel's eyes feeding on his own ambition. Captain Cannon, they had called him then, the funny little *chef de brigade* who took himself so seriously, even if no one else did, and who had to leave his hat in the Cafe Procope as payment because he could not afford to pay the reckoning. Well, no one was laughing now, or if they were, they made sure he didn't find out about it.

He focused on his more immediate surroundings, or what he could see of them through the window of the carriage. In the cold light of day the houses along Oxford Street and most other streets in London had looked darker and dingier than when he was last home, though perhaps he had changed more than they. He had read that the King's ministers had been obliged to make peace because the country was on the brink of bankruptcy, deep in debt and taxed to the hilt. Nathan was inclined to think it was because there was not a single general in Europe who was a match for Bonaparte and his citizen soldiers.

But it was true that the country was exhausted. Exhausted and divided – and desperate to resume trade with continental Europe. Even in Sussex the Tory landowners complained of the low price of wool and the high taxes, while in London . . . But London was what it always had been, lurching between the extremes of wealth and poverty, the elegant and the grotesque. A hopeless, garish Gillray cartoon of a city, but still the greatest in Europe, for all its squalor.

And right on cue, they came out of darkness into light, a blast of sound, a hopeless tangle of carriages. And here was the Pantheon, built as assembly rooms for the rich, a venue for balls and concerts, but now a setting for extravaganzas of the most ludicrous nature, and a magnet for all classes of society. Nathan looked out on a crowd that would have made the perfect cast for a Gillray, a bizarre mix of the well-heeled and the downtrodden, beggars, whores, street musicians and pickpockets, though he was making an informed guess about the latter for they did not advertise themselves. There were plenty of pickings for them. For all its vulgarity the Pantheon still attracted members of the *ton*, though perhaps of the seedier sort, and the rookeries of St Giles was a mere half-mile away, the worst nest of thieves and cutthroats in the capital.

The carriage made a right turn into calmer, darker streets, and moments later they were in Soho Square. His mother had made her home here for several years now, since she had been obliged by the decline in her fortunes to move from St James's. It had once been listed among the most fashionable areas of London and the houses still had a faded grandeur about them which Nathan rather liked. His mother was less sure. She would have preferred rather more grandeur and less faded. For all her radical politics, Lady Catherine valued a certain status in society, and in recent years she had been obliged to make do with more limited resources. Even so, it was a far cry from poverty, as Nathan had frequently pointed out to her.

The carriage set them down at the front door of Number Two and the footman jumped down to lower the steps.

'Are you not coming in?' enquired Lady Catherine when she saw that he was still sitting there.

'I thought I might join a few friends at Brooks,' he said. This was only partly true. *Eat, drink and make the love*, the man had said, and he was right. What else was there to do, now they were at peace? It was time to stop agonising over the past and make what he could of the future. Perhaps he could learn to fly balloons.

3

The Admiral's Coffin

'Why Peake, is it you?'

The once-familiar voice halted Nathan in his tracks. He had been tacking unsteadily homeward across Saint Martin's Fields after a night spent in a manner his mother would have tactfully described as 'carousing' when he observed a commotion in the road ahead. A crowd of ruffians, who appeared to be even worse for wear than he was, were in the process of removing the horses from a carriage that was stranded in the middle of Saint Martin's Lane, while the coachman and a gentleman in a beaver hat and striped brown overcoat watched helplessly from the pavement.

As neither of them looked to be in any immediate danger of assault and being in no fit state to get involved, Nathan had been about to cross to the far side of the road when the gentleman addressed him. Bringing himself sharp about he recognised the distinctive features of his former commander, Admiral Lord Nelson.

'It is, my lord,' he replied, removing his hat and making a bow.

'How very good it is to see you,' said the admiral, with apparent sincerity.

This was gratifying, for it had been several years since they had last met, and though they had enjoyed amicable relations up to that point, Lord Nelson's fame was now such that had he not been hailed by him, Nathan would not have presumed upon their previous acquaintance.

'I do not suppose you have brought a company of marines with you?' the admiral enquired wearily.

Nathan confessed that he had not.

'But if these fellows are troubling you,' he began, taking a firmer grip upon his cane and regretting that he was in civilian dress and had not thought to equip himself with sword or pistol, or even a small cannon, for at a rough estimate they were above a score in number.

'No, I fear we must let them have their fun,' Nelson sighed. 'They mean well, poor fellows, but it happens whenever I come into town and I do find it a trial at times. It is impossible to proceed from one place to another without a mob of unruly seamen descending upon one's carriage, removing the horses, and drawing it through the streets of London, often in the wrong direction.'

For the first time Nathan saw that at least some of those occupied in this endeavour wore the blue jackets and Barcelona scarves that advertised them as British seamen, and very likely in the King's service, or at least recently so.

'I suppose one must consider oneself to be honoured, and indeed one is,' Nelson conceded in the same weary tones, 'but it is a confounded nuisance all the same. Another few hundred yards and I would have arrived at my destination and now they would be offended if I attempted to walk there.'

Above a dozen seamen had now taken the place of the horses while the rest prepared to push from behind, and one was standing at the open door of the carriage with his hat off and a horrible smirk on his face, inviting the admiral to resume his seat inside.

'Would you care to join me, Peake?' Nelson proposed, 'and you can entertain me with an account of your recent adventures – or have you better things to do?'

Nathan did not have better things to do, and even if he had he would have known better than to do them, so with a smile and a nod for the self-appointed footman he followed Nelson into the carriage and took the seat opposite. With a whoop and a holler and a chorus of *Hearts of Oak* their inebriated hauliers proceeded up Saint Martin's Lane, with the coachman following on with the horses and a great fanfare of huzzahs from the people at the sides of the road who had stopped whatever they were doing, even coming out of the shops and houses, to show their appreciation of the nation's hero as he passed by.

It was astonishing to Nathan just how much of a celebrity Nelson had become of late, even given his victories at the Nile and Copenhagen, for it far surpassed the adulation accorded to other admirals of repute such as St Vincent, Duncan and Rodney who had enjoyed significant success over the Spanish, Dutch and French fleets in recent memory. His triumph at the mouth of the Nile had been particularly spectacular, of course, and Nathan had been there to see it, but even so, this was something more than appreciation of the man's genius in battle – he had attained the status of a god, a kind of British Achilles.

It was a rather different image that imposed itself on Nathan's brain, however, as they proceeded up Saint Martin's Lane, for in common with Achilles, Nelson had his vulnerable heel. Nathan had heard stories of the admiral's liaison with Lady Hamilton even as far afield as India, but he had not appreciated the full extent of the scandal until his return to England and saw the cartoons. By then the affair had reached the proportions of a national lampoon, in successive hilarious instalments.

Nelson had met the lady in Naples shortly after his victory over the French fleet at the Battle of the Nile and fallen hopelessly in love with her. The fact that she was married to the English ambassador and Nelson had a wife back home in England would not have raised so much as a lifting of the brow in genteel society had it not been for the lady's own background and circumstance. Emma Hamilton, née Lyons, was a blacksmith's daughter from Neston, on the Wirral, who had achieved a certain celebrity, if not notoriety, in her younger days as an artists' model and, some said, courtesan. She had become the mistress of a young aristocrat and when he had felt constrained to marry an heiress, he had palmed her off on his uncle, Sir William Hamilton, a veteran diplomat and collector of beautiful objects, who was then the British envoy to the royal court of the Two Sicilies, in Naples. To the astonishment of his peers, Sir William took her back with him as his consort and then married her. The difference in age and rank – and Emma's propensity for acting out classical roles in the scantiest of clothing for the entertainment and instruction of their guests – had made the couple a subject of salacious interest throughout Europe. Then along came Nelson.

He had by all accounts fallen passionately in love with Emma, and she with him, a situation to which her husband apparently reconciled himself, either because he was indifferent or unable to stop it. Apparently the three of them were now living in Merton, a few miles from London, Nelson having left his wife and provoked the rebuke of his king and the revulsion of polite society. The newspapers had descended like vultures. The cartoons portrayed Emma as a voluptuous hoyden – this was the polite word – in skimpy muslin, Sir William as an emaciated old cuckold obsessed with his collection of Etruscan vases and Nelson as a funny little man in an overlarge cocked hat, with one swivel eye and one arm. This in no way diminished his iconic status as national hero, but he had become national hero as figure of fun.

Nathan had known the Hamiltons in Naples, a year before all this happened, and like most seamen, he had enormous respect and admiration for Admiral Nelson. He was by no means an imposing physical presence, but he had a noble countenance, a generous spirit and his personal courage was beyond dispute – quite apart from his genius in command. And yet every time you picked up a newspaper you saw this odd little satyr making a fool of himself with an oversized Emma while a thin, old man with horns peered at them myopically from behind a vase.

Inevitably, it was this image which Nathan saw now as they sat opposite each other in the carriage. He could think of nothing to say. Everything that came into his mind seemed inappropriate or to have some salacious double meaning. He sat there in an embarrassed silence, with a fixed grin on his face. At first this did not matter. Once they were on the move – and apparently in the right direction – Nelson seemed happy enough to acknowledge the plaudits of his admirers, but eventually he sat back in his seat and regarded his companion with a curious expression. Possibly Nathan's grin disconcerted him. It was disconcerting Nathan, but it had fixed itself there and did not seem to know how to remove itself.

'Well,' Nelson said.

'Well,' said Nathan, still grinning. It was as if he was enjoying some enormous joke at the admiral's expense.

'I am glad you find this so amusing,' said the admiral.

'Oh, it is not that,' Nathan assured him hastily, managing with a great effort to achieve a more earnest expression. 'No, I am just – ridiculously pleased to see you,' he finished lamely.

Nelson bowed his head in brief acknowledgement of this compliment. Silence resumed.

'Are we going far?' Nathan enquired at length.

'No. Indeed, we have arrived,' replied the admiral rather worriedly as he glanced out of the window. He banged on the roof of the carriage with his cane, but he had forgotten there was no coachman on the box, and it made not the slightest difference. If the sailors heard it at all, they took it as applause. As the coach continued on its merry way the admiral was obliged to thrust his head out of the window and bellow in a voice trained up by the exigencies of wind and weather: 'Vast heaving, you whoresons, you have sailed past the fucking berth.'

The carriage came to a halt and was hastily backed – a manoeuvre accomplished far more proficiently by the matelots than it would have been by the horses – and stopped again.

Nathan looked out of the window.

'This is an undertakers,' he observed.

'That is correct,' replied the admiral as he distributed coin to the leader of the hauliers. 'They have charge of my coffin and have some material to show me for the lining. You might care to advise me on the choice, as you were involved with Ben Hallowell, I am told, in the original conceit.'

Nathan was stunned.

'It had nothing to do with me,' he protested. 'It was entirely Hallowell's idea.'

Ben Hallowell had been captain of the *Swiftsure* at the Battle of the Nile, and had conceived the idea of making a coffin out of a section of mainmast from the French flagship, so that he might present it to Nelson as a tribute to his glorious victory. It was true that he had mentioned the idea to Nathan at the time, seeking his opinion on how the admiral might take it. Privately, Nathan had considered that Hallowell might be more than a little touched in the head, possibly by the sun. He had made very little comment, however, other than to say he should wait until Nelson had fully recovered from the head wound he had received in the battle, lest he consider the gift of a coffin unduly premature.

This could in no way be construed as a joint decision, Nathan thought.

He had heard later that Nelson had been quite appreciative of the gesture and had for a time kept the coffin in his cabin, even having it propped up behind his chair at the head of the table when he entertained his fellow officers to dinner, until they had begged him to have it removed on grounds of taste. But whatever Nelson's views on the subject, Nathan did not wish to be given any credit for the gift, tribute or no tribute. He suspected he had been slandered by association because Hallowell was born in Massachusetts and Nathan was known to be half-American and both were therefore tainted with the spirit of rebellion and, almost as bad, if not worse, vulgarity.

'Oh well, I was clearly misinformed,' said the admiral. 'But come and see it now. I think you will agree it is a very fitting compliment.'

They entered the premises together. France & Beckwith it said on the front, Undertakers, Cabinetmakers and Upholsters, by appointment to His Gracious Majesty, King George III.

The proprietors were awaiting them in the front office. They both looked astonishingly young – they could almost have been schoolboys, one fat, one thin. There was a strong smell of wood shavings and beeswax, but not of death, Nathan was relieved to note. He had had quite enough of the smell of death.

They were shown the coffin, which was about six feet long and the sides rounded, as they would be if it had once been a ship's mast. This had been a particularly large mast, for L'Orient had been a 118-gun ship of the line. Nathan remembered when it had blown up, and large parts of it had rained down from the sky. Parts of its people, too.

A selection of lining materials was brought for Nelson to choose from. He said he rather liked the red.

'What do you think?' he enquired of Nathan.

Nathan, with his head still filled with the carnage of the Nile, thought that blue might be more appropriate.

'Why is that?' Nelson frowned.

'Well, the Navy, the sea . . .' Nathan replied vaguely, trying to affect an interest – 'And of course you are a Vice-Admiral of the Blue.'

'There is that,' Nelson agreed thoughtfully. 'What do you gentlemen think?' he asked the two schoolboys.

Mr France favoured white silk stretched over wool for padding.

'Why white?' enquired Nelson.

'It tends to set the body off to more advantage,' Mr Beckwith replied, 'once we have applied the rouge of course. And if it is to be an open coffin, laid in state.'

'True, very true,' said Nelson. He had always wanted to be buried in Westminster Abbey, Nathan recalled. It had been his battle cry when leading the boarders onto the deck of the San Nicolas at the Battle of

Cape St Vincent. 'Victory or a tomb at Westminster!' Nathan had been close behind him at the time and had not thought much of it, even then, as battle cries go. 'What do you think, Peake?'

'Would it not show the stains more?' Nathan queried.

'Stains?'

'Well, of what happens after . . .' Nathan just stopped himself from saying, 'after death.' 'I mean, if you were to lie in state, in an open coffin,' he struggled.

'Oh, really, Peake.' The admiral looked at him askance. He caught Mr France's eye. 'They are brutalised, these fellows,' he said. 'Desensitized by war. Dear me.'

But he went for the blue.

When they were finished, they found the sailors gone, the horses restored to their traces and the coachman back up on his box.

'Where can we drop you off, Peake?' the admiral enquired.

Nathan told him he was staying at his mother's house in Soho Square, but as it was only a short walk.

'Get in, man, get in!' the admiral commanded.

'So, you resolved not to remain in India?' he prompted him as they resumed their journey.

'I was only temporarily assigned to the Bombay Marine,' Nathan replied. 'I was still officially attached to the Mediterranean fleet.'

Nelson inclined his head in what Nathan assumed to be polite interest. In fact he was more interested in the doings of his subordinates than most admirals of Nathan's acquaintance, but he could not be expected to keep track of all their meanderings, and Nathan's had been more meandering – and secretive – than most.

'I took passage in a homeward-bound East Indiaman,' Nathan went on, 'and prevailed upon the captain to land me at Gibraltar where I hoped to report to Lord Keith. However, I discovered he was engaged with the fleet at the siege of Acre and so rather than charge about the Med in pursuit of him, and the Falmouth packet being ready to sail, I resolved to return to England and apply to Lord Saint Vincent.'

Saint Vincent had been his previous commander when he was with the Mediterranean fleet and was now First Lord of the Admiralty. Both he and Nelson had not enjoyed the best of relations with him in the past. Possibly this explained the admiral's frown.

'A pity,' he said. 'Keith would have given you a ship, even a squadron. No doubt about it. Not after your action in the Andaman Sea.'

'Thank you, my lord. I am gratified to hear you say it.'

Nathan wondered if this was the right time to tell him about his difficulties over the prize money but decided not. There would probably never be a right time. Besides, Nelson had only recommended him to the governor; it had not been in his power to confer a command.

'And have you spoken with Saint Vincent?'

'No, my lord. By the time I arrived in England the preliminaries of a peace had been agreed. And shortly after, most of the fleet was laid up in ordinary. I have as much chance of obtaining a ship as of flying to the moon.'

Astronomy was something of a hobby with Nathan, so he had some notion of the odds.

'Pity,' said Nelson again. 'A great pity.'

Though whether he was referring to peace with France or Nathan's present prospects of a command was open to question. Probably both.

They had arrived at Soho Square. Nelson peered out of the window. 'So you are staying with your mother?'

'I am,' said Nathan. He offered no further explanation. He loved his mother but he knew the opinion held of her by his superior officers was neither favourable nor greatly supportive of his career. Her admiration of the French Republic and her support for Republicans in England did not endear her to men who had spent the best part of their lives in the service of the King.

He thanked Nelson for the lift and ventured to hope that it would be many years before he would be needing the services of Messers France and Beckwith.

'Doubtless it will,' Nelson agreed miserably, 'if this peace holds.'

But then as Nathan moved towards the door he said: 'See here, Peake, why do you not come to Merton? See my new house. The farm, I call it. Stay a day or two. Stay as long as you like. I have the Hamiltons staying with me at present – Sir William and Em – Lady Hamilton – I recall that you met them in Naples.'

Nathan sat down again and regarded him cautiously. He was touched by the offer. Yet there was a look that was almost pleading in the admiral's eye. Or possibly challenging. Perhaps both.

'We do not have many visitors,' Nelson went on, 'but we are very cosy there. The air is excellent – and you will not go short of entertainment, I assure you.'

Nathan did not have to be convinced of that – he remembered Emma's Attitudes from his stay in Naples. There had been an incident when, dressed in a thin muslin shift – he forgot what role she was supposed to be playing – she had fallen down in an affected faint and one of the guests had removed the flowers from a vase and thrown the water over her. It was as good as a comic Opera. I am recruited into the ménage, he thought, but he could not find it in his heart to refuse, even if he could have found the words. He had great respect for Nelson, and was genuinely flattered by the invitation, but all that he had heard about the admiral's relationship with the Hamiltons argued the advantages of staying with his mother.

'I would like that very much,' he said. 'I am honoured that you . . .'

'Excellent!' Nelson beamed. 'Shall we say tomorrow? I will send my carriage for you, shall we say at midday? It is only an hour's journey.' Then a different expression crossed his face. It was almost crafty, Nathan thought later, but not, unfortunately, at the time. 'In fact, we have another visitor you should meet who would, I think, very much like to meet you.' He tipped his hat. 'Until tomorrow, then.'

4

The Admiral's Friend

Nathan awoke the next morning with a sense of spring in the air, though in truth it must have been a sixth sense for it was not readily discernible to any of the others. The view from his bedroom window showed a sky dimmed by the smoke of a hundred thousand coal fires, while the trees in Soho Square looked like they had been struck by lightning or blight, possibly both. But a yellowish tint in the murk to the south-east suggested that somewhere in the world the sun was shining, and he told himself he might not have to go far to find it. Merton was a mere eight miles from London Bridge, but pretty much in the heart of the Surrey countryside, and he took a notion to ride there. He could hire a hack from the livery around the corner in Frith Street, with a groom to bring it back, and the chaise that Nelson was sending for him could carry his bags.

Thus decided, he dressed in his riding gear and packed enough clothes for three or four nights away. He took the new uniform and boat cloak he had ordered from his tailor as soon as he arrived back in London, along with most of the kit that had been sent on with his trunk from Gibraltar. Although Merton was a long way from the sea, you never knew what might turn up where Nelson was concerned – the last time they had met he had been sent to India – and that parting shot of his was at least as promising as the hint of a sun in the London sky. If there was no other use for it he could always wear the uniform for dinner – he assumed his host wore his, though he had never seen him in a domestic setting before. He told himself it would be an interesting experience but admitted to a degree of nervousness. There was a lot about Emma Hamilton that Nathan liked. It took a lot of guts – as well as beauty and resilience – to attain her present station in life, given where she had started from, but there was no disputing the fact that she could be painfully embarrassing at times. And that was before she met Nelson.

From what he had heard, they made no secret of their passion for each other, though Nelson referred to her as 'his good friend' – at least in public. God alone knew what he called her in private, though He might not care to. They mooned over each other like lovesick adolescents, according to Nathan's mother – for a woman who claimed to abjure gossip and could not abide the newspapers she was remarkably well informed but how much of it was true? Did she really cut up his meat for him at dinner? Feed him morsels from her own plate? And how did Sir William deal with the situation?

Well, he would soon find out.

The carriage arrived precisely at noon, as Nelson had promised, and he saw his two bags stowed safely in the boot before mounting his hired hack. His mother came down to see him off and seemed unusually down about it, but he assured her he would be back before she knew it. She gave him a look that suggested a degree of scepticism on this account, and it was true that past experience would not have filled her with confidence, but this time there was no obvious diversion. It wasn't as if there was a war on, and even in the fraught history of Anglo-French relations it was unlikely that hostilities would resume quite so soon after peace had been signed.

They headed south across Westminster Bridge and Nathan stayed with the chaise through Lambeth as far as Clapham Common where he gave the hack its head. It was a big, heavy grey, name of Dandy, and it needed the exercise even more than he did – he had not been out riding since he had left Sussex – but after a sluggish start they made a decent fist of it between them. The sky had gradually cleared and was now a pale shade of blue streaked with high wispy cloud which usually foretold fine weather to come, or at least fine for February. The gallop was exhilarating and blew away at least some of the cobwebs that had formed while he was in London, or perhaps it was the fumes of drink, for he had been hitting the bottle more than usual latterly, and certainly more than was good for his health. It felt good to be out of the city again and free of family ties, for though he loved both his parents and tried not to take sides, the continuing tensions between them could be a trial at times.

He raced the groom as far as Balham Hill, where they waited for the carriage to catch them up, their mounts blowing hard and steaming after their run. There were woods here, the trees still bare of course, but he felt the hint of spring in the air even if there was no sign of it on the ground. For the first time in weeks he felt other than pessimistic for a future without the prospect of war. There were plenty of opportunities in peace even though they might not be obvious to him. It was time he found a wife, his mother had told him over dinner the night before, and though it would be going too far to say he agreed with her, he would not at all mind falling in love again. Perhaps he would meet someone at Merton Place, he thought. Stranger things had happened.

They arrived within the hour that Nelson had predicted. Nathan's first impression was of a sturdy country house of two stories built of red brick and somewhat resembling a priory, though it cannot have been more than a century or so old. It might have been the home of a wealthy merchant, or a clergyman with a good living, possibly not unlike the Norfolk country rectory where Nelson had been born and bred.

All three of them came out of the house to greet him. Emma was as vivacious and exuberant as he remembered her from his time in Naples, though there was a good deal more of her than there had been then, and he could not help but wonder if she was with child. There was a story that she had given birth to one by Nelson already – a girl, who had been farmed out to a family in London – but Nathan tried to put the rumours and the scandals and the cruel cartoon images out of his mind. She had always had a trick of mixing what would have seemed obvious flattery with genuine warmth and they had dealt well with each other in Italy.

'What a handsome lad he is,' she gushed, 'Just look at that there jacket – and the boots. Oh la! And how well his breeches fit his bum. You must give me the name of your tailor, my dear.' Laughing at Nathan's embarrassment.

Even Sir William managed a smile, though he looked to have aged a lot more than the four years since they had last met, when all he'd had on his mind was Bonaparte's progress through Northern Italy and whether Vesuvius would have one of its periodic eruptions. Happy days. He was worn and fragile, that tall elegant frame reduced to that of a stooped and thin old man, but then he must be at least seventy now. Thirty-three years older than Emma, twenty-five more than Nelson. In fact, the admiral looked tired and under the weather. He was wearing his heavy boat cloak and a thick woollen muffler, though it was by no means cold. His concern for others, however, whether guests or crews, was as apparent as ever – he had sent a servant to fetch a jug of warm, spiced ale for both Nathan and the groom as soon as he saw that they had ridden here, and he gave instructions to the servants to see that the groom was fed before he was sent back to London, though Emma was clearly anxious to get him back inside the house as soon as possible.

'I am sorry to say Our Dear Lord is not at all well,' she confided in Nathan the first chance she had. 'He has had a chill since coming back to England and is very low at times. Your presence will cheer him.'

He seemed cheerful enough as he and Lady Hamilton showed Nathan around their new abode, Sir William having retired discretely to the library. His 'good friend' had seen to the purchase, Nelson informed him, patting Emma on the bum, while he was otherwise engaged on the South coast ('In defence of the realm,' added the good friend in an aside, in case Nathan thought he was off gallivanting). They inspected the grounds from one of the upper windows while she listed their many amenities – a dairy and an ice house, an orchard and orangery, the ruins of Merton Priory, and a small stream which she had named the Nile, 'in honour of Our Dear Lord's greatest triumph.'

'*She crams him with flattery by the trowel-full and he takes as quietly as a child does pap.*'

Nathan remembered the words of Lord Minto, who had stopped the night at his father's house shortly before Christmas.

'*The whole place and the life they lead there – it fair makes you want to greet.*' Minto was as outspoken as many Scots of his class, especially when the drink was flowing. He had been viceroy in Corsica when Nelson was stationed there and they had maintained cordial relations ever since, but their latest meeting had clearly tested Minto's patience and his tolerance of the lower classes had never been especially benign.

'I am very sorry to say it, but he makes himself ridiculous with that woman,' he had complained, 'and that beanpole of a husband of hers, dripping around the place, ne'er saying boo to a goose.'

'What on earth does he see in the woman?' Nathan's father had wondered, who only knew her from those vile cartoons of Gillray and his associates.

'Gan away wi' ye, man, is it no obvious? Married to that dried up hackit of a wife, and that one throws herself at him. Oh, and she was a bonny lass in her day, trained in the arts of love, they say at the House of that Doctor fellow on the Strand, what was it, you'll know?' – He looked at Nathan who did, as a matter of fact – it was the Temple of Health and Hymen and the proprietor was Dr James Graham who was as much a doctor as he was. He saw his father looking at him and shook his head. 'They had an electric bed, you know, that gave you shocks while she danced around you naked. Why, he did not know what hit him!'

And yet . . .

Nathan had known Adelaide Correglia, the courtesan from Genoa, who had lived with Nelson for the best part of two years on his flagship in the Med, and Nathan would have thought she was at least as well versed in the arts of love as Emma Hamilton, though he had no means of knowing for sure. But looking at them now, gazing out over the grounds of the house she had chosen for him, seeing how she trailed the backs of her fingers down his arm and how he bent his head to hers, he thought, it is not just that, it is her kindness, her warmth and her talent for mothering. Nelson's mother, to whom he was apparently devoted, had died when he was only nine years old, and three years later he had entered the service as a midshipman aboard his uncle's ship of the line. He can't have had a lot of mothering in life thereafter.

As if in confirmation of this, Emma linked an arm through Nathan's and marched him off to show him the guest room he was to have, as he might want to have a wash and change of clothing before luncheon. 'Every bedchamber has its own powder room,' she informed him proudly, 'and I know you Navy men are used to dining early at sea, so we won't let you starve till six o' the clock.'

Nathan's heart warmed to her for he had never adjusted to the landsman's practice of having dinner at six and of despising luncheon as an indulgence for the ladies.

'And if you fancy a bite of something, just ask one of the servants to bring it up to your room,' she instructed him. 'Or wander down to the kitchen yourself, for we keep no ceremony here.'

Nathan began to feel a lot more relaxed about his visit – and the room they had given him increased his satisfaction, for despite Minto's jibe it was furnished in the best of taste – no portraits of either host or hostess, or even naval engagements, only a couple of rustic scenes – and with a fine view over the park.

'And if there is anything else you require, just give the bell a pull,' Emma told him before leaving him to the reflection that as a hostess, Emma was far superior to many others he had known, for all their pedigree.

He did not linger over his toilet and joined them a few minutes later in the dining room where a number of dishes had been laid out on the table for them to help themselves along with several bottles of French wine. Nelson had been taught by his mother, apparently, to hate a Frenchman like the Devil, but he clearly did not despise their wines, which flowed rather more freely since the peace was signed.

Both Sir William and Lord Nelson were quite abstemious, but not Emma, who applied herself to both food and drink with characteristic gusto and urged Nathan to do the same. It was something of a jolt then, when having consumed two large portions of chicken and ham pie and a quantity of bread and cheese, accompanied by the usual relishes, and washed down with four bumpers of hock, Sir William suggested he might care to join him for a spot of fishing 'in the Wandle'.

Whatever 'the Wandle' was, the only thing Nathan really cared to do was have a long lie-down and a spell in the 'powder closet' as Emma coyly described it, before dinner, but it was difficult to refuse. He shot a glance towards their hostess in hopes of a rescue but for once she was remiss in her duties though she had surely heard the exchange. Instead, she announced that this was a splendid idea, as 'Our Dear Lord' needed his rest in his current state of health and she would not care for their guest to be bored. Clearly guest and spouse were to be packed off for the remainder of the afternoon, though Nathan was not sure if rest was precisely what Nelson had in mind, even if she did.

And so, half an hour later, he was to be seen in the company of Sir William, trudging across the park in the general direction of the ruined priory with fishing rods at the shoulder and a servant traipsing along behind pushing a wheelbarrow loaded with chairs, umbrellas, and what other equipment was considered necessary for an afternoon's fishing.

It turned out the Wandle was the name of a river – or at least a large stream – which rose in the Surrey hills, Sir William informed him, and joined the Thames at Wandsworth.

'I believe the waters are somewhat polluted by industry closer to the junction,' he declared, 'but it is tolerable fishing hereabouts.' Said with a heavy sigh. 'It has been one of my few diversions of late, though the weather is not always to one's liking.'

The thought of the poor fellow being turned out of the house every afternoon, rain, frost or shine, to accommodate Our Dear Lord's need for rest rather depressed Nathan, and – his brain still somewhat dulled by drink – he heedlessly enquired if Sir William missed the Palazzo Sessa, his beautiful home in Naples.

Hamilton shot him a look. 'Well, what do you think?' he said.

Nathan could only look pained for him. They walked on in silence for a while, the servant trudging dutifully behind with the wheelbarrow, and Nathan desperately trying to think of something to lighten the mood, but finally it was Sir William who spoke.

'I was, as you may know, obliged to leave many of my treasures at the Palazzo, when we resolved to return overland to England,' he announced.

'No, I did not know that,' replied Nathan, affecting interest. What he did know was that Nelson had joined the couple on this overland journey, without leave of absence and in the middle of a war. He had no idea what route they had taken to avoid French territory but he was aware that it had taken rather a long time and that Nelson had been feted in practically every town they visited as the saviour of Europe while his commanding officer, Lord Keith, was ranting about having him court martialled.

'The vases were shipped to England in due course,' Hamilton went on, 'but, alas, many were lost with the *Colossus* when she went down off the Scillies.'

'I did not know,' Nathan said. 'I am very sorry.'

'I am forgetting that you have been in India,' the baronet sighed, 'so perhaps there are many things you do not know.'

Nathan desperately thought of something to say, but it was not easy. They were passing the ruins now and a sentence formed in his mind concerning the Dissolution of the Monasteries, but before he could put it into words, Sir William spoke again.

'Since our return we have lived in London,' he said. 'And now here.'

'Well, it certainly has the benefit of cleaner air,' Nathan floundered, 'and of course, the Wandle.'

Rather wishing he could drown himself in it.

That look again. 'We came to an arrangement, of course, about the expenses, though I am obliged to maintain my house in Mayfair. So – yes – to answer your question, I do miss the Palazzo Sessa.'

Hamilton lapsed into silence, for which Nathan could only be grateful. It had been a somewhat uncharacteristic response for a man raised in discretion and schooled in diplomacy, but perhaps he felt the need to put the record straight. It must be hurtful and humiliating enough to know that your wife was having sex with another man in the house you were sharing with them without every visitor thinking that you were being kept at the fellow's expense.

Hamilton suddenly stopped in his tracks, so suddenly in fact that the gardener, whose mind was clearly on other things, ran the wheelbarrow into the back of his legs causing him to fall into it. Nathan and the apologetic gardener helped him to his feet, but Hamilton did not appear to be aware of the indignity. 'As you may observe,' he said to Nathan, 'if you have not already, I am obliged to submit to a great deal of nonsense to avoid coming to an explosion which would be attended with many disagreeable effects, and would totally disturb and destroy the comfort of the best man and best friend I have in the world. So be assured there will be no eruptions in Merton, Captain. Not during your stay here, nor ever.'

He walked on.

A few minutes later they reached the Wandle. A pleasant little river, clear enough to see the long ribbons of emerald grass rising from the riverbed and streaming off with the current. On the far side were water meadows with grazing cattle and on a slight rise, another house, slightly more elegant and more substantial than Merton Place.

'Wandle Bank House,' Hamilton announced following Nathan's gaze. 'Home of Mr Parry, editor and proprietor of *The Morning Chronicle*.'

This was a surprise. The *Chronicle* was his mother's newspaper of choice, and was staffed almost entirely by radical journalists, many of whom supported the ideals of the French Revolution. Not Nelson's politics for sure. Nathan wondered how the *Chronicle* had dealt with the affair of Nelson and Lady Hamilton, and what Perry was like as a neighbour. He was aware that when Nelson had endeavoured to thrust Emma onto

London society they had been ostracised, all three of them, certainly by the ladies. Their company had been confined to gentlemen who came alone, or leading ladies of stage and opera. Nathan had supposed those living in the country would be worse. Certainly, when they had gone on a kind of national tour, they had been greeted coolly by those above a certain rank, and sometimes snubbed. There was a story of their chaise being halted at the lodge of Blenheim Palace when they had gone to visit the Duke of Marlborough and submitting to the humiliation of having sandwiches sent out to them.

'This looks a good spot for you,' said his companion, indicating a dismal-looking willow, a long way from leaf. Nathan nodded his agreement, and the servant unloaded the wheelbarrow.

'Good luck,' said Hamilton, trudging off to find a spot further upstream.

The effects of the drink having worn off by now, Nathan felt himself sinking into gloom. He wrapped himself in his boat cloak, settled in his chair and within a minute he was asleep.

'Captain Peake?'

Nathan opened his eyes. Hamilton was standing over him, the servant a few steps behind. The river was in shadow and the sky to the west a glorious pallet of reds and pinks and purples.

'Ah.' He smiled. 'Afraid I nodded off. All well?'

'Well, some of us are,' remarked his companion, looking into Nathan's empty basket. He himself had caught four decent trout. 'One for each of us,' said he. Then his face fell. 'Oh, but I am forgetting. We have another guest.'

'Oh, and who would that be?' enquired Nathan, remembering Nelson's remark when he dropped him in Soho Square.

'I am not sure,' said Hamilton wearily. 'An American, I believe.'

They walked back to the house.

Nathan heard the coach arrive while he was changing, finished tying his stock and went downstairs to find the new guest with Nelson in the drawing room. He turned at Nathan's entrance to reveal the familiar features of a man who had tried to kill him at least twice, or maybe three times, not counting a farcical duel on Lincoln's Inn Fields over a woman's honour.

'Why, Captain Peake,' he said, with that familiar drawl and an ironic bow. 'How delightful to see you again.'

'Imlay,' said Nathan without affection or hatred, or even mild surprise. You did not show surprise when you saw your nemesis. It conferred too much satisfaction.

5

The Confidential Agent

When Nathan was a lad, before he went to sea, his father had a dog called Benj, which was presumably short for Benjamin, though no one ever used the polite form. Benj was one of many dogs at Windover House. Some of them were guard dogs, some were farm dogs, some were for hunting and some were all three. None of them were pets, though people had their favourites, and they were known collectively as 'the hounds'. There were many different breeds of hound, and many that were no breed at all, the most common being a lurcher.

People had different explanations of what a lurcher meant. Nathan's father had explained that it was from the Norman-French or Middle English *lurch*, meaning to lurk, or to loiter furtively in one place, but the shepherds told Nathan it referred to the breed's ability to 'lurch', or turn suddenly in pursuit of its prey, which was usually the hare and the house servants said it came from Old English for prowler, swindler and thief. Benj answered to all these descriptions. There was something beyond sly about Benj, something that suggested that he had just committed a crime or was just about to. He was a dog who was always weighing up the main chance.

It was said of Benj that if you were asleep and Benj came up and licked your face, which he was prone to do, it was not to show affection but to check if you were dead. If you did not bat him away with a kick or a curse or do something else to demonstrate that this was not the case, he would start to eat you. Nathan thought this was giving a dog a bad name, but he was not going to take a chance on it. You could lose a nose.

It was many years since Nathan had last seen Benj. Probably he just came on leave from the navy one day and Benj was no longer there, and no one knew when or where he had gone. Run off with the gipsies was the usual comment. But sometimes – in his more fanciful moments – Nathan thought that Benj had just spent a little while as a hound to study human behaviour, and when he reckoned he had a fair grasp of it, he metamorphosed into Gilbert Imlay.

'I think you gentlemen have no need of an introduction,' said Nelson.

'No,' said Nathan. 'We have had our moments.'

Nelson arched a questioning brow. 'But no bad feeling I trust?'

He must surely have known something of the history.

'Not on my part,' said Imlay.

'Nor mine,' said Nathan with a smile.

They were both practised deceivers.

They had first met in Paris in the spring of 1793, during the dark days of the Terror, when there were massacres in the prisons, and the guillotine was despatching enemies of the people daily in the Place de la Revolution, and neither of them was who he said he was. Nathan had assumed the identity of an American sea captain called Turner, from Nantucket, while Imlay – Imlay was whoever you wanted him to be. The Revolution had attracted all kinds of people to Paris, from many different countries. Revolutionaries, of course, idealists, rogues, opportunists, observers, misfits and writers. Like Benj, Imlay was something of a lurcher in this regard, a bit of everything. He was an American, on that people could be agreed, he said he was from New Jersey, originally, and that he had served as an officer in the New Jersey militia against the British in the Independence War – he still called himself 'Captain' Imlay. Nathan discovered many years later that he had been the corps paymaster and that he had absconded after a few months with the pay. There was a story that he had gone over to the British and was widely despised in New Jersey as a traitor and a thief, though some said that he had been put up to it by his superior officers and sent into the British camp as a spy.

Either way, after the war he had spent some time on the western frontier with the pioneer and mountain man, Daniel Boone. He had written a book extolling the virtues of settlement in the region which was published by Debrett of London to considerable acclaim. It even made some money. He followed this up with another book – a novel this time called *The Emigrants* about the trials and tribulations of an American pioneering family in Kentucky. It contrasted the decadence of Europe with the utopian promise of the American West. It also had a sensational love affair, and a rape. When he came to Europe his personal charm combined with his experience of the frontier made him something of a celebrity. Comparisons were made with Rousseau's noble savage. On his arrival in Paris in 1792 he was embraced by literary society. Literally in one case. He became the lover of the English feminist Mary Wollstonecraft, author of 'A *Vindication of the Rights of Women*', who had come to the French capital to write about the Revolution. When England and France went to war, they were married in a dubious ceremony conducted by the American ambassador in the U.S. embassy – to give her the benefit of U.S. citizenship and save her from arrest, Imlay later said. At the time he talked of them buying a farm in the Ohio Valley, combining writing with working the land and raising a large family. Mary loved the idea, but instead they moved to Le Havre where he set up in the soap business. There was a great shortage of soap in Revolutionary France and a great deal of money to be made from importing it, he thought. But this meant running it past the British blockade. So, Imlay, the soldier, spy, frontiersman, writer and businessman, now became a blockade runner. He ran soap and gunpowder. It was in this guise that he first met Nathan, who was then smuggling counterfeit currency on behalf of His Majesty's Government. Imlay was quite useful to Nathan, and to others engaged in nefarious enterprises. His status as a U.S. citizen allowed him to visit both Britain and France – and indeed any other country in the world. Mary, however, remained in Le Havre where she was delivered of his child. When Imlay's visits to London became more prolonged that she might have wished, she employed some smugglers to take her across the Channel and found him living with an actress in Soho. Imlay suggested they all live together. Mary tried to kill herself. Twice. On the second occasion Nathan became involved, mainly because Mary was a friend of his mother's. This was when he and Imlay fought their duel in Lincoln's Inn Fields. It was inconclusive.

Their subsequent relationship had remained fraught. He had presented himself to Nathan at various times as a confidential agent for the governments of the United States, Great Britain, France and Spain, sometimes all four at the same time despite the circumstance of two or three of them being at war with each other. Many years later, it had been impressed upon Nathan by someone who claimed to be 'in the know' that Imlay's principle loyalty was to the United States, and that he was one of a select band of agents known informally as 'Washington's Boys' – paid out of the general's secret funds and willing to do anything, to resort to any device or subterfuge, to advance the interests and security of the United States.

Nathan's own opinion was that Gilbert Imlay was willing do anything to advance the interests and security of Gilbert Imlay. He had gained a little weight since Nathan had last seen him – when was it, three years ago, just before the Battle of the Nile – and his face had the bland, podgy, slightly florid look of a prosperous merchant. What had he been doing in the last three years, Nathan wondered, but it was probably better not to know.

'So,' Nelson raised his glass. 'All friends together. Past disputes forgotten I trust.'

There may have been a question mark there somewhere. Imlay smiled. Nathan inclined his head thoughtfully. They all drank.

'Excellent,' said Nelson, turning to Nathan, 'because I believe Captain Imlay has a proposition for you to consider.'

Nathan did his best to look interested. If he had known Imlay was the 'someone' he wanted him to meet he would never have come near the place.

'Shall we wait until after dinner?' Nelson was saying, 'or is now as good a time as any?'

'I think now, if your lordship is in favour,' said Imlay. 'If dinner is not imminent.'

Dinner was apparently not imminent.

They adjourned to the library *'where we have left the maps.'* Nathan followed them with an uncomfortable feeling that he had been set up. The candles had been lit and there was a fire in the grate. Nathan also noticed the recumbent figure of Sir William Hamilton in an armchair by the fire, apparently asleep. The other two behaved as if he were not there.

'I have been explaining the situation to Lord Nelson,' Imlay said, 'but if your lordship does not object to going over it again.'

Nelson made a sign for him to continue. The maps to which Nelson had referred were on the desk, mostly rolled up, but one spread out and weighed down at the corners with books. It was of North America and the Caribbean.

'You may know something of this already,' Imlay was saying. 'There has been a deal written about it in the English newspapers. For the past few months, since the preliminaries of peace were signed, Bonaparte has been sending ships and men to the West Indies. The biggest contingent sailed from Brest in December, but since then there have been regular departures from every port on the French Atlantic coast. We estimate that there are as many as eighty ships at sea, including forty men of war – and some twenty thousand troops. It is said to be the largest armada ever to leave the shores of France.'

Nathan had indeed read something of this, but he had taken no more than a passing interest, mainly to wonder at the thought of all those French ships at sea after so many years being locked up by the British blockade. Under the terms of the recent peace treaty, several West Indian colonies had been restored to France, he had read, and the purpose of this expedition was to bring them back under French control.

Imlay was bending over the map. 'Their first stop is Saint-Domingue,' he said, 'on the island of Hispaniola.'

He indicated a large island in the Antilles, to the east of Cuba. It was not a name you heard much of these days, but Nathan seemed to recall that it was where Columbus had made his first landfall in the New World back in 1492, claiming the island for the Spanish Crown. It had since been divided between Spain and France – the Spanish San Domingo in the east, the French Saint-Domingue in the west – but during the recent conflict, with both powers fully engaged in Europe, the whole place had been overrun by rebel slaves. It was reported that a number of white plantation owners and their families had been massacred and thousands had fled to Cuba. A force of British troops had been sent from Jamaica to seize the island for King George, but the rebels had put up such a strong resistance the expedition had ended in defeat. But this had been several years ago. Imlay proceeded to bring him up to date.

'Bonaparte has stated that his only concern is to restore order and to resume the trade in coffee and sugar. This is understandable. Before the war Saint-Domingue was the richest colony in the Caribbean. Said to be the greatest jewel in the French crown. It produced about forty per cent of the sugar and sixty per cent of all the coffee consumed in Europe – more than all the British Caribbean colonies combined.'

Nathan thought he probably had known this at some point in his career, though he may not have been able to quote the exact figures. His first appointment as post captain had been in the Caribbean, when he had taken command of the frigate *Unicorn* in Havana, after its previous captain had been murdered by members of the crew. It was perhaps fair to say that the economy of Saint-Domingue had not been among his principle concerns at the time.

Imlay was still talking.

'At present the colony is under the control of a former slave called Toussaint Louverture – perhaps the name is familiar to you?'

He had detected a flicker of interest in Nathan's eyes, for the name was indeed familiar. Louverture was something of a celebrity in the abolitionist circles frequented by his mother. He had led the first successful slave rebellion since Spartacus, she had informed him, though Nathan's recollection from his sparse classical education was that Spartacus and the surviving members of his rebel army had been defeated by the Roman general Crassus and crucified along the Appian Way. Thus far, Louverture had avoided a similar fate. The new French Republic had not only abolished slavery but also appointed him governor general of Saint-Domingue.

But this was before Bonaparte came to power.

'So far as Bonaparte is concerned the whole thing is a mess,' Imlay declared. 'And as we all know Bonaparte don't like a mess.'

Nelson made a huffing sound. He had seen how Bonaparte tidied up a mess in Italy. Nathan said nothing. He had his own problems where Bonaparte was concerned, and they were rather more personal.

'Louverture has played into Bonaparte's hands by appointing himself governor for life,' Imlay went on.

'Man after his own heart, you could say,' offered Nelson.

'Indeed, though I doubt if Boney would see it that way. He says he won't restore slavery, but I don't know many who believe him, even in France. This is one reason he has sent so many ships and so many men. However – it is not the only reason . . .'

He paused and glanced pointedly at the slumbering figure in the corner of the room.

Nelson raised his voice. 'Sir William?' He raised it a little louder, nothing like the volume on the quarterdeck, but quite loud for an English country house. 'Sir William!'

Hamilton awoke with a start and looked about him in some confusion.

'You may wish to prepare for dinner, Sir William,' said Nelson in a kindlier tone. 'It will be served in about half an hour.'

'Ah. Yes. Indeed.'

The old man rose with an effort, bowed in their general direction and shuffled stiffly to the door. Watching him, Nathan reflected that it was only four years since he had been one of the most senior diplomats in Europe, and one of the most respected. Was this how it would be for all of them if they lived long enough?

'The fact is that for all his apparent openness in this matter, Bonaparte has a secret agenda,' Imlay resumed as soon as the door had shut, 'and that is to build a new French Empire on the North American mainland.'

Imlay had unrolled the map further to the west, to reveal most of the American mainland, with the individual states of the Union marked in different colours. They covered about a third of the continent, from the Atlantic coast to the Mississippi River. To the west, there was nothing.

Imlay traced a finger along the length of the Mississippi, from the Canada border to the Gulf of Mexico.

'This, gentlemen, marks the westward boundary of the United States – the Mississippi River. The territory to the west was formerly claimed by the French which is why it is called Louisiana, but it was ceded to the Spanish some years ago. As you see, it extends from New Orleans to the Canada border and westward to the Rocky Mountains, an area of about eight hundred thousand square miles, but there are only a few thousand Europeans in the entire territory. Most of the inhabitants are Indians.'

A shrewd glance and the hint of a smirk in Nathan's direction. One of their early clashes had been in the region of New Orleans when Nathan had been captain of the *Unicorn* and Imlay had been a French agent, though even then his true loyalties were unknown. The region had long been of interest to the Americans.

'So, now to the point.' Imlay was no longer smirking. 'As Captain Peake will know, the French have been keen to recover this territory for many years. Well, they have finally done so, at least on paper. We have had intelligence that about a year ago Spain and France made a secret agreement to this effect. I think they were offered a small part of Tuscany in return.'

A mirthless laugh from Nelson.

'Possibly they thought they had the best of the bargain,' Imlay went on. 'However, Bonaparte has a different view. He sees a great future for French settlement in America, and we have secret intelligence that as soon as his forces have restored order in Saint-Domingue, they will move on to New Orleans, and then on up the Mississippi, building a chain of forts to establish the French claim to the entire region.'

They stared in silence for a moment at the map. It was too vast an area, too ambitious a concept for Nathan to get his head around. You needed a head like Bonaparte's, he supposed.

Nelson broke the silence. 'Can they do it?'

'There is very little to stop them. Even if they progressed no further than New Orleans it would be a disaster for the United States. Something like three-fifths of our trade passes down the Mississippi, and then out through New Orleans. If they put a stop to that, or even impose tariffs, it will bring ruin to thousands of our citizens in the region.'

Nathan was aware that Imlay himself owned land on the Ohio and that he had spent a great deal of time and energy trying to attract settlers there. It was the main reason he had written books about it.

'Besides, a French army on the Mississippi is unthinkable. It would be like the bad old days of the French and Indian Wars – without the British Army on our side. And of course, it would put paid to any dreams of expanding westward to the Pacific, which would not please a lot of people in my country, I can tell you.'

'You got rid of the British,' Nathan pointed out, 'when we became a problem.'

'And we will get rid of the French, too,' said Imlay. 'That is why I am here.'

Nathan doubted if it was that straightforward, but he held his peace.

'So, what are you planning to do?'

'Officially, nothing. Jefferson is one of Bonaparte's greatest admirers, as you probably know. He don't want a war with Bonaparte. But unofficially, it has been agreed that the place to stop him is here.'

He drummed two fingers on the island of Hispaniola. Rat-a-tat-tat.

'If the French army meets with serious resistance in Saint-Domingue, there will be no more talk of building forts on the Mississippi.'

'Is that likely?' Nathan queried.

'Louverture has seen off the Spanish and the British in the past few years. Not in such numbers, admittedly, but if the French try to re-impose slavery, he will have no shortage of recruits. But they need guns – muskets, rifles, whatever weaponry we can give them – artillery most of all.'

'When you say "we" . . . ?' Nathan queried.

Imlay frowned. 'Did I say "we"?'

'You did. I take it you mean the American government.'

'Good God, no!' Imlay appeared shocked. 'There can be no official involvement in this. And not just because it would mean war with the French. If it were known in the southern states that the Federal government was supplying rebel slaves with guns . . . You can imagine the reaction.'

Nathan could. He was not that well up on U.S. politics, despite his mother's best efforts, but he knew that no president could remain in power without the support of the southern states – and they were all slave states.

'So, if it is not the Federal government.'

'All I can tell you, between these four walls, is that I have been authorised to secure enough in the way of weaponry to give Louverture what you might call a fighting chance. And the ships to deliver it. I have one waiting right now in the Downs, a fine sloop of sixteen guns, crewed up and ready to sail, and another in America – and there will be more. All we need now is someone to command them.'

'Well, the country is full of unemployed naval officers . . .'

'You know my meaning.'

Nathan knew his meaning.

'I am not a gun-runner,' he instructed him firmly. 'You can find any number of men who can run guns in the Caribbean.'

'If it were that easy, I would not be here,' Imlay retorted. 'We need someone who has had experience of supporting an army from the sea . . .' He paused for a moment and Nathan noted the swift glance in Nelson's direction. 'As you have when you served under Lord Nelson in the Mediterranean. And I should say that the financial rewards will be commensurate with the risk.'

'I may be on half-pay,' Nathan replied a little tartly, 'but I still hold the King's commission. I am not free to go off on a jaunt to the Caribbean on some clandestine mission for the Americans, official or otherwise.'

Imlay's glance flicked across to Nelson again. Nathan wondered how much of this had been discussed by them beforehand. Most of it, probably. Nathan looked at him too, a question in his eyes.

The admiral had the grace to look embarrassed. 'It is really nothing to do with me, Peake,' he said. 'It is entirely your decision. However, I can tell you there would be no objection from the Admiralty, none at all. On the contrary.'

'So, the Admiralty knows about this?'

'It has been discussed.' Nelson's reply was terse. The question could be regarded as impertinent in a junior officer. But then he relented.

'This is in strict confidence you understand?' He waited for Nathan's nod of assent. 'But I can tell you that Mr Imlay has shared this information with the First Lord and one or two other gentlemen in the Ministry, and while a breach between the United States and the French Republic would be welcome in some quarters' – a look and a resigned shrug in Imlay's direction – 'it was thought to be in the best long-term interests of His Majesty's Government if Bonaparte's ambitions were to founder on the rock of Saint-Domingue, as it were. Or to be plain, to contrive a situation where it becomes a constant drain on French resources while allowing us to replenish our own and rebuild our alliances on the continent of Europe.'

Nathan nodded thoughtfully. This all made sense, but he had another question – best asked of Imlay. 'So, when did you think to involve me in this?'

'When I saw you at the American embassy with your mother. Until then I believed you were to be still in India.'

'You were there?' Nathan was astonished. 'At the balloon symposium?' How could he have missed him?

'Alas, I was obliged to miss the event, but I observed you as you were leaving. And yesterday I had the good fortune to run into Lord Nelson at the Admiralty and your name came up in conversation.'

Imlay at the U.S. embassy, Imlay at the Admiralty and now Imlay at Nelson's house. This was how it worked; it was how it had always worked. Fortune had little to do with it.

'The fact is, Peake, we need someone we know we can rely upon,' said Nelson, 'but is not afraid to take independent action . . .'

If he had left it there, Nathan might have basked in the glow for some considerable time, but scarcely drawing breath he added: 'Someone who is something of a loose cannon, ha ha.'

Someone who could be described as such if it all went badly wrong, thought Nathan. Someone it would not be difficult to disown.

'*Oh, he has always been something of a loose cannon. To be perfectly honest, we have never known where his true allegiance lies.*'

From another part of the house came the sound of a bell. Dinner was served.

'Can I sleep on it?' said Nathan.

6

The Fire

L'Ocean, off Cap Francais, Saint-Domingue

She woke in a panic thinking the ship was on fire. But it was not the ship, it was Le Cap.

The whole city was ablaze. Cap-Francais, the old colonial capital of Saint-Domingue, the place they had once called the Paris of the Antilles, the place that was to be her new home. She watched from the French flagship, a mile or so from the shore, the flames dancing and leaping all along the coast and way up into the hillside, flames a hundred feet high, and sometimes higher.

You will be the Queen of the Americas, her brother Napoleon had told her. Queen Pauline. You will have your own court in Cap-Francais, as brilliant as any court in Europe. She did not believe him of course. They would play these games as children, usually with their brothers and sisters, building up their hopes and dreams only to knock them down and laugh at them. They both had a streak of cruelty in them. The only difference between them was that she was ashamed of hers and tried to be a better person. She did not think that was true of Napoleon, but he would not think this was funny; he would be enraged.

'How did it happen?' she asked, as if anyone would know. But they did.

'It was the blacks,' they said. 'When they saw the fleet and they knew they could not fight us, they set fire to it.'

There were explosions on the shore and they stood further out to sea as a precaution. There was nothing they could do but watch. The entire crew and all the passengers were out on deck or up on the rigging. The fire seemed to be spreading along the coast and up the hillside. It must have covered an area of two or three miles, and they could hear the roaring, like a giant furnace.

Then she heard another sound, curiously like bells.

'They *are* bells,' someone told her. 'Church bells.'

'But who is ringing them,' she said, 'in this heat?'

She imagined some fanatical monks, hearts set on martyrdom, tolling on the bells as the flames reached out for them. Or the ghosts of the dead. She was not the only one who thought that, and a great fear swept through the ship's company, as if it foretold the end of the world, but one of the officers said it was the upward rush of the hot air inside the bell tower, making the bells swing on their yokes. When the flames consumed the wooden beams, the bells would fall.

Indeed, soon after this, they stopped ringing.

'Where are all the people?' she said. She would have thought they would make for the sea, to jump in the water, or escape in the ships, but she could not see a single person along the waterfront, and there were no ships, just the French fleet standing off the shore.

But no one knew what had happened to the people.

'Evacuated it is to be hoped,' said the admiral. 'Gone to the hills above the port, but you cannot count on it.'

Her husband, Leclerc, had landed earlier. He was ashore somewhere with the army, fighting their way up the coast, she had been told, though there seemed little point. Le Cap was lost, with or without a battle. She watched the flames leaping up the hillside to the outer suburbs. And on the hills above the town there were more fires. Sugar plantations, they told her.

'Why are they doing this?' she said.

Leclerc had meant to read a proclamation from her brother, assuring the people of liberty, equality, fraternity. The ideals of the French Republic. There would be no return to slavery, he gave them his word. At least until reinforcements arrived.

'They do not know what is good for them,' the admiral said. His name was Villaret and she did not like him. He was over fifty years old and suffered from gout, like they all did. One of the old guard, and probably a Royalist. He made it very clear what he thought of the blacks. 'Slaves they were and slaves they will be again.'

She shivered and her maid fetched her a coat. Despite the fire it was cold out at sea. There was a stiff wind blowing inshore. They said it was the heat of the blaze, sucking out the air, so that more rushed in to fill the vacuum. She could see the ships of the fleet all around them, heaving on the swell. Even *L'Ocean*, the flagship, the biggest ship in the French navy was struggling to hold her station in the wind. Pauline was starting to feel sick. Even after the long voyage across the Atlantic she had never become used to the sea. She doubted if she ever would.

'What will we do now?' she said.

'Carry on as we mean to,' said the admiral grimly. 'They could burn the whole island and it will not make the slightest bit of difference. I advise you to go below, Madame, and get some sleep.'

It was the night of 4 February 1802.

7

Night Watch

Sleep did not come easy for Nathan, that night at Merton Place.

He could sleep in a cot rolling through a forty degree arc, or standing up on deck with his arm twined through the mizzen shrouds like a dosser in a twopenny flophouse, he could sleep at the masthead, or in the saddle. But not here.

He had too much to think about. Imlay, Saint-Domingue, Nelson and Saint-Vincent . . . The uncomfortable feeling that he had not been told the whole story, though there was nothing unusual about that. And it did not help that he was stuffed with food and wine, or that the after-dinner entertainment had filled his mind with images so bizarre that when he did slip beneath the surface it was to awake within seconds, startled by dreams of Emma Hamilton, in one or other of her many incarnations.

She had always been an accomplished actor, Emma, a mime artist of exceptional talent. Visitors to the home of the British envoy in Naples would be entertained by her performances of scenes from the classics, with the minimum of props – and clothing – and invited to speculate on her identity as she threw herself into the most erotic and alluring of poses, transforming herself from haughty goddess to tragic heroine with the clever manipulation of a shawl, a pose, a facial expression . . . She was a living gallery of statues and portraits, a Roman maiden making an offering, a martyred saint, a Medea slaying her children . . . Young men on the Grand Tour came to Naples to see Vesuvius and Emma. They carried away stronger memories of Emma. But that was in Naples and Emma in her glorious prime. Now . . .

In his sleepless state, Nathan plunged into a lonely and ultimately futile debate on the nature of beauty, propriety, vanity, adultery, the age-ing process, and the sadness of declining powers . . . He felt there were infinite truths that he was on the edge of grasping, if only he were not so tired, or distracted by the thought of Gilbert Imlay and his offer of employment.

Eventually he gave up the unequal struggle, for he was vastly outnum-bered by demons, his own and others, and he wrapped himself in his dressing gown with the bedspread over his shoulders for added warmth, and shuffled over to the window to see what the sky was doing. But it was not doing very much. The moon was there, a great horned beast chasing Venus through dark, ragged clouds, but most of the stars were playing hide and seek. He followed the handle of the Plough to Polaris, or at least where he should have found it, but if it was there, and he was quite certain it was, it was keeping its light very dim. After straining his eyes for a few minutes in search of this and other heavenly bodies that might have been familiar to him he returned his gaze to earth and out towards the river where he had been fishing with Sir William Hamilton, but this, too, was indistinct, not even a silver snail's trail in the darkness. A mist lay low across the fields and meadows and the trees that rose from it looked as if they were draped in a ghostly shroud. Occasionally, he heard the hoot of an owl and the trilling of a night jar, and once the cry of a vixen. This was the England he was fighting for, or so he had been told. A pastoral idyll, Milton's Eden. From out in the mist the owl gave another hoot. Or it might have been his mother. Either way, it was derisory.

And yet, ironically, the rebellion in Saint-Domingue was a cause his mother would almost certainly have approved. She had been campaign-ing for the abolition of slavery for as long as Nathan could remember, lon-ger even than William Wilberforce and his Clapham Sect, and for once he and she were in accord, if not total agreement. Nathan had always detested slavery – he might have imbibed this with his mother's milk, save that she had almost certainly put him out to a wet nurse – and what he had seen for himself in the West Indies and Louisiana had angered and disgusted and shamed him beyond measure, beyond anything else he had ever seen, anywhere else in the world. Well, now he had an opportunity to do something about it.

But there was another reason why he might want to give Bonaparte a bloody nose, as Nelson had put it. During one of his clandestine trips to Paris, he had saved the man's life.

It was not intentional. He had been sent to Paris by the Earl Spencer, who was then First Lord of the Admiralty in hopes of discovering if a secret deal had been signed between France and Spain. He was to pose as a wealthy American sea captain called Turner who was a great supporter of the Revolution and favoured a permanent alliance between the United States and France. His main contacts had been two women – Madame Tallien, the wife of one of the two most powerful men in France, and Rose Beauharnais, the mistress of the other, Paul Barras. But while he was in the city, he had been caught up in a counter-Revolution – a Royalist bid to seize power from the Republicans. Sent by Barras with a message for a young colonel of artillery called Napoleon Bonaparte, he had ended up following him around the centre of Paris with a street map while the colonel organised the defence of the government area. It was one of his least useful functions as a secret agent, or indeed, any other role that life had called upon him to play. From time to time Nathan would hold open the map while Bonaparte consulted it, but as it was raining heavily, the map began to disintegrate in his hands. He was trying to rescue the important part, when he noticed that someone had given the colonel a horse. He had thought at the time that this was probably a mistake, and the next minute the horse slipped on the wet cobblestones and bolted towards the Royalist mob, dragging Bonaparte with it, his foot caught in the stirrup. Without thinking, Nathan had jumped forward and grabbed the reins. His hat had been shot off and the horse shot through the head, but Bonaparte had survived. Shortly afterwards, he blew the Royalists apart with his cannon and that was the end of that. But for Bonaparte it was just the beginning. He had gone on to command the army of Italy and invade Egypt, and then he had returned to Paris and seized power through a military coup. He was called First Consul, but he was effectively a military dictator.

Imlay had spoken of the coup at dinner and declared that it had brought the Revolution to an end.

'I was never a supporter of the Revolution,' he had said, presumably for Nelson's benefit – he had not told Mary Wollstonecraft that, and he would not have said it to Thomas Jefferson, either. 'But all those people who fought and died for it, you could at least say they died believing in *something*, even if it was misguided. But after all that bloodshed and passion, all that *conviction brio*, to end up with Bonaparte . . .'

And Nathan had sat there, in silence, thinking about that moment he had saved the dictator's life. The *deus ex machina* who had assisted his rise to power. Not many people knew about this, certainly not in England – he had chosen not to include it in his report, but Nathan knew. If you save a man's life, it was said, you are responsible for what he does with the rest of it. Bonaparte had called Nathan 'his lucky star'. How many people had died since as a result of what happened that day in Paris, how many would die in the future?

He thought about it now as he kept his lonely night watch in the window of Nelson's new flagship. Here was his chance to make amends. If Bonaparte could be stopped in the West Indies, it might well stop him in America, and even in Europe. The French did not take kindly to failure in their leaders. And he would be doing his own country a great service, Nelson had said. So many uncertainties of course, but then . . .

He looked out across the dark fields, but he did not see them, or even the mist that veiled them. In his mind's eye, he saw a ship. A ship at anchor. But where? The sea was grey and choppy, and it was raining. An English rain. Then it came to him. Gosport, to the west of Portsmouth Harbour, and the ship was the *Peregrine*, the first ship he had served upon, the old *Peregrine*, 64, Captain Pobjoy. And he was a midshipman, just thirteen years old. And yet he remembered, even after nearly twenty years, the smell of the sea and the sound of the rain – and that strange mix of feelings as he was ferried out to her, that sense of – what? It was not excitement or adventure, or even apprehension, though all three were probably there somewhere. But what he remembered most strongly was the sense of uncertainty. Of not knowing what lay in store for him, out there, in the rain and the darkness.

Later, when he took an interest in philosophy, and astronomy, and even music, he considered that some level of uncertainty – or mystery, to give it a more attractive name – was for him an essential ingredient of life, for without it there was only the certainty of death, and a dull, dark plodding towards it. Step by step, season after season, year after year. Like one of his father's oxen, or they being ignorant of the process, the men who drove them.

He turned away from the window and hobbled back to bed, trailing his bedspread behind him. He knew what he would do in the morning, he did not have to sleep on it.

8

The Ship

She was lying in the Downs, off Deal. The *Falaise*, of sixteen guns, a newish French corvette taken in the last summer of the war by a British squadron off Rochefort on her maiden voyage. The navy had no use for her – there being a prejudice in the service against corvettes on the grounds that they were too lightly armed, though more likely, Nathan thought, because they were a class of ship thought of as specifically French and damned for that alone – so she had been sold off to a London-based consortium of merchants and shipowners who planned to operate her as a privateer – a private ship of war under a letter of marque permitting her to 'cruise upon the enemy'. However, a few weeks after their purchase the preliminaries of peace had been signed in Paris and her cruising ended before it had properly begun. The owners were considering turning her into a slaver when Imlay turned up with his offer: 'And so we have already contributed to the fight against the Abominable Trade', he informed Nathan dryly, as they jounced and bounced along the sunken lanes of Surrey. Nathan declined to comment. He took most of what Imlay told him with a large pinch of salt.

They travelled post, stopping for a brief lunch at Westerham, and then on to Canterbury for the night. Nathan slept for most of the journey, but over dinner in Canterbury – a very fine Dover sole followed by a duck from the Pevensey marshes – he put Imlay to some serious interrogation about this enterprise of his, which Nathan had thus far only promised to 'consider' with no commitment made. It was hard work, of course, for one had no means of knowing if what Imlay said was true or false, or a fairly random selection of the two. In Imlay's world there was no moral distinction between either commodity – they were just that – commodities, or rather currencies, to be used according to whatever would buy him the most advantage in whatever difficult situation he happened to be in at the time. However, he seemed tolerably well informed about the situation on Hispaniola. He had spent some time there as a young man, he said, trading in rum and molasses with both the French and the Spanish planters. In those days, back in the 1870s, there were about 30,000 Europeans in the French sector alone, and some 800,000 African slaves who were treated abysmally, Imlay said, even by the standards prevailing in most countries where slavery was the established form of labour. Floggings, hangings and other brutal forms of punishment were routine – more specialised executions included being staked out in swamps to be eaten alive by mosquitos, crucified on planks and drowned in sacks, but most of the deaths occurred simply because of the appalling conditions in which the slaves were housed and fed. Roughly about 50,000 of them died every year and were replaced by regular shipments from West Africa, notably Dahomey and Benin, accounting for about a third of the entire Atlantic slave trade.

Then suddenly, in 1791, inspired it was said by the French Revolution, the slaves of Saint-Domingue threw off their chains and exacted a violent revenge. Over a thousand plantations were burned to the ground and many thousands of colonists slaughtered or forced to flee to San Domingo and Cuba. After a period of total chaos, the rebels had come under the unified command of a freed slave by the name of Toussaint Louverture. When the new government in Paris abolished slavery he declared his allegiance to the French Republic and was recognised as governor general of Saint-Domingue, fighting both the Spanish and their British allies and gradually winning control of the whole island.

'I met him recently,' Imlay announced airily over dinner – to Nathan's frank astonishment. Imlay never ceased to astonish him either as to the extent of his perfidy or his impressive network of contacts in various countries. 'He is a fine man, a devout Roman Catholic, educated by Jesuits, I believe. He has worked very hard to improve the economy and security of the island, maintains a large standing army, very well-disciplined from what I have heard – and seen for myself, in fact – modelled on the

Revolutionary French Army – and he has restored the plantation system, replacing the slaves with paid workers.'

'You met him where?' Nathan enquired.

'In Cap Francais, which they call the Paris of the Antilles,' Imlay smiled.

'And when was this?'

'Oh, a couple of months ago, on my way to England.'

Nathan decided to return to this later. 'So, if he is such a paragon, why are the French trying to get rid of him?'

'Ah, but you must ask your friend Napoleon that,' said Imlay slyly, for he knew of Nathan's association with the young Bonaparte – though not that he had saved his life. 'Possibly because he does not have a high regard for black men. And certainly not when they appear to have a high regard for themselves. He was not overly pleased when Toussaint appointed himself Governor-for-Life. Also . . .'

He appeared to consider for a moment and a subtle change came over his features which Nathan had learned to recognise over the years as indicating an element of prevarication on his part, or at least a reluctance to disclose too much relevant information, but then he went on: 'Louverture has made certain trading agreements with Britain and the United States which Bonaparte might consider a threat to his future plans and even a challenge to his own authority.'

This was something else to bear in mind for the future. Wherever trade was involved there was money, and wherever money was involved, Imlay's motives became rather more complicated – though in some ways a lot clearer.

'So, what did you discuss with him when you met,' he asked, 'if it is not to betray a confidence?'

'Well, it is a matter of some confidentiality of course,' Imlay affirmed, dropping his voice, though they had bespoke a private room and it was hard to imagine that many of those staying at the inn, or indeed, in the entire city of Canterbury can have been much interested in the affairs of a distant Caribbean island. 'But as we are now associates, I can tell you that we did discuss some specific requirements in the way of munitions, and the means by which they might be delivered.'

Nathan suppressed a shudder at the word 'associate'. He had only agreed to 'take a look' at this ship that was lying in the Downs and give Imlay's proposal his further consideration. He was still a long way from thinking of himself as an 'associate'. However, he was also uneasily aware that the more they talked about it, the more he felt drawn into whatever dubious enterprise Imlay had in mind. It would not be the first time he had been led astray by one of Imlay's intrigues – there was a certain chemistry between them that sometimes reminded him, uncomfortably, of that between Faustus and Mephistopheles, though he would never wish to concede that Imlay had that much power over him, or even any at all. Still, he cautioned himself to maintain a cool reserve. He had drunk far too much wine, eaten a great deal too much of the duck and their present surroundings, with the low, blackened beams, the guttering candles and the smoky warmth of the open fire, lent itself to an air of conspiracy that he found all too alluring. They were like a pair of smugglers, he thought, arranging their next run across the English Channel.

As if to countenance these suspicions, Imlay was now waxing lyrical over the buccaneers who had been drawn to Hispaniola in a previous age, and the numerous secluded bays and inlets where they had hidden their ships.

'The second longest coastline in the Caribbean,' he informed Nathan, 'and a perfect environment to play hide and seek with the French Navy.' Leaning across the table to top us his glass.

He was less forthcoming about the munitions they were to deliver and where these were to come from. But it was 'all in hand', he said, confidently, and they could discuss the details later when Nathan felt properly committed. He did admit, however, that none of the ship's officers or crew had any idea of where they were bound or what plans he had for them once they arrived. He had thought it best, he said, to wait until they were well on their way so that no word of their mission could be passed to the French.

Nathan retired to bed uneasily aware that he was sliding inexorably into something over which he had little or no control. But then he could not remember a time when it had ever been much different.

They left Canterbury at dawn and arrived at Deal in time for a late breakfast at the Royal. The sun was shining through patchy cloud, and the sea unusually calm for the time of year. Another good omen, said Imlay, who clearly felt that Nathan was in need of encouragement. Nathan was not especially encouraged. He knew Deal of old and was not enamoured of the place, or the waters off it.

The port was strategically placed at the point where the English Channel met the North Sea and sheltered from the full force of both by the proximity of the Goodwin Sands – a ten-mile length of sandbank just off the Kent coast, which provided a natural anchorage for ships waiting for the right wind to continue their journey. When it came, there was a frantic rush to up anchor and set sail, with a consequent risk of collision as several hundred ship's captains fought for precedence. But the main reason Nathan disliked the place was that for all the protection given by the Sands, it had one grave shortcoming – the seabed on this part of the English coast was composed of fine sand on a bed of chalk, and in anything more than a fresh breeze it was not uncommon for a ship to drag her anchor and run upon another ship, or upon the shoals themselves. Many hundreds of vessels had been wrecked on the Goodwin Sands over the years, and the boatmen of Deal made a good living from the salvage, while the printers and stationers of the town did a lucrative trade in maps, showing every wreck marked with a cross, the name of the vessel and the date of its demise which were very popular in households that had no connection with the sea. It was a ship's graveyard, full to overflowing, and not the most propitious of places, in Nathan's opinion, to begin any voyage, let alone one that involved Gilbert Imlay.

And yet, gazing out from the forecourt of the Royal Hotel, he felt a familiar lifting of the spirits at the sight of that vast armada of ships, stretching for as far as the eye could see, some with bare poles, others with their sails hung out to dry, all rocking gently on the incoming tide, with the jollyboats and bumboats moving among them. It could have been a painting on the theme 'Ocean Trade' and it was this, he supposed, rather more than the water meadows of Merton, or the country estates of Old England, for which he had been fighting over the past nine years, though there was obviously a strong link betwixt the two. In a few more years, he reflected, if he lived long enough, he might be coming down here to buy a house of his own, on the cliffs beyond the town, and set himself up with a telescope like all the other retired sea captains to watch others go about earning the wealth of nations. It was not a prospect that appealed to him overmuch, but then Imlay could probably be relied upon to save him from it.

'And where lies the *Falaise*,' he enquired, anticipating the usual pre-varication, for Imlay was surprisingly ignorant of nautical matters for one who had made his living at various times by either smuggling or blockade running – though in the particular enterprises in which Nathan had been involved, or knew anything about, he usually confined his activities to making the deals while others took the risks at sea. For once, though, Imlay admitted he had no idea. But not to worry, he assured Nathan complacently, for he had arranged with the landlord to have one of the local boatmen ferry them out in a cutter as soon as they had finished breakfast. The local boatmen, as Nathan was aware from previous visits, knew the name and location of almost every vessel moored in the Downs, and probably a good deal more, for they made their living from servicing them with whatever was required in the way of food, drink and other luxuries during their stay here, and salvaging what was left of them when they were blown on to the Goodwin Sands.

Nathan now knew a little more about the *Falaise* than when he had started out from Merton. He had even examined some of the ship's papers that Imlay had thought to bring along with him. Thus, he had learned, with some disquiet, that when she was taken off Rochefort, she had been called the *Mutine*, which was extraordinary even by the standards of the French Republican Navy. It is true that the word had two meanings in French – mischievous and mutineer – but to choose a name that was even capable of such an interpretation seemed to go well beyond the realms of common sense so far as Nathan was concerned, whether your country was in the hands of royalists, regicides or downright anarchists. The previous owners had obviously thought so, too, and defied convention, and an ele-ment of nautical superstition, by changing her name to the *Falaise*, the town in Normandy where William the Conqueror had been born, which might be useful when it came to playing hide and seek with the French navy in the waters off Hispaniola, especially if they had the odd tricolour in the flag locker.

At any rate, she had been launched in May 1799 in Le Havre, the first of a new class of corvette, armed with 16 eight-pounders and probably in-tended as a cruise raider. Shortly after her launch she had sailed south to Rochefort where she was taken by the inshore blockading squadron with-out having fired a shot in anger. Nothing else Nathan read about her was exceptional. She was 95 feet long and 26 in the beam with a displacement of 400 tons, and she carried a crew of 156, fully manned. In the Royal Navy she would probably have been classed as a sixth-rate, the lowest rate there was. Not that Nathan held that against her. On paper she was ideal for the purposes Imlay had in mind, though Nathan would reserve judgement until he saw how she sailed. He had great respect for French shipbuilders – on the whole they turned out much better craft than the British yards, certainly in terms of their sailing qualities and they were beautiful to look at. It was their crewing that was the problem, in recent years at least, and the fact that they never had a chance to practice at the guns, being locked up in harbour for years on end by the British blockade.

As to the present crewing of the *Falaise*, this was another area of concern to him, and rather more so than his unease about her original name. She had been sold to Imlay fully crewed and most of the men had agreed to serve under the new owner – almost certainly because with the ending of hostilities they would otherwise have been unemployed, and Imlay was paying them twice what they would have earned on a merchant ship. But there were certain anomalies here that Nathan had yet to resolve. A great many of the crew were Americans who had been pressed into the service and released when there was no further need for them. But that must have been when peace terms were agreed, so why had the previous owners taken them on? One man for every twelve tons was the usual calculation when it came to crewing a merchant ship, maybe twice that for a slaver. So the maximum they would have required was seventy. The present complement of the *Falaise* was more than twice that. It was possible, he supposed, that they had other slavers to crew, or that they planned on a raiding expedition into the interior, but if they had gotten that far with their preparations, why sell her to Imlay at a bargain price? So far as Nathan could make out from Imlay's vague – evasive? – responses, the Americans accounted for near half the crew.

As for the rest, they were 'mostly British', said Imlay, though that covered a multitude of sins, and if they were anything like most privateer crews Nathan had encountered in the course of his career they would be drawn mostly from the smuggling fraternity, with a sprinkling of naval deserters and other renegades from the law, and perhaps a few 'gentlemen' adventurers fallen on hard times and drawn to the prospect of prize money. They would be no better or worse than crews in the Royal Navy, which was overly dependent on the sweepings of the prisons and those unfortunate enough to be seized by the press gangs, but on a King's ship a captain had the authority conferred by the Articles of War, enforced by a great number of commissioned officers and warrant officers, and anything from a squad to a whole company of marines. All Nathan had was the authority of Imlay.

Once he had started thinking along these lines, his natural pessimism asserted itself and he started to consider other problems that might be waiting for him should he accept the American's offer. How was he to introduce himself to the men, for instance? He was not even using his real name. He had decided it would be prudent to use that of his *alter ego*, Captain Nathaniel Turner of Nantucket, in case word should carry to the French that a ship running guns to the rebels in Saint-Domingue was under the command of a post captain in His Britannic Majesty's Navy. For this reason, he was not wearing his uniform – just his boat cloak over a plain blue jacket and breeches. No epaulettes, no medal ribbons, he was not even carrying his sword – all he had retained from the service was his hat. So he would not be able to rely on his past reputation to give him a degree of authority.

Then there was the question of where he was to berth. The *Falaise* was too small a ship to have a cabin of equal size for himself and Imlay, and there was no question of them sharing, not so far as Nathan was concerned. As for the other officers, there hardly seemed to be any. The ship's master had been part of the consortium that had previously owned her – a senior partner in fact – and he had declined to accept a diminished role – 'not that he was offered it', said Imlay, hastily – and taken his chief mate with him. That left just two others, the second mate, Mr Keppler, and the third – Mr Cole. Both had previously held the King's commission, Imlay said, but that appeared to be the full extent of his knowledge, or all he was prepared to reveal. Nathan would have liked to know what rank they had held and what circumstances had caused them to quit the service – or more likely, to have been dismissed – for they had joined the ship some time before the war had ended. He would be far more reliant upon his junior officers than he had ever been in the past when it came to the maintenance of discipline. There would be no marines with their red coats and fixed bayonets, no master at arms with his minions, no midshipmen, and he had no personal servants – having lost them one way or another in the course of his wanderings about the Mediterranean and

Asia. He did not even have his own store of provisions, or stock of wine. He was beginning to wish he had stayed with his mother.

Then the cutter came round the stern of a fat East Indiaman and he saw a flush-rigged ship of war almost dead ahead, with eight black chequers on the white band that ran from stem to stern, and Imlay gave him a nod and a smile, and said: 'Behold your new command.' This was presumptuous of him in the circumstances, but still, now that he had seen her, Nathan felt considerably less displeased with him and the situation in which he found himself. She looked what she was, a long, lean predator, redolent of menace and an infinite range of possibilities for a man who was in his soul, as Imlay well knew, a buccaneer.

More to the point, he noted that she was double anchored to ensure against dragging, her rigging taut and her sails neatly furled, no loose ends hanging down, no foul streaks from the scuppers, not even the heads; in fact she looked fresh painted. There were a few men fishing from the waist but this was fair enough if they had no other duties to perform, and she was clearly keeping a look out for as they closed on her there was a cry from the deck and the boatman enquired of Imlay: 'What shall I answer, sir?'

'*Falaise*,' replied Imlay, a clear indication that they had the ship's captain aboard, though Nathan gave him a glare to show that this was far from agreed, at least in his own mind. Imlay did not appear to notice.

It took a moment for this information to be relayed and absorbed, then across the water came the clear, shrill sound of the bosun's whistle calling all hands and a rush of feet across the decks. This was a good sign but before Nathan had a chance to think about it and weigh it in the balance, the cutter swung neatly across the bows and he looked up to see the ship's figurehead.

'Good God!' he exclaimed aloud, for though it bore the face of a woman, there was something so utterly depraved or deranged, or possibly both, about her expression it caused him considerable disquiet. He assumed she was meant to be the spirit of mischief, or possibly Revolution, for the unknown sculptor had given her a Phyrgian cap, or *bonnet rouge*, much favoured by the Paris mob, to perch upon her snakelike locks. Doubtless this was considered appropriate for a ship designed to wreak havoc among the enemies of the Republic, but Nathan wished the new owners had considered changing it along with the name. Possibly it was too much trouble for them, or they had sold the vessel before they could make the effort.

Nathan was still a little stunned as the cutter came up on the larboard side and shed the wind, keeping just enough way to reach the entry port. A ladder had been lowered for his convenience complete with side ropes, and several heads peered down at him from the rail as he stood up in the sternsheets and made his way forward. 'No slips', he silently commanded himself, for it had been the best part of a year since he had last come aboard a ship in this way, and an unkind fate had no better opportunity to damn him in the eyes of the entire ship's company, but then the boatman's lad hooked onto the chainplates and Nathan swung on to the ladder and ran up onto the deck as confidently as he had been doing since he was thirteen years old, which of course, he had.

Another wail of the bosun's pipe and as it faded, a cry of 'Off hats' from one of the several officers and warrant officers who waited on the gundeck to greet him. One of them stepped forward.

'Mr Keppler, second mate. Welcome aboard, sir.' A youngish man, probably in his early twenties, with fair hair and a weathered complexion, wearing a plain blue pea jacket with no insignia. He spoke confidently enough but his eyes betrayed a level of uncertainty, even apprehension, for he could not have known until a minute or so ago that the owner and his new captain were coming aboard, and his mind would be filled with a whole host of faults they might find. Nathan should have announced himself and asked Keppler to name the other officers to him, but he felt suddenly deprived of the power of speech, not from any shyness or lack of confidence, but from the sheer effrontery of what he was doing, and an unwillingness to begin whatever he was beginning here with a lie. Though God knows it would not be the first time, by any means.

'Permit me to introduce your new commander,' said Imlay, stepping into the silence: 'Captain Turner – of Nantucket.'

9

The Muster List

Captain Turner of Nantucket sat at the captain's table in the stern cabin of the *Falaise a*nd inspected the ledger that had been placed before him. It was the ship's muster list and it took less than a minute to tell him much of what he needed to know, which was that Imlay was up to his old tricks and this whole enterprise was very likely as much of a sham as he was.

Thus far, Nathan had found little to complain about, at least so far as the ship itself was concerned. The *Falaise* might not up to the standards of the Royal Navy in many respects – the decks were not holystoned to a state of cleanliness that he might have dined off them, the brass work not so burnished that he might have shaved in it – not that he had ever been tempted in twenty years of service to do either of these things – and there was a good deal of squalor below decks that he put down to the fact that he had come aboard with little more than a moment's notice. He did not go poking his nose into the crew's quarters but he saw enough to inform him that there were a number of women aboard, but then he would have anticipated that, even on a King's ship, so close to port. Mr Keppler, who conducted him on his tour of inspection, was clearly embarrassed to be caught with his pants down, so to speak, but in all essential respects everything appeared to be in good order. Being a relatively new ship, launched no more than a year or so ago, her timbers were sound, her masts, sails and rigging in prime condition and her guns looked as if they had never been fired, though the gunner, Mr Caine, assured him that they had, if not in anger, and that in her first two or three weeks as a privateer, before they heard that the war was over, they had practised every second day with powder and shot and achieved a creditable two broadsides in five and a half minutes. Nathan thought they would have to do better than that before they fired at anything at all capable of firing back, but he kept this opinion to himself for the time being and confined himself to appraising their condition in repose, which was as good as on any ship he had commanded, and a lot better than on some he had not. He noted with approval that they were fitted with flintlocks – rather than the old-fashioned linstocks more commonly used in the French navy – with wad hook, rammer and a powder ladle and horn to every gun, side tackles neatly frapped, muzzles lashed to a pair of eyeholes above the gun ports . . . and all moving parts, including the wheels of the trucks, thoroughly greased with cook's slush. The shot lockers were amidships, just forward of the pump well, with fifty rounds of iron shot per gun, Mr Caine informed him, five of grape and three of chain shot – for use against the enemy rigging, he added unnecessarily – and Nathan was about to utter a sardonic response when he recalled that the poor man had no idea what ships he had commanded before if any, and might even be someone Imlay had run into on the way here.

He was a younger man than was usual in a master gunner – mid-twenties at most, Nathan would have said – and he admitted on their way to inspect the magazine that his last situation had been as gunner's mate on the old *Centaur*, 74, until she was paid off in Chatham within a week of the war's ending. But he seemed to know his guns, and apart from that one remark about the chain shot said nothing that Nathan might have taken amiss.

The magazine was not, of course, guarded by an armed Marine, but was at least kept under lock and key and appeared to be equipped with all the necessary safety precautions—no fire or iron allowed, a separate light room to illuminate the inner chamber through a pane of glass, and the deck fitted with small panels of charcoal to absorb the damp. The powder was kept in stout wooden casks with copper hoops and the one he had opened for him had even been corned—wetted and formed into grains to improve its consistency—but then he almost literally stumbled upon the first real surprise since coming aboard – a rack of hollowed-out cast-iron balls filled with powder and fitted with a short fuse. Explosive shells. A projectile he had not seen before on any ship of war other than a bomb ketch. He gave Caine a look. For once the gunner appeared a little thrown.

'They came with the ship,' he replied, with a glance toward the second mate.

'But – for what purpose?' enquired Nathan, for they were far too large to be fired from the eight-pounders, even if anyone could be found reckless enough to take the risk – they had a tendency, he had heard, to explode in the breech or within a few feet of emerging from the barrel, to the detriment of all within the vicinity.

'For the murderers,' said the gunner, mysteriously.

Mr Keppler led him amidships, and there, nestling among the casks of rum and barrels of flour were two large objects which even in the gloom of the orlop deck Nathan recognised as naval howitzers – or mortars, murtherers or murderers, according to custom and tradition – each mounted on a wooden gun carriage and secured to rings on the deck, though of course there was no gun port for them to fire through. He gazed at them in wonder as the light from the hatchway gleamed on their short, bronze muzzles. *Obusiers de vaisseau*, the French called them – a large-calibre but light piece of naval ordnance capable of firing round shot or an explosive shell at low velocity – designed in response to the British carronades or 'smashers', which were particularly lethal at close quarters. But he had heard that the French had given them up as ineffectual, as well as being a danger to the ship firing them.

'They were with her when she was taken,' Mr Keppler informed him. 'There are fittings for them on the quarterdeck, but we thought it best to keep them down here until we knew what to do with them or had instructions from the owners.'

Nathan gave a nod, which was the best he could do for the time being. It occurred to him that Imlay might be keeping them for the rebels in Saint-Domingue though they would not thank him for it if they had to drag them across a mountain range covered in forest.

For reasons he did not care to disclose he was keen to inspect the armoury where the small arms were kept when not in use. This, too, was on the orlop deck, directly under the gunroom where they would have been secured in the distant past before it was taken over as accommodation for the officers. Most of the weapons were stashed away in boxes, save those lying on the workbench to be repaired, but Mr Caine's itinerary listed 76 muskets, 40 pairs of pistols and a lethal assortment of the edged weapons required for boarding – 30 poleaxes, 100 cutlasses, 50 pikes and a couple of dozen tomahawks. There were also a number of hand grenades, Mr Caine informed him, which he kept in the magazine because of the powder. Again, no sentry, and the lock and clasp on the door could have been broken in seconds by anyone determined enough, armed with a simple crowbar. But again, Nathan said nothing of this.

They made their way back to the upper deck and Nathan gave a curt nod to the waiting and clearly anxious group on the quarterdeck, but while he was reasonably satisfied with the state of the ship, he was not at all pleased with what he had seen of the crew. Not all of them, by any means, but enough to increase his edginess. There was a lot of standing around without any obvious form of employment which Nathan found intolerable, for there was always something to do on a ship, even when she was moored, and if there was not, it had been instilled in him as a young midshipman that the maintenance of discipline required for it to be invented, even if it was scraping the rust off the chain cables. But it was not simply the standing around, or the leaning over the side, or the extraordinary amount of conversation that bothered him so much as the way they looked at him: those sly, sidelong glances, and the smirks that accompanied them – as if they knew something that he did not, or there was some joke that he was not privileged to share. This could be put down to his own sense of insecurity – his suspicions of Imlay born of long experience – but he was determined to get to the bottom of it before he committed himself any further. And so when he returned to the stern cabin and Imlay asked if he was content with what he had seen – with the clear indication that he expected no less than an enthusiastic endorsement – he confounded him by requiring to see the purser, and for him to bring the ship's accounts with him.

For a moment he thought Imlay was going to refuse, but then he met Nathan's eye, saw something there that he had perhaps seen before, and gave a shrug of assent.

In bustled Mr Babb, a stout, very purserly looking man with a round, red face and a little powdered wig, and his clerk following with a great pile of books and papers which he dumped on the table for Nathan to examine. Nathan regarded them bleakly. Accounts of provisions shipped and returned, slops issued, sick book, gunner's and carpenter's expenses, a vast quantity of receipts, logs, order books . . . enough to occupy him all the way to Hispaniola and back if he was so minded. In short, the usual purser's ploy to prevent anyone from seeing the wood for the trees. But Nathan was having none of it. He interrupted a babble of inconsequential rubbish disguised as explanation.

'And where is the muster book?'

He knew from the silence that followed this request and a significant alteration in the man's demeanour that he had hit upon it. There was a pretence of searching for it among the great pile of papers but of course, the clerk had to be sent to find it and at length it was laid before him.

He did not need long – he could tell by the difference in the colour of the ink – but he went through the whole thing just to be sure.

'I see here,' he said, 'that you have taken on near seventy men in the past fortnight.'

Mr Babb looked to Mr Imlay for a response.

'Have we?' said Imlay with a raise of the brow. 'I did not think it was that many.' He came over to the table with a look of concern.

'Come, sir,' said Nathan looking him in the eye. 'These men have been signed on since you were the ship's owner and they are all American.'

'Do you object to that?'

'No, I do not object to that,' countered Nathan, though his tone was mild, 'but I was told you took over the ship fully crewed. This appears not to be the case, unless there has been some confusion over the dates.'

Imlay begged Mr Babb to give them a moment. His clerk began to gather up the books. 'You can leave them here,' said Imlay.

'We were short crewed,' Imlay explained when they were alone, 'and there is no shortage of Americans in British ports looking for a passage home. It seemed a pity not to take advantage of that.'

'And doubtless every one of them pressed into the King's Navy,' Nathan conjectured, 'and paid off when the war ended.'

'There is no record of that, but very likely, yes. What of it?'

'So, what did you tell them, may I ask, that made them sign up for a cruise aboard a privateer in peacetime?'

'Passage to a port in North America at twice the normal wage after dropping off a cargo on the way,' replied Imlay with a shrug.

'And do they know the nature of this cargo?'

'Of course not. I told you that on the way here – and the reason for an element of discretion.'

'So, when do you plan to tell them?'

'When we pick the guns up – in the Azores.'

So that was where the guns were – in the Azores. Portuguese territory, but a thousand miles into the Atlantic.

'And what if they object?' Nathan enquired.

Imlay sighed. 'When have you ever known a crew object to the cargo they were carrying, whether it be guns or opium?'

'Some of these men will be from the southern states,' Nathan pointed out. 'Slave states. Do you not think it possible that they might object to running guns to rebel slaves?

'Possible,' agreed Imlay, 'but unlikely. Besides, the great majority are from New England and anxious to return there.'

'So, when we have dropped off the guns we are to proceed to Boston or some other port on the mainland?'

'No.' A faint smile. 'Not immediately. But before I say more, I must know if you are with us or not. Have you come to a decision?'

Nathan had, but it would it not be prudent to let Imlay know what it was while he was still aboard the ship. He would not put it past him to have him confined in the chain locker until they were at sea.

'I need a little more time to think about it,' he said, 'and to make preparations for leaving England.'

Imlay gave him a hard look. 'How much time?'

'Three days?'

Imlay frowned. 'Very well – but I must insist that you do not discuss this enterprise with anyone – least of all your mother.' Nathan opened his mouth to object. 'Or you will have to answer for it, not just to me and my associates in the American embassy, but to Lord Nelson and Lord Saint Vincent, as I am sure you understand.'

Nathan travelled post to London – an expense that further diminished his dwindling supply of sovereigns. But he knew he would not be going back, whatever inducement Imlay was prepared to offer. What surprised him was the level of regret that he felt. It had hit him as soon as he stepped off the ship and it stayed with him for most of the journey. He had scarcely been aboard the *Falaise* for more than a couple of hours, but from the moment he had been piped aboard he had felt his heart lift. Now it was back in the doldrums again. Apart from his own disappointment, there was the feeling that he had left people down, people whose good opinion mattered to him, none more so than Lord Nelson.

He would have to write to him, of course, to say that he had declined Imlay's offer, and at least hinting at some of the reasons why. He could not say the man was a complete scoundrel that it was impossible to trust, but there must be some way of suggesting this. He phrased the letter in his head. *I regret that on my arrival aboard Captain Imlay's vessel I found that more than half the crew were Americans, who had been illegally pressed into the King's service and harboured so great a resentment I feared that as soon as we were out of sight of land they would cut my throat and feed me to the fishes?*

Hardly. The problem was he could not explain his distrust of Imlay without giving grounds for it, and that would mean revealing something of their past history when they were both pretending to be people they were not.

He was tempted to tell the coachman to turn about and take him back to Deal. But surely it would be the height of folly, having been double-crossed by Imlay in the past, to repose the slightest confidence in him now. The fact was, he should never have embarked on the journey in the first place – and all because he felt he owed it to the world for saving Bonaparte's life. But he could hardly tell Nelson that, either.

He was still pondering the problem when the coach reached the top of Shooter's Hill, and there was the whole of London spread out below them, a great constellation of lights in the descending gloom. It did not appreciably lift his spirits. By the time they crossed London Bridge it was raining, and the city looked even grimmer and more woebegone than when he had left it. It was close on nine o'clock when they arrived at Soho Square and he stepped down from the carriage and hurried towards the front door, wondering if his mother had guests and hoping not. He desired nothing more than some supper, a bottle of wine and his bed. The door opened before he reached it and a gentleman stepped out, pulling on his hat against the rain.

'Evening,' muttered Nathan, touching his hat and hoping to get inside without further intercourse, for he assumed it was one of his mother's gentleman friends – but it was not. It was Martin Tully. They both started in surprise, but Nathan found his voice first.

'Good God!' he exclaimed. 'What are you doing here? Not that I ain't delighted to see you,' he added hastily for Tully was the one person capable of cheering him up at the present moment, 'but I thought you had other plans.'

Tully had returned to his home in Essex with the notion of choosing a bride. There was, Nathan believed, someone particular he had in mind.

'It is bad news I am afraid.' Tully's expression was grim. 'Perhaps we had better step inside, out of the rain.'

10

The Highwaymen

His first thought was that it was his mother and that Tully had been sent to find him. He moved towards the door.

'No. It is not your mother.' Tully laid a restraining hand on his arm. 'Your mother is quite safe and well, and with company.'

'My father?'

'With his sheep in Sussex, I should imagine.'

His two parents being thus accounted for, and in predictable circumstances, Nathan permitted himself to relax a little.

'Let us step inside,' he agreed.

They gave their hats and coats to the footman, Vincent, and Nathan asked him if there was a fire in the library. There was. 'Then be so good as to bring us some wine and perhaps a bite to eat,' he requested, 'and please to tell my mother I am home and will wait upon her presently.'

He waved Tully into a chair near the fire and invited him to continue.

'It is George Banjo,' said Tully.

Next to Nathan's mother and father, and Tully himself, and Sara, this was as bad as it could be.

'Oh God, he is not dead?'

'He is not dead, but he soon will be if we don't act sharp.'

George Banjo. The name conjured up so many incidents from Nathan's recent past it was impossible to make a coherent picture of them. They had first met in Louisiana shortly after Nathan had assumed the

81

captaincy of the frigate *Unicorn*, and George – or Jorge as he was then – was a slave in the service of the governor of New Orleans. Having purchased his freedom, Nathan had entered him on the muster roll of the *Unicorn* under his Yoruba name, Banjo, and in the course of time he had attained warrant rank as gunner's mate, though he had long since appointed himself Nathan's unofficial bodyguard, in which role he had saved his life on a number of occasions. Besides his prodigious strength, he was a man of considerable intelligence – he had learned to speak four European languages as well as his native Yoruba, but he possessed a number of eccentricities, one of which was an exaggerated fondness for English nursery rhymes, discerning in them a metaphorical significance which frequently escaped lesser men, though he did not always quote them accurately. However, he had a very quirky sense of humour and you never knew with George whether he was being serious or luring you into some elaborate private joke for his own amusement. This did not go down well with some people. And if he had a fault, it was that he did not suffer fools gladly. It would, as Nathan had warned him, get him into serious trouble someday. And it had.

'He is in Newgate prison,' said Tully, 'awaiting transfer to Portsmouth to face a court martial.'

'On what charge?'

'The same as it was then,' said Tully. 'Striking an officer.'

'The same officer or another one?'

'The same.'

'But it was, what, five years ago?'

'It does not go away.' This was true and Nathan knew this as well as Tully. As well as George Banjo, too, for that matter, so what in God's name was he doing back in England? 'I am named as a witness for the defence,' said Tully, 'and so are you.'

Nathan was still trying to get his head around this. 'But . . . what possible defence can there be?'

He cast his mind back five years to the time of the incident. They were in the Ionian Sea, off the island of Corfu, and had been practising at the guns. Just rolling them out and going through the motions, no powder or shot. Nathan had been below deck at the time. The officer of the watch was the second lieutenant, Mr Bailey. A pompous dolt of a man who covered up his inadequacies with bluster and bullying. The practice had ended, and the guns were being secured when George had become involved in a dispute, something as ludicrous as the right way to frap a muzzle to the gun port. He should have known better, but he had a very proprietorial attitude to the guns. This was bad enough, but when Lieutenant Bailey had called him a 'fucking black bastard', George had struck him. Or so Lieutenant Bailey claimed. Several of those present said that George had just walked away, but that in so doing he had caught the lieutenant with his shoulder causing him to trip over a rope and fall to the deck. It amounted to the same thing.

'They'll hang him,' Nathan said simply.

They would have hanged him then if Nathan had not contrived his escape during the chaos that had followed a cutting out. Later, he had arranged for his employment with the British Consul in Corfu, Spiridion Foresti, who combined his official duties with gathering intelligence throughout the Levant and was more in need of a body-guard than Nathan, even. In fact, in his usual fashion George had so far exceeded his brief as to become the finest undercover agent in the Levant.

Both men had been part of Nathan's escort on his overland journey to India and he had not seen either of them since, though he had thought of them often. He had even imagined joining them some day on Spiridion's home island of Zante, enjoying wine, women and song in the manner of Odysseus after his adventures – though Nathan's knowledge of the Odyssey was limited, and if there had been a sequel he had not read it. He had an idea there was a wife in it somewhere.

'But why in God's name did he come to England?' he asked Tully.

'It is a long story,' sighed Tully, 'but apparently, he was on his way to report to Nelson in Naples when the ship was taken by the French. They took him for a common seaman, and he has spent the last year or so as a prisoner of war in France. When the war ended, they sent him back with the rest of the prisoners.'

He was lucky. If the French had known who he really was they would have hanged him and saved the navy the trouble.

'He arrived in Dover in the middle of January,' Tully went on. 'Not a penny on him or a friend in the world. In England at any rate. All he had was the address of some shipping company in Wapping – some friends of Spiridion's apparently – so he came to London. On foot.'

Nathan shook his head. 'But why did he not come to me – or you?' Nathan would have been in Sussex then, at Windover Place. He would have been a little surprised to see George Banjo there but would have done his best to make him feel at home.

'How would he have known we were in England? For all he knew we were still in India. Besides . . .' Tully hesitated.

'What?'

'He has his pride. He would not have wished to turn up penniless on our doorsteps, in need of assistance.'

'Why not? After all he has done for us.'

A shrug. 'You would have to ask him that. At any rate, he was staying with these people in Wapping when someone informed on him. Apparently, there is a thief-taker by the name of Mellors – he has a side-line chasing up deserters and the like for the Navy. Employs a small army of informers and bullyboys. So, George was hauled before the local beak and remanded in Newgate until a court martial was convened.'

'In Portsmouth, you say? Why . . .'

'You know the Navy. It will be for some impenetrable reason. The officer he struck – Bailey – is based down there. He is the principle witness against him, though I believe there are others.'

'How do you know all this?'

'I learned most of it from his lawyer – then I spoke to his friends in Wapping.'

'So, he has money for a lawyer?'

'His friends do.'

'What are they like?'

'What you might expect of Spiridion's circle of acquaintance. Merchants with interests in less lawful activities.' Smugglers, most probably, and spies. 'Our kind of people.'

In other circumstances Nathan might have objected to this, but it was true, of course. He had fallen a long way from respectability over the years. And mostly in the service of His Majesty's Government.

'And this lawyer . . . ?'

'Datchett.'

'Does he have any hope?'

'He said that would rather depend on you – as his commanding officer.'

'On me? What am I to say? The charge was logged. Striking an officer. And then he does a runner. They will hang him, whatever we say. You must know that.'

They would hang Nathan, too, if they knew what he did. At the very least he would earn a severe reprimand for letting him escape.

'What else can we do?' Tully said.

Vincent came in with a tray of cold pie and a cheese he had found in the pantry. There was also a decent bottle of French wine. Nathan told him he would see to the pouring of it.

'When is this court martial?' he asked when the servant had closed the door.

'The day after tomorrow.'

'But he is still here in London?'

'They are taking him down there tomorrow.'

'How? I mean, how are they travelling, do you know?'

'Mellor's men are taking him. In a prison van. Another of their services.'

Nathan shook his head. 'How many thief-takers are there in London?'

'About the same number as there are thieves. Some say the exact same.'

'Could you find out when they are leaving?'

'I could try but what are you thinking?'

'Nothing as precise as a thought. Let us see if we can find out a little more about it first. I will come with you but I had better pay my respects to my mother first. Will you spend the night?'

They were not back until the early hours. Nathan let himself in with the key he had to the scullery. The house was dark and silent, the servants all abed. Nathan wished he was, though he was probably too agitated for sleep. He found the bottle of wine they had drunk from earlier and the rest of the pie, and they sat round the kitchen table with their coats still on.

'I tell you this, Martin,' he said, as he poured the wine. 'I am thinking of trying my hand at a highwayman.'

'You could do worse,' Tully considered. But then he realised what Nathan meant. 'I take it you mean on the road to Portsmouth. Well, I am game for that.'

'Oh no, I am not having you joining me in this,' Nathan informed him firmly.

'And why is that, pray?'

'Well, you are getting on a bit, you know,' Nathan pointed out. They were much of an age in fact. A thought occurred to him. 'Besides, you are to be married, are you not? It is no way to start married life being hanged for a highwayman.'

'I am assuming we do not intend to be caught. Besides, what makes you think I am getting married?'

'I thought that was your intent. Indeed, I am sure you told me so, on the way back from India. You said there was a woman you were going to marry. A childhood sweetheart. Just as soon as you returned home.'

'Did I?' Tully thought about it. 'Was I in my cups?'

'Probably, but you seemed serious about it.'

'Yes, well, unfortunately she was married already.'

'Never. Oh, dear me, I am sorry, Martin. And was there no-one else?' Tully rolled his eyes at the ceiling.

'Well, be that as it may, this is not something for you to be involved in,' Nathan insisted.

'I am offended,' said Tully. 'My credentials are far better than yours when it comes to breaking the law.'

This was a matter of dispute between them. Tully was the son of a Guernsey smuggler, but Nathan was from Sussex where free-trading was bred in the bone. He had served his apprenticeship as a tubman for the Jevington gang in Birling Gap and had been shamefully thrashed by his father's steward, Gilbert Gabriel, when he found out about it. Gabriel had been a highwayman in an earlier life and had taught Nathan many of the tricks of the trade. Not only that but he took a cut from the free-traders for storing contraband in the cellars and priest holes of Windover House. But he had been in the navy, too, and was a great believer in the service idiom: Do not do what I do, do what I say. Gabriel was someone else Nathan had lost in the course of his travels. He was a careless employer.

'I will not argue with you,' said Nathan. 'I am too tired.'

'So, do you have a place in mind?'

'Fortunately I have been on a reconnaissance,' said Nathan, thinking of his ride out to Merton, which had followed the Portsmouth Road for the first few miles, 'and I am of the opinion that there is nowhere better this close to London than Wimbledon Common.'

'In broad daylight?' They had been informed that George was to leave Newgate at nine in the morning.

'The best time there is for a highway robbery,' pronounced Nathan, thinking of Gabriel. 'The busier the better.'

'You have done this before?'

'No, but I have taken advice. It is not over-complicated. You ride up, point your pistol, and tell them to hand over the gee-gaws. Or in this case, prisoner. It is advisable to wear a mask.'

'Ride?'

'Naturally. I am afraid that is in the nature of being a highwayman. It does not work anything like so well if you jump out from behind a tree. It is all a matter of first impressions, and that does not give a good first impression. And if they keep going you will never run fast enough to catch them, not with the weight you are carrying. You can ride, can you not?' It occurred to him that coming from Guernsey, Tully might well not. But he had been brought up as a gentleman, so it was not entirely out of the question, even in Guernsey.

'I can. It was the mounts that concerned me. Do you have any?'

'Not here, but I know where to get them. There is an excellent livery in Frith Street which opens at seven o'clock in the morning.' He wondered if he should take the groom with him. He might be a help. But it was probably best to keep the numbers down, and he might blab about it later. 'We won't get much sleep,' he said. 'In fact, I advise we stay awake. I'll open another bottle.'

It was not a pleasant morning. Not like the morning of his ride to Merton. No blue skies, no frost on the fields, just a dank English drizzle and a bitter wind. They sat in the lea of a belt of trees on the edge of Wimbledon Common where they could watch the London Road. There was not a lot of traffic, and what there was moved fairly briskly.

Tully voiced another concern.

'What do we do if they do not stop?'

'We fire a shot in the air,' said Nathan. 'It is normally sufficient.'

'And if it is not?'

Nathan did not think he had discussed this at any length with the Angel Gabriel. His impression was that they stopped more often than not. Again, it was probably a matter of how determined you appeared.

'You simply ride along beside them,' he improvised, 'and threaten to blow off the driver's head. They always stop then. Why would they not? It is just a job for them. They will not wish to die for it.'

'What if they fire back at us?'

'I think that is unlikely,' Nathan said.

It seemed to him that Tully was raising too many imponderables here. Besides which it was a little late in the day. They should have discussed all this before starting out, but they had nodded off at the kitchen table and did not awake until disturbed by the screams of the downstairs maid who had the duty of making up the fires in the morning and who had taken them for intruders. They had been obliged to make haste to pick up the horses and had not even had time for breakfast.

'But there will be a guard, will there not?' Tully persisted. 'And he will be armed with a blunderbuss, I should think, the size of a small cannon. What if he raises it to fire? It is not unimaginable. Would you shoot him?'

'I have shot Frenchmen who were probably better men than he.'

'Yes. But that was at a time of war.'

Nathan thought about it. 'I would not necessarily shoot to kill,' he said.

'You would be confident of winging him, would you? On horseback?'

The short answer to this was no. Especially not with the pistols Nathan had been able to procure from his mother's house. He was not even sure if they would fire at all in this rain. He took one of them out of the saddle holster and examined the firing lock.

'This damned rain,' he said.

'Trust in God and keep your powder dry,' said Tully.

'What?'

'It is what Cromwell said.'

'Was he a highwayman?'

'I do not think so, but . . .'

'Well then, what would he know about it?' But Tully had got him thinking.

'Cold steel is probably a better bet,' he said. 'In this weather. Cold steel and a boarding party.'

Tully looked about them. 'You have concealed them well,' he remarked.

'What I mean is, if one of us was to leap up onto the back of the van with a cutlass, or put a pistol to the driver's head, it would probably have more of an impact.'

'Could you do that?' Tully enquired. 'From horseback? Because I am not sure I could.'

'For God's sake, Martin, it cannot be more difficult than jumping from ship to ship in the midst of a battle.'

Tully did not look so sure.

'It would be better if it were not moving that fast,' Nathan admitted. Nor was he sure they could rely on the mounts they had hired. He had managed to get Dandy, the same old grey he had ridden out to Merton, but though reliable on the flat, it was not a horse that liked to be taken by surprise. He did not know how it would react to him standing on the saddle preparatory to jumping onto a coach roof. And then there was the spare they had brought for George Banjo; they would have that to worry about, too.

Then it came to him.

'What?' said Tully.

'Come,' said Nathan, shaking the reins and giving Dandy a kick with his heels. 'I have thought of a better place.'

There had been a bridge at Kingston-upon-Thames since Anglo-Saxon times and although the original wooden structure had been replaced many times, the current stone edifice was in such drastic need of repair, a toll booth had been erected at each end in hopes of raising sufficient funds to pay for the work. This had made a notorious bottleneck even worse, and on most weekday mornings the approaches to the bridge were clogged by a long line of carriages and carts, packhorses and drovers with an assortment of domestic animals. This morning was no exception and tempers were running high.

Among the resulting chaos was a carriage much resembling a stagecoach in appearance, save that it was completely enclosed at the sides with a locked door and a barred window at the rear. As it finally emerged from the ruck of traffic at the southern end of the bridge and the coachman prepared to whip up the horses, a gentleman in a buttoned-up pea coat and a cocked hat emerged from the shadows of the toll booth and jumped onto the narrow step beneath the door. After peering briefly through the bars into the interior of the vehicle, he adjusted his scarf to conceal the lower part of his face and swarmed up on to the roof, an activity that passed unnoticed by the two attendants until he pressed a pistol into the neck of the guard and removed the blunderbuss from his faltering grasp. At his forthright command, the driver urged his horses into a reluctant canter, proceeding down the Portsmouth Road for a mile or so before a further instruction caused him to turn into a muddy lane leading to the village of Thames Ditton. After continuing for about half a mile, the vehicle then halted in the lea of a small copse, apparently to wait for a lone rider who was following them at some little distance leading Nathan's mount and the spare.

'Very nice,' he said, as he approached.

Nathan acknowledged this compliment with a small bow. 'Keep an eye on this one,' he said, indicating the driver, before instructing the guard to descend from the box and open the double doors at the rear. Inside sat two men with their arms and legs shackled to a metal bar that ran along the centre of the vehicle a little above the level of the floor. Mr Banjo was on the right. Nathan inclined his head in that direction. 'Him,' he said.

The guard unlocked the shackles and Banjo stepped awkwardly down to the ground, rubbing his wrists.

'What about me?' said the other man, who had been watching this with interest.

The guard looked enquiringly at Nathan, who shook his head.

'That ain't fair,' said the prisoner.

'Life ain't fair,' said Nathan.

'Come on, mate,' the man appealed to his former companion.

'Not up to me, mate,' said he.

'For pity's sake,' the prisoner persisted, 'you are not going to let them hang an innocent man.'

'We do not know that,' said Nathan. 'You might be a mass murderer for all we know. What is he accused of?' he asked the guard.

'Sodomy,' said the guard. 'Aggravated.'

'Which is a gross and malicious slander,' the prisoner protested, 'perpetrated by the ship's cook on account of I would not let him have his way with me. And that I was a better cook.'

'I am sorry,' said Nathan, reflecting that the man's vocabulary was unusual in one of his rank, while his accent, though hard to place, was not of the common sort. 'But true or not, we can only take one at the moment.'

The prisoner noted some reluctance in his tone. 'Oh, come on, governor, have a heart. I don't take up much space.'

This was true. The man was as slight as a street urchin and did not look much older than one.

'Can we move on?' requested Tully, who had been listening to this exchange with some impatience. 'Before they set up a chase.'

'What do you think?' Nathan asked Banjo who was massaging some life back into his chafed wrists.

'Seems a decent enough cove,' said he. 'Says his name's Kidd.'

'How are you rated?' Nathan asked the alleged sodomite.

'Able. And I was the captain's steward on my last ship.'

'Very well,' Nathan sighed. He nodded to the guard.

'What are we going to do for a mount?' demanded Tully.

'He will have to ride behind Banjo,' said Nathan.

Mr Banjo having no objection they sat Kidd on the flanks of his mount. Then they obliged the driver and the guard to climb into the back of the wagon and locked the door. Nathan threw the bunch of keys down by the side of the track where they might easily be found by the next person who came along, and they jogged off down the lane in the direction of Thames Ditton. But now that the most difficult part of the venture was over, Nathan realised he had no clear idea of what to do next.

'You had better take your scarf off,' Tully advised him. He had already removed his own. 'You would not want to be taken for a highwayman.'

Nathan saw that his eyes were brimming with tears. This set Nathan off and they stopped the horses and doubled up with mirth, Mr Banjo joining in.

'Hey ho, the cat jumped over the moon,' he announced when he was capable of articulate speech.

If this was a metaphor for his escape, it failed on several counts, Nathan thought.

'It was a cow,' he told him. 'The cat played the fiddle.'

This set them off again. Kidd watched them with astonishment. He had fallen among madmen. But after the release of tension, Nathan sobered up considerably. Recriminations were in order, he thought. He and Tully had gone to considerable trouble on Banjo's behalf and it could so easily have been avoided.

'Why did you not come to us as soon as you arrived in England?' he demanded.

'I thought you were in India,' said Banjo with a shrug.

'As well for you we ain't,' Nathan assured him coldly.

'I'll not dispute that,' said Banjo. 'I could feel the noose around my neck. So where now?'

The answer was obvious, of course. Nathan was surprised he had not thought of it before. There was, after all, little alternative.

'First we drop the horses off in London,' he said, 'and then post to Deal. I have a ship waiting in the Downs, bound for the West Indies, unless you have something better to suggest.'

11

The Journey Out

Ship's log. March 27th, 1802, Saturday. Course WNW. Wind NEbE. Lat 18.26N Long 67.37W. Gentle breeze and hazy weather with slight swell as before. Studding sails set on main alow and aloft.

Nathan closed the log and crossed to the larboard rail of what he chose to call the quarterdeck, taking what comfort he could from the shade of the awning they had rigged against the sun. They were barely five bells into the forenoon watch and already he could feel the heat rising from the decks. If it was this hot in late March, he dreaded to think what it would be like in two months' time. He had dispensed with his coat but the linen shirt he had put on for the first time that morning was already damp with sweat. He had nothing to do. Tully was running the ship, in as much as she needed running. The weather was mild, the sea relatively calm and they were still 300 miles from Saint-Domingue and what he supposed one must call French waters. He could go below right now and instruct Kidd to bring him a jug of something cold and wet, or at least wet, throw open the stern windows to catch the breeze and set himself down for a quiet nap until dinner and no one would give a toss, or even notice that he was not on deck. Tempting though the thought was, he dismissed it to the back of his mind. It would diminish him in his own eyes if no one else's. And Tully would notice, of course, and put it down as yet another sign of his inevitable decline into senility. He would be thirty-four on his next birthday.

He lifted his eyes to the southern horizon, or where it would be if he could see it for the haze. They were crossing the Mona Passage, the narrow strait between Puerto Rico and Hispaniola, an important trade route between the Atlantic and the Caribbean, but there was not a sail in sight. He told himself it was unlikely that the French would patrol this far out into the Atlantic, and legally the eastern part of Hispaniola was still Spanish territory, though Imlay said the rebels had overrun the whole island. He had posted lookouts in all three tops, but he doubted they could see more than two miles in this haze, assuming they were still awake in the heat.

However . . . heat apart, he felt reasonably content with his lot, or as content as a man of his cynical nature ever would be. There were several reasons for this. Tully was one, of course, presently taking the watch in his role as ship's master, having stubbornly refused to be left behind at Deal. 'What reason have I to stay in England?' he had demanded, and Nathan had not tried very hard to find one. Another was Mr Banjo, who was at the helm, though his actual role was somewhat vague. 'Coxswain', Nathan had informed the purser when he was entered on the muster roll, though it did not much matter. Imlay had been happy enough to take all three of the new recruits without question, and doubtless any other renegades from the law that Nathan cared to bring him, though Nathan had not disclosed the precise details of their recruitment. So now there were at least two members of the crew that Nathan could trust. Three if you counted Kidd, but that would be a little premature. All he knew about Kidd for sure was that he was shaping up to be as good a cook as he had indicated when they first met, and thus far had shown no overt signs of the predilection of which he had been accused.

In fact, the entire crew was shaping up a lot better than Nathan had expected when he first came aboard. He still did not like the slanticular, smirking way they had of looking at him, but he was coming to accept this as an American thing, a measure of their independent spirit. They did a lot less standing around than they had in the Downs and you could not fault their seamanship – they could hand, reef and steer as well as any crew he had known, if not better.

And then there was the ship. The British Admiralty would never admit it, but a good French-built corvette was as fast a sailor with the wind on her quarter as any ship in the world. If the *Falaise*, or the *Mutine*, as she then was, had evaded that British inshore squadron coming out of Rochefort and escaped into the Atlantic shipping lanes she would have played the very devil with allied trade. There was not a King's ship that Nathan knew of that could catch her on the open seas, and not a merchant ship smaller than an East Indiaman with the guns to fight her. If she had a fault – and he was keeping this to himself and Tully for the time being for fear of being called a grouch – it was a tendency to fall off the wind, and though he had not yet put her to the test, he had a feeling she would struggle to impress on a bowline. But so far they had been very lucky with the winds. The north-east trades had held to the very end of March and it was barely thirty-five days since they had rounded Ushant, even with the time lost in picking up the guns.

Even that had proved less of a problem than it might have been. The supply ship had been waiting for them where Imlay said it would, just off Corvo – the smallest and most remote of the nine islands of the Azores She was a large barquentine called the *Sao Paolo*, flying the Portuguese flag, and Imlay had gone aboard alone, taking with him a small chest, presumably containing the required coinage, and had returned without it, looking pleased with himself and flushed with drink. Shortly afterwards, they had taken the cargo aboard – 200 port wine crates and 50 casks stamped with the name of a Portuguese grape distillery in the Duoro Valley. In fact, according to Imlay, they contained 1,000 Spanish M1752 muskets, 100,000 rounds of ammunition and 2,000 lbs of powder. For once, Nathan took his word for it.

When they had been securely stowed below decks, Imlay had assembled the entire crew in the waist, had his minions distribute a double ration of rum and made a brief speech, outlining the purpose of their mission. This could roughly be summed up as delivering a consignment of munitions to the governor general of Saint-Domingue with which to equip his new army, after which they would continue to Florida where the voyage would end and they would receive their recompense for handling a dangerous cargo – twice the monthly pay of the average merchant seaman plus a bonus of $20 a head if everything went according to plan. Nothing about what the French would do to them, of course, if it did not.

When mildly accused by Nathan in the privacy of their shared quarters of being 'a little disingenuous', Imlay had protested that he had told nothing but the truth. Toussaint Louverture *was* the legitimate governor of Saint-Domingue, appointed by the French government and ratified as such by the National Assembly in Paris. If Bonaparte had other plans, he had not yet disclosed them, either to Imlay, Louverture or the National Assembly. At any rate, the men showed no outward signs of dissent, or even of any interest in the matter. Possibly they did not care who the guns were intended for, or to what purpose. Certainly, not a single one of them had accepted Imlay's invitation to terminate his contract and depart for Lisbon in the *Sao Paolo*. When he gave the details of their remuneration, they cheered.

But if Imlay had been proved right in his estimation of the crew, it had not resolved other of Nathan's doubts. What bothered him most was why the American had decided to ship the cargo in a small sloop-of-war. Why not a merchant ship, with the capacity to take a much greater number of guns? A thousand Spanish muskets might look a lot stashed away on the orlop deck of the *Falaise*, but they would not go far to equip an army, especially not one that was expected to take on 20,000 crack French troops, blooded on Bonaparte's victories in Europe. The corvette was fast, for sure, and her guns might be useful – but only in a fight with a ship her own size, or a garda costa. She could not take on a ship of the line or even a sixth-rate, and there were plenty of both waiting for them in the waters off Saint-Domingue if what he had read in the English newspapers was even half true. Thirty-five ships of the line and twenty frigates, by some accounts. It would have made far more sense to Nathan to ship a much greater load of munitions in a pair of fast Baltimore clippers.

But who was he to argue? Imlay was the ship's owner; Nathan was just the delivery boy, though Imlay assured him that he would have plenty to do when they reached their rendezvous. He would be commodore of a flotilla, he said, charged with delivering arms and men to wherever Louverture and his subordinates required them. Nathan had attempted to discover more of these requirements, but Imlay was characteristically vague on detail. For once this was understandable. It was four months since he had met Louverture in Saint-Domingue, and the situation could have changed considerably since then.

Seven bells rang. Half an hour closer to Nathan's dinner. For once he did not feel particularly hungry, though copious quantities of liquid refreshment might change that. Nathan had a strict rule about dinner, though like many of his strict rules he had been known to break it on occasion. But in general he waited until the two watches had been fed in succession and then the officers, before he sat down to his own meal in the captain's day room. This meant that he rarely got to eat until halfway through the afternoon, and on a voyage like this, time did tend to drag, and he had so little to think about except food.

He became aware of a presence at his right shoulder and he turned to observe Kidd who had sidled up to him in his usual manner – which rather resembled a cat closing on its prey – and was awaiting his attention. This usually meant food or drink or both, and not for the first time Nathan wondered if his new steward was a mind reader, though as he was usually thinking about one or both, it did not perhaps require any supernatural gift on his part.

'Yes, Kidd?' he enquired hopefully.

'I have prepared a jug of lemonade, sir,' announced the steward in the mournful tones he apparently considered appropriate to his present role, at least in public. 'Would you care to take it on deck or in your cabin?'

'I will take it below if you please,' replied Nathan. It was unthinkable that he would refresh himself on the quarterdeck in this heat, in front of the sweltering officers and crew. Besides, the first issue of grog would be served just before noon. 'I will be down directly,' he said, if only to avoid appearing too eager. He caught Tully's eye and thought he detected a glint of amusement. Tully thought Kidd was taking him for a ride, and he probably was, but you could not deny that he had his uses, not least in his capacity to entertain, for he was an accomplished storyteller. Or, as you might say, liar. He claimed to be descended from the notorious pirate captain William Kidd, who had terrorised the Spanish Main in the latter part of the seventeenth century and had been hanged for it – in Wapping. This might well have been true, but the story did not end there. According to Kidd, his grandfather had purchased an inn overlooking the river, close to the spot where the hanging had occurred, and erected a memorial in the backyard in the form of a gallows. This was where young Kidd had been brought up, he said, and where he had learned his culinary skills – from a French chef who had worked for the royal family at Versailles and had been forced to flee by the Revolution. But at the age of fifteen, beguiled by tales of his infamous ancestor and the more recent exploits of those fighting the French, young Kidd had run away to sea and spent the next few years in the service of King George until the misfortunes that had lately attended him.

It seemed unlikely to Nathan that a French chef of that stature would end up in a pub in Wapping, with or without a Revolution. However, he valued Kidd's stories more for their entertainment value than their veracity, and you could not complain about the quality of the service or the food he served up. There was just that sense that he was making game of you, toying with you – yes, like a cat – before delivering the death blow.

'I am going below,' Nathan said to Tully. 'When the watch ends do you come and join me?'

Then, with a nod to Banjo, he went below to his cabin.

When he had made his deal with Imlay, the matter of his accommodation had been a serious consideration. The *Falaise* boasted a relatively spacious rear cabin for the exclusive use of the ship's captain, but that was when she was assigned to the French navy. As a private ship of war, she provided no accommodation for the ship's owner if he was aboard. The only alternative quarters that were available were the cramped cabins available to less godly individuals on either side of the gunroom. Imlay's solution had been to have the ship's carpenter construct a false bulkhead down the middle of the stern cabin, running fore and aft, so they could share the light from the stern windows. Although this halved the space available to him, it still provided Nathan with room for a cot, a writing desk, a table with seating for up to six people and an armchair where he could relax in the cotton *chogha* he had brought back from India with a long pipe of tobacco and a bumper of Madeira – and for the first time since he had been made post he did not have to share his cabin with a cannon, or even a pair of them, French officers being noted for their refusal to countenance so barbaric a practice.

Additionally, although the *Falaise* was officially described as flush-decked, like all of her class, the afterdeck had been raised fourteen inches to provide that much extra headroom for the captain's quarters – a puzzling concession to anyone raised in the Spartan traditions of the King's navy. At a little over two yards tall, Nathan still had to avoid banging his head on the beams supporting the upper deck but he was not obliged to stoop as much as he might have been. He particularly enjoyed the light which flooded in from the stern windows and the reflections of the water which bounced off the deckhead above and on to the polished cherrywood of the table. It was a shame having to share the space with Imlay but there it was, and they had not exchanged a harsh word since his return from London, which was an important consideration when you had fought a duel with a man, and been on opposite sides in a global conflict.

On entering this sanctuary, Nathan removed his hat, sent it spinning in the direction of one of the hooks affixed to the bulkhead for this purpose – one day it would land where he had intended but not today – and dropped with a relieved sigh into the armchair. Kidd was there in an instant – he had a small galley which he shared with Imlay's steward – bearing a tray with the promised jug of lemonade, a glass of Venetian crystal, a dish of olives in brine and a small plate containing a number of thin almond biscuits.

Nathan took the glass appreciatively.

'Chilled?'

"Of course,' with a superior raise of the brow.

'It was not a question, it was an observation,' Nathan assured him, 'though I will not ask how you contrived it.'

Nathan had purchased a small store of personal provisions before they left the Downs, but it had not included ice. He knew that a limited stock had been shipped in straw to cool the stash of hock that had been laid down on the orlop deck for Imlay's private consumption, but he would have been surprised if Kidd had been permitted access to it. Not by Imlay's steward at any rate. This was a Frenchman called Pellett who was exceeding jealous of what he considered to be his own territory and treated Kidd, and everybody else on the ship apart from his lord and master, with barely disguised contempt.

Nathan took a long draught of the lemonade and closed his eyes with a sigh as he sampled the chill, sour liquid. Just the right amount of sugar, not too much, not too little. He reached out to select an olive. They were a little wrinkled from the brine, but not so much he needed to issue a complaint. Kidd was picking up his hat and putting it on the hook. Nathan inclined his head in the direction of Imlay's half of the cabin and dropped his voice. 'Is he there?'

This was a daft question, though probably Kidd would refrain from pointing it out, for he had not seen Imlay on deck or skylarking about the rigging and there were few other places he was likely to be unless he had fallen overboard during the night. Kidd replied by putting a hand to his cheek at an angle of forty-five degrees and resting his head upon it in an attitude of torpor.

One of Kidd's many uses to Nathan was as an informer, though he took care to limit the power this conceded to him, and he had to remind himself to filter out the steward's prejudices. Kidd was inclined to see people very much in terms of angels and demons, and most of them were of the latter persuasion. However, his information had helped Nathan become somewhat better acquainted with the ship's crew than when they had been lying in the Downs.

Roughly half of them were British, though this term hid a multitude of sins and nationalities. They had been recruited by the previous owners in the last month or so before the peace, and had mostly served on privateers before, so they were more or less legalised pirates.

'Cut your throat soon as look at you,' according to Kidd.

The rest were the Americans Nathan had noted in the muster roll. Every one of them had been taken off a ship flying the American flag and pressed into service illegally on the grounds that they were deserters from the King's navy, or the even more spurious assumption that despite the Independence War they were still the King's subjects, which possibly explained the looks Nathan had been getting. Being half-American himself he did not at all blame them, though it did not make him feel any more at ease, particularly as Kidd assured him that many of them were infected by the spirit of the French Revolution. He had not bothered to attempt the accent he assumed from time to time in his role as Captain Turner of Nantucket. It might work in Paris, but it would never fool an American, certainly not one from Rhode Island and there were plenty of them aboard the *Falaise*.

'To be sure they know you are English,' Kidd had informed him with a faint sneer. 'They are just trying to work out what your game is, or whether you are a bit soft in the head. With respect.'

There were no overt signs that they were planning to cut his throat, but it remained a possibility. Like most sailors he was prone to superstition, and he was still troubled by the knowledge that the ship had originally been named the *Mutine* – and of course by the image of that terrible face on the ship's bow. He had not seen her up close since that first encounter at Deal, but the memory stayed with him and had even appeared several times in his dreams, startling him out of sleep. While going through the ship's papers he had discovered that she was modelled on a Greek goddess called Até, in the French, which was uncomfortably close to the English word 'Hate'. Further research (a conversation with Tully who was impressively erudite on some subjects) revealed that Até was the eldest daughter of Zeus who, after a family row, had been cast down to earth 'to walk on the heads of men' and wreak havoc and delusion. Her speciality, he said, was to tempt a hero into an action which would lead to his death or downfall. She was thus known as the goddess of mischief, ruin and folly.

Nathan was horrified.

'Why in God's name would anyone want to put *that* on the prow of a ship?' he had demanded.

'Well, perhaps because it was not in God's name, but the name of Revolution,' Tully proposed. 'And in the expectation that she will terrify its enemies.'

This did not help Nathan sleep any easier at night. As a precautionary measure, he kept a pair of loaded pistols next his cot, and he had stationed Tully and Banjo in the cabins closest to him on either side of the gunroom. His only real security, however, was the knowledge that he was unlikely to be murdered before the crew had been paid off in Florida, and by that time he would have either won their approval or the French would have done the job for them.

As for the two officers who had been dismissed the service, Kidd told him they had been done for duelling in Keppler's case and blasphemy in Cole's, which seemed equally unlikely to Nathan or there would hardly be an officer left in His Britannic Majesty's Navy. However, Tully, who had an easy way with him that invited confidences, told him they had fallen foul of the Earl St Vincent when he was commander of the Mediterranean fleet, a man of notorious ill temper married to a strict sense of discipline. Nathan had fallen foul of Old Jarvey himself in the past, so he had resolved to give them the benefit of the doubt while keeping a wary eye on the pistols and the bottle, but neither he nor Tully had observed an undue attachment to either since they had left the Downs.

Immediately below them in rank were a number of specialists who would have been warrant officers in the navy: the surgeon Mr Drew who was not the usual butcher, according to Tully, but a real doctor and a gentleman who had been in practice at a rural parish near Dover but for some quixotic reason decided that pursuing his vocation on a privateer suited him better. Possibly he was drawn to a life of adventure – he was young enough, being barely out of medical school – but Kidd said he had been romantically involved with the local parson's wife and been denounced from the pulpit. Again, this sounded like one of Kidd's stories, but it was an interesting possibility. Nathan had hardly exchanged more than a few words with him on the voyage, and while he stayed healthy, he doubted he would. He seemed pleasant enough on casual acquaintance, but Nathan maintained a wary distance from most doctors he had known in case they had to cut him up some day – it was bad enough to be screaming for your mother while they sawed off your leg or some other vital part of your anatomy without the embarrassment of counting them among your intimates, though it was possible that in such circumstances you would not care a jot one way or another. He had inspected the sick bay and it seemed as clean and well equipped as on any naval vessel he had ever sailed in, and better than some; lots of knives and saws and pincers arranged in immaculate order, shelves of bottles and jars with stuff in them that might kill or cure you but all neatly labelled with their Latin names which convinced most mariners they would do the latter. There were several boxes of guns in there, too – apparently, they were useful as an operating table, though there was nowhere else to stow them anyway.

The boatswain, Mr Jarred, was definitely not a gentleman and the only man aboard who had a face grimmer than the monster up in the bows. He was a Norfolk man like Nelson and kept pretty much to himself except when he was bawling someone out for something or other. He was another ex-navy man according to Kidd, dismissed for persistent drunkenness. The carpenter, Mr Penn, and the sailmaker, Mr Jones, also kept to their own company. Nathan had no complaints about the quality of their work, though they did enough complaining on their own account, mostly about the cramped conditions on the orlop deck where they kept their stores and which was now a hold for Imlay's guns. Kidd had nothing to say about either of them. He had plenty to say about the cook, however, who was the one he had the most dealings with, a black-bearded, one-eyed giant of a man called Masham who looked the most piratical of anyone aboard, and a thoroughly nasty piece of work according to Kidd. The space he shared with Pellet was too cramped and limited in its facilities to prepare anything more ambitious than cheese on toast and the occasional soup, so for the main meals of the day he had to negotiate with Masham for a share of the range in the ship's galley. This invariably led to altercations and Kidd had his revenge by carrying tales of Masham's little swindles to Nathan, which were mostly to do with the bribes he elicited for access to the range, and the distribution of the semi-liquid fat known as cook's slush which was most useful for greasing the guns but was valued as a vital ingredient of bread and dripping – regarded as a delicacy by many on the lower deck, despite all the warnings that it induced scurvy. According to Kidd, Masham had once been the proprietor of a molly-house in Smithfield but fled to sea after poisoning his business partner with rat poison, which might or might not have been true – half the crew were probably on the run from the law, including Kidd himself. Nathan and Tully, too, if you were going to be particular about it.

There was no schoolmaster or chaplain on a privateer, and no master-at-arms, so the only other warrant officers were the gunner, Mr Caine, his mate, Mr Bentham, and the purser, Mr Babb, who had been among Nathan's earlier acquaintances when he had first come aboard at Deal. The only one of these Nathan had much time for was Caine, who had much the same feeling for his guns as Masham had for his stove, but though Nathan could not fault him for the condition they were in, he was able to knock no more than a few seconds off their firing rate, even after practising five or six times with powder and shot during the voyage out. He had discussed this with him at length, along with Tully and the other two officers, without coming up with much in the way of a solution. Tully felt the gun crews were too respectful of the powder, taking overlong with the swabbing and worming out, but the main reason, Nathan thought, was that they just did not have the ambition for improvement. Perhaps they did not think their lives would ever depend upon it, and they could be right about that: they were not at war, and they clearly did not think they would ever have to take on the French navy in the waters of the Caribbean. Nathan took a different view and he would have liked to set Mr Banjo to the task, but it would have put Caine's nose seriously out of joint, not to speak of the two officers, and after what had happened the last time he had let Banjo loose on the guns, it was probably best to keep him and them apart, at least until it became a matter of life and death.

He heard the bells go for the end of the watch, and then a few moments later the bosun's call for 'Up spirits!' and the drumming of feet on the deck as the starboard watch came up from below.

'Here, Kidd,' he raised his voice. 'Put a dash of rum in this stuff, will you? Mr Tully won't be pleased if we're the only two aboard who ain't had any.'

This was received with another noticeable arch of the brow, but the jug was taken away for the necessary improvements and a moment later a brisk knock announced Tully's arrival. He removed his hat and pitched himself down on the bench in the stern windows, cocking his head enquiringly in the direction of Imlay's quarters. Nathan made much the same gesture as Kidd had, but neither of them would count on Imlay's torpor. If there was anything they did not wish Imlay to comprehend they would slip into a patois known as Guernésiais, a form of the old Norman language spoken on Tulley's home island of Guernsey, the rudiments of which Tully had taught him over the years and which had proved useful when they needed to discuss anything in private. Imlay spoke French but his comprehension was not nearly as good as that of a native, particularly if it was spoken fast, and he was quite lost with Guernesiais, or at least they hoped so.

The carpenter, Mr Penn, had left a narrow gap between the end of the wooden partition and the stern bench to permit access to the quarter-gallery where they performed their ablutions – the powder room as Emma would have called it. When they had divided the space up, Nathan had insisted that Imlay, as the ship's owner have the convenience on his side – the larboard – though his real reason was that Imlay would also have the smells, and would not come trespassing on his territory every time he wanted to use it. On one occasion, squinting around the end of the false bulkhead to see if Imlay was there, he had observed him with his head pressed against it in the hope of overhearing the conversation on the other side. It must annoy him considerably that he and Tully spoke in their impenetrable patois, but as they only did so when they had no other company, he could hardly voice an objection.

Kidd appeared with the new jug of lemonade, now well laced with Jamaica rum – and Tully drank gratefully. He was looking older, Nathan thought, and had been more reserved during this voyage than he was normally. In repose, if he did not know you were observing him, his face often looked melancholy. Nathan was inclined to think it must be the woman in Essex. He had met her on his last leave and Nathan knew he had been writing to her from India. He never spoke of it, but her marriage could have hit him harder than he was prepared to admit.

He had known Tully nine years now and had very little idea of his true feelings about women; but then he had very little idea about his own. Or perhaps it would be fairer to say he had many ideas, but they had not yet coalesced into what you might call a working proposition. He had been very much in love with Sara – he was in no doubt about his feelings there – but it had been during the time of the Terror in Paris when their lives were in mortal danger on a daily, if not hourly, basis, and they were at a heightened level of emotion, which is how Imlay had put it in his irritating way. He considered himself an expert on women and all associated subjects – one of his books had been known in the trade as a 'bodice-ripper' – and he had probably been thinking of his own relationship with Mary Wollstonecraft who he had so cruelly betrayed.

After Sara, the only woman who had come close to engaging Nathan's emotions, if not his passions, was the woman he thought of as Sister Caterina, who had been an actress and a courtesan and a nun, more or less successively but combining at times all three vocations with remarkable success, but he had only realised he was falling in love with her when she had found God and then it was too late. Tully's dealing with the fairer sex had been much more straightforward, at least as far as Nathan was aware. When they first met he had been engaged to a young woman in Rye, where they had been based at the time, but she had died of typhus fever while they were in the Mediterranean – Tully had only found out a year or so later. He did not talk about it.

'All well?' he enquired when the steward had left them. Another daft question, or Tully would not be down here and Nathan would be up on deck trying to pretend he was essential to the safe running of the ship, but he replied politely that the wind was holding up well, and that if it stayed as it was they should pass Cap-Français tomorrow evening, just after sunset, and reach their rendezvous on the island of Tortuga early the following morning.

'Could hardly be better,' said Nathan, raising his glass.

And at that precise moment they heard a shout from one of the lookouts.

'Sail ho! Six points on the larboard bow.'

12

The Chase

There were two of them, not one, emerging from the haze to the south-west. They had almost certainly come through the Mona Passage, and could easily have been merchant ships out of Panama save that they were in line ahead and no more than a cable's length apart, as if joined by an invisible thread. No merchant ships sailed like that, unless they were East Indiamen, and they were a long way from India.

Nathan had joined the lookout in the maintop the better to see for himself. It was a fighting top with a two-pounder swivel gun for sweeping an enemy deck and he used it to rest his arm on while he trained his Dollond glass. They were both under a full press of sail and he could just make out the line of gunports on the lead ship, but that meant nothing. Most merchantmen had gunports painted on the side as a deterrent to pirates or other nautical predators, even if they did not mount anything heavier than the gun he was using as an armrest. But they were much closer than he would have wished – three miles at most – and on a course that would bring them across his bows in a little less than half an hour if he did not alter their own. He could not blame the lookout – it was this damned haze – but it left him precious short on time.

'What do you think?' he said to Tully who had climbed up beside him.

'The one in the lead is a two-decker,' said Tully after a moment's study.

Nathan swore and looked again. He could just make out the two white lines now along her hull. A bad sign but not definitive. He swept the

107

glass slowly along her top deck from stem to stern, looking for another clue, but she was still too far away to see any sign of a gun, much less a uniform. Up to the top of the masts. She had top gallants and royals set which usually required a bigger crew than most merchantmen carried but again it did not put the matter beyond reasonable doubt. He could not see a flag either at the masts or the ensign staff. He swept the glass back along the deck to the bow and suddenly, leaping into focus, he caught a clear glimpse of the distinctive warship beak. He shut the glass with a snap and thrust it into his shirt.

'All hands,' he said to Tully, 'and clear for action.' Not that he was going to fight them, but it was as well to be prepared. He descended to the deck at a speed which would doubtless impress the crew no end, but for once he had more important things to think on.

'What do you think?' said Imlay. He wore his worried look.

'Well, they are not merchantmen,' Nathan told him, but his eyes were on the rigging. They would have to take those studding sails in if they ran close to the wind, and it looked like they had no other choice. If they were French and insisted on coming aboard it would not be easy to explain why they had a thousand Spanish muskets packed in wine crates on the orlop deck.

The bosun was piping all hands and the starboard watch came spilling up on deck, squinting against the sun.

'Take in stuns's and cast loose the guns,' he told Tully quietly, 'but leave the ports for now.'

'You think they are French?' This from Imlay, still a frowning presence at his side. Nathan felt like swotting him, like a troublesome mosquito.

This close to San Domingo they could easily be Spanish, or British even, bound for Jamaica, but he would be a fool to take a chance on it.

'I could not see their colours,' he said, 'but best to think the worst. And we should think to our own,' he added.

'We have discussed this,' said Imlay sharply. 'Portuguese. It was agreed.'

They had agreed no such thing. When Nathan stopped arguing, it did not mean he agreed – only that he considered it a waste of time continuing. Stopping a ship on the high seas was an act of war, but the maritime powers did it all the time, especially the British. The fact was if you had a big enough navy you could do pretty much as you liked, and conversely, if you flew British colours you were far less likely to be stopped by anyone else for fear of the consequences. No French captain would risk the displeasure of Bonaparte by risking another war with the British before he was ready for it. But they would not think twice about stopping a ship flying Portuguese colours if they thought she was up to no good.

Nathan had made this point to Imlay, but he claimed he had been told 'at the highest level' that they were on no account to fly British colours, not if they were engaged in gun running. The British and the French had come to an agreement, he said, during the peace talks in Paris. Bonaparte had signalled his intention to send a battle fleet to the Caribbean to restore order in Saint-Domingue, and the British had agreed not to interfere.

'I gave my word to Saint Vincent,' Imlay said now, speaking low. It was the first time he had named the First Lord of the Admiralty as a co-conspirator in this affair and he obviously thought it was his trump card. In fact, so far as Nathan was concerned it was a red flag to a bull. He was damned if he was going to be hanged or even spend a few years in a French prison to save Old Jarvey from being embarrassed. But he shied from having a full-blown row with the owner in front of the entire crew, and every minute they spent arguing brought the French a cable's length closer.

'Then we will have to run,' he said.

Tully had the stuns's in and was waiting at the con.

'North by West,' Nathan told him.

Only the slightest flicker of an eyelid betrayed Tully's opinion of this, but Nathan knew what he was thinking. It was as close to the wind as they had ever taken her, and that only once, by way of an experiment, soon after they left the Downs. It had not been what you might call an unqualified success, but with the wind in its present quarter they had no other option if they hoped to stay out of range.

Tully raised his voice: 'Hands to the braces.' And then to the helmsman, an ox of a man from Cornwall by the name of Cuff: 'Course nor' by west.' Then in an undertone, 'but ease her off if you have to.'

They watched the edge of the sails as the bows came round. The last thing they needed was to be laid in irons, especially not now. Four points, five . . . and they started to flap like a line of washing. Cuff eased her off half a point. Tully shot Nathan a look between apology and resignation. Nathan nodded but he was chewing his bottom lip. He looked over at the two-decker hopefully. But already she was changing course. Not by much, but enough to show her intent. And the other ship was coming out from behind her stern. He had only caught a glimpse of her before, but now he could see she was a frigate – of up to forty guns, almost certainly eighteen-pounders. But it was not so much the guns that worried him as the long, lean look of her, and the press of sail she was carrying. She would give them a race of it with the wind on any quarter but close hauled . . . He ran part way up the mizzen shrouds for a better look, and at that instant she broke out the tricolour – from her foretop, so they could see it clearly, streaming away to the south-west. How often had he seen that in the past nine years, but never before with such a sense of anxiety – and at a time of peace. Then she began to pull away from the other ship, and the chase was on.

Nathan returned to the quarterdeck. Another look to the sails. They were holding steady now, but this was as close to the wind as she would allow, and she felt sluggish for the first time since they had left the Downs, apart from that one brief trial in the English Channel. He glanced at the compass again, just flickering on NbW. Nothing ahead but the open sea and the sky, all the way to the Carolinas. There was nowhere for them to hide, except the Turks and Caicos Isles, and they were far to the north-west. The sloop would be much happier if he headed in that direction, but so would the French. They could bring their entire broadside to bear and use her as target practice.

He crossed back to the larboard rail. The frigate was gaining. Not by much, but enough. About a cable's length a minute, he reckoned, a tenth of a mile since he had last looked. He could see her bow chasers quite clearly now without the aid of his glass, and even as he looked the starboard gun fired. A tongue of flame out of a maw of black smoke as the dull boom of the explosion carried across the intervening stretch of water. He did not see where the shot went but the meaning was clear. He called Mr Cole over.

'Break out the Portuguese flag,' he said, suppressing a sigh.

At least it would give them something to think about. There would have to be an exchange of signals, too, for it was odds on the senior of-ficer was aboard the two-decker. What would he be going through his head? Nathan tried to put himself in his place. He would know from her lines that she had been built in a French yard and was almost certainly a

British prize, so why was she flying a Portuguese flag – and what should he do about it? She could have been sold on by the British, or it could be a ruse. Either way, why was she running from them if she had nothing to hide?

Still they ran on, all three of them, close-hauled to the north, the *Falaise* about a mile and a half ahead, the frigate gaining little by little, the two-decker lumbering along in her wake but the gap between them, widening all the time. Two bells rang. One o'clock. The cook would have had dinner ready for about an hour now. He should send the watch below, he thought. There was nothing else they could do; they might as well have their dinner. He opened his mouth to give the order, but at that moment there was another spurt of smoke and flame and this time he saw the shot skim off the swell, a very short distance off their larboard bow. He felt the tension in the air. Imlay was standing two or three yards along the rail, staring out at the frigate with one arm across his belly, and the other resting on it with his clenched fist drumming on his chin. Tully was watching the sails. Half the men standing to the guns, the rest up in the rigging. He had ordered the gunports opened but the guns were still not run out. There was no point. The sloop was leaning so far to leeward they would be firing into the sea. Not that Nathan had any intention of firing them, not unless he absolutely had to. And then in a flash it all changed.

A flash and a bang, in fact, and this time a splintering of timber as the shot smashed into the rigging above Nathan's head. It was a lucky shot, though not for everyone. It struck one of the heavy lift blocks for hoisting the mizzen yard and it came hurtling down, through the small gap in the awnings they had hung against the sun – and struck the helmsman Cuff on the top of his head.

They heard the crack as it split his skull open, but he fell without a sound.

Mr Banjo stepped up to the helm while Nathan was still staring at the body. Tully said something and two of the hands dragged it over to the scuppers, leaving a long smear of blood on the deck. Everyone could see it was not a job for the doctor. Nathan was looking at the blood. Well, he thought, so that is how it is.

'Back the fore course,' he said to Tully. And to Mr Cole: 'Strike the colours.'

Imlay gave him a look. Nathan was not sure if it was a look of shock or relief.

'Unless you have a better plan,' he said, but as soon as Tully had given the order to brace by he took him aside. 'Keep them at the braces,' he said, 'and load up the larboard guns with chain.'

If he was to be hanged for a pirate he might as well act like one.

With the fore and main sails countered they were lying dead in the water, and the frigate was closing on them fast. Nathan waited until she was off their larboard quarter at little more than three cables' lengths before he gave the order.

'Brace full! Run out the guns!'

The yard came round, the fore course filled, flapped and then filled again.

'Are you mad?' Imlay was still at his side.

'Very likely,' said Nathan. He crossed to the rail and raised his voice to carry the length of the gundeck: 'Maximum elevation Mr Keppler.'

The bows were coming round so very slowly, and yet still the frigate came on, as if blind to their intent – and pray God she was, if God did not mind being drawn into such a quarrel. He could see the figurehead at her bow, a golden-haired angel or goddess with a serene, guileless face, so unlike their own. He raised his voice again: 'Fire as you bear!'

It was not quite the rippling broadside he might have hoped for, more a series of sharp barks, such as a lapdog might utter, but every gun aiming high and at a range where they could hardly miss.

There was a long moment when he thought they had. The frigate, finally, was falling off the wind and from where he stood, he could see the full extent of her broadside, count every gun if he wished. They had not yet come to bear but they would soon enough – she did not have to keep pace with them, only keep falling off the wind, and they would keep pounding shot after shot into her until she was a dismasted, bleeding hulk. He could not strike his colours a second time. He had committed one of the worst crimes in the book, pretending to surrender and then fighting on – but then so had they, firing on another ship when they were not at war. All he could do was climb up the mizzen shrouds and wave a white flag, and hope they showed mercy, if he was still alive to do it.

And then, slowly, almost nonchalantly, her foretopmast started to lean forward, was held by the rigging for a moment and then came crashing down into the sea, bringing the jib and the flying jib and the fore topmast staysail with it, dragging her bows round to leeward and acting like a great sea anchor, holding her by the head.

Nathan felt the sloop gather way as she felt the wind on her quarter, her bows pointing to the north-west and freedom.

He heard the men cheering at the guns and he did not have the heart to berate them and tell them to get on with the business of reloading. The two-decker was a good mile and a half to the south. Firing at that range would be a waste of powder and shot. He caught George Banjo's eye and shook his head in a kind of bemusement at his own luck. The cat had jumped over the moon again, but it was becoming profligate with its nine lives.

He heard Imlay's voice at his shoulder.

'What shall we do about Cuff?' he said.

Nathan looked at the body of the helmsman sprawled in the scuppers, and the trail of blood leading there. He suppressed a sudden wave of anger. It was amazing that he had hit Imlay only once in his life, but there was still time.

'Swab the deck and bury him,' he said in a voice as cold as his eye, 'when we have time to make a decent job of it. What flag do you want us to use? Or did you not discuss that with Old Jarvey?'

13

The Isle of the Turtle

Ship's log. March 29th, 1802. Monday. Course SWbW. Wind ENE. Lat 20.16N Long 72.47W. Gentle breeze. Studding sails alow and aloft. Off Tortuga.

They sighted the island at first light, as Columbus had over 300 years before. It looked to him like the shell of a turtle rising from the sea, so that is what he called it – Tortuga in the Spanish – claiming it for the dual crown of Aragon and Castile and as there was no one at the time to dispute it, least of all the local inhabitants, that was the name by which it was known – at least by the Europeans – until the French took over and changed it to Ile de la Tortue, but most people, even the French, continued to call it Tortuga. It was Nathan's first sight of land since the Azores.

He viewed it from the foretop of the *Falaise* through his Dollond glass, with the rising sun tinting the tops of the hills, and the shoreline still in shadow, feeling a vicarious pride in the excellence of Tully's navigation, and the wondrous nature of navigation itself, to have brought them across 3,000 miles of ocean to this remote dot on the map – their future base for whatever operations Imlay had planned for them, if he had such a thing as a plan. Thus far it had not been discussed.

'Let us get just there first' was all he would say when Nathan broached the subject on the journey out.

Nathan knew the island, at least by repute, from his last visit to the Caribbean, but this was the first time he had actually seen it. He did not think it looked particularly like a turtle, but then Columbus had come at it from a different angle, and if anyone had challenged his perception – 'Don't be a sap, Cristofero, it don't look nothing like a turtle' – it had not been entered in the ship's log. Nathan knew from his charts that it was less than thirty miles long and no more than four miles wide, and from his history that it had once been the most notorious nest of pirates in the Caribbean. It was now barely inhabited, though only a narrow strait – the Tortuga Channel – separated it from the coast of Saint-Domingue. The perfect location, Imlay had assured him, for running guns to the rebels. It was one area of expertise where Nathan was prepared to concede that Imlay probably knew best.

Since their encounter with the French they had kept well out to sea, heading towards the Caicos Isles and changing course during the midwatch to make their approach from the north-east, ready for instant flight should they run into another French patrol. The Turks and Caicos were in British hands, and provided a sanctuary, it was to be hoped, if Tortuga turned out to be occupied by the French.

From Nathan's present vantage, however, it appeared to be free of occupation by any species of human. The hills rose sharply from the sea and were covered in dense jungle for as far as the eye could see – and he could just make out a host of brightly coloured birds flitting above the forest canopy. A paradise, he thought, dimly recalling what might be a line of poetry, untouched by the hand of man. Except that it was anything but. Its position at the northern end of the Windward Channel between Cuba and Hispaniola had made it an ideal base for the hordes of adventurers and renegades who had flocked to the region in the seventeenth century, either to escape the law in their own countries or to make their fortunes from piracy and other degenerate pursuits. Rum was plentiful, women were imported or abducted from more populated islands and there was a plentiful supply of food from the herds of wild pigs and feral cattle that roamed the interior. Once butchered, the carcasses were usually smoked over a slow fire in wooden huts that the French called *boucanes*, thus providing the pirates with the name they most liked to be known by – the buccaneers. There were others less flattering. Initially they preyed on the Spanish galleons, homeward bound through the Windward Channel, and raided the coastal settlements on the Spanish Main or the colonial islands, taking whatever they could carry away, including the residents, who they either ransomed or kept for whatever service they could provide. Despite, or more likely because of their violence and lawlessness, they were considered useful by the other European powers, especially the French and English, who issued them with letters of marque, giving them a flimsy legal cover for their activities, and even provided them with safe havens in Jamaica and Martinique, but when their own ships were targeted and their barbarity became excessive, even by the flexible standards of their allies, they united against them. They exterminated the pigs and cattle they lived on, bombarded their forts and burned their settlements. Those that were not killed in battle were hanged or otherwise disposed of whenever they were taken alive, and by the end of the century piracy was all but eliminated, at least in the Caribbean. Kidd's alleged ancestor, Captain William, was one of the last to 'dance the hempen jig', as the pirates called it, though he was probably hanged in chains and left to be covered by two tides, in the English tradition. Tortuga had been free of them for over a hundred years, but they had left their mark in a few ruined forts along the coast and the one port of any size on the island – Cayona. Much of their plunder, it was said, lay buried under the sand of the now deserted shores.

The *Falaise* was close enough now for Nathan to hear the birdsong, and to see the great number of seabirds fishing in the waters close to the shore or foraging along the edge of the tide, though the only ones he could name with any confidence were the pelicans and terns and boobies, for he was no ornithologist. It strengthened his perception of an unspoiled wilderness, however, and he was just thinking how thoroughly nature reclaimed its own if given the opportunity, when they rounded the cape at the eastern tip of the island to reveal a small bay with a waterfront of clapboard hovels and the ruins of a stone fort on a rock above the harbour – and two tall ships – one a brig, the other a barque of a type that he had heard called a 'Baltimore clipper' – and he knew they had reached their rendezvous: the little haven the buccaneers called La Roche, and had been renamed by the rebels, Porte-Liberté.

Even this early in the morning it was a hive of activity, both on the waterfront and on the water itself, with a fleet of small boats ferrying goods between ships and shore and a great number of people waiting to unload them. The goods in question were mostly casks and crates, very similar to those stored on the orlop deck of the *Falaise*, and raising his glass to the hillside he could see a long line of men and mules snaking up a narrow, winding track through the forest, most of them wearing white – or at least whitish – cotton shirts and ducks and broadbrimmed straw hats, but not a few in blue uniform jackets and black shakos, very like those worn by the French army. The whole scene, with the two ships at anchor, their sails hung out to dry in the morning sun, the palm trees along the shore and the ruined fort, brought back memories of the books he had read as a child with their lurid illustrations of swashbuckling pirates and buccaneers, and stirred the romantic longings that had led him to join the navy, though strangely this was the first time he had seen anything like it for real.

He was disturbed in these fanciful thoughts by the arrival of a stout figure in a Panama hat, heaving itself through the lubber's hole to join him – Imlay, come to inspect his little fleet, and feeling very pleased with himself to judge from the broad beam on his sweltering face.

'I take it those are our ships,' said Nathan, handing him the glass.

'Yes.' It came out as an exultant breath and for the first time Nathan began to appreciate just how much of a gamble Imlay had involved him in, though he would probably call it a game of chess as he moved his pieces about the globe. Hoping they would not be blown away by the first French broadside.

He was sweeping the glass from one ship to the other. 'The brig is the *Mohawk*, Captain Scott – sixteen guns. The clipper is the *Delaware*, Captain Lowell.' His voice was exultant. His moves had been successful, even if they were just the opening gambit. 'They were to sail from Boston on the 15th – I did not expect them so soon. And unloading the guns already, I see.'

'Some of the men on shore are wearing French uniform,' Nathan pointed out. 'But I take it they are not the French army.'

'I hope not,' said Imlay lightly, 'or we have come a long way for nothing.'

He raised the glass to the hillside and announced that they were Louverture's men.

'He was in the French army himself until very recently,' he said. 'His men wear the uniform of the French National Guard.' A barking laugh that could have been nervous. 'It is a strange war we are fighting here.'

Tully was taking in sail and Nathan climbed down to join him at the con.

'We will moor close by the brig,' he said. 'I expect the two captains will be coming aboard to report.' He looked about him. 'Have you seen Kidd?' He raised his voice. 'Kidd. Kidd, there.'

'Right here, sir.'

Directly behind him, as if he had risen through a trapdoor in the deck like the demon in a comic opera. If there had been red smoke and a smell of sulphur Nathan would not have been entirely surprised.

'Coffee, if you please,' he said, 'in my cabin. And some breakfast, too, I think. And if any boats come out from the shore, as I expect they will, see if you can get some fresh fruit.'

He looked around the decks. They were as good as could be expected. Their visitors would not expect much in the way of spit and polish. But they should be piped aboard. He looked for the boatswain.

'We arrived yesterday, just after midday,' said Scott. 'The thirteenth day out of Boston. I hope it will not prove unlucky, ha ha.'

'It will for some,' murmured Lowell softly, gazing at a space just above his fellow captain's head.

They could have been called Captains Chalk and Cheese; they were as different in manner as they were in appearance. Scott, a stout, ruddy-faced man of fifty or so, sweating profusely in the heat. He had come aboard in a cocked hat and a powdered wig, but taken them both off when they went below, and was presently mopping his shining, bald pate with a large handkerchief. He wore a weathered blue jacket with medal ribbons and his black stock was like a sweat rag. He was a veteran of the Independence War and the more recent naval conflict with France that the Americans called the quasi-war because neither side had bothered to declare formal hostilities. Solid as a rock, said Imlay as they watched them being ferried across in their respective launches. But it was clearly a rock that dined well.

Lowell was a much younger man, perhaps no more than thirty, tall and lean with hawkish features and the air and dress of a beau. He wore a buff-coloured tailored coat over a white shirt with an immaculate white stock and tight white breeches, all spotless, and a straw planter's hat with a wide brim, and he came aboard looking as cool and composed as if he was entering a plantation ballroom in Georgia. In fact, the Lowells were from Boston and one of that city's oldest and richest families, according to Imlay, and 'young Will', as he called him, was a rising star of the younger set and the darling of the assembly rooms.

'So, what in God's name is he doing here?' Nathan had wanted to know, 'and the captain of a barque?'

'In search of adventure, I guess,' said Imlay, 'like a great many of us. Then, too, he is a committed abolitionist, so doubtless that will have played its part. Something of a romantic, I believe, and a gifted poet.'

He noted that this did not go down as well as it might with a more sensitive soul and added more seriously: 'Also, he killed a man in a duel and was advised to lie low for a while.'

'There are probably safer places to keep your head down,' remarked Nathan who was still thinking about all of this, but Imlay assured him that nothing could catch a ship like the *Delaware*, and no one would ever hang a Lowell, not even the French, as they were much more valuable alive.

Nathan's greater concern was whether he could captain a ship, but apparently it was not his first time at sea – he had financed and commanded an expedition in search of the north-west passage when he was in his early twenties, Imlay said, and though he had not come anywhere near finding it, he had at least come back alive and brought most of his crew with him.

'He has the money to employ the best,' he said. 'And he has a very reliable first mate called Tom Kiernan, who is now in his forties and has been at sea since he was a boy of twelve. A natural born seaman, you will like him a lot.' Not the least of the traits Nathan disliked in Imlay was a tendency to presume the tastes of others. 'Done a fair bit of smuggling, too, I believe. His last job was running guns to the United Irishmen in Newfoundland to use against the British.'

Nathan was not entirely reassured, but then nothing involving Imlay was ever reassuring and he was still not at all sure what he was doing here himself. Imlay had introduced him as 'Captain Turner', but he presumed they knew he was English even if they knew little else about him, and he made no attempt to pretend otherwise. They seemed to accept him readily enough, though it was hard to tell, and they addressed most of their remarks to Imlay who had taken charge of the proceedings.

On their arrival, the two vessels had hoisted the Portuguese flag above the tricolour of the French Republic, as Imlay had instructed. Some two hours later a boat had come out from the shore bearing a gentleman in French uniform who had introduced himself as Citizen Dubois, the representative of General Louverture. He had obviously been expecting them.

Imlay nodded as if the name was familiar to him, but he asked the captain what he looked like.

'Well – he was black,' said Scott, clearly a little thrown by this directive.

Imlay looked pained. 'Yes, most of Louverture's people are,' he murmured. 'Any other distinguishing features?'

'Mulatto, most likely,' drawled Lowell, as if the effort of speaking was a serious bore but if someone had to do it he was probably the most qualified in the room, and for a considerable radius beyond. 'What used to be known in these parts as a free man of colour, I believe. Mighty sure of himself for a person of that – ilk. Speaks good English with what I would say is a Virginia accent if I did not know better. Civilian dress of a certain – regional style. If he were not black, you might say he was a planter.'

'He is a planter,' said Imlay. 'If he was indeed our man. He farms a coffee plantation in the interior, just a few miles from here, though he calls it a cooperative.'

There were no French forces on the island, Dubois had told them, but there had been sightings of French ships in the Tortuga Channel, and there were large numbers of both ships and men at Port-au-Prince, just over 100 miles to the south, and at Cap-Français, which was even closer. He suggested they unload the guns the following morning at first light.

'It seemed a reasonable suggestion,' Lowell said, 'in the circumstances.' Imlay nodded. 'But he said they had lookouts posted on the high ground to give us plenty of warning if there were any French ships in the vicinity.'

'Did he say when he would be coming back?'

'He said he would receive word of your arrival, so I assume he will be joining us shortly. If his lookouts are as good as he says they are.'

Apparently, they were. Pellet thrust his head into the cabin to say there was an official-looking boat approaching from the shore flying the tricolour at the stern.

"We should be on deck to receive him,' announced Imlay, standing up and reaching for his hat. 'And with all due ceremony if you please, Captain, as befits the emissary of a Governor-General.' This to Nathan who nodded coolly, though he wondered what exactly Imlay had in mind.

'What do you think, sir?' murmured Lowell in his ear as they shuffled out of the cabin. 'Twenty-one gun salute?'

This was clearly meant to indicate Lowell's support, as one seaman to another, but Nathan did not require Lowell's support for the time being and gave him no sign of encouragement.

They reached the deck as the boat came up on their starboard side. It was crewed by eight oarsmen and a coxswain, all wearing the blue jackets, white duck trousers and broadbrimmed sennit hats of the French navy – though it was to be presumed that like the soldiers on the shore they were not – and just forward of the steersman was the man he presumed was Louverture's emissary, wearing a dark suit and a top hat. But to Nathan's surprise there was a woman seated next to him, dressed all in white and sheltering herself from the sun with a parasol. This was an added complication. He had instructed the boatswain to lower steps with side ropes, but if she could not manage them, they would have to use a sling or a harness. He looked for Jarred, but Imlay was badgering him again.

'Are we ready to pipe him aboard?'

'We are,' said Nathan wearily. He had instructed the officers to assemble the hands in the waist and to wear their uniform jackets. There was little else he could do in the time available to him.

'We must treat him with the greatest respect,' Imlay murmured, 'for he is as close to Louverture as anyone, and we need him on our side.'

But Nathan was no longer listening. His attention was entirely focused on the woman, for despite the parasol he could see her face quite clearly now and to his astonishment he realised it was a face he knew – and the last time they had met she had sworn to kill him.

14

The Witch Queen
and the Philosopher

'Captain?'

Nathan became aware that Imlay was gazing curiously at him.

'I am sorry.' Nathan dragged himself back into the present. 'Is there a problem?'

'I said, do we have a chair for the lady?'

'A chair?'

'So that she might come aboard.'

There had been no indication that he knew the woman, or that he knew Nathan had once known her. He was looking down at the boat with a troubled frown – but that might be prompted by his fear that she might fall in the water. Not that there was any need for concern. As the boat came level with the steps, she stood without aid, handed her parasol to her companion and gathering her skirts in one hand, and reaching out for the steps with the other, climbed nimbly aboard.

Nathan took a step back, deeper into the shade of the canvas awning. Could it really be her? It was seven years ago, and their acquaintance though passionate had been brief. He watched her as she gazed about her, half smiling and biting her lower lip, as if this was quite a good joke but she must not disgrace herself by laughing out loud. Very like the Adedike he remembered. But she wore a broadbrimmed straw hat with a blue ribbon tied under the chin and her face was in shade. Imlay stepped up to greet her, bowing low and removing his own hat, but still there was no sign of recognition between them. He was introducing himself as 'Admiral Imlay, ma'am, at your service.'

Admiral? This was the first Nathan had heard of it. Where had he got that from? The American president, or had he awarded it himself? But his thoughts were mostly occupied with the woman he had once known as Adedike, courtesan, rebel and priestess of Lucumi, the forbidden faith of the Cuban slaves.

She was talking to Imlay but if she gave him her name, Nathan did not catch it. She could not possibly be Adedike. It would be too great an irony, as if the Lucumi gods were playing tricks on him, for they were very like the Greek gods in their capacity to toy with mere humans as a cat with a mouse – just like that bloodthirsty fiend on the front of his ship. Then she saw him, and he saw the look in her eyes. Just for an instant. And there could no longer be any doubt.

He was in a daze. Things were happening around him, but he was only half aware of them. He felt like a character in a comic opera, or a tragedy, who has forgotten his lines, or wandered onto the stage by accident and does not know how to leave it.

The man had come aboard – Dubois. Nathan had almost forgotten him, and how important Imlay had said he was. Fortunately, Jarred had not, and the boatswain's pipe was sounding its fiendish wail of respect. He heard the shout of 'Hats off' from Tully. Imlay bowed and addressed their visitor in French.

'This is Captain Turner,' he was saying. 'My second-in-command.'

Nathan made his bow and as his head came up, he found himself looking straight into the man's eyes and they were looking into his with an intensity – and a curiosity – he found discomforting. He was a man of middling years with strong, distinctive features, a broad brow and a strong jaw, wide mouth, thin nose. It could have been the face of a Greek god, save that it was black. What was his relationship with Adedike, Nathan wondered? And would she tell him about their own brief association, and what she perceived as his betrayal in the Bay of Serpents?

Imlay continued with the introductions. Nathan continued thinking about the past, and how it had a way of catching up with you. He had such a clear image of it in his mind.

The Bay of Serpents on the east coast of Cuba. The eight-gun brig that had once been a Liverpool slaver anchored beneath the guns of the fort.

The black flag of piracy flying from its masthead. The red and black flag of the Army of Lucumi above the fort. The reception committee waiting for him on the shore. And the statuesque figure of Adedike. *She who answers our prayers.*

They had made a deal. She would persuade her people to give up the pirates, and in return Nathan would supply her with a few muskets and pistols from his own ship's armoury to continue her war against the Spanish. But she had wanted him to stay with her, to train the Army of Lucumi to use the cannon they had captured from the Spaniards, and perhaps to satisfy her own more personal desires. Nathan had been vain enough to believe that – then. But faced with the choice of breaking his promise to Adedike or his oath to King George he had chosen his sovereign – with a little help from Tully who had literally held a pistol to his head so that it would look like he had no choice.

The last he had seen of her she was standing on the shore with her arms stretched out to him, screaming curses. At least he had assumed they were curses because shortly afterwards he had been overtaken by the most violent stomach cramps. He had thought he was going to die. The ship's surgeon said it was a build-up of wind and gave him a laxative. It seemed to do the trick.

He had never thought to see her again. He still could not believe it. She looked as lovely now as she had seven years ago, and hardly a day older. But what was she doing here on Tortuga?

He had thought about her many times over the years, mostly to recall the physical part of their relationship, and in truth there was not much else to it. He had assumed that if she was still alive, that she was still in Cuba, up in the mountains fighting the Spaniards, or hiding from them. But Cuba was a mere fifty miles across the Windward Channel, La Bahia de las Serpientes not much more. Then he recalled what the Spanish agent Brother Ignatius had told him:

I am told she came from Saint-Domingue with a boatload of refugees . . . It is thought that she was the mistress of one of the French planters, an aristocrat, who granted her freedom in his will. He was butchered by the rebels – though there are those who say that it was she who killed him after first making him sign a document to make her free.

'Captain?' Imlay was looking at him again. What had he been saying now? He dredged it up from the shallows of his mind, where it had been sinking into the mud. A proposal that they should adjourn to his cabin. It would probably be cooler to set up a table here, beneath the awning, he thought, but he found he did not have the energy even to make the suggestion, and besides, Kidd and Pellet would probably have everything arranged below decks. At least, he hoped they had.

He need not have feared. Kidd might have his faults, but he was an excellent steward and for once he and Pellet must have worked in unison. The table was laid in his cabin with six chairs set. Fresh fruit and jugs of lime juice had been prepared, with more than a hint of rum judging from the smell. But despite the open windows it was decidedly sultry. Scott for one looked as if he might expire at any moment. Even Lowell was wilting. Only Adedike and Dubois appeared at all composed. But Imlay, though he was sweltering and clearly nervous, made a reasonable job of host and though there were undercurrents of tension in the air – or perhaps that was just in Nathan's mind – the atmosphere was convivial enough.

Kidd and Pellet circulated behind the table filling their glasses and Imlay proposed a toast.

'To life, liberty and the pursuit of happiness.'

Nathan was not sure if a subject of King George was permitted to drink to this, but he was supposed to be American, so he raised his glass anyway.

'And now, sir,' Imlay addressed Dubois. 'Perhaps you will bring us up to date with the present situation in Saint-Domingue. I will translate for you if you wish for the benefit of my associates who do not speak the French.'

'Thank you, but that will not be necessary,' said Dubois in perfect English with a strong American accent. He saw the two captains look at him in surprise and then at each other. It was the accent of the Southern states, of Virginia perhaps; they would probably know, even if Nathan did not. It crossed his mind that he might have once been a slave there.

He snatched a quick glance at Adedike, who had been seated at one end of the table. They had conversed in French when they last met. She also spoke fluent Spanish, but not more than a few words of English. Had she learned more since then? There was no way of knowing from her expression. She was sitting back in her chair still wearing her wide-brimmed hat, her face in shadow, her eyes, what he could see of them, drifting lazily over the company.

Dubois was telling them about the arrival of General Leclerc in Port-au-Prince at the beginning of the year, with thirty-three ships and 8,000 French soldiers. They knew they were coming, and that this was just the first of many. The expedition had been preparing for several months and they had regular reports from their agents in France. Until then their relations with the Republican government in Paris had been perfectly amicable. More than that. Louverture and most of his men were enthusiastic supporters of the French Revolution. Liberty, equality and fraternity. 'Who would not be?' said Dubois. No one challenged him, least of all Nathan, who alone among them had been fighting the French for the last nine years. Louverture's troops were proud to serve in the Revolutionary Army, to fight the enemies of La France, including the British and the Spanish. They had fought them both and won, wearing French uniforms and singing the songs of the Revolution. But when Leclerc arrived, he issued a proclamation naming himself governor general, with the authority of the Directorate in Paris – which meant Bonaparte. Otherwise, his tone was conciliatory. He was here to restore law and order, he said, but not slavery. He offered to make Louverture his lieutenant, and to incorporate his troops into the French army.

'I suspect this was a *ruse de guerre* to keep us quiet until reinforcements arrived from France,' Dubois told them. 'But the General rejected the offer and issued a call to arms.'

However, more French ships were arriving on almost every tide. Within two months, it was reckoned there were over 20,000 troops from France and her allies, and 10,000 trained soldiers who had rebelled against Louverture and taken refuge in French or Spanish territory.

'And how many ships?' Lowell put in.

'Thirty-two *vaisseaux*' – Dubois corrected himself for the benefit of those who did not speak French – 'that is, ships-of-the-line, and twenty-two frigates and sloops of war.'

Nathan was astonished. Could this be true? This was two-thirds of the entire French navy. There had been only thirteen French ships of the line at the Battle of the Nile. It was far more than the French needed to reimpose their authority on a small Caribbean colony with no ships of their own. This was a fleet to conquer a continent.

'You are feeling heavily outnumbered, *Capitaine?*' Dubois addressed Nathan directly – and again there was the hint of a twinkle in his eye and the sense that he knew exactly who he was. 'Think how we were feeling when we saw the sails off Port-au-Prince.'

But their main concern was the number of soldiers they had brought with them.

'Veterans of the French wars in Europe, victors over the Austrians, the Prussians, the Dutch, the Spanish – the British.'

He glanced again at Nathan. Had his accent given him away? He could not possibly know otherwise unless Imlay had told him. Or Adedike. And yet there had been no opportunity for Imlay to communicate with either of them since they had come aboard, at least not openly.

'There was no possibility of fighting them in open battle, so the General decided on other methods – to fight as the Americans fought during their own War of Independence.' This time his smile embraced them all. 'Fire at them from cover and then run. Deep into the forest where they cannot follow.'

This was probably not the most flattering summary of Washington's tactics, Nathan reflected, but none of the Americans bothered to put him right on the matter. Imlay just asked how the fighting was going.

Badly was the simple answer, though Dubois did not put it quite so bluntly as that.

'As you know when you came here, there are many divisions among our people,' he said to Imlay, who had said nothing of this, of course, to Nathan. 'It was necessary for the General to make them return to work on the plantations. Many did not wish to do so, even if they were paid for their labour. Also, there were laws against sedition – the freedom to speak out against the government. There were some who called Toussaint a dictator. So when Leclerc arrived, there were many who greeted him as *libérateur*, especially among the free people of colour who were still moved by the spirit of the Revolution – *liberté, égalité, fratenité* – which the French seemed to have forgotten. And also, the middle class in the towns – we have a middle class,' he said, with that smile again, 'though that might surprise you. A quite affluent middle class, in fact.'

It was Lowell who had looked surprised. Though it was closer to an amused contempt. He might be an abolitionist, as Imlay had said, but he was clearly a long way from accepting equal status with a former slave, though he probably felt the same way about Nathan, or any mortal who was not a Lowell.

'They think the French Army will restore order,' Dubois went on. 'The whites, of course, support him because they think he will restore slavery. And they will regain all their former privileges, which they consider to be their rights. When the French landed, we had sixteen thousand men under arms. Now, I doubt it is more than half that number.'

'I had no idea it was that bad,' said Imlay. For once, Nathan thought he was probably telling the truth. He looked shocked.

'I am afraid it is true. Even the General's own family is divided. When the French came, they brought his two sons with them from France where he had sent them to be educated. Bonaparte's own orders, I am told, to show good will. But now the older brother, Isaac is with Leclerc, the younger, Placide, with his father.'

'This is very bad news,' said Imlay, and he did not mean about the two brothers.

'I am sorry, but it is better you know how it is, and the situation will improve, now that you have brought us these guns. And there is one other thing. The French, too, are divided. They are fighting those who wear the uniform of the French Army, women, too, who are like the women who fought the Revolution in Paris, except that they are black. We go into battle singing the same songs they sing in France at the time. The *Marseillaise, the Ça Ira* . . . This is not good for them. I have heard one Polish regiment has refused to obey orders.'

'Polish?' Again, from Lowell, with that characteristic lift of the brows.

'Yes. There are many Polish troops here. From what the French call the Legion of the Danube, recruited from among the prisoners taken in the battles against the Hapsburgs. They joined the French Army to fight for liberty and equality – and to free their homeland from the Austrians and the Russians – and what happens? They are sent to Saint-Domingue to destroy the liberty of another oppressed people. This is the reality of the Revolution, gentlemen, as it is today under General Bonaparte. But if we win one battle – just one – everything will change, you will see – and that is where you gentleman can help us.'

Imlay extended his arms in a gesture of what might have been benevolence or despair. 'Anything we can do, Armand, you know that. We are at your service.' But Nathan had seen that look on his face before. Shortly before he put the boot in, or the knife. 'We have brought the guns that were promised – and we will bring more.'

'It is not just guns we need, Gilbert.' He pronounced it the French way – *Guilber*. It was originally a French name, Nathan recalled. Or French-Norman. He had heard him called this before, in Paris when they first met, but hearing it here, for some reason, discomforted him. Perhaps because it reminded him that the last time they had been in the Caribbean together, Imlay had been a French agent.

'We need your ships – to bring us to where the French do not expect us, to take them by surprise.'

'And where is that?' Lowell again. Nathan wondered at his relationship with Imlay. He did not seem the least subservient to him, but then if you could believe Imlay he felt himself subservient to no one.

'I am waiting to hear from my General. But it will be in the south, closer to Port-au-Prince, to make the French shift most of their forces from the highlands, and the plantations.'

Imlay seemed to be considering this, but Nathan had the impression that it did not come as a surprise to him, and that there was an element of theatre to this whole exchange. It felt rehearsed. He caught Adedike's eye for the first time since she had been sitting at the table. He had seen that look before, too. She was smiling, like Dubois, but the look in her eyes was worrying. How much of their conversation had she understood?

'I will have to discuss this with my associates,' Imlay was saying. He looked at the two Americans. 'But it does make a certain amount of sense.'

'I am glad to hear it,' said Dubois, still smiling. 'But let us discuss this later, shall we, when we hear from my General.'

'And in the meantime?'

'In the meantime, I trust that you will dine with me, at my house, this evening on the hill above the harbour. You and your captains.' The smile became a beam, embracing everyone around the table.

'You are very kind,' said Imlay, 'but is that wise with the French so close?'

'We will have plenty of warning,' Dubois assured him. 'My house is but a short distance from here, but the view is spectacular. We could see a French ship leaving Le Cap. I exaggerate, but I promise you, they will not take us by surprise. We call it *Le Belvédère*. In English I think the translation would be the Beautiful View, but also I have heard it called the Lookout.'

He reached for his hat and started to lever himself up from his chair. '*Attention à la tête,*' said Nathan quickly. '*Les poutres.*'

'*Ah.*' Dubois raised his eyes to the deck beams just above his head. '*Merci, mon Capitaine, vous me sauvons le coup de tete.*'

Nathan caught Adedike's eye again, and this time she winked.

'What was all that about moving troops?' said Nathan. 'We are not troop transports. Did you know about this?'

'Of course I did not know about it.' Imlay retorted. He appeared to be on a short fuse. 'How could I have known about it? We have only just got here.'

They were in his cabin still – just the two of them, the other two captains having returned to their ships.

'It did not come up when you were last here?'

'No. Not at all. We were simply to supply guns and ammunition. That was the deal. However – as I said, it does make a degree of sense.'

'What makes sense?'

'To divert the French to the south, away from the plantations.'

'You will have to explain this to me,' Nathan said.

Imlay sighed. 'Most of the coffee and sugar plantations are in the north, in the highlands. Obviously, it makes sense to keep the fighting in the south if we can.'

'Why? I thought the important thing was to keep the French fighting everywhere so they would not move on to North America.'

'This is true, but . . .' Nathan sensed his hesitation and pressed him. 'But what?'

'If Louverture wants guns he has to pay for them, and the only way he can pay for them is by trade.'

'Guns for coffee?'

'And sugar of course.' A crooked smile. 'You cannot have coffee without sugar.'

There was a crooked man, he had a crooked smile . . .

No, it was not that.

There was a crooked man, and he walked a crooked mile.

He found a crooked sixpence, upon a crooked stile.

There must be a deeper meaning to the rhyme, a political meaning. Banjo would know. But at least half the nursery rhymes in England could be applied to Imlay if you thought about them long and hard enough.

He might have known, of course, that money was involved. It always was where Imlay was concerned.

'So, you are seriously considering a request to move Louverture's troops around the island – with two-thirds of the French Navy in the region?'

'Well, we would obviously have to plan it very carefully, move by night, perhaps – but this is just an idea. We need to hear from Louverture.'

'And meanwhile we keep the guns aboard the *Falaise?*'

There had been no proposal to unload them, as they had with the other two ships.

'What is the point, if we have to load them back again in a day or two?'

'And what about the crew?'

Imlay frowned. 'What about them?'

'You told them when we left the Azores that once we had dropped off the cargo we would proceed to North America where they would be paid off.'

'Did I?'

'You did.' It was possible that he had forgotten. Imlay made so much up as he went along, he sometimes forgot his lines.

'Well – we will.'

'When?'

Imlay thought about it. 'If there is a problem, I will offer them more money,' he said. 'If that will not content them, we may have to send some of them to Florida in the *Delaware.*' He changed the subject. 'What do you make of this thing tonight?'

This was another problem that Nathan had been considering. If Adedike did want revenge for what she perceived to be his betrayal in the Bay of Serpents, this would be the perfect opportunity. But he had to be careful about this. He still did not know how much Imlay knew about him and Adedike. If anything.

'What do *you* make of it?' he said.

'Is it safe, do you think, to leave the ships?'

'We will put out boarding nets,' Nathan said, 'and keep the guns loaded with grapeshot. Besides, Dubois said we would have plenty of warning.'

Imlay dropped his voice. 'But what about the crew? What if they take it into their heads to take over the ship?'

'You said that would not happen.'

'I know, but – one can never be sure.'

'But they will not be paid until they are landed in Florida.'

'They could take the money themselves and sail the ship anywhere they wished.'

'You mean you have it aboard?'

'Of course I have it aboard. It is in the strongbox in my cabin. Where else would I have it.'

Nathan shook his head in despair. 'Then let us not go. But it was you who said we must seek his approval. I doubt we will succeed if we refuse an invitation to dine with him.'

'No. No, I am being foolish. The news from Dubois has made me anxious.'

'You mean about the fighting?'

Imlay nodded. 'I had not anticipated that. I thought they would hold their own for a while – in the north at least. As they did with the Spaniards and the British.'

'How close is Dubois to Louverture?'

'Very close. One of his inner circle. Dubois is his chief adviser on matters of trade and finance. He is the only man on the island, I think, black or white, who knows the first thing about economics.'

'Not a soldier, then.'

'No. Not a soldier. Except – a soldier of Jesus, maybe.'

'Where does Jesus come into it?' Nathan was mystified.

'He was a Jesuit. That is what they call themselves, is it not – soldiers of Jesus.'

'A priest?'

'I am not sure if he was a priest. A reverend brother, perhaps. But he spent about ten years teaching in a Jesuit college. In Virginia.'

That would explain the accent, of course, but Nathan was struggling to come to terms with this. It stirred a deep, almost atavistic sensitivity. The Jesuits had been enemies of England since the Reformation.

'I thought they had been suppressed,' he said, 'by the Pope.'

'Not in the United States. Nor the Russian Empire, I believe, or Prussia, or China . . . They have never been allowed in England, I think, not since they tried to blow up the King and Parliament . . .'

But the Gunpowder Plot was not Nathan's chief concern for the time being. 'So – Dubois was a Jesuit priest – in the United States?'

'As I say, I am not sure if he was ordained, but he was trained and taught there. Philosophy, I believe. I think he may even have been a professor.'

'A professor of philosophy?'

'Yes. Why does that surprise you. Because he is black. I believe Saint Augustine was black, was he not?'

Nathan had no idea. And his query had nothing to do with colour. He did not think he had met a professor of philosophy before. The navy can be limiting in some ways.

'But he is from Saint-Domingue – originally?'

'Oh yes. I think his parents sent him to the States as I child. To be educated by the Jesuits. It is not unusual. They were free people of colour. In Port-au-Prince. Quite wealthy, I believe. From merchandising.' His tone was vague, almost dismissive. As if he had other things to think about, which he did, of course. He had his fingers pressed to his temple above one eye and was massaging it as if he had a headache.

'So – what is he doing back here?'

'Playing his part in the Revolution, I expect. Or maybe the Jesuits sent him. They might be suppressed; it has not stopped them interfering in politics. Though they would probably say it was the work of God.'

Presumably, Imlay was no more a friend to the Jesuits than the Pope was. He was from New Jersey originally which almost certainly meant he was a Protestant. And very likely Presbyterian. Though if he had any religion now, he had never spoken to Nathan about it. Or Mary Wollstonecraft, so far as Nathan was aware.

'So – a philosopher,' Nathan mused. He asked another question in his mind: 'And what is he to Adedike?'

'Who?'

'Adedike. The woman. You must have noticed her.' His tone was sardonic. Not for the first time he had the sense that Imlay was playing games with him,

'Is that her name? I did not quite catch it. Or she did not tell me. I have no idea. His woman, I expect.'

No sign that he had met her before today. It was possible, Nathan supposed, that he had not. All that Adedike had said at their previous

encounter was that Imlay was a French agent and that he had promised
to supply the rebels in Cuba with guns. She had not said that he had
made the promise to her, personally. And there was no reason why Imlay
should have known of Nathan's own association with her.

He wondered if he should tell him now. But perhaps not. He thought
about the wink she had given him. Did that signify malign intent? It had
not seemed malign. But she was tricky, you could never be sure of her
intentions. He shook his head at himself. It would not be the first time
his past had caught up with him. It could have proved lethal before; he
might not be so lucky next time.

'He seemed to like you,' said Imlay thoughtfully.

'Who?' Nathan was startled.

'Dubois. Who else have we been talking about?'

'I stopped him from banging his head on the deck beams, that was all
the converse we had.'

'No, but I could tell. And the woman she kept looking at you, did you
not notice?'

'No.' Nathan was startled. 'Did she?'

'Well, I caught the odd "covert" glance. Maybe you should do most of
the talking tonight.'

'Me?' Now he was seriously alarmed. 'What would I talk about?'

'Oh – him, her, the food . . . Philosophy? Just keep the conversation
going. I am not at all sure I am up to it. I have a terrible headache. In fact,
I think I had better rest for a while. Have Pellett wake me, if you will, half
an hour before we are due to leave.'

He lurched off back to his cabin leaving Nathan wondering where
they went from here. Obviously not to Florida. Not by the morning tide
at any rate.

15

La Belvédère

'You will understand now why I am confident the French will not take us by surprise,' Dubois was saying. 'Not by sea, at least. And if there is another way, I have yet to hear of it.'

Clearly, he was not acquainted with Monsieur Garnerin and his balloons.

They were standing on the veranda of his house near the top of what he called Le Belvédère. The Beautiful View, or the Lookout-point, as Nathan preferred to translate it. They could see the little bay far below and their three ships lying at anchor, and the sea beyond as far as the coast of Saint-Domingue. The sun was setting, the sea calm and the wind patterns on the water were like the brushstrokes of a divine painter. Rather more prosaically, there was not a sail in sight. Yes, he could understand why the French would not take Dubois by surprise, but they would have to arrange a system of signals before he felt entirely relaxed, if that happy state ever awaited him in this life.

It had not been easy to get here. It had involved a steep climb up a winding track through the forest – probably the same track that had been used to carry away the munitions earlier in the day. Happily, Dubois had sent a guide with four mules for their convenience, and an escort of eight soldiers for their safety. In his present mood, Nathan found the escort anything but reassuring. He felt with every upward step of his mule took him into the elaborate trap that had been set for him.

The first sight of the house did something to relieve his apprehensions. It was a far cry from the grim Spanish donjon where he had last met Adedike. It might have been a rich planter's house, but so closed in by trees and overhung with lianas and other creepers, some flowering, it was impossible to perceive from any distance. In fact, they would not have seen it until at the doorstep had it not been for the lights that blazed within and without – in great crystal chandeliers in the rooms or in lanterns on the veranda and the surrounding trees. It gave the place a look of enchantment that would not have been out of place in a production of A Midsummer Night's Dream, he thought, with Adedike in the role of Titania, queen of the fairies. She greeted them on the veranda, looking radiant in a West African kaftan of many colours, flowers in her hair, a welcoming smile on her face and Dubois, at her side, also wore African dress, though in less brilliant colours – and his smile was more enigmatic. He was accompanied by several men and women whom he introduced as family members, including his sister and her husband, and also his two young children – a boy and a girl – who were whisked away before Nathan had a chance to ascertain if Adedike was their mother. He assumed not for they looked to be about seven and eight, and he was fairly sure she had not had young children when they met in Cuba.

They ate indoors, for though it was still warm, the flying insects, Dubois said, would eat them alive, and the dining room was scented with smoke from several chasubles burning an incense that he said made an effective repellent. Their conversation was in French, which his visitors all spoke to a greater or lesser extent – much lesser in Captain's Scott's case, though he may have been happy enough to give the conversation a miss and focus on the food and drink. It was all local fare, Dubois informed them, and rather more refined than the smoked pork or beef of the boucanes. In successive order came courses of chicken stuffed with banana, fried pork with spices, red snapper and lobster marinated in lime and peppers and various vegetable dishes, some of which Nathan recognised, but most not, delivered by a host of servants and accompanied by French wines and jugs of rum, lemon and sugar, which the navy would have called grog but probably had a more civilised name in Le Belvedere.

Out of respect for the food and the company, they tried to avoid talk of the war, though it must have been foremost in everyone's mind. Aware of the responsibility that had devolved upon him, Nathan tried to draw

Dubois out about his life in Virginia, but inevitably this turned to the subject of slavery – 'the troublesome property' as he said many Virginians called it.

'I have always thought it odd that the Virginians, who think of themselves as the most civilised and genteel race on earth, should continue to uphold so barbaric a practice,' observed Captain Lowell, as if to himself. Certainly, he did not look at anyone else as he spoke, the implication being that they could fall upon his gems as manna from heaven, or not; it was all one to him.

'Oh, but they do not think of it as barbaric,' said Dubois, 'any more than the Greeks did, or the Romans. Even when they crucified them.'

'Did they crucify them?' said Lowell, with that faint crease of the brow.

'Oh yes if they became a little too "troublesome". After the Spartacus affair I believe they crucified six thousand rebels along the Appian Way, one every thirty-five yards.'

'That must have made it very difficult to read the signposts,' remarked Lowell.

Dubois observed him carefully. 'You are an abolitionist, I believe,' he said.

Nathan wondered how he knew that, but perhaps Imlay had told him.

'I am,' said Lowell, looking directly at his host for once.

'So how would you deal with the troublesome property, once it has been abolished, so to speak?'

'How do you mean?'

'Well, the Europeans have been transporting slaves from Africa to the Americas for three hundred years. There are now many millions of us distributed widely across the Americas. Four million is it, in the southern states? Half a million in Saint-Domingue. And I expect people will be talking about what is to be done with us for the next three hundred years, even if we are freed.'

'When you are freed, you may do as you wish,' said Lowell. 'That is the point of being free, is it not?'

'Life, liberty and the pursuit of happiness.'

'What is wrong with that?'

'Nothing at all if you have the means to pursue it. It rings a little hollow, I fear, if you work in the sugar fields for thirty sous a day.'

'What is your point, sir?'

'My point, sir, is that it is not enough to give a slave his freedom, you must also provide him with the means to live. And even to pursue this happiness that Mr Jefferson extols.'

'Pay him a wage he can live on,' said Lowell. 'That would go a long way to solving the problem.'

The gently, mocking smile again. Was it mocking, or even gentle? It was certainly ironic; it might have been dangerous.

'We tried this after we had our Revolution,' Adedike put in quietly. Far too quietly for her, Nathan thought; he wished he could tell Lowell to shut up. 'But what if they do not wish to work in the sugar fields? What if they choose to come into the towns and the cities to work as porters, and packers or even pimps, or to sit around in the sun all day and drink rum? Some might even set up in business and make a fortune. Some might turn to politics, or religion. What if that is their idea of freedom? While the sugar cane rots in the fields.'

'Is that what happened?' put in Imlay, before Lowell could ask another question, or suggest a solution, which would probably be worse. He was looking at Dubois, not Adedike.

'I am afraid it is. We tried to force them back to work, but that incited them to rebellion, and now they have turned to the French, much good that will do them.'

'Was there no alternative?' persisted Lowell, ignoring the look Imlay gave him, or more likely not noticing it. 'To forced labour, I mean. Could you not have paid them more?'

'I expect so, but to pay the workers we need money, and to get money we need to sell our sugar, and before we can sell out sugar we need to harvest it, and to harvest it, we need workers. It is what you might call a vicious circle.'

'Could you not borrow the money, and pay the interest from the profits you will make from the sale of sugar?'

'Now that is a good idea,' said Adedike in mock innocence. 'But where would we borrow it from?'

'A bank? It is what most people do.'

'That is what most *white* people do. You should try it if you are black.'

'Armand had a better idea,' said Imlay quickly. 'Did you not, Armand?'

Dubois merely inclined his head, with his little smile.

'He proposed turning every plantation into a cooperative,' Imlay went on regardless, 'and giving the workers a share of the profits, but this was too revolutionary, even for a revolutionary junta. This is right, Armand, is it not?'

'If you say so, Gilbert,' said Dubois. 'And now we go to Hell in the handcart, as they said in the Great Plague, but not before we have the dessert. Yes, Simone?'

He raised his head to the servant at his shoulder who bent her own head to convey a message, but it was not about the dessert.

'There is a courier,' he announced, 'come from Cayona. I must attend to him, if you will excuse me.'

'At this hour?' Imlay was clearly alarmed.

'I will be but a few moments.'

Adedike followed, leaving them to make conversation with those who remained. They discussed the relative merits of whisky and rum as a cure for minor ailments, and some major ones. It was a long few moments.

'I am afraid it is not good news,' said Dubois when he returned. They knew this already from his face. 'The General has gone to Le Cap to parley with Leclerc. He wishes me to join him there, as soon as possible. And I think you should come, too,' he said to Imlay. 'He will want to meet you. And it is important you meet with him before he agrees to terms.'

'But – what about the French?' Imlay frowned.

'They have nothing against the Americans,' said Dubois, and the smile was back. It was not reassuring.

'The *capitaine*, too,' said Adedike, looking directly at Nathan. It was the first time she had addressed him since their reunion. If, indeed, he was the one addressed. It was in the nature of a command.

'Me?' Nathan was startled. 'But – why would he wish to meet with me?'

'Because of your great service,' she said, as if surprised he should ask, 'to the Army of Lucumi.'

16

Le Cap

They could smell Le Cap before they could see it, and it was the smell of burning, or rather of charred wood when you stir it with your boot. As they came closer, they saw the reason why. All along the shore and up into the hills there were burned-out buildings amid great swathes of blackened forest, some almost totally destroyed so that only the stone chimneys remained; others that had been built entirely of stone, still standing, but with the roofs and windows gone, so that they resembled gaunt, blinded giants, staring with their sightless eyes out to sea; and the offshore breeze stirring the black ashes around them.

They had taken the *Delaware* for the short journey from Tortuga. If they were to sail into the heart of the French camp, the more innocent they looked the better, Imlay reckoned, and though the *Delaware* carried a few light cannon and swivel guns, she looked far less like a ship of war than either of the other two vessels available to them. As an extra precaution, she flew the flags of both the United States and the French Republic.

'We will represent ourselves as a trading mission,' he informed Nathan. 'Sent by the President in the hope of restoring commerce now that the colony is back under French control.'

But if this was French control, Nathan thought, it would be a long time before the island regained even a fraction of its former riches.

'Sadly, it was necessary to fire the port to deny it to the French,' said Dubois who had joined them at the rail.

'This was your doing?' Imlay's tone was shocked.

'I believe it was the general's decision when it was clear we could no longer defend it against the French.'

'And the people?'

'Gone to the hills, where most remain, if they are still alive.'

But then the *Delaware* stood out to round the point and they saw a different sight. The whole bay was filled with ships: a great armada of two- and even three-deckers, frigates and sloops of war, brigs and cutters, transports by the score. There must have been a hundred or more of them. Nathan would not have known the French had so many ships, all the years they were locked into their ports along the Atlantic by the British blockade. If they could have put such a fleet together then, in one place, they might have given us a fight, he thought, with our creaking, leaking wooden walls. There were Spanish flags among them, he saw, and Dutch, both allies now, sucking up to the new power and the glory of Republican France under Bonaparte.

They took in sail and cruised slowly between the long lines of ships, hoping not to be too much noticed as the sun went down. There were lights showing here and there as the sun sank down behind the western headland and the shadows reached out across the water. Nathan could hear voices, in French and Spanish, shouted orders, and he was braced for the gun ports to open, the guns run out, the shattering broadside, but they stayed closed. He read the names on the sterns of the bigger ships, some he knew – *Dexaix, Intrépide, Duquesne, Jupiter, Alexandre, Brave*. He consigned them to memory, as if he was a spy, thinking to report back to the Admiralty, but the French were no longer the enemy – the expedition had been given the stamp of approval by the British government, much choice they had – and who would read his reports? And yet it was said in some circles that Bonaparte had made peace so that he could send his fleets to sea at last, finally freed from the shackles the British had set upon them, so they could practice their sailing skills and their gunnery for the next war.

As a former artillery officer, trained at the Military School of Paris, Bonaparte could never understand why the gunnery of the French navy was so poor. Nathan recalled a conversation he had once had with him, when he thought he was talking to Captain Turner from Nantucket, an admirer of the French Revolution.

'*You are a seafaring man, do you know why this is?*'

'*It is because they never go to sea,*' Nathan had told him. '*They have not learned to account for the rise and fall of the waves. It is not a steady platform, as it is on land.*'

'*They cannot practice in harbour?*'

'*Not without reducing the harbour to rubble.*'

He was not sure that Bonaparte considered this a legitimate restraint.

If he had not known differently, he would have assumed the French had been practising their gunnery on Le Cap, but as they came closer he saw that a lot of what he had taken for devastation was in fact construction work. It had stopped now, as the day ended, but he could see that many of the buildings were encased with wooden scaffolding. The whole town was being rebuilt, and in straight lines, climbing up the hillside from the harbour. The smell of charred timber was still there, but so was the smell of mortar and lime, and rope and wood shavings. Some of the buildings along the waterfront had been completed, or spared the flames, and there were lights in them, he could even hear music. And further along the shore, and on both sides of the river that flowed into the bay, he could see hundreds of tents, presumably of the French army, the real French army and not the troops of General Louverture.

Here, too, in the mouth of the river, and off the mole there were a number of merchant ships, maybe up to a score, some flying the flags of Britain and the United States, some Danish, at least one Russian. Supply ships, Nathan assumed. Imlay was not the only man who ever made profit from a war, though he doubted if soap was much in demand. But an army of 30,000 men would need a lot of supplies, and the French army would not fight on what was available to them on the islands. They dropped anchor next to an American brig called the *John Adams* of Ipswich and Dubois said he must send one of his people ashore to make contact with the general.

'Do you know where to find him, amongst all of this?' Imlay was still looking as if he was struggling to come to terms with the devastation and wondering what it meant for his mission.

'No, but we know how we can send word to him. And we must do it now before dark.'

The French had imposed a curfew from an hour after sunset and so a boat was lowered and the messenger – a woman – rowed ashore.

'We should report to the harbourmaster,' Kiernan fretted as they waited for her return.

'Leave it till the morning,' said Imlay, who still had the instincts and inclination of the smuggler and a great aversion to authority. 'There is no hurry, and we may want to unload some of our cargo before we make our presence known.'

By cargo, he meant Dubois and his people, presumably, but they were in no hurry either, until they heard from their general.

'He may no longer be here,' said Dubois. 'He comes and goes. It is how he stays alive.'

But the woman was back within the hour. She had not met with the general, but she had met with someone close to him.

'He will send word when and where we are to meet,' she said. 'But I was told it would be soon.'

And so the waiting continued.

Nathan was standing at the rail, looking at the lights along the waterfront and their reflections reaching out across the water towards him. He could hear singing. Male voices mostly, accompanied by an accordion. A Cajun song from Louisiana. He could not hear the words, but he caught the rhythm. No curfew there, then. He felt a rare need for company. Wine, women, song . . . And almost as if he had conjured her up – or more likely she had conjured herself up – he heard the voice of Adedike at his shoulder.

'You would not like it. Too many French.'

It was true that the only people he could see moving on the shore wore French uniform.

'I quite like the French,' he said, still looking out towards the shore.

'But it does not stop you killing them.'

'Only because they are usually trying to kill me. But that is over now.'

'Ah oui, bien sûr!' He heard the irony in her tone. 'I had forgotten.'

He looked at her then – as much as he could see of her in the light of the stern lanterns. The tilt of that strong jaw, lifted towards him, with the suggestion of a challenge, as always. The wide mouth and the eyes, the glint of fire in them from the lamps. They had spoken French together, as they had when they last met, and her tone was as familiar as if it had been yesterday and there had been no animosity at their parting.

'How are you?' he said.

'I am very well, thank you, how are you?' The mockery in her voice and her eyes. He grinned, a little sheepishly. He wondered if she was remembering that last meeting before it turned ugly. Perhaps he should apologise for breaking his promise. Perhaps not.

'When did you come back to Saint-Domingue?' he said.

'About five years ago, in the early days of the Revolution.'

She would have been here during the fighting with the British, when they came from Jamaica to restore order, and seize the colony for themselves. The French would have been her allies then.

'You know the General,' he said.

'I do not think anyone knows the General,' she said. 'Not his wife or his children. Or himself.'

'Not Dubois?'

She laughed, the deep chuckle that he remembered, and he felt what Imlay would call in his bodice-ripper, a stirring of the loins.

'Oh, I cannot speak for Dubois. Dubois knows everyone.'

He could not tell if she was being sarcastic or not. Now was the time to ask, and what is Dubois to you, and you to him? But he knew he would not. Instead he asked the other vital question on his mind: 'Why do you want me to meet him, your General?'

She looked away from him, across the water to the town.

'He needs to know that the English are supporting him,' she said.

'How will he know that I am English?'

'He will know.'

She left him to ponder this. He did not come to any helpful conclusions. But it was good to know that she no longer appeared intent on revenge for what had or had not happened in the Bay of Serpents. Or if she did, it was not the first thing on her mind.

He was sorry she had gone. It was an impossible situation, but he was as much under her spell as he ever was. No. He was older now. He was like one of those battered, creaking hulks off the French coast. But battered by more than gales. He would never be as bewitched as he was then. But he felt sad about it.

He stood there for another half hour or so, leaning on the rail, listening to what he could of the Cajun music from the shore, the lilting, rhythmic sadness of it. It spoke of love and loss and longing. The French had brought it down from Canada with them, from the place they called Acadia, down the Mississippi in their oxcarts and their flatboats, after Wolfe took Quebec. Seeking a new homeland in the bayous and the swamps of Louisiana. But they had lost that too. And now they were coming back, to their lost colonies in the Americas.

He went below, to the tiny cabin they had given him, but for a long time he could not sleep. He was thinking of Adedike of course, and then of himself and the role he was supposed to be playing. Neither captain nor commodore, fish nor fowl. He had no purpose here, except perhaps to reassure the rebels that they had Britain on their side. And yet they had been fighting the British before the French. And who was he to speak for Britain? He could not even speak for himself.

He slept at last but was awoken almost immediately, it seemed to him, by a rapping on his cabin door, and Kidd's face peering round it. It could have been a bad dream. He looked like a bad dream, Kidd's impish face a gargoyle, moulded to the walls of a church to scare the demons. But he had brought Kidd with him in the *Delaware*, and Banjo, too. There was a glimmer of daylight seeping down from the companionway.

'What is it?' said Nathan. 'Are we under attack?'

He was being flippant, though in truth they might have been, they were in the middle of the French fleet.

'He's here. They want you up – toot sweet.'

'Who's here?'

'His nibs,' said Kidd, and in case this was not explicit enough: 'The General.'

Nathan still did not get it. He thought he meant the promised emissary to take them to him. But no, he meant the General.

He had come in person to hold a council of war, or peace.

17

The Black Jacobin

They were in Lowell's cabin; Imlay and Lowell at one end of the table, the three Africans at the other – Dubois, Adedike and a third who must be Louverture. Nathan had no notion of what he looked like – he had seen no portraits of him, not even a crude engraving – and when he walked into the little cabin, the picture that came to mind was a sketch David had made in the early days of the Revolution, of Marat conspiring with Danton and Robespierre in a wine bar. This was odd in many ways, for Marat had been notoriously pale, but there it was. Their features were not so dissimilar, and they had the same hunted look, combined with an intensity, a kind of burning energy, even in repose. Also, like Marat the figure at the table was so slight, he looked like you might snap him in your hands. Nathan recalled that as a child he had been called *Fatras-Bâton*, Creole for a stick so thin it should be thrown in the garbage. Perhaps that was one of the secrets of his success. His enemies had always underestimated him, and he was not so easily broken. He had led the first successful slave revolt in history, defeated the armies of Britain and of Spain and created a legend as enduring as that of Spartacus.

But now he looked like a fugitive.

He was dressed as a simple working man, a cutter of sugar cane, in cotton shirt and culottes, a straw hat on the table in front of him, presumably necessitated by the need to come aboard incognito. But in contrast to his body, he had a strong face with a long, lean jaw, a high forehead and a

Roman nose, though his eyes looked tired and the skin under them was darker than the rest, and looked bruised. L'Ouverture – the Opening. A nickname, some said because he opened the way, others that it came from the gap between his two front teeth.

There was a welcome smell of coffee – they all had cups in front of them – and Kidd followed him in with a fresh pot which he placed on the table before making himself scarce.

'This is Captain Peake,' Imlay introduced him. No more pretence then, on his part. If this was a surprise to Lowell, he did not show it. Nor did the others.

'I am glad to make your acquaintance, Captain,' said Louverture – he spoke French with a strong, Creole accent – 'I have heard much about you.'

This *was* a surprise, and slightly alarming. Who had told him? Adedike?

When he was last in the Caribbean, Louverture would have been fighting the British troops sent to Saint-Domingue to claim the colony for King George, and Nathan had been captain of the *Unicorn*, hunting down French naval forces in the region. If Louverture had heard of Captain Peake then, it would have been through French sources and they would not have been complimentary.

'And I have heard much about you, my General,' Nathan replied with a bow.

In fact, what Nathan knew of him was sketchy, derived mainly from what Imlay had told him on the voyage out, and in a few sparse reports in *The Times* and other English newspapers. Despite his slight stature he was reputed to have astonishing stamina, spending whole days in the saddle without tiring, and he was famous for appearing where you least expected him and then vanishing just as suddenly. This had been a characteristic of Marat, too. In the days when Louverture had been fighting the British, *The Times* had called him the Black Jacobin, describing him as a fanatical revolutionary and an admirer of Robespierre, but lately they seemed to have changed their tune. It was said that Sir Thomas Maitland, the general who had led the British forces against him, had offered to acknowledge him as King of Hispaniola, and defend the island with the British fleet, if only he would abandon his loyalty to the French. He had politely declined the offer, but since then he had been supportive of

British interests in the region, even to the extent of alerting the authorities to an attempt to free the slaves in Jamaica, led by the Sephardic Jew Abraham Sasportas.

It was virtual certain that approaches had been made to him by British agents in the recent past, and Nathan knew he would have to tread carefully. He did not want any adverse reports of his conduct carried back to the Admiralty to further poison the First Lord's perceptions of him.

He joined them at the table, gratefully accepting the cup of coffee Dubois had poured out for him. There was a lantern lit but the rising sun was flooding in through the skylight to the deck above, and he could hear the crew at work with the holystone. Lowell kept the *Delaware* as smart and trim as any ship in the British navy, or the American for that matter.

'I am afraid you have come too late to save us,' said the general, 'if that was your intention. Or did you wish to make us a part of the British Empire?'

Clearly someone, probably Imlay, had given him a false impression of Nathan's importance, but now was probably not the time to set him straight, not if they wished Louverture to fight on, and he supposed they did.

'I think the British government has learned its lesson, so far as that is concerned,' he replied cautiously. 'But why is it too late?'

'Because I have begun talks with General Leclerc, with a view to ending hostilities.'

He spoke quietly but the words were like a shock on the air. Presumably the others had heard them before Nathan had joined them, but he could sense the tension around the table.

What was he supposed to say? He glanced at Adedike, but her eyes were lowered.

'I understand the war has not been going well for you,' he managed awkwardly, 'but now we have brought new weapons . . .'

'We need a lot more than weapons,' said the general sharply. 'We need numbers, and we do not have them. The French have defeated us in every battle and my men are deserting me. I have fewer than five thousand left under arms.'

Again, Nathan glanced around the table, but no one seemed willing to meet his gaze, let alone reply. They were clearly waiting on him, as if he was their only hope. If he was, they were in worse trouble than they knew.

It seemed to him that 5,000 men, fighting in difficult terrain, might hold up the French for some considerable time, but even if this was what Imlay wanted him to say, the words stuck in his throat. How could they even think of persuading Louverture to fight on, if all it meant was more death and destruction, and no hope of winning? And yet why else was he here?

He asked a different question.

'And what of yourself, your Excellency? What will happen to you?'

The general smiled, either at the question or the title, but there was no humour in it. It was more a wry acknowledgement of defeat.

'I am to retire to my plantation at Ennery and grow sugar.

He had been born into slavery, Nathan recalled, though he had been freed long before the Revolution and gone on to own his own small plantation. Some said he had even kept slaves himself. At any rate, he had been a wealthy man at the start of the Revolution, Imlay said. Possibly this was what prompted Nathan to ask his next question.

'And what of your people?'

Perhaps it came out too quickly, too sharp. Certainly, it was not diplomatic, but Nathan had never considered himself to be a diplomat. There may have been a flash of anger in the look the general gave him. He had been the sole authority on the island for the past three years or more; he was not used to being questioned. But he replied equably enough.

'My men are to retire with a pension or join the French Army with the same rank as before. As to the rest of our people . . . I have made it clear that there must be no attempt to restore slavery. No. Absolutely. If that were the case I would fight on, whatever the cost, but Leclerc assures me there is no possibility of this.' His words were for the others in the room, Nathan guessed – Dubois and Adedike most of all. 'I have Bonaparte's word for it. "Black, white, all are the children of the Republic" – that was his proclamation. He abhors slavery as much as any man alive, Leclerc says.'

'And do you believe him?'

The question was more curious than challenging, and he was thinking more of Bonaparte than Leclerc, but Louverture did not take it well.

'What choice do I have?' he flared angrily. 'I no longer have the means to resist. But to attempt to restore slavery to the islands . . . It would not only be foolish, it would be totally opposed to the values of the French Revolution – and I believe, to Bonaparte's own personal beliefs.'

From their short acquaintance in Paris, Nathan had formed the impression that Bonaparte believed only in himself – and what he called his Destiny. It had probably suited him to support the Revolution in the early days. Why would he not? He was a poor officer cadet from Corsica, more Italian than French, with an accent his fellow cadets openly mocked and no influence he could bring to bear. The Revolution was the one means he had of advancing his career. But he had no great belief in liberty or equality, and his only sense of fraternity was to his family, and his followers. As for the institution of slavery, Nathan doubted if he had given it much thought. So long as he and the French had their coffee and their sugar, he probably did not care whether the people who brought it to them were free men or slaves, provided it did not cost more.

'He sent his sister, Pauline, here – his favourite sister.' Louverture was saying. 'The wife of General Leclerc. Is that the action of a man who wants war? You did not know that?'

He had seen the surprise on Nathan's face. No, he did not know that. Pauline? That would be the youngest sister. Bonaparte had spoken of her once, but Nathan was damned if he could remember what he had said. He had not considered it important at the time; she would have been a child then. Nor had he known that she had married Leclerc. But then why would he? He did not follow these things. As for coming to Saint-Domingue, she probably stamped her little foot and insisted. Or more likely, Bonaparte's wife wanted her out of Paris. The Bonaparte family was as complex in its jealousies and its feuds and intrigues as the seraglio in Constantinople. Even so, it was an odd thing to do, even for the Bonapartes.

'His younger brother too. Jérôme. A naval cadet, eighteen years old. I met him in Port-au-Prince. A fine boy, he reminded me of my own sons. Would he have done that if he meant to betray us? Force us into an endless war of attrition that would leave tens of thousands dead, French and African. Because that is what will happen if they try to bring back slavery. Or do you think we will kneel and stretch out our arms' – he put his wrists together and stretched them out across the table – 'and let them put back the chains and the manacles?'

There was silence around the table. No one knew, that was the problem. Or no one wished to contradict him. He is trying to persuade himself, Nathan thought, as much as us. He *has* to believe in the word of Bonaparte.

'Just a few weeks more and it will be the rainy season.' Imlay said. 'Then we will have the yellow fever back. It decimated the British and the Spaniards, it will not spare the French.'

The general looked at him. He shook his head. 'These were my tactics when the French came in January – to hold out until May and wait for the rains to fall and the fever to descend. But we have lost too many men. We cannot wait for the fever to save us. Or the Americans and the British.'

It might have been a question or an accusation. Either way, Imlay was silent. It was Adedike who spoke.

'We cannot trust anyone but ourselves,' she said firmly. 'But why will the people not heed us?'

Nathan looked at her in surprise. It was unusual for her to sound plain-tive, or to ask a question to which she did not already know the answer. He wondered if it veiled a note of criticism. If so, it was not veiled thinly enough for the general.

'You think that is my fault?'

'No,' she said, but the look she gave him was defiant. 'But I wonder where we went wrong.'

He stared at her for a long moment, but she held his gaze. 'We were the first,' he said. 'We broke the ground. Even if we made mistakes, we showed it could be done.'

'He is fooling himself,' said Imlay to Nathan as they stood at the rail of the *Delaware* and watched the slight figure of the general being rowed ashore. 'They will crucify him. And his people.'

The Spartacus solution. A crucified corpse every few yards along the local equivalent of the Appian Way. But Bonaparte would avoid that if he could, Nathan thought. He would rather pay him a pension and let him die in peace on his plantation. They might even make a statue of him some day, and set it up in Le Cap, or even Paris to demonstrate their continuing belief in the ideals of Revolution. Liberty, equality, fraternity.

'So, what now?' he said.

Their mission had failed, but he felt surprisingly relaxed about it. The sun was rising above the hills to the east and bathing the bay and its hundred ships in the glow of a new dawn. The shore was a hive of enterprise as thousands of black labourers applied themselves to building a new Paris of the Antilles, bigger and more beautiful than the last, or were applied to it by the French, for there were almost as many soldiers guarding them as there were men working. But the workers, though entirely black, did not appear to be slaves. They wore no chains at any rate; there were no overseers with whips, no barking dogs and harsh words of command, the atmosphere seemed almost cheerful. The hammering of nails, the sawing of saws, great lengths of timber born upwards on pulleys to reaching willing hands, a city of scaffolding stretching up into the hills. From where he stood it looked like a great Roman amphitheatre.

They were building the future. And good luck to them.

It was time to move on, to leave the people of Saint-Domingue to the French, and their own destiny. If their mission were to stop the French moving on to North America it was time to look to the next line of defence. New Orleans perhaps. Or maybe they should sail up the Mississippi and distribute their guns to the Red Indians.

But Imlay had other plans. He looked along the rail to where Dubois and Adedike were standing and lowered his voice.

'Perhaps it is time we spoke to another general,' he said.

18

Venus and the Lucky Star

'I have had a reply from Leclerc.'

Nathan, who had been reclining peacefully in a hammock on the afterdeck of the *Delaware*, raised the brim of his straw hat to observe the document being waved before his face. He looked above and beyond to the figure of Imlay who was holding it between finger and thumb. It had hitherto been a reasonably pleasant day.

'We are invited to dine with him aboard the French flagship.'

Nathan took this calmly. He was, however, surprised.

'What did you do to merit this?' he enquired.

'I sent him a letter from the President,' Imlay told him, 'for use in emergencies. Besides, I met him in Paris after the coup. He knows I have connections.'

Nathan would have liked to pursue this, particularly that reference to 'the coup', but he had just taken in the use of the first-person plural.

'When you say "we" . . . ?' he began.

'Why, you must accompany me, of course.'

'Why? In what capacity?'

'As an observer for the British government.'

Nathan swung his feet to the deck. Reclining in a hammock, while agreeable in many ways, did not confer much in the way of an advantage when it came to serious conversation. A glance about his surroundings assured him that nothing significant had changed since he had taken up residence here an hour or so ago. The *Delaware* swung idly at her moorings off the mole of Le Cap, with canvas awnings rigged against the sun, the position of which informed him that it was either just before or just after four bells in the afternoon watch. There was not a breath of wind and the French fleet did not appear to have moved since he last looked. In fact, it had not moved since their arrival over a week ago. It was the town that had moved, extending ever further up the hillside. Work was continuing even now, even in the afternoon heat.

'What do you mean – an observer for the British government?' 'What am I to observe?'

Imlay led him to the starboard rail where they could speak looking out to sea, out of the hearing of whoever might be interested or bored enough to listen.

'I do not wish to give Earl Saint Vincent the impression that I am playing false with him,' Imlay confided in lowered tones. Nathan could understand this. It was the last impression one would wish to give the Earl Saint Vincent. 'If I were to meet with Leclerc in private, especially if I were to dine with him and his wife, certain – assertions – might be made against me.'

This was undoubtedly true. The same assertions might be made against Nathan. However, it was probably better to be there than not. At least he would know what Imlay was up to and what further complications might occur as a result. But he had picked up on another word.

'His *wife?*'

'Pauline Bonaparte – though I suppose we must now call her Madame Leclerc. You will recall that Louverture mentioned her. I knew her in Paris, too' – he smirked – 'though she was then betrothed to Stanislas Fréron.'

Fréron was another name known to Nathan from his own sojourn in Paris on behalf of His Majesty's Government. He was a former journalist who had been one of the architects of the Terror until he turned against Robespierre, largely to save his own skin, and helped to bring the whole edifice crashing down, guillotine and all. But there were more important things on Nathan's mind than the machinations of the terrorists, or even the love life of Pauline Bonaparte.

'So, remind me again why are we meeting with the Leclercs?'

'We need to get something out of this,' said Imlay, as if this should have been obvious, even to Nathan.

'And what, precisely, did you have in mind?'

Imlay shrugged. 'I am open to offers.'

'Why should he offer anything?'

'To keep Britain and the United States off his back? I think he would offer quite a lot.'

'But Britain and the US are not on his back,' Nathan pointed out. 'Not officially. They have given the French carte balance to do what they like in Saint-Domingue. So far as Leclerc knows, at any rate.'

Imlay made a contemptuous noise with his lips. 'He knows what the score is. And so does Bonaparte. They know very well that whatever the British and Americans say in diplomatic circles, they will do everything they can to make things difficult for them in Saint-Domingue.' This was probably true, though it was the first time Imlay had admitted it. 'If Leclerc can neutralise the threat without an open confrontation, he will jump at it, believe me.'

'And what about our mission?'

Imlay frowned. 'What about our mission?'

'To make things difficult for the French in Saint-Domingue. The reason we are here,' Nathan reminded him.

'Yes, well, that was entirely dependent on keeping our boy up to the mark. But he has thrown in the towel. You heard him. He has gone back to his plantation to cut sugar cane.'

This probably summed up Imlay's true feelings about Louverture and the fight for freedom, but Nathan let it pass for the moment.

'So, what are you going to do – sell the guns to Leclerc to use in North America?'

'No, we will keep the guns for the time being. I have not given up on Saint-Domingue yet. There may be other ways of keeping Leclerc embroiled here, even without stirring up the blacks.'

'Such as?'

Imlay was stroking his jaw, never a good sign. 'There is a lot more money in Saint-Domingue than there is in Louisiana,' he said. 'At least in the foreseeable future. If I know Leclerc, he will want to see some of it for himself before he moves on to a hellhole like New Orleans.'

Interesting way of putting it, but entirely in character, so far as Nathan was concerned. Imlay might write about the American frontier in terms that would have his readers sighing for a log cabin and a few thousand

acres of virgin forest, but he was not much of a one for it himself, whatever he had told Mary Wollstonecraft to the contrary. He was a lot more
at home in the salons of Paris and London than in the waterfront bars of
New Orleans, let alone a waterlogged shack in the swamps of Louisiana
listening to the bullfrogs and the alligators – if alligators made a noise
before they took your leg off.

'You mean line his own pockets?'

'That is exactly what I mean. And the only way he can do that is by
getting things up and running again – and I don't mean just in Le Cap,
I mean the trade in sugar and coffee and indigo and whatever else they
brought the slaves here for. And no matter what he and Bonaparte say in
public, they ain't going to do it without 'em.'

Nathan gazed out across the waters of the bay to the vast building site
that was to be the new Le Cap. Ten thousand workers were employed in
the rebuild, he had heard, and it was scheduled to be finished in time for
the tenth anniversary of the French Republic in September. Dubois had
seen the plans, apparently, which were displayed outside the shell of the
old Government House. The streets were set out in a grid pattern running
back and upwards from the harbour. There were to be two public squares
with elegant fountains, two hospitals and a large barracks. A thousand
new buildings in all, mostly built from the bricks and stones of the old
ones. No, Leclerc was probably not going anywhere soon.

'So, when is this dinner?' he said.

'Tomorrow evening. At a civilised hour. When the heat has gone out
of the day.'

'And am I Captain Peake or Captain Turner?'

'Good question.' Imlay considered. 'I think you had better be Captain
Turner for the time being. As you were in Paris.' He grinned wickedly.
'You never know, they might have heard of you.'

*

The French flagship was well named. She was a three-deck Leviathan of
120 guns, the biggest ship in the French navy so far as Nathan was aware,
and by far the biggest he had ever seen, let alone set foot upon. It was also
the first time he had ever been piped aboard a French warship – though
this honour must of course be intended for Imlay, in whatever capacity
he had presented himself. Minister Plenipotentiary to the president of the

United States was not beyond Imlay's imagining, or his vanity. There was even a marine guard.

But not Leclerc.

The captain general awaited them on the poop deck, an aide informed them, if they would be so good as to follow him. Imlay gave Nathan a look to indicate that he thought this a little high and mighty, but when they ascended the two flights of steps they saw that an even more impressive reception had been staged. A hundred or so officers in all the finery of their rank, and not a few women in rather more revealing apparel, were assembled at the stern of the vessel beneath a great canvas awning hung with lanterns of many colours and flanked by potted palms and other tropical plants. The rails were decorated with bunting in the red, white and blue of the French Republic. There was even an orchestra playing chamber music, while white-coated servants circulating with trays of drinks and tropical delicacies. If this was in Imlay's honour, he had clearly been promoting his importance beyond even Nathan's expectations.

'L'Amiral Imlay et le capitaine Turner,' announced their escort.

With only a slight delay, two of the more illustrious figures – judging from their appearance – detached themselves from the crowd and came over to greet them. One wore the uniform of an admiral and though Nathan was less confident about military rank he judged the other to be in the higher echelons of the French army. Nathan had done his best to make himself presentable, but he felt like the skipper of a Newcastle collier. It hardly mattered. Neither of them looked at him.

'My dear Gilbert,' said the military gentleman, 'welcome aboard.'

This, presumably, was Leclerc. Nathan had first come across the name back in November when Bonaparte appointed him to command the expedition, not thinking then that he would ever come any closer to meeting him than in the columns of *The Times*. He was described as a professional soldier who had met Bonaparte in the early days of the Revolution when they were both junior officers at the siege of Toulon and followed him to Italy, like most of the inner circle – the band of brothers, *The Times* said, though Imlay had put it less flatteringly on their way over here in the *Delaware*'s gig.

'One of his favourite toadies,' he had said, 'which is why he had him marry his sister, even though she was in love with someone else at the time. They say she leads him a merry dance as a result, though I would not know about that. What I do know is that Leclerc played a major part in the coup that put Bonaparte where he is now.' He looked up to the towering sides of the *L'Ocean*. 'This is his reward. He has just turned thirty. The blond Bonaparte they call him, and don't he play up to it, the scrub.'

'You have done me proud, Charles,' said Imlay now.

Leclerc looked surprised for a moment, but then he beamed if a little uncertainly.

'Very good,' he said, clapping Imlay on the arm. 'I forget the American sense of humour. We are commemorating the battle of Montenotte, Gilbert, my brother's first victory as General of the Army of Italy, at which I had the honour to be present.'

Poor Imlay. Nathan did not dare look at him. Instead he looked at Leclerc, wondering if he knew that Imlay had been serious. It rather depended on how well the two men had known each other in Paris. The blond Bonaparte. He did have something of the look of his brother-in-law. The long thin face, the aquiline nose and thin lips, but he was nothing like as sallow or as sickly – Nathan remembered Bonaparte as looking pretty much like a drowned rat most of the time, even when he was in relatively good health. Leclerc had the fresh, ruddy complexion and fair hair of a Northerner. He looked older than thirty, though, and while he was obviously making an effort to be jovial, there was a strain about his features and a wariness in his eyes.

'But forgive me,' he was saying. 'This is my friend, Admiral Joyeuse de Villaret, who commands our fleet.'

A much older man, probably in his fifties, his hair powdered white, hook-nosed and jowly, nothing of the Boney about this one; in fact, he reminded Nathan a little of the Earl Saint Vincent, though his career had been considerably less illustrious. After leading the French fleet into several disastrous engagements with the British he had wisely taken up politics and managed to get himself elected to the Council of Deputies. But even then, he had managed to back the losing side, and his alliance with the Royalist faction had led to his being exiled to the Isle of Oléron for several years. Quite what he was doing commanding the largest French fleet ever assembled was something of a mystery, at least to Nathan. *The Times* had speculated that it was due to his membership of the right-wing *Club de Clichy*, a faction promoting slavery and the colonies. If that were so, it would not suggest the best of intentions so far as the former slaves in Saint-Domingue were concerned.

Nathan had ample time to run through his knowledge of both these dignitaries, for he had still passed notice, but now Imlay, who had managed to hide his chagrin at not being the reason for the festivities, introduced him as '*le capitaine* Turner' leaving the rest to their imagination.

Nathan made a bow commensurate to his insignificance, and as he came up from it, with a polite word of greeting, found himself face to face with a vision of loveliness that literally took his breath away. He felt as if he had been punched in the stomach. She had the face and figure of a Venus in the full bloom of youth and she was draped in a dress of pale blue muslin that did very little to disguise her charms, which was very probably the point of it. He had been about to say something, not at all consequential but possibly very witty, but whatever it was went completely out of his head. All he could do was try to breathe. And strangely, the vision seemed equally taken with him. Certainly, she was staring at him with an intensity he could only find promising. She had eyes like that of a startled doe. For all of two seconds Nathan thought his luck had changed. Then Leclerc spoke.

'And this,' he said, 'is Madame Leclerc, my wife.'

Of course she was. What else could he have expected? It was entirely in accordance with the fortune that had pursued him from India. The luck of Até. This must be the former Pauline Bonaparte. Pauletta, her brother had called her when he had mentioned her to Nathan in Paris. She had been fourteen then, and an impossible flirt according to Bonaparte with the morals of a *pika*, which Nathan gathered was a Corsican mammal somewhat resembling a rabbit. He had added, confusingly, that of all his brothers and sisters she was the one most like him. This was not true of her appearance, however. Her complexion was rather more peaches and cream than rotting olive, she had excellent teeth and her eyes were more, well pika than rat. The only Bonaparte feature he could discern was her nose which was quite aquiline, but he could forgive her that. What he could not forgive was her being the wife of General Leclerc.

She was speaking to him. 'Did you say Captain Turner?'

Nathan was smiling like an idiot.

'But no, it cannot be. Surely you are an imposter.'

This showed a level of precognition that was as divine as her person. Nathan struggled to find the words of rebuttal. It was entirely beyond his present capacity, however. He looked to Imlay for rescue, but Imlay was frowning at him as if he were the first to have been imposed upon and it demanded explanation. The other two gentlemen appeared merely bemused, but any moment now they would be calling out the guard. The marines were probably still there, on the upper deck. He considered making a dash for the rail and plunging into the sea, leaving Imlay to do the explaining for him, but it was a long way down and a long swim to the *Delaware*. They would launch a boat and catch him before he was halfway there, even if he survived the dive.

'Or perhaps Turner is a common name in America?'

'It is not uncommon,' agreed Nathan, clutching at this helpful straw.

'But – you are just as he described – tall, dark – American?'

Nathan agreed that this was the case.

'And you were in Paris in Vendemiaire, in the Year Four.'

Or in the King's English, October 1795. Nathan wondered if he might deny it, but there was a serious risk of being found out. Besides, it did not sound like a question.

'I think I may have been,' Nathan frowned, as if it were just coming back to him.

'Then you are the man who saved my brother's life!' The vision beamed at him in delight. 'His lucky star who came from nowhere!' She turned to her husband. 'You remember the story? My brother told it many times. He was in Paris, with no money, no job, no future, and this mysterious American came to his lodgings to tell him he was called upon to defend the Revolution. Like an angel who appears to him! Marvellous, is it not? The Royalists, they had thirty thousand men marching on the Tuileries, where the representatives of the people were gathered. It was his moment of destiny. And then, in the hour of victory, his horse fell and began to drag him into the mob, and the American comes again, from nowhere, to save him. And look – *Voila! Le mystérieux Américain! Le capitaine Turner.*'

'All I did was hold his horse,' murmured Nathan, but no one was listening; they had ears only for Madame Leclerc.

'He tried to find him afterwards to thank him,' she told them, 'but he had disappeared.' She addressed Nathan again: 'He became convinced you were his lucky star, come down to earth to lead him to his destiny. I will write to him to say I have found you and that you are quite mortal. Are you mortal?' she added, poking him in the belly with a slender finger. 'Oh, that feels solid.'

Nathan stretched his lips into the ghost of a smile.

'So now we have something else to celebrate!' announced Leclerc signalling to a waiter. Nathan took the proffered glass of champagne as Leclerc raised his own.

'To our honoured guests from America.'

They drank to that.

'And to our beloved General Bonaparte!'

They drank to that, too.

'But what are you doing here in Saint-Domingue?' Pauline wanted to know.

'They have come to talk to us about trade, my dear,' said her husband. 'But not tonight,' he added with a look at Imlay. 'This is not a night for business. I will instruct my secretary to arrange a meeting later in the week.' He clapped Imlay on the arm. 'And you must bring Captain Turner with you, our lucky star.'

But now the admiral was murmuring something in his ear. Nathan caught the one word, *Tortue.*

'Oh, but I am forgetting!' exclaimed Leclerc. 'On Thursday we sail for La Tortue. Today, I accepted the sword of General Louverture. He has surrendered,' he informed his guests. 'Tonight, we celebrate our own victory as well as that of my brother Napoleon. And now we can harvest the fruits of peace.' He raised his glass again but found it empty.

'La Tortue?' Imlay repeated faintly, though he knew perfectly well that it was the French for Tortuga.

'It is a small island just a few hours sail from here,' the admiral informed him. 'Once the pirate capital of the Caribbean.'

'And now to be the finest botanical gardens in the world,' said Leclerc, reaching for another glass.

'And the most famous menagerie,' said his wife. 'Do not forget the animals, Charles. There will be lions and tigers and oh, every animal you can imagine. It will surpass the Jardins de Paris.'

'It will be our Garden of Eden, my love,' said Leclerc fondly. He caught Imlay's eye. 'I am afraid our meeting must wait, monsieur.'

'But they must come with us,' declared Madame, clasping her husband's arm but gazing with shining eyes at Nathan. 'You can have your talks, and our lucky star will guide us. He can help us build our Garden of Eden!'

19

The Garden of Eden

Six Months Later

Quem Iuppiter vult perdere, dementat prius. The Polish officer spoke the words in Latin, for he was a learned man – a former student of the University of Paris – though this was not greatly appreciated by either his superior officers or those under his immediate command who were more inclined to respect his considerable bulk and his capacity for swearing at them imaginatively in their native tongue.

'I am sorry you have lost me,' said Nathan. He could understand Latin, just about, from his time at Charterhouse but he had to concentrate, and his mind had been elsewhere.

'Whom Jupiter would ruin, he first makes mad,' the officer translated. His name was Florjan Bruski and he was a captain in the Legion of the Danube as the Poles called it, though to the French it was just another brigade of foreigners in the service of the Republic. There were many such. This one had been formed from volunteers among the Polish prisoners of war who had previously been fighting for the Hapsburg emperor. Bruski's hope at the time, which he shared with most of the volunteers, was that they would help bring *liberté*, *égalité* and *fraternité* to the whole of Europe, thus freeing their homeland from the tyranny of Imperial Russia. In this they had been cruelly deceived. They had not been told they were bound for Saint-Domingue until they were halfway across the Atlantic.

Florjan Bruski had then been a mere corporal, but his coolness under fire and his qualities of leadership had led to his rapid promotion, though Death had played the major role in his advancement. The Danube Legion, which had numbered almost 6,000 men at the turn of the year, was now reduced to a little over a thousand, and Bruski had been appointed captain of the personal bodyguard to Madame Leclerc, who had expressed a preference for the Polish contingent over her own French countrymen. Thus he had come to his present posting at the *Habitation Labattut* where he had met the man he knew as Le Capitaine Turner, whose official function was not so well defined as his own but was perfectly clear to Captain Bruski and most of his men.

He did not appear to hold this against him. In fact, they had become good friends in the short time they had been here. He told Nathan that his family had been aristocrats and that in his native Poland, if it existed, he would have been Count Bruski. Nathan called him Jan and they normally spoke in French.

'Did you have anyone in particular in mind?' he asked him now.

'All of us,' said the captain. 'All of *this*.'

He indicated their present surroundings. The former plantation house was set on a forested hillside above the sea with extensive gardens planted with tropical flowers and herbs, and even some vegetables. It was close to being considered an earthly paradise, but it was presently disfigured by a multitude of wooden cages, some small, some large, each containing a solitary prisoner – animal, reptile or bird. Strolling among them, as if they were guards, or visitors to the zoo, were a number of peacocks, who occasionally flaunted their finery while emitting the usual peacock noises, somewhat between a whoop and a shriek. This visibly agitated some of the larger animals who would have made short work of them had they been released, even for a few seconds.

Nathan viewed the collection thoughtfully.

'She is thinking of letting them go,' he said. 'Back into the wild. She knows she will never have her garden. Not now.'

Bruski did not have to ask of whom he was speaking.

'That is sad,' he said. 'But probably not for them.'

They gazed about them at the captive creatures. There had once been talk of lions and tigers, but they had been deemed inappropriate. All of the ones here were native species. Apart from the peacocks, of course.

'She has hundreds of detailed drawings,' said Nathan, 'of both plants and animals which she will send back to Paris to be made into a book. That is her consolation.'

'And what about you, my friend?' The officer turned to regard his companion. 'Is she thinking of releasing you any time soon?'

Nathan rewarded this sally with a thin smile. He had been here for almost six months now, and it had not, thus far, been necessary to cage him. In fact, like the peacocks he more or less had the run of the place. The time had passed pleasantly enough, compared to other times when he had been forced into a long spell of inactivity – on the voyage home from India, for instance. Or the time he had been in command of the *Nereus* sloop on smuggler watch in the English Channel. He knew men who had spent years on blockade duty in the Bay of Biscay, in sight of land but never setting foot on it, constantly ploughing the same furrow of ocean. You found things to do, ways of occupying yourself. Played music, or cards, or chess. Ate, drank, counted off the days. In the past, Nathan had diverted himself with a fantasy of travelling alone through space, in a craft he called a spaceship, powered by magnetism. He had made extensive notes and was thinking of turning it into a book. It would have philosophical passages, mathematical calculations and speculations on the nature of time and space, enlivened by encounters with creatures from other planets . . . Like Voltaire's *Candide*, it would be an observation on the human condition, a form of satire. He had done some work on this during his stay here but not very much. He had been uncharacteristically idle. He thought sometimes that he was under a spell, an enchantment similar to that which had been placed on the mariners in *The Tempest*. At other times, when he was less cheerful, scenes from another play by the same author came to mind, when Anthony had been in thrall to Cleopatra.

Either way, he felt abandoned. Shipwrecked. Even if by his own choice, though he felt he had been manipulated into the situation by Imlay.

After hearing of Leclerc's plans for Tortuga, Imlay had sent the *Delaware* gig back to the island to warn Scott and Tully that the French were on their way. The weapons so recently unloaded had been crammed into the holds of the *Mohawk* and both she and the *Falaise* had fled to the sanctuary of the Turk Isles while they waited upon developments. Imlay had since joined them, leaving Nathan with the vague instruction to offer whatever assistance might be required of him by Madame Leclerc in her pursuit and categorisation of the island's flora and fauna. This appeared to be his new strategy for keeping the French occupied on Saint-Domingue. A few weeks later he had sent the *Delaware* back with a message to say that he had off-loaded the cargo – whatever that meant – and was bound for Washington to seek guidance from his political masters, taking both the *Falaise* and the *Mohawk* with him under the command of Scott and Tully. He would return before too long, he said, with new orders. And that was the last Nathan had heard from him.

Dubois and Adedike were back at Le Belvedere, he had been told, but they did not appear to desire his company and for various reasons he did not seek theirs. Banjo and Kidd were staying with him at the *Habitation Labattut*, but Nathan rarely saw them. Banjo had developed an unexpected interest in the local flora and had gone on long expeditions with the botanists and illustrators that Madame Leclerc had brought with her, attaching himself to one in particular, a woman of colour from Port-au-Prince called Céline, who had studied botany at the Jardins des Plantes in Paris. Kidd fulfilled the few duties he had as a servant and went on frequent 'fishing trips', as he called them, usually but not always with Nathan's permission. Sometimes he brought back fish. Banjo told Nathan that the steward was searching for buried treasure left here by his pirate ancestor. This might have been his idea of a joke. To Nathan's knowledge, Captain Kidd had never set foot on Tortuga, but he was not an expert on the subject. The *Delaware* was often at sea – making a hydrographical survey of the island on behalf of the U.S. Admiralty, Lowell reported with a straight face when Nathan asked him. He did not for a moment take this to be true. What Lowell was really doing was a mystery to him. He suspected it was on Imlay's behalf, unless Lowell had his own agenda, which would not surprise him. He did not much care.

As for Leclerc, captain general of the French expeditionary force and governor general of Saint-Domingue, he had devoted the first few weeks to the collection of flora and fauna. *Whom Jupiter would ruin, he first makes mad.* But then urgent news from his subordinates had forced him to return to Le Cap in *L'Océan*. Leaving Madame Leclerc to continue her pursuit of the local wildlife.

'You must protect me as you protected my brother Napoleon,' Madame told Nathan, linking her arm through his, as they watched the French flagship sail into the sunset. That night she had summoned him to her room at the *Habitation Labattut* and they had become lovers.

Nathan was unable to justify this to himself. He doubted if he would be able to justify it to Imlay who was still, officially, paying his wages, though they were now in arrears by almost six months. He hoped he would never have to justify it to General Leclerc.

He told himself that he was in love. This made it a little easier on his conscience. He told himself he was playing his part in keeping the French involved in Saint-Domingue, and Bonaparte from conquering the world, but he knew that his reasoning was at best disingenuous. In fact, he did not know what he was doing here, or why, any more than he supposed the peacocks did.

From time to time Pauline heard from her husband and she would pass on the news to Nathan. He had mixed feelings about this. It added to his guilt, and yet he told himself it was extremely useful to know. He even compiled a detailed despatch to Imlay on the subject but had no means of sending it to him.

The French were winning the war, the general reported, but losing more and more men. They lost most of them, not in battle, but to an enemy the French called *fièvra jaune*, the Poles *zotta febra* and the British, who had already lost the best part of one army to it, yellow fever.

As enemies went, few could rival its power to turn a conquering army into an army of the dead and the dying within a matter of weeks. It came on suddenly with a fever and headache. Muscle pain and vomiting followed, with aching muscles and eyes blinded by light. Then the fever passed, the victim appeared to recover, some did, but for many this was followed by a second, and much more serious attack. This brought the yellowing of the skin which gave the disease its name, along with bleeding from the mouth, nose, eyes and ears. Then came paralysis, then death. The hospitals in Le Cap and Port-au-Prince were filled to overflowing. The workers had stopped building the Garden of Eden on La Tortue and started building an isolation hospital there instead. Hundreds of stricken soldiers were ferried across from the main island every day. Most died. The island paradise had become a graveyard.

In his letters to his wife, there was no more talk of winning the war against the rebels. Leclerc estimated that he had no more than 2,000 men left who were able to bear arms. This had encouraged many of Louverture's former soldiers to revive the liberation struggle, even without their leader who was still in retirement on his estate in Ennery. Those of an African heritage appeared to have an immunity to the disease.

No one knew what caused it. There was a theory that it was spread by miasmas rising from stagnant water, and that it was dispelled by fresh breezes. Perhaps this was the reason it had not spread to La Tortue, apart from among those soldiers in the hospital. It did not seem to travel across the sea, beyond a mile or so from land, but the larger ships of the French fleet were now being used as floating hospitals in the Bay of Le Cap and many of the sailors had gone down with the disease. Pauline said that Leclerc wrote constantly to her brother, begging him to send reinforcements. He received encouraging replies, praising his efforts, but no extra men.

'You know what my brother values most in his generals?' Pauline supplied her own answer: 'Luck. He will think poor Charles does not have any.'

Her own feelings about her husband were difficult to work out, at least for Nathan. She seemed fond of him, but in a vague, almost sisterly way. They had a child, a little boy called Dermide, who was three years old. He was with her on the island and she seemed fond of him, too. But it was very difficult to know what went on inside Pauline's head. Or her heart. At times she was astonishingly vain and shallow, and yet she was prone to violent displays of temper or despair or passion. At other times she would surprise Nathan with her thoughtfulness, or with some insight, or concern for someone of her acquaintance, or even strangers she had just heard about who were going through a bad time and she would want to move heaven and earth to help them, but the next day she had forgotten all about them. She was easily distracted. Her interest in flora and fauna was typical of the way her mind seemed to work. Sometimes she showed a genuine interest in the collection, particularly the detailed drawings that were being made. She talked of doing for French botany what Sir Joseph Banks had done in Britain. At other times it seemed her prime concern was to outshine her sister-in-law Josephine who was a patron of the Jardins des Plantes in Paris. She would create a new Garden of Eden on Saint-Domingue, she said, but without any snakes in the grass. She was like a spoiled child. Or a character in a tragic opera who was so fickle and thoughtless you wanted her to die in the First Act, and so beautiful and passionate and vulnerable, you would give your life for her.

As for his own feelings – he knew it was a kind of madness.

And he knew this was an excuse, too.

He would wake in horror sometimes as if from some terrible nightmare and think, what am I doing here? What have I become?

He knew he had to stop, to find some excuse to leave, to join Lowell on the *Delaware*, if he would let him. And then he would think of making love to her. He would think coming into her room, in answer to a summons from her maid, and seeing her lying on the bad, naked through the thin veil of the mosquito netting, turned away from him as if she had forgotten she had sent for him, and then looking at him over her shoulder with an expression of such pure promise and promiscuity it made him forget all of his reservations, or most of them.

But it was not all physical. She told him about the time in Corsica, after the Revolution, when the Bonapartes had lost everything. They had backed the wrong party in the civil war and expected every day to be their last. But the worst of it, she told him, was not the fear of death, but the poverty. They had been respectable bourgeoisie, and this made their sudden deprivation worse, or certainly more shameful. She told him that her mother had been obliged to take in washing and that she and her sisters were enrolled as laundrymaids, though they had never done a day's work in their lives before. She showed him her hands as they were now and told him to imagine them red and stinging from the lye, and the cracks and blisters on her skin. She had received no formal schooling; what she had learned she had learned from her mother, Letitia, and it was not all good. Her ignorance of some things was as astonishing as her knowledge of others. She told him that the whole family had crossed to the French mainland in a small boat, arriving in Marseilles as refugees, with no money and no food and only the clothes they stood in.

He told himself that it was not just her beauty that captivated him; he admired her spirit and her *sang froid*. She was a survivor and a fighter. And she was a Bonaparte – that played its part. There was a magic attached to that name, and he was not immune from it. She told him things about her brother Napoleon that probably no other Englishman knew. And probably no Frenchman outside the family.

He told himself that it would be very useful for Admiral Lord Nelson and the Earl Saint Vincent to know these things – if he ever saw them again.

She would ask him about the time he saved Bonaparte's life.

'Did you really turn up at his lodgings and tell him he was needed to save the Revolution?' she asked.

'I was sent to find him,' he said. 'By Barras.'

Barras had been the effective ruler of France at the time, though effective was probably not the right word. He had given the young Bonaparte command of the artillery at the siege of Toulon and when Paris was threatened by a Royalist mob he had turned to him again – only he had no idea where he lived, and Nathan did.

'And what happened to you afterwards, when you saved his life? He sent Junot to find you.' Junot had been Bonaparte's sergeant and aide de camp. Now he was a general like Leclerc, and his wife Laure had been Pauline's best friend in Paris. 'He asked at the American ambassador's house, but they had not heard of you.'

This was because Nathan had been nowhere near the American embassy during his time in Paris. They would have known within minutes that he was not American. In any case, by then he would have been on his way back to England, to make his report to the Admiralty, who had sent him there.

'He wanted to thank you properly,' she said. 'Even to give you a reward. He might have made you an admiral. So now it is left to me.'

He felt like a satyr who had been swept up, by accident, in her collection.

He was convinced he was going to die here. This would be his act of atonement for saving Bonaparte's life. And as useless as everything else he had done since he came to Tortuga.

And to think he had thought Nelson pathetic.

Suddenly she was there, plonking herself down on the steps between them, barefoot, with her hair down, and still in her nightdress, though it was early evening. Or perhaps it was a day dress, there was often very little difference.

'My lovely boys,' she said. 'What are you talking about?'

'Not you,' said Jan. 'So, you will not be interested.'

Was that the way the captain of the guard talked to his mistress? Unless she was a different kind of mistress. She pouted but Nathan could see she was amused.

He felt a desperate jealousy. Had Florjan Bruski been the last man to have her before him? Perhaps he still did. She was not with Nathan every night.

He despised himself for the thought, even if it were true.

How had this happened to him? Was it all down to Até, goddess of delusion and mischief, folly and ruin? But you cannot always blame the gods. Or the goddesses. If his mother and father were agreed upon anything it was that you are responsible for your own actions.

Mea culpa, as the Papists said, beating their breasts, *mea maxima culpa*.

He woke early the next morning. Pauline was still asleep. He gazed at her for a moment, his head propped on one elbow. She was turned away from him, the sheets tangled around her thighs, her long dark hair spread across the pillows. He had seen paintings like this, of artists' models, the long haunches they favoured, the impossibly smooth skin. If she had not been the sister of Napoleon Bonaparte, she might have become an artist's model, like Emma Hamilton, or his own Sara in Paris. It was better than taking in washing. He brushed his lips lightly across her shoulder and then parted the mosquito netting and slipped out of bed. He put on his robe and padded out of the room in his bare feet, and out onto the veranda. The birds were singing away in their cages, his fellow prisoners greeting the dawn of a new day which would almost certainly be no different from the last. There was no sign of the peacocks, but he could see two of Jan's guards smoking their pipes at the edge of the trees. And beyond them, far, far below, the sea. He leaned on one of the columns of the veranda and breathed in the morning air, lost in an immeasurable sadness. And then he saw the ship rounding the headland to the east. The *Delaware* no doubt, back from her latest trip to God knows where. He felt such an intense longing then to be out there with them, the deck of a ship under his feet again and the wind in her sails. It was almost worth putting up with Lowell. He felt as if he was being torn apart, one part of him pulled by the sea, the other by the siren in the room he had just left.

But sailors always blamed the sirens.

And then he looked again and saw it was not the *Delaware*. It was the *Falaise*.

20

Out of Eden

He could not find Kidd – off on one of his 'fishing trips' no doubt – but he roused George Banjo and they descended the steep path to the harbour and found a boatman to row them out to the *Falaise*. She looked even more beautiful than when he had first seen her under the grey skies of the Downs, but it was probably the setting, and the mood he was in. Even the monstrous face of Até appeared to smile down upon him, though as he came closer, he saw that it was a smile of malicious pleasure as if his poor, feeble humanity had now been thoroughly exposed to her satisfaction. Her Phyrgian cap had been restored to the original red, he saw. He did not know why – prolonged exposure to the Americans, perhaps – but it suited her better. It looked like her hair was drenched in blood.

He went aboard up the pilot's ladder and there was Tully to greet him, beaming broadly. Nathan swept him an ironic bow, but he could have fallen to the deck on both knees, he was so pleased to see him. Other familiar faces: Keppler and Cole, Caine, the gunner, and Bentham, the gunner's mate, Mr Drew the surgeon, one or two he did not recognise or whose names he had forgotten, all seeming as pleased to see him as he was to see them. Then suddenly Imlay was there, looking like mine host disturbed in a furtive liaison with one of the chambermaids by the arrival of an unexpected guest and doing his best to appear welcoming.

'Louverture has been arrested,' he said to Nathan when they convened in the stern cabin, restored now to his exclusive use. 'They have sent him to France, almost certainly to spend the rest of his life in prison.'

He seemed to know more about the current situation in Saint-Domingue than Nathan did, which was surprising as he was not sleeping with the governor general's wife. He said he had picked up the news from a British naval officer in Nassau where he had stopped on his way back from the States. The British, he said, were keeping a close eye on things. No one believed the peace with France would last more than a few more months at most and they would become the enemy again, a situation which, on the whole, the British preferred.

'There are rumours that Bonaparte is planning to bring back slavery,' he reported. 'They have passed new laws in Paris. At present they apply only to Guadeloupe and Saint-Martinique, but everyone believes it will be Saint-Domingue next. It has provoked insurrections all over the island, though mainly in the northern highlands above Le Cap.'

This had been mentioned to Nathan by both Pauline and Bruski, but the reports from the British were more detailed, and more catastrophic for the French.

'The rebels are led by Dessalines and Christophe – Louverture's lieutenants until they went over to Leclerc,' Imlay went on. 'And they have thousands more men. The French cannot venture out of the main towns and a few forts in the highlands. They still control the main road from Le Cap to Port-au-Prince, but only by day. The plantations are burning again. I am told you can see the flames from Le Cap. All that sugar gone to waste.'

And Imlay's commission with it. But it was what Imlay, and his political masters in Washington, had wanted. A long war of attrition, and the rebels holding their own. Though in fact, it was the disease that was doing the fighting for them. According to Imlay's informant, Leclerc had even fewer men available to him than he had reported in his letter to Pauline.

'And he is not well himself,' said Imlay. 'Not well enough to fight, at any rate.'

'He has not caught the fever?' Nathan was alarmed. He did not want Leclerc to die. He felt guilty enough already.

Imlay shrugged. 'He has never been well, by all accounts, not since he was in Ireland with Humbert in ninety-eight.'

But Nathan knew this. This was something else that Pauline had told him: how Leclerc went to liberate the Irish and came back a broken man, older than his years, who would sit huddled by the fire, wrapped in a blanket, drinking hot spiced wine to sweat the fevers out of him, muttering of the endless rain and the bogs. Ireland broke his heart, she said, and his body. He was not the first man this had happened to and would probably not be the last. And now he had been sent to Saint-Domingue. Some people had all the luck.

'He has effectively passed on the military command to his number two – Rochambeau. The word is that he has been told to restore French power by any means available to him. They will find him a much tougher enemy than Leclerc.'

He spoke as if he knew.

'How so?'

'I have met him before.' Imlay looked grim, as if he was remembering something distasteful to him. 'He was in America during the Independence War. His father was the commander of the French forces sent to assist Washington. An honourable man and a distinguished soldier. The father, I mean. I would not say the same for his son. Not by any means. The man is a vicious bully. The only way he knows how to make war is by the indiscriminate use of terror. They say he has bought hundreds of killer dogs in Cuba, specifically trained to hunt and kill negros. It is getting to be like France in the worst days of the Terror. Remember the stories of the Royalists drowned in the Loire?'

Nathan remembered. Like Imlay, he had been in Paris at the time.

'Well, there are stories of them loading prisoners up on ships and taking them out to sea and throwing them overboard. Some of the officers and crews protested, but they have been made to serve with the army, which is a death sentence in itself.'

He brooded on this for a moment and then looked at Nathan as if recalling where they were now, and why. 'So, how are you?' he said. 'How have you been keeping? You look well.'

Nathan was thrown by the change of subject, still thinking of the atrocities Imlay had described. It made his own life appear that much more dissolute. 'We have been idling our lives away in the Garden of Eden,' he said. 'Wondering what was keeping you.'

'I am sorry. I was much longer than I intended. I had to spend some time in Washington. People could not agree.' Agree on what, Nathan wondered? And what would it mean to him? 'Then we had to pick up more crew.' He seemed to cheer up. 'I have a hundred new men for you, all able seamen – mostly English and Irish from New York and Boston, looking for a passage home.'

'And did you tell them they were going to Saint-Domingue this time?'

'Oh, yes. I was quite open with them.' Nathan very much doubted that, but there was a first time for everything. 'They are all eager to join in the fight against slavery.'

Nathan kept his expression carefully neutral, but while he had known many British seamen who were eager for a fight, the issue of slavery had not cropped up in general conversation with them. He might, of course, have been speaking to the wrong seamen.

Imlay was still talking, and he did his best to pay attention. It was never wise to let your mind wander when Imlay was talking; you might miss something that could cost you money, or lose you your life.

'We loaded up a thousand guns from Brunswick. In Georgia, that is.' There were a great many Brunswicks in what had once been the thirteen colonies, named in honour of the British ruling family. The Americans had not bothered to change them. Perhaps they did not know George III was a member of the House of Brunswick. Perhaps they did not care. 'Eight hundred Brown Bess muskets, two hundred Ferguson rifles, with powder and shot for a hundred rounds a man. So, we are back in business.'

He clapped Nathan on the shoulder, but Nathan was looking thoughtful. These were all British guns.

'Ex-British Army,' Imlay said. 'Put into store after the Independence War. Last used at the siege of Charleston, I believe. But they are in prime condition.'

Why was he so particular about this, Nathan wondered? It was unusual in Imlay to be that interested in the guns he sold – other than the price he was getting for them. But perhaps he was being unfair. In Imlay's case, absence had not made the heart grow fonder.

'So – are you ready and rearing to go?' Imlay was regarding him in a way that made him wonder if he had been receiving regular reports from a spy strategically placed in the Garden of Eden.

'Where did you have in mind?' he enquired with as much nonchalance as he could contrive.

'Hands to weigh!'

The wail of the bosun's call and the rush of feet from below. Nathan, back in his blue coat, looked quickly to the shore, searching out the white house among the fringe of trees on the top of the ridge far above. He thought of Pauline, still asleep or just waking. He wondered how she would take it when she discovered he had gone. Furious rage, grief, indifference?

At a somewhat lower level of concern, Kidd was still missing. But he could probably look after himself, at least until their return. Imlay said they would be only a few days at most.

'Rig the capstan!' The pigeonholes emptied, the bars shipped and pinned. 'Bring to the messenger!'

The fiddler leapt to the drumhead and bent his bow.

'Heave round!'

'When I wuz a young'un I sailed wid de rest
On a Liverpool packet bound out to the west.
We anchored a day in the harbour o' Cork,
Then put out to sea for the port o' New York.'

The tide still on the flood and the sloop butting her head a little into the restive waves as she hove short to the anchor.

'At long stay!'

Up to the mainmast shrouds now, and he could feel the sloop shaking off her stays, or was that him?

'Heave to, cheerily now!'

'Singin' ro-o-o-oll, ro-o-o-oll, roll, bullies, roll,
Them Liverpool judies have got us in tow!'

He was still not used to the singing – working shanties being banned in the King's navy, though there were exceptions made far from the frowning brow of the Admiralty. He had made them himself in the past when a bit of a song cheered the men up. Most of the lads they had taken on in Boston seemed to be from Liverpool. There were as many of them among the crew, now, as there were American, Tully said.

'At short stay!' Alongside the fore shrouds now.

'Make sail!' cried Tully.

'Away aloft!'

The shrouds were alive with men as the larboard watch raced to the yards.

'Lay along topsail sheets and halliards, jib halliards! Lay out and loose! Stand by!' A moment when the wind held its breath . . . 'Let fall!' And the canvas came tumbling down.

'Up and down, sir,' from Cole at the forecastle. And then the cry they had all been waiting for: 'Heave and aweigh!'

He felt, as the sloop did, the moment they tripped the anchor: the wrenching free of shale, shell and shingle, or whatever earthly substance held her in thrall, and the bows rising and falling as they met the incoming tide. Always a poignant moment, this, after a long spell ashore, it held a special significance now, and he felt his heart lift with it – but there was sadness, too, for what he was leaving. Or at least regret.

He looked once more to the house on the hill, and then to the bumboat halfway to the shore with his hastily scribbled note. Urgent call to Port-au-Prince, back in three days or less. Coward that he was. He knew that he would never be back, and if he was it would not be to stay.

'Heave and in sight!'

He could see in his mind's eye the cloud of muddy water rising to the surface about the rising anchor, and yet he had not seen it with his own eye since he was a midshipman, posted on the forecastle for that very purpose, on the old *Hermione* in the South Seas, was it seventeen years ago, and was he happy then? He thought so, but what did he know? One more look back, and was there a figure in white up on the distant balcony, and should he wave, or at least raise a hand in salute?

'Heave and awash!' The anchor ring in sight, the last of the cable coming aboard . . .

'Sheet home and hoist away topsails.'

'Haul taut, brace abox, brace up!'

'Man the jib halliards!'

As the wind filled the sails, the bows came round and she fell off towards the reef, and he could almost feel her shaking off her shackles and heading for the open sea, as of her own free will, but it was never that.

'Course West by South, Mr Tully.'

And they were headed for the Windward Channel and whatever awaited them beyond. And there was probably now no looking back.

21

The Sea of Silence

They consulted the chart in the privacy of the stern cabin.

'Apparently, we are to rendezvous with the *Mohawk* here – in the *Baie des Garcons*,' Nathan told Tully, tracing a finger from their present position in the Windward Channel to a point some 120 miles to the south, on the southern shore of the Gulf of Gonâve.

'At our present rate we should get there in the early hours of tomorrow morning,' he estimated. 'The plan is for us to lay up for the day, and then land the guns tomorrow night at the mouth of the River Anse-à-Veaux – here.' He indicated a small notch in the coastline some twenty miles to the east of their rendezvous with the brig.

Tully was looking thoughtful. It was not hard to see why. The Gulf of Gonâve was a large indentation in the western coast of the island, dividing the colony into two more or less equal halves – the Northern Peninsula, with Le Cap and most of the sugar plantations, and the poorer Tiburon Peninsula, to the south – with the Gulf between like the gaping mouth of a giant fish. But at its eastern end, the Gulf was itself divided by a large island – known as La Gonâve – with Saint Mark's Channel to the north and the Gonâve Channel to the south, both fringed by shoal waters and coral reefs that did not leave much room for manoeuvre. And of even greater concern, about fifty miles east of their landing point, was Port-au-Prince, the capital of the colony – with its French garrison and a large part of the French fleet.

'It will be tricky,' Nathan acknowledged, 'even without the French Navy.'

'Did he say why it had to be here?' Tully wanted to know. 'Or did he just want to make it more of a challenge for us?'

'He' was Imlay, who had stayed behind at Le Roche because, he said, he needed to consult with Dubois and might have to go into Le Cap.

'Apparently the rebels are preparing for an attack on Port-au-Prince,' Nathan said. 'They have about ten thousand men available to them, but half of them are armed with machetes. He says our guns will make all the difference.'

He knew what Tully was thinking. How did Imlay know this when he had just come from the States?

'Apparently, he had instructions from one of Dessalines's people in Nassau,' said Nathan. He was aware that he was using the word 'apparently' rather a lot.

'And do we know how many ships the French have in the area?'

'All we know is that they have stripped the crews to serve with what is left of the army, and that they rarely venture out of Port-au-Prince. When they do, they tend to use the northern channel. So' – he shrugged – 'we may be lucky. If we are not – we will have to run for the open sea.'

Tully nodded, but he still looked thoughtful.

'Let us take a look at these guns,' said Nathan.

They equipped themselves with a couple of lanterns and descended to the orlop deck, taking the gunner, Mr Caine, with them and the armourer, Newton, and not without some misgivings, George Banjo, who would very likely know exactly what Nathan was curious to know but might cause certain noses to be put out of joint in the process of revealing it. The orlop was filled with casks and cases, much as it had been on the voyage out – but they were no longer stamped with the name of a Portuguese grape distillery in the Duoro Valley; instead the casks bore the name of a distillery in Louisville, Kentucky, and the cases that of Taylor & Sons, suppliers of Nuts, Bolts and Agricultural Tools, Brunswick, Ga. They opened three of the latter at random – two were packed with Brown Bess muskets, the third with rifles.

It was the rifles that were of particular interest to Nathan. He had heard of the Ferguson rifle, but had never seen one before, and was not even sure they existed until now. His father's steward, the Angel Gabriel, claimed to have used one at the Battle of Brandywine in the American Independence War when he had been briefly attached to a light infantry company. Or so he said. He had told his young follower that they were the invention of a certain Major Patrick Ferguson, and were the only breech-loaders ever issued to the British army. Nathan, who was ten at the time, had seen no reason to dispute this, though this was not his habitual stance, but thus encouraged, Gabriel had gone on to make the further, astonishing claim that with such a weapon an expert rifleman, such as himself, could fire nine rounds a minute – two or three times the rate of a trained infantryman with a Brown Bess musket, and that this feat had enabled the British to win the battle with minor losses. Despite which, the British army, which was led by fools and scoundrels, had disbanded the company, and declined to order any more of Major Ferguson's miraculous inventions, thus making a major contribution to the loss of the American colonies.

But Gabriel was a notorious teller of tall stories – or liar as Nathan's father would have put it more bluntly – and even at age ten Nathan had learned to take his tales with a large pinch of salt.

He lifted one of the rifles out of the greased sacking. It was about five feet long, barrel and stock, much the same as the Brown Bess musket, and about the same weight. He had expected it to be hinged at the breech, like some of the early cavalry carbines he had seen from the English Civil War, but he could see nothing resembling a hinge or swivel, only a thick, iron screw that appeared to join the barrel and the breech just below the gunlock. But it would surely take longer to unscrew it, insert the cartridge and screw it up again than it would to load a gun from the muzzle. He handed it to the armourer to see what he could make of it, but after turning it over in his hands a few times and trying to break it open with brute force, he declared himself stumped. Nathan took it back and gave it to Mr Banjo who had been watching with barely contained impatience and took about ten seconds to discover that the trigger guard served as a crank to turn the screw. One complete turn dropped it low enough to insert powder and ball into the breech, and then you turned it the opposite way to close it up again. He demonstrated this with his usual competence.

'Very neat, sir,' said the armourer sourly, 'but I wonder how long that screw would last in a proper ruckus.'

'Interesting to find out,' said Nathan idly. 'What have we got in the armoury in the way of rifles?' he asked him.

'Well, sir, there is a dozen Frenchie guns,' he said without enthusiasm. 'Come with the ship, so to speak. Carabines, they calls 'em. Made in Ver-sails.'

'Versailles,' Nathan corrected him automatically. 'Any good?'

'Beautiful made,' Newton conceded. 'But you'd be dead and buried the time it takes to load and fire 'un, sir.'

Nathan could not resist giving Banjo a look as if for confirmation of this intelligence. He inclined his head in considered agreement. 'That's what Boney thinks,' he said. 'He won't tolerate them in the army. But he don't mind if the navy uses 'em.'

How did he know something like that, Nathan wondered? But it was sometimes better not to ask. He also wondered why Imlay had chosen British guns when he could surely have found more of the Spanish muskets in the States, and the rebels could have used the same ammunition. But if they were left over from the Independence War, perhaps he had picked them up on the cheap. Certainly, there would be some advantage to him personally and it was as like to be financial as not.

'Tell you what,' he said, turning to the gunner. 'Take a pair of these and put two of the carbines in their place. I'll sign the paperwork.' He was fairly confident that Imlay would never read it. He had a desire to try one of the Fergusons for himself, if only in honour of old Gabriel, and to see if he could match the same rate of fire. He could make it a contest between himself and George Banjo; it might entertain the crew and if Banjo won, which he very likely would, it might reconcile the gunner and the armourer to his superior knowledge of the weapon.

They were on their way to the upper deck when the lanterns flickered on a gleam of bronze and his gaze fell on the two howitzers he had first seen when the ship was riding in the Downs. *Obusiers de vaisseau.* He stopped dead, obliging the others to pile up behind him.

'What are they still doing here?' he said.

'I don't rightly know, sir,' replied Caine. 'Not having no orders to dispose of 'em, so to speak.'

Fair enough. Either Imlay could not find a buyer for them or he had forgotten they were here. He may never have known about them in the first place. Nathan doubted if he had ever come down to the orlop deck.

'Do we still have the shells for them?' he asked the gunner.

'Aye, sir, I keep a regular check on them in the magazine,' said Caine, on the defensive now. 'Can't say as I'm too pleased to have 'em there either, sir.'

The shells, of course, were the problem, being notoriously prone to going off by accident, or a few feet out of the muzzle, causing great slaughter to the gun crew. He almost had second thoughts, but it went against the grain to have two 36-pounders stowed away in the orlop. He could always use canister with them, or grape shot.

'Get them up on deck,' he said. 'Let us have a look at them in the light.'

The gunner looked taken aback.

'You mean on the quarterdeck, sir.'

'If that is where the fittings are.' The 'fittings' were no more than four ring bolts on the deck but there was plenty of spare tackle. 'Would you mind having them on the quarterdeck?' he asked Tully in Guernésiais.

'*Naon*,' said Tully, but he showed his surprise. '*Mais pourquois?*'

But Nathan did not rightly know himself.

'Have Mr Banjo help you,' he said to the gunner. 'I am sure he knows what to do with them.'

They were on their way back up to the deck when they heard the shout from one of the lookouts: 'Sail on the larboard bow.'

Nathan studied her through the glass from his favourite perch in the foretop. She was a brig, under staysails and a single topsail, coming out from the land on a course that would converge with their own in a little more than half an hour at their present rate of progress. He could not see her colours, or any guns. Not a ship of war, for sure, and therefore no threat unless she ran athwart of them, and they both had plenty of time and sea room to change course. She was headed diagonally across the Windward Channel in the direction of Jamaica, but she did not appear to be in any hurry to get there, or she would have set more sail. Nor could he see any movement on her deck or any sign of people up in the rigging. He looked beyond her to what he could see of the main island. They were just off Cap Saint-Nicholas, or Mole Point as it was marked on the English charts, where Columbus had made his first landing in 1492 and where the *Santa Maria* was said to have run aground. The sun was almost directly overhead. It was almost time for the ritual of grog before the first watch went below for dinner, and there was no justification for delaying either, other than a vague sense of unease, something between concern and curiosity.

'Let us take a closer look at her,' he said to Tully when he joined him back on deck. A very slight frown crossed Tully's face, but then he must already think that Nathan had exposed himself to ridicule, and perhaps had too much sun, for dragging the *obusiers* up from the orlop and making it impossible for anyone to move around the quarterdeck without tripping over them, and the extensive amount of tackle that Caine and Banjo had rigged up between them. He gave the order to alter course a point to larboard.

'What are they playing at?' Nathan said, when they were close enough to observe her with the naked eye, but he could have asked the same question of himself. The brig was heeling slightly to the northerly breeze, but she was hardly making way. Rather more mysteriously, there was still no sign of anyone on board, not even at the helm, but if she were in distress, or even abandoned, he was hardly in a position to take her in tow. There was no longer any danger of running into her, and he was about to resume their previous course when Tully said thoughtfully: 'Why are there no birds?'

It took a moment to sink in. They were normally so prevalent this close to shore you did not give them a thought. If you could not see them, you would certainly hear them. In fact, in these waters you would expect a whole flock of laughing-gulls to be trailing the brig in the expectation of picking up scraps of food or refuse. But not now.

It was possibly their absence, and the silence that went with it, that was making him feel so uneasy. He recalled what Imlay had told him about the rebel prisoners being drowned at sea. It was not without precedent. He had heard similar stories at the time of the terror in France. Except then, they had used rivers.

There was one story in particular that preyed on his mind. Reports had reached the capital of suspected Royalists, including priests, nuns and many women and children, who had been loaded onto barges drilled with holes and sunk in the middle of the Loire, not far from the city of Nantes. It had become known as 'the national bathtub'. Some of the survivors had been rescued by the crew of a French warship in the area, but they were forced to hand them over for execution. He remembered reading an account of the drownings by a gunner called Wailly. We heard the screams, he said, and then a terrible silence. The ship he was on was called *La Samaritaine*.

But throwing men overboard would not explain the absence of sea-birds.

'Lower the gig,' said Nathan. 'I am going aboard.'

They came under the stern of the brig to approach on her lower side, and he saw the name *Donna Elena* which indicated she was Spanish, or had been once upon a time. She was clearly an old tub, the timbers pretty well rotting, he suspected, and he wondered if she had been sent out to sea by the owners and then abandoned by the crew in order to claim the insurance. However, he was wary of there being contagion aboard, particularly the yellow fever, and he left most of the men in the gig until he could be sure it was safe. He took George Banjo and the surgeon with him, though, by their own choosing.

There was no one on the upper deck, but the wheel had been lashed and the needle of the compass pointed south-west, which would have taken her out into the Caribbean Sea and very likely wrecked on some rock or island. Beyond the absence of a crew it was the silence that affected him most. It was not a total silence, of course, but the sounds he could hear – the groaning of the ship's timbers, and a rope or door creaking from somewhere below deck – only made it seem more eerie to him. She was equipped with gunports but no guns – though he could see the metal ring bolts in the deck for securing them. The rigging was not exactly Bristol fashion, but it would have passed inspection on most merchant ships, and the ropes and tackle had been secured in the correct manner with no loose ends. Whatever had happened to the crew they had left everything in good order. The gratings to the lower decks had been covered with tarpaulin but there was nothing unusual about that; it would happen in any heavy sea. Except that the sea was not heavy, and it would make it very dark and airless on the lower decks.

He noticed something lying on the deck, near the mainmast. It was a dead bird. He went closer and saw that it was a booby, with no sign of any physical injury. He raised a brow at Mr Drew who bent to inspect it and shook his head, looking puzzled.

'Well, if it is the fever, it will be the first bird that I have heard of being affected,' he said. He wrinkled his nose in disgust, but it was not at
the dead bird. It was at a smell that seemed in to be rising from the lower
deck through the covered hatchway: a foetid human smell, not quite of
corruption but something close to it.

Banjo, with his usual efficiency, had thought to bring a lantern and
they followed him down below, taking the precaution to tie kerchiefs
across the lower part of their faces. As soon as they reached the lower
deck and their eyes adjusted to the light, they saw the bodies. They were
lying in more or less straight lines all down the deck from stem to stern,
and also on a kind of platform, like a half-deck, running along both sides,
such as you might see on a slaver. There appeared to be hundreds of
them, of both sexes, all black, scantily clad or naked and chained by the
ankles to the deck. Nathan almost choked on his own vomit. God knows
he had seen enough dead bodies in his time, many torn apart by chain
or shot, but nothing like this. It was like a slave ship filled with corpses.
There were also a number of dead rats, he noted, which increased his fear
of the fever and he wanted no more of it. But despite Nathan's note of
caution, the surgeon had already stooped over the body nearest to him.
He examined it briefly while Banjo held the lantern, and then moved to
the next, and the one after that.

'It is not the yellow fever,' he said. 'But I know not what else it can be.
I think it may be a kind of asphyxia. There is precious little air down here,
but I would have thought there was enough to keep them alive, even with
the hatches battened down.'

They descended to the deck below. There was even less light here,
save what came from the companionway, but there was enough to see
more bodies, though probably not as many as on the deck above, and confined to both sides, leaving a space in the middle which was occupied by
a great pile of rocks or shale, such as one might use as ballast. There were
gratings in the deck above, but they had been left uncovered, and there
were several large objects hanging down from them. Nathan advanced a
little closer and saw they were stone jars, or amphora, like those used to
store olive oil or wine, or hide the forty thieves in Ali Baba. They had
been lashed to the gratings upside down, and the cork seals had either
been loosened or punctured in some way so that the contents had dripped
onto the rocks where it had formed a thick, viscous sludge covering most

of the deck. The dripping seemed to have stopped, but only because the jars had been drained of their contents. The lantern light glinted on a long, sticky trail from each jar, like a stalactite.

Nathan looked enquiringly at Drew again and the doctor advanced cautiously towards the pile of rocks and scooped some of the sludge up with a pocketknife. Banjo held the lantern close while he peered and sniffed at it.

'I think it is oil of vitriol,' he said.

'And what is that used for?' Nathan wanted to know.

'It is a kind of acid, used in certain fabric dyes, I am not quite sure why, but I know it is used with indigo. And it was thought by the ancients to have certain medicinal properties, to cure convulsions in pregnant women, for instance, and for certain intestinal disorders.'

Nathan cut to the quick. 'And can it kill you?'

'Well, like most medicines, yes, if used for the wrong purpose and in excessive quantities.' Drew was unusually frank for a ship's doctor. 'However, it is mostly used for industrial purposes. I believe that it can corrode certain types of rock – limestone for instance, which I think you will find this is – which is of course useful in certain . . .' He sensed that Nathan did not wish to know the full extent of its uses, either for medicine or manufacture. 'But I believe this process releases a noxious gas which can be fatal to animals, and I suspect, humans. You would have to be in an enclosed space, however, and for some time . . .'

But Nathan had heard enough. He was having difficulty breathing, his limbs felt heavy and he had the beginnings of a headache.

'Let us talk about this on deck,' he said.

Back on deck he took a few minutes for them to fill their lungs with air and then he sent the gig back to the *Falaise* with instructions for Tully to bring the sloop alongside. When she was close enough for them to talk, or at least shout, from rail to rail, he told him what they had found.

'We need to find out if any of the poor wretches are still alive,' he said.

They agreed that this called for volunteers, rather than a direct order, and assembled the crew on the gundeck for Nathan to explain the situation. He assured them there were no signs of yellow fever, or any other contagious disease, and that the victims had likely suffocated for lack of air, but that common human decency demanded they ensure there was no one alive before they continued on their way. To his frank surprise they had far more volunteers than they needed. The ships were close enough for them to leap directly from one to the other, and they swiftly uncovered the hatches and opened the companionways leading to the lower decks. Then they started to bring up the bodies. There were just over 300 of them, and the doctor and his loblolly boys went from one to the other, with the same dismal result. But not always. Although they were unconscious, he founds signs of life in six of the victims, four men and two women. They were carried aft and laid on a bed of canvas where he applied *sal ammoniac* and when they showed signs of recovery an emetic. Nathan was anxious to find out from them what had happened, but they were clearly in no fit state to be questioned and besides Tully came with more alarming news. Some of the crew had reported to him that the sludge down in the orlop deck appeared to be rotting the ship's timbers.

Nathan ordered everyone back to the *Falaise*.

'I think we should set fire to her,' he said to Tully. 'I do not like the idea of letting them drift around the Caribbean Sea until she sinks or drifts up on some island somewhere.'

They made a pyre on the main deck with scraps of wood and canvas, casks of paint and tar and whatever other combustibles they could find. Then Nathan assembled the hands again and read a part of the Service for the Dead, concluding with the words he had read over so many of his shipmates in the past few years, though never in such circumstances.

'We therefore commit their bodies to the deep, to be turned into corruption, looking for the resurrection of the body when the sea shall give up her dead, and the life of the world to come, through our Lord Jesus Christ who at his coming shall change our vile body that it may be like his glorious body, according to the mighty working whereby he is able to subdue all things to himself. Amen.'

He nodded to George Banjo on the deck of the brig who put a touch to the pyre and then leaped back onto the *Falaise*.

They could still see the flames from two or three miles away, but then suddenly she was gone.

22

The Rendezvous

They reached the *Baie des Garcons* with the first hint of dawn appearing in the sky over the Tiburon hills. But there was no sign of the *Mohawk*. They came up into the wind and dropped a single anchor just off a small island, marked on the charts as La Grande Cayemite, with its little sister, La Petite Cayemite, to the west. The shores were fringed with white sands and the charts showed reefs of rock and coral just below the surface. It looked like another earthly paradise, untouched by human hand, but Nathan felt nervous. In any earthly paradise he anticipated the presence of the serpent.

The location had been chosen for its remoteness, Imlay had said, and because the island concealed them from any shipping in the Gonâve Channel. And from here it was but a short cruise to the mouth of the Anse-a-Veaux – where they were to land the guns.

Nathan had asked the obvious question: 'Why do we not land them at the rendezvous point? Or go straight to the river?'

But Imlay said the rebels had insisted on both ships landing their cargoes at the same time to cut the risk to themselves, and Captain Scott had reckoned the *Baie des Garcons* was a safer anchorage than the river mouth if one ship had to lay up for any length of time to wait for the other.

This made a kind of sense, but Nathan knew from his own experience, both as a lookout for the smugglers when he was a boy and an officer of the King's navy, that the more complicated you made things, the more chance there was of them going awry. You went in fast and came out even faster. He hated waiting off a hostile shore in broad daylight, and if a French warship came upon them it would be the devil of a job to beat up the Gonâve Channel against a north-west wind.

He diverted himself by consulting Mr Caine and Mr Banjo about the howitzers they had pulled out of the orlop deck. The gunner clearly wanted nothing more to do with them. He had heard that the shells were liable to explode either before they were fired or at the point of firing them, either of which misfortune would very likely kill the crew and cause serious damage to the ship if it did not destroy it entirely. Besides, they were notoriously inaccurate, he said. Fine for lobbying shells into a town or fortress; hopeless at hitting a moving target, such as another ship. Mr Banjo was more sanguine, of course, as he usually was when it came to firing guns and hitting anything with them. He advised using a slow match to ignite the cartridge, instead of a flintlock, to cut down the risk of a misfire, but he saw no reason why they should be any less accurate than a carronade, at least up to about a mile range. He obviously thought that working out the correct elevation was something of a challenge, but then he had always liked a challenge. He had invented a form of range finder that looked a little like a sextant, but without the mirrors and shades. He was obviously eager to practise with the guns, but Nathan would not permit it in their present position. It might attract unwanted attention from the shore, he said. Mr Caine looked relieved.

Nathan left them discussing fuse lengths and went down below to consult Mr Drew about his patients. He thought one of them might be in a fit state to talk, but he only spoke Creole, which was a local form of French, as impenetrable in its own distinct way as Guernésiais. With Tully's help, however, Nathan managed to form a more or less coherent picture of what had happened.

His informant was a man of about forty who said his name was Fabien Ducasse and that he had been he had been brought up as a slave on a sugar plantation in the northern highlands. He had briefly served as a soldier, he confessed, but only when Louverture was the legitimate governor of the colony. More lately he had been working as a carpenter in Port-Paix, just opposite Tortuga. He had played no part in the current rebellion, he said, but about two months ago he was arrested by the French and incarcerated with a great many other citizens in a former leper colony, charged with being rebel sympathisers. The place had become desperately overcrowded as the weeks went by and finally several hundred of the prisoners had been marched down to the harbour and loaded onto the brig where they were chained down on the lower decks, much as in a slaver. In fact, they thought they were being taken to Cuba or Jamaica to be sold in the slave markets.

The hatches were battened down so that there was very little light or air, and the brig put to sea. At first, they could hear sounds of the crew moving around on the upper deck, but after a while there was silence apart from the creaking of the ship's timbers. It became more and more difficult to breathe, people complained of having headaches and their limbs feeling too heavy to move. Many were vomiting. At first, he had thought it was the lack of air and the motion of the ship. There were shouts from the people on the deck below that they were being poisoned by something dripping out of stone jars above their heads, but he could not make any sense of it. People began to lose consciousness. Fabien was close to the companionway and he and those nearest to him were shouting for help, but there was no response from the crew. He thought they had been abandoned and was more terrified than at any time since his arrest. Then he himself lost consciousness.

Nathan assured him that he was safe now and that when he and his friends were sufficiently recovered, they would be put ashore, far from any French garrison. He did not seem greatly reassured by this.

Nathan went back on deck to find that Banjo and the gunner had achieved a kind of harmony, or at least truce, and were keen to try out their new toys, Banjo probably more than the gunner. He decided to let them fire a round from each gun, but took the precaution of removing all of the crew, and himself, to a safe distance, if any distance could be said to be safe on a ship the size of the *Falaise*. As a target they chose the Grande Cayemite, which appeared totally deserted and big enough to give them a reasonable chance of hitting it. They loaded the first howitzer with cartridge and then lit the fuse on the shell, dropping it carefully down the short, stubbly barrel. Then Banjo quickly applied a slow match to the trail of powder in the touchhole and they beat a hasty retreat. Mr Caine took the additional precaution of throwing himself down to the deck. Banjo, to his credit, only crouched a little. A moment of great tension, then a flash and a bang. Then, after a short hiatus, an even bigger bang on the distant beach, throwing a great deal of sand into the air. Nathan caught Tully's eye. Tully looked away, biting his lip. The performance was re-peated with the other gun and with much the same result. The two men looked very pleased with themselves and shook hands. Nathan returned to the quarterdeck and congratulated them.

'But what are you going to use them for?' Tully asked him privately. 'Are we planning to bombard Port-au-Prince? Or will we stick to unin-habited islands?'

'No, but it will give us a sting in the tail if we are obliged to run for it again,' Nathan replied coolly. He had been concerned about the lack of this facility in their encounter with the frigate. It would only take one shell to land on the deck of a pursuer, he thought, to make them lose any further interest in the chase. Tully still appeared sceptical.

And so the long day passed without incident – except when one of the lookouts reported seeing a reflection from the shore which might have been someone spying on them with a glass. Nathan looked with his own glass, but the reflection was coming from a group of rocks surrounded by dense foliage and he could see nothing definitive; it could have been a discarded bottle.

Dusk fell. Still no sign of the *Mohawk*. Nathan gave it three more hours and then decided he had waited long enough. Imlay's instructions had been explicit for once. If Scott had not turned up by sunset, they were to proceed to the landing point under cover of darkness and wait for the signal from the shore – three flashes of a single light, repeated at a five-minute interval.

The wind had shifted to NNW and they fairly crept along the coast, arriving at the landing point just after midnight, at the beginning of the black watch. It was an open stretch of shore a little to the west of the Anse-a-Veaux which could loosely be translated as the calf's buttocks. The tide was on the ebb and they backed the mizzen yards to deaden way and waited for the signal from the shore. After an hour or so they were drifting so far off their position Nathan reluctantly gave the order to drop anchor. Still no flashing light. No light at all, in fact, on that dark, almost featureless shore. They could not even see the mouth of the river. The night passed even more slowly than the previous day. Nathan had a chair brought up on deck and wrapped himself in his boat cloak and slept fitfully, but he would not go to his cabin. At the end of the black watch the tide turned, and the ship swung at her anchor until she was pointing directly at the shore. The wind had freshened a little and moved a point further to the north. At two bells in the morning watch he decided to send Cole ashore in the gig with a few armed men to see if they could find any sign of human activity. If not now, then in the recent past.

'But do not venture far from the boat,' he warned them.

It was almost an hour before the gig came back, by which time there was a distinct lightening of the sky to the east. Cole had nothing useful to report. No signs of activity; no signs that there ever had been. It had just struck four bells when there was a shout from the lookout in the maintop. A sail to the north-west.

A natural-born pessimist has moments of wild optimism. The Devil's idea of a tease, Nathan called it, but he was not entirely immune from the condition. For a moment he thought it might be the *Mohawk*. But he did not really believe it, and he was right. She was a ship of the line, a two-decker of seventy or eighty guns, and she had crept up against the dark mass of Gonâve Island to the north unseen by the lookout until she was little more than a mile away, well within firing range of her twenty-four-pounders. There could be no doubt that she was French.

'Cut the cable,' Nathan said to Tully. 'We will run to the north-east.'

Tully began to bark out orders, but they both knew there was very little chance of escape, either to the north-east or any other point of the compass.

Nathan had a clear picture of the chart in his head – he had been studying it off and on for the last twenty-four hours. He had observed that the Gulf of Gonâve was like the maw of a large fish, with the bottom lip extending a little further than the top, and the Island of La Gonâve in the middle, like a fish being swallowed. And further to the east, at the hinge of the jaw – perhaps sixty miles from where they were now – was Port-au-Prince. To run east would take them deeper into the trap. Their best route, all things being equal, was due west, out into the Caribbean Sea – but all things were not equal, for that would mean running directly past their stalker at a distance of less than a mile, exposing the little *Falaise* to her full broadside of thirty or forty guns. You did not need to be a pessimist to know that this would leave them a shattered hulk. The only alternative was to run close-hauled to the north-east in the hope of rounding the eastern end of La Gonâve – then coming about and heading westward up St Mark's Channel. But the chances of doing that without running into another French warship or being crippled by their pursuer were not good.

And yet he had to try. There were two men with axes hacking at the anchor cable and the rest of the hands ready aloft, or at the braces ready to trim the yards round the moment he gave the order. And he had one more trick he could pull – or what had he called it? A sting in the tail.

He called George Banjo over.

'Let us see what your howitzers can do,' he said, 'with a moving target.'

The cable parted and Tully was calling out a stream of orders that had them moving away from their mooring, but painfully slowly. The two-decker was barely a half-mile off their larboard quarter and closing, and the sky was becoming lighter by the minute. Nathan was braced for the first broadside. He could not understand why they were holding their fire unless they hoped they had not yet been spotted. But surely, they knew now, as the *Falaise* began to make way and head for the centre of the channel. They did. A flash and a bang as she fired one of her bowchasers. A warning shot, probably. George Banjo was at his side, touching his cap, unusually for him.

'Whenever you give the order,' he said.

Nathan nodded. 'Very well.'

He knew it could bring the full weight of the broadside on them, but what else was he to do? Even if he were to surrender without firing a shot, the French would very likely hang them for running guns to the rebels.

He had no idea where the first two shells went, or the next two. Certainly, they did not hit the target, or explode in the air. But the French must know they were being fired at; why did they not fire back?

At last they did. The bowchaser again. This time they saw the shot hit the water, a few yards ahead of the glaring goddess. A serious warning to heave to, but they were being remarkably tolerant.

'Why do they not come up into the wind,' said Tully at his shoulder, 'and give us a broadside?'

Nathan had no answer to that.

The howitzers fired again, and again to no effect. But at least they had not blown the stern off. Banjo was aiming his rangefinder at the Frenchman, his face a picture of intense concentration. He adjusted the elevator on the howitzer and nodded to one of the guncrew to load again.

Two flashes now from the two-decker and two great rents appeared as if by magic in the main topsail. But they were firing very high, even for the French.

The larboard howitzer went off again. He looked to the two-decker, closer and clearer now in the growing light of day. He could see her guns run out on both decks, but still she did not bring them to bear. Why? And then it came to him.

'She is shepherding us,' he said, as much to himself to Tully. 'Herding us into a trap. They want to take us alive.' He looked along the length of the deck and beyond, but the sea was clear, at least from his present vantage. He opened his mouth to call to the lookout in the maintop, but then there was an almighty explosion, and it was not from one of the howitzers. It came from the forecastle of the Frenchman. And it was followed within seconds by another.

He looked at Banjo in amazement, and a measure of disbelief, as if he were a conjuror and what he had seen but an illusion, a trick of smoke and mirrors. But Banjo had his eye firmly fixed to the rangefinder. Another small adjustment to the *obussier*. Another flash of fire and that distinctive bang from the short bronze muzzle, more strident than the roar of the cannon. Seconds went by. And now at last their pursuer was turning into the wind, bringing her full broadside to bear. Or at least that was surely the intention. But then there was a third massive explosion on her forecastle and slowly the foremast began to topple forward and to starboard, bringing topmast and staysails with it. There were flames, too, licking along her decks, up into the rigging. Nothing caught faster than a fire aboard ship. He could see men hurling buckets of water into the flames, and they had a fire engine going, pumping water into the rigging, he could see it from where he stood, the silver stream of water in the light of the rising sun. The howitzers fired again, but the distance between the two ships was increasing, and both shells exploded well short while still in the air.

'Avast firing!' he ordered, unwilling to tempt fate. The men in the rigging were shouting that they could see flames on the lower decks of the Frenchman. Nathan swarmed part way up the mizzen shrouds to get a better view. He thought he could see a red glow through the gun ports on the lower deck, but it could be the sunlight glinting on metal. But the upper deck was an inferno. Despite their efforts the flames had set the main course alight. The ships boats were alongside – she must have been towing them behind her. He could see men swinging down to them on ropes, others jumping into the sea.

Then there was an explosion that he could only compare later to the sudden eruption of a volcano hurtling fire and debris high into the air. A massive fireball appeared to race across the sea towards him, then a blast of hot air almost tore him from his perch in the shrouds and bent the sloop over on her beam ends before she righted herself and began to pitch violently on the heaving sea.

Almost blinded, he groped his way back down to the quarter-deck. He had seen this before, just once before at the Battle of the Nile, when the French flagship *Orient*, exploded. The fire must have reached her magazine. He could not feel exultant but only a sense of shock, and the hands must have felt the same. There was no cheering. It had been the same at the Nile. All those lives lost in a fraction of a second – and then a silence that seemed to last for minutes before the battle resumed.

But now he heard shouting. There were men in the water.

'Shall we pick them up?' said Tully.

'Yes, yes, pick them up,' he said.

They came about on the starboard tack and lowered nets. The hands were climbing down them to help the men in the water, but there were not many. Then they spotted a ship's boat, part-wrecked and water-logged, with five or six men clinging to what was left. Nathan brought the sloop alongside and the hands hauled them up on deck. Half-drowned, the shock in their eyes.

'Get them below,' he said. It would be standing room only in the sick bay.

They were searching for more survivors when there was a cry from aloft.

'Sail to the north-east. Two sail. Three!'

So, he was right about being herded into a trap.

'Course west-nor-west,' he said. And they headed up the Gonâve Channel towards the open sea.

He looked out George Banjo and the gunner. He could have hugged them, but he shook their hands instead, nodding grimly. They appeared just as grim, crushed almost. He did not think it was the handshake.

'The surgeon's compliments, sir, and could you have a word with him below? He cannot leave off his work at present, he says.'

'There is one of them Frenchies says his brother will pay a king's ransom to save his life,' said the man on their way down the ladder. 'A young officer cadet.'

'Is that so?' said Nathan, unimpressed. 'And is his brother a king?'

But his brother was not a king. He was greater than that. The officer's name was Jérôme Bonaparte.

23

Return to Tortuga

The French sailors were being accommodated on the orlop deck, among the cases and casks that constituted the sloop's cargo. Hopefully, they would be put ashore before they found out what they contained. There were fourteen of them, wrapped in blankets and clutching mugs of what smelled like straight rum. All were in varying states of shock, and several had suffered some physical injury. The surgeon was attending to a head wound when Nathan arrived, and he waited in the shadows until he had finished.

'I could not accommodate them in the sick bay with its current occupants,' Drew explained. 'They would have likely killed each other.'

Nathan had not considered the survivors from the brig. He had better not put them ashore at the same point, he thought now.

'Which is the one who claims to be a Bonaparte?' he asked.

The surgeon indicated the man he had just been attending to, who was now sitting on a cask with his bandaged head in his hands while one of the other survivors knelt at his side and offered him a mug of rum which he declined. He was no more than a boy really, perhaps of sixteen or seventeen. Nathan would have taken him for a midshipman on a British ship of war, though no midshipman he had ever known would have declined a mug of rum, no matter what misfortune he had suffered. In the French navy he would be an *aspirant* or ensign. Junior though he was, he appeared to be the only officer among the survivors.

'He is terrified of what the blacks will do to them if we put them ashore,' the surgeon said. 'He is begging that we take them into Port-au-Prince or Cap-Francais. He says General Leclerc will pay a handsome reward.'

'Any evidence that he is who he says he is?' Nathan asked him.

'He showed me a locket with a miniature of his brother on one side and his mother on the other, if that is any guide. The man certainly looks like Boney. I cannot speak for the woman, but if anything, she looks more frightening than he does. There is also a letter he had in a pocket which he says is from his brother, Napoleon, but it has been in the water and the ink has run. I have put it to dry in the sick bay if you would care to see it.'

They went into the sick bay. The survivors of the *Donna Elena* were looking almost as anxious as the newcomers. They would have heard the sounds of battle, of course, but have had no idea what was happening. Nathan gave them a summary in French which they mostly understood.

The letter was lying on one of the munitions cases. At the top was a crest he did not recognise and the address of the Chateau de Malmaison, which was Bonaparte's home near Paris and one of the places he used as his headquarters. There was also a signature at the bottom which had run a little but looked like it could be that of Napoleon.

The contents did not tell him much.

My beloved brother, he read, *it gives me great pleasure to hear* . . . Unreadable . . . *excellent report from the captain of the Guerriere* . . . *your conduct* . . . Unreadable . . . *of the utmost importance that* . . . *at least I have one brother who shows an interest in gunnery* . . . .

It sounded like Captain Cannon, but it was not definitive.

'Is he fit to be brought to my cabin?' Nathan asked.

'Oh, I should think so. The physical wound is slight – it is more the shock and the fear . . . He has a servant who seems quite devoted – can he accompany him?'

Nathan thought about it. 'No. The more shocked and frightened he is the better,' he said cold-heartedly. 'I will send Mr Banjo for him.'

He went up to the stern cabin and was about to call for Kidd when he remembered that the scoundrel had gone missing on Tortuga and he had not had time to appoint a replacement. Imlay had taken Pellett with him on the *Delaware*. He found a bottle of cognac in the galley and a couple of decent glasses. First show him the instruments of torture, then pour him a drink.

'*Bonjour, monsieur*,' he greeted him cheerfully when Banjo escorted him into the cabin. '*Comment ca va?*'

Stupid question. His ship had blown up killing several hundred of his shipmates, he had been fished out of the water like a half-drowned rat and now he was wrapped in a blanket, shivering uncontrollably from cold or terror, probably both, and expecting to be butchered any minute by ex-slaves or pirates. He dismissed Banjo with a word of thanks.

'*Asseyez-vous*,' Nathan said, gesturing to the easy chair he himself relaxed in when he was in need of comfort and consolation, but it crossed his mind that he should invite him to make use of the seat of ease in the quarter-gallery for a few minutes first.

He poured him a large glass of cognac and a smaller one for himself. He was beginning to think that the man's brother had not been entirely fanciful in referring to him as his 'lucky star', except that he now appeared to be extending his divine radiance to the whole family. Certainly, there appeared to be some strange link between their destiny and his, though he was aware that it might as readily be described as a curse. He handed him his drink which he just about managed to hold in two shaking hands.

'I am Captain Kidd,' said Nathan, using the first name that came to mind. He had better not use Turner, he thought, in case he needed to make use of it again. 'I am an American. That is, a citizen of the United States.'

The boy looked at him properly for the first time.

'You have had a terrible shock,' Nathan went on in a voice of gentle concern. 'You have lost many of your friends and shipmates. I regret that immensely.' Did he? He probably did, though not as much as if they were his own. 'I could never have imagined such a thing happening.' What else did you think would happen when you lobbed live shells at a ship of war? 'It was the magazine, I suppose?'

The boy stammered something unintelligible and went into a fit of coughing. The cognac had probably been a mistake. Nathan was about to take it off him but a few more sips loosened his tongue, as Nathan had hoped it might.

When the flames had spread below decks the *capitaine* had almost thrown him into one of the boats, he said, but they had scarcely pulled away from the ship when it exploded. They had been struck by a spar and been swamped, but they had managed to cling to the wreckage. Another spasm of coughing and this time he spewed up a quantity of sea water, laced with cognac. He apologised miserably. Nathan passed him a towel to wipe his chin.

'Your first battle?' he said.

A tearful nod.

'I fought my first battle when I was about your age,' Nathan lied. 'Against the British in America. Alongside the French.'

'Did you, monsieur?' He looked at Nathan with hope in his eyes. But then he frowned. 'But now you are with our enemies?'

'I am not your enemy, lad, who told you that?'

'We were told you were running guns to the rebels.'

That was interesting. And did they know where and when? But one thing at a time.

'Is that why you fired upon us?'

'It was a warning shot only,' said the boy.

'Why not a full broadside?' Nathan pressed him. 'That would have made short work of us.'

'We were told we must take you into Port-au-Prince. We did not think you were able to fight back. *Nous ne savons pas que vous avez les obus.*'

We did not know you have the bombshells.

'So, you were expecting to find us at the mouth of the Anse?'

But he was pushing his luck. The boy only shook his head.

Nathan changed his tone, leaning back in his chair and regarding him with a smile, 'I am told you claim to be the younger brother of General Bonaparte?'

'Yes, monsieur, and if you land me in Port-au-Prince or Le Cap, I will ensure you are well rewarded.'

'So I have been told but I cannot do that I am afraid, especially now that I know the authorities have an interest in us.'

'But I can assure you of your safety, monsieur . . .'

Nathan held up a hand. 'I will think on it, but in the meantime, I must have your parole, so I do not have to lock you up.'

'You have it, monsieur,' the boy agreed. He looked so sorry for himself that for the first time Nathan saw a vague resemblance to his brother when he first met him in Paris. That look of a badly used spaniel, nursing his grievances, waiting for the chance to sink his teeth into someone.

He called for Mr Banjo and told him to put the officer in the cabin his steward had recently vacated, which was more of a cupboard, but would have to do until he decided what to do with him. He would have to consult Imlay, he supposed. The other Frenchmen would have to share their accommodation with the ship's animals on the orlop deck.

When he joined Tully again, he saw they were about to clear the western edge of La Gonâve though it was no more than a smudge on the horizon. They would soon be out into the Caribbean Sea. But it would be a long haul to Tortuga.

It took them two days, fighting the wind all the way. On the second day he invited young Bonaparte for dinner in the stern cabin with himself and Tully. He looked only a little less anxious, but at least he wore his cadet uniform in preference to a wet blanket and it looked like it had been sponged and pressed after its encounter with salt water. He now reminded Nathan not so much of his brother Napoleon as his sister Pauline, but only slightly. He was certainly a lot more subdued than she tended to be, even under stress when she was as likely to throw plates at him as sulk, but he became more loquacious as the meal went on.

In the absence of Kidd and Pellett, they were reliant on the ship's cook, Masham, and it was relatively simple fare, but at least he did not disgrace them. They began with a turtle soup and some fried tilapia, which had been caught during their lay up in the *Baie des Garcons*, and when it was removed they had a pie made with Dutch beef and onions, a duck fresh killed from the livestock they had picked up in Washington, a smoked ham, some pickled tripe, carrots and French beans and a sheep's cheese from Virginia which had aged better than might have been expected on the voyage south and went very well with pickled cucumber. This was washed down with a cask of Imlay's claret and a bottle of Sillery, and they had a molasses tart for pudding with Spanish fritters and cream from the Jersey cow, currently sharing its quarters with the French prisoners. Well before they were finished young Bonaparte became positively merry, and it certainly loosened his tongue to a level that Nathan found educative, though its owner might have regretted it when he thought about it later, if he was capable of remembering.

It was not a surprise to hear that the war was going very badly for the French, but this was not just because of the yellow fever, he said, it was because his brother-in-law General Leclerc was a *branleur*, which Nathan translated privately as tosser.

'He complains to my brother that the blacks fire one round then run away into the forest. Like the Arabs in Egypt.' He frowned. 'Except it would be the desert, but you know what I mean?' They nodded wisely.

'You mean they do not stand in line waiting to be shot at,' said Tully sympathetically.

'*Exactement!* And Leclerc does not know what to do about it.'

'General Gage had the same problem in America,' Nathan reflected.

'What *could* he do about it?' Tully wanted to know. 'Leclerc.'

'He should be more ruthless,' the young man insisted. 'Rochambeau knows this. Leclerc knows it. But he does not have it in him. My brother says the application of extreme force at the right time can save many lives later.'

'A whiff of grapeshot,' said Nathan, remembering how Bonaparte had used cannon on the mob in Paris. Something even King Louis would not consider. Which was why he had gone to the guillotine and Bonaparte to the Tuileries.

'You have it! But Leclerc does not have the stomach for it.' He shook his head sadly and belched. Tully refilled his glass. They were drinking the Sillery, with the cheese and pickles so a few belches could be forgiven. 'He is not the right man for a war like this and he knows it, poor fellow. My brother did him no favours there.' He put on a voice which was presumably an imitation of his brother's. 'I have good news for you, Charles, I am giving you Saint-Domingue and my sister, Pauline. *Bon chance!*'

Tully grinned. Nathan studied his glass of Sillery carefully.

'Handful is she?' said Tully. Nathan had not told him about Pauline and the only other men aboard who knew about them was George Banjo who was not the type to gossip. Hopefully.

'Ha. You could say that.' The boy brooded. 'It is in her nature. Strange thing is, I think she loves him, deep down, or could do if she would let herself. But she will never forgive him for marrying her because her brother told him to. "Take her before she makes a fool of herself with that evil old leche Fréron." And so she is punishing them by being – Pauletta. I think she will go back to Paris soon, with him or without him.' He was becoming morose. He would be asleep soon.

'And what will happen in Saint-Domingue?' Nathan asked him, more to get off the subject of Pauline Bonaparte than because he thought he had anything useful to say on the military situation.

'Oh, we will hang on to it somehow I expect, if my brother sends us more men. We have sent most of our crews to fight on land because the army has lost so many to the yellow fever. So, what happens? They catch it, too.'

He reached for the bottle but missed it, overbalanced and fell off his chair. They picked him up and put him to bed.

They sighted the island early the following morning and smelled it shortly after. The smell of Saint-Domingue when it burns. Unlike Le Cap, however, the fires were more recent. Every plantation they could see on their journey along the coast had been burned to the ground and much of the area around it. But their greatest shock was when they reached the port of Cayona, where the richest planters had lived, and where the French had built their new hospital. They came close inshore and Nathan took the measure of it through his glass. He could see what looked like dead bodies lying in the open and the dogs and carrion feasting on them. But no sign of any human life, white or black.

'We will have to make sure,' he said without much hope.

He took three boats and thirty armed men, and they walked up the main street to the hospital above the town. There were dead bodies everywhere, the bloated carrion flapping off at their approach, the dogs retreating a little and snarling. Nathan had the Ferguson rifle he had acquired, though he had not quite got the hang of using it yet. The *Falaise* was covering them from the sea, but he knew it would go badly with them if they ran into the rebels, assuming this was their doing. Some of the buildings were still smouldering despite the rain which fell three times a day at this time of the year, regular as clockwork. It was raining now as they walked.

The hospital was burned out, and there were a lot more bodies, lying in and out of the gutted buildings. Those that were not blackened by fire were white. As far as Nathan could tell their throats had been cut, and they were badly mutilated by machetes, in as far as you could tell after the dogs and the birds had been at them. He did not want to look too closely. Some of the victims had been hanged from trees, but even they had not been safe from the carrion. There had been over 500 patients here, he had heard, at any one time, and over fifty doctors and nurses. There were too many dead to bury. He was in a fret now, to get to the *Habitation Labattut* where he had left Pauline but feared what he might find there.

It was late afternoon when they reached the plantation. That, too, had been burned to the ground, but there were no bodies – only empty cages, scattered about the gardens. No sign of the animals and birds they had contained, dead or alive, or of the peacocks.

He sent the men off to patrol the perimeter and viewed the remains of what had been his home for the past few months, or his prison. He knew that Jan and his Poles would have fought to the death to defend their mistress. It was possible they had turned the house into a stockade, and their bodies were under the ashes and the blackened wood, along with Pauline and the servants. He took a few hesitant steps in but could no further, not only because of the hot ashes.

He was standing there, undecided, when he heard shouts from the far side of the ruin. A man had emerged from the trees.

It was Kidd.

He was unharmed but in some distress after two days hiding in the forest. They sat him on one of the empty cages and the doctor gave him a salve for the insect bites which seemed to cover most of his body. He had been away gathering herbs for cooking, he said, when Nathan had left in the *Falaise* – an explanation Nathan some-what doubted – and he had watched helplessly as the corvette sailed away. But then Céleste – Madame's maid – had informed him that *le capitaine* had left a note to say that he would be back in a few days. Madame was furious that he had left without her permission, she told him, and Kidd had kept out of her way in case she took it out on him. Later that day a French frigate came into the bay and an officer came up to the house with a group of French marines. They left an hour or so later with Madame, her guards and most of the servants, and the ship sailed off in the direction of Le Cap.

A little later the *Delaware* sailed into the bay and he saw a boat go out to it with Imlay and several negroes, including the man and woman who had come out to the *Falaise* when they first arrived on the island. Then the *Delaware* set sail, also in the direction of Le Cap.

The only people left at *Habitation Labattut* were the plant collectors, he said. They had no idea why Madame had left so suddenly. She had left no message for them. That night they saw flames in the sky over towards Cayona and one of the local inhabitants brought news that hundreds of rebels had crossed over from the mainland and attacked the French hospital. The following morning, they arrived at Le Roche.

Kidd had fled into the forest with the botanists and spent two days and nights in makeshift shelters among the trees. When he saw the *Falaise* down in the bay he had made his way back to the *Habitation*, knowing it would be the captain's first port of call.

Nathan was vastly relieved to hear that Pauline had escaped the massacre, but Kidd had given him a lot to think about.

'The couple in the boat with Imlay,' he began, 'are you sure they were the same people who came out to the *Falaise* when we first arrived?'

He was. He had seen them several times since, he said, at Le Belvedere. And the children were with them. With their nanny.

'The children?'

'Patrice and Jeanne. The boy and the girl.'

It sounded like he knew the family rather better than Nathan.

'What were you doing at Le Belvedere?' he asked him.

A shrug. Visiting an acquaintance, he said. They had been here six months, one had to pass the time somehow, with a look that in other circumstances Nathan might have considered impudent.

He let it go, for the time being. There were more people coming out of the forest, including a young woman who ran straight to George Banjo and was greeted in a manner that left Nathan in little doubt as to the nature of their relationship. It seemed they had all found ways to pass their time on Tortuga.

In all, eleven of them had survived the massacre, most of them connected with Pauline's Garden of Eden. They corroborated Kidd's story, but Nathan was puzzled about Dubois and Adedike. Why had they gone into Le Cap, always assuming this was their destination? And why so soon after Pauline's departure? Unless this was a coincidence.

There was probably only one way to find out – and there was little point in staying on Tortuga.

24

The Butcher of Le Cap

He took the gig into Le Cap, leaving Tully to cruise off the coast. It was late afternoon when he arrived, and they sailed between the long lines of warships as he had on his last visit in the *Delaware* six months ago, but the lines were perhaps not as long and many of the ships looked like prison hulks. Many had lines of washing on the upper deck and streaks of rust and refuse down the sides, while others appeared to be entirely abandoned. The merchant vessels that had been moored close to the harbour were gone, and the waterfront itself was like a morgue.

Nathan went ashore with George Banjo and they walked up the Rue St Jacques toward the grand edifice of Government House – rebuilt since the fire. Here, at least, there were people – rather more than Nathan would have expected, and all moving in the same direction, though it was not Government House they were making for, but a group of buildings set back a little way from the street behind a line of palm trees.

A crowd of about a hundred was waiting at the entrance to this compound and Nathan stopped to ask one of them what was going on, but he shot a glance at Banjo and turned away with a shrug and a muttered aside.

'What is this place?' Nathan asked another man.

'Les Religieuses,' he replied, which Nathan took to mean a convent.

'So, what is it,' he persisted, 'some kind of festival?' He used the word fête.

A bark of a laugh. 'You could say that. An auto da fête.'

Nathan exchanged glances with Banjo, and they joined the end of the line.

There were soldiers at the gate checking passes. They eyed Banjo with suspicion. He was not the only black man there, but he may have been the only one with a pair of pistols and a dagger in his belt. They showed the passes they had been given at the *Habitation*, identifying them as auxiliaries of the French Republican Army. Nathan was a captain, Banjo a sergeant. The guards saluted and they headed through an archway into what appeared to be the cloisters. There was a large open space of red earth in the centre resembling a parade ground or playing field, with a single wooden pole in the middle. The cloisters surrounding this area were packed with spectators – perhaps a couple of thousand altogether, mostly male and white, though there was an area at one end that appeared to be reserved for black people, fenced off from the arena and guarded by a line of soldiers with fixed bayonets. The rest of the convent seemed to be empty. At one end of the concourse there was a band playing martial music, and another line of soldiers. Next to them was a wooden platform with steps leading up to it.

Nathan had guessed by now that the spectators had come to watch some form of punishment, like a flogging or an execution. He had an uneasy, if irrational, fear that it involved Dubois or Adedike, possibly both.

There was a drumroll and a uniformed figure ascended the platform. The uniform and plumed hat announced him as a person of some importance, a general at least, but it was not Leclerc. There were loud and prolonged cheers from the crowd which he acknowledged by taking off his hat and bowing. Other officers, in less elaborate uniform, joined him on the platform, and one of them stepped forward and made an announcement, reading from a scroll. His voice barely carried to where Nathan was standing but he caught some words about a servant of the chief of staff – and the word traitor.

Another drumroll and a squad of soldiers appeared escorting a prisoner – a black man, stripped to the waist, with his hands tied behind his back. It was not Dubois. The crowd went wild with rage, hissing and shouting insults. The soldiers led him to the pole in the centre of the square and tied him to it, facing outwards. Then they retired.

The band struck up a martial tune and two men wearing leather aprons, like butchers, and carrying long whips stepped up to the platform and opened a door in its base. From it, in a frenzied, barking rush, emerged a pack of dogs. Gasps and roars from the crowd. Cockades and flowers were thrown into the arena. The dogs separated enough for Nathan to see that there were six of them. Large, ugly brutes, something between a mastiff and a hunting dog. He began to feel sick. He felt Banjo tense beside him, his hand dropping to one of the pistols at his belt. Nathan reached out his own hand to check him.

After running around in circles for a moment or two, snapping at each other and barking at the crowd, the dogs rushed up to the man tied to the pole. His head was hanging down, his eyes closed and his lips were moving in what might be a prayer. The dogs sniffed at his feet, one or two leaped up at him. But they did not attack. After a while they backed off and stood motionless, looking around them, as if they did not know what was expected of them. The crowd urged them on and then, when they did not respond, began to yell and jeer. The two men in aprons advanced into the arena and began to crack their whips. The dogs ran in circles again, barking and snarling. The crowd was now angry and directed their venom at the officers on the platform. The two men conferred. Then one of them produced a knife, advanced to the man on the pole and slit his stomach open. Nathan caught one glimpse and turned away, staring hard at the men on the platform as if committing them to memory. He could hear from the roars of the crowd what was happening in the arena. When his eyes went back to the prisoner all he could see was a whirl of red dust and the dogs among it, in a frenzy, tearing at something on the ground. He took Banjo firmly by the arm and they walked away.

They continued up the road towards Government House. Neither of them was in the mood to speak. There were half a dozen soldiers at the outer gate. Nathan showed his pass and said he had an urgent message which he must deliver personally to Captain Bruski, of Madame Leclerc's personal guard.

A sergeant took his name and instructed him to wait. After a few minutes Bruski appeared. His manner was tense and his opening words not encouraging.

'What are you doing here?'

'Good to see you, too.' Bruski just stared at him, waiting, so Nathan said he had just come from Tortuga.

'Well?'

'Have you not heard what happened there?'

He had not. Nathan told him what he had seen at the hospital and the house. It was clearly a shock, but he looked like a man who has heard worse.

'So, what is happening here?' Nathan asked him. 'Why did you leave so suddenly?'

Bruski seemed to make his mind up. 'Come with me,' he said. He led them into the building, and they sat down on a long stone bench running around the side of the lobby.

'We had news that General Leclerc was ill,' he said. 'He has the yellow fever. Well advanced. I doubt he will last the night.'

'Where is – Madame?'

'Where do you think? With her husband.'

'And how is she taking it?'

'She is desolate with grief – and very possibly guilt. So where did you run off to?'

'I had to go to Port-au-Prince in the *Falaise*,' Nathan told him. 'Acting on orders.'

'Orders from who?'

'Imlay. My superior.' In other circumstances this would have hurt. 'He had just come back from Washington.'

'So, you take orders from Washington now?'

'I have always taken orders from Washington. We are hoping for a trade deal with the French – remember?'

'So why do you go to Port-au-Prince when the Governor-General is here in Le Cap?'

'I was wrongly advised.'

A cold stare. Nathan persisted. 'I was told that Imlay had come here to Le Cap. In the *Delaware*. Just after you and your people left. I have to find him.'

'Then I suggest you ask down in the harbour. We have enough on our minds.'

There were obviously bridges to be built here, but before Nathan could figure out why and how, the door was thrown open and a group of officers came in led by the man in the general's uniform who had opened proceedings at the convent. The real butcher of the show. Bruski leaped to his feet and saluted. Nathan and Banjo stood up rather more slowly. The general glanced at them briefly before striding on towards the ornate staircase, but then he stopped and looked at them again, longer and harder. He said something to one of his underlings who came over and spoke to Bruski.

'The general wants a word,' Nathan heard him say.

He watched the two men conversing, the general glancing once or twice in his direction.

'Let us go,' said Nathan. He headed briskly for the door. There was a shout of 'Garde!' and within seconds they were surrounded by French soldiers.

Nathan raised his hands, nodding to Banjo to do the same. They were relieved of their weapons and led to what appeared to be a guardroom where they were searched and locked in a small cell, more like a cage. It was about half an hour before they came back for him. Banjo was left in the cage.

Nathan was marched up the stairs and into a large stately room on the first floor where the general sat at an equally large and stately desk smoking a cheroot and talking to a couple of his subordinates.

Nathan was stood in front of him. He crossed his arms in front of him, holding his hat in his hands, and waited. He felt like a peon. It did not improve his mood. The general looked at him with an expression of cold contempt, though this might have been his normal expression when attempting conversation.

'You speak French?'

'I do.'

'What is your name?'

'Captain Nathaniel Turner.'

'Captain of what?'

'Lately – of the barque Delaware.'

The general appeared to think about this for a moment.

'Do you know who I am?'

'No.'

'Tell him.'

'This is General Rochambeau,' said one of the underlings. Nathan nodded his appreciation of this intelligence.

'And what are you doing here in Cap-Francais?'

'I am looking for a friend,' said Nathan.

'Instruct him how to address a general officer in the French Army,' said Rochambeau in a bored tone.

The blow – a back-handed swipe to the side of his head – took Nathan by surprise and almost knocked him off his feet.

'You address a general officer in the French Army as my General,' said the man who had struck him – one of the men who had escorted him from the guardroom. For a moment Nathan thought about hitting him back but decided against it.

'But you are not my General,' he pointed out reasonably. 'I am an American.'

The man hit him again, the same way as before. It might kindly be called a cuff across the ear, but it was delivered with such force he was knocked to the floor.

'Stay there,' said the general as he began to get up. 'Unless you wish to be knocked down again.'

Nathan stayed there, on his knees.

'I take it you are the gentleman who has spent the last few months on La Tortue, at the home of Governor-General and Madame Leclerc.' He spoke precisely and with distaste as if the words disgusted him.

'That would be correct – General.' He compromised by dropping the personal pronoun, bracing himself for another blow for this lack of respect, but it did not come.

'For what purpose?'

'I was asked to assist the Governor-General in his foundation of a botanical and zoological garden.'

'You are a botanist?'

'No – General.'

'A zoologist?'

'I regret not.'

'Then what use could you possibly be in establishing a, what did you call it, a botanical and zoological garden?'

'I did point this out to them, but they did not seem to be bothered. General. I think they enjoyed my company.'

The general gazed at him for a moment. Nathan had the impression he was trying to make up his mind. He tried to help him by looking confident, in as much as he could while kneeling on the floor.

'Leave us,' he said to the guards. 'Sit down,' he said to Nathan.
Nathan sat down.

'Where did you learn to speak French as you do?'

'I had a French tutor as a child.'

'Why?'

'My mother was half-French. She thought I should speak the language.'

'It is a useful facility for a spy.'

'I am not a spy.'

'You say you are not a botanist either, or a zoologist, so what are you?'

'I am a sea captain, as I have said.'

'And do you have any other talents that might endear you to the Governor-General – and his wife?'

Nathan pretended to look puzzled. In fact, he was thinking quite hard, and not just about the question. Bruski had known about his affair with Pauline. Had he told Rochambeau about it? It seemed unlikely in the brief time they had spent conversing in the lobby, though it was possible, of course, that he knew about it already. Clearly, he was not concerned that he might be reprimanded for treating Nathan like any other prisoner. This could mean a number of things, but Nathan needed more time to think about them. His head was still ringing from the two blows he had received, and his ear felt like it was on fire. There was a trickle of blood running down his neck into his collar.

'This – friend – you are looking for in Le Cap. Who would that be?'

'His name is Captain Imlay. Envoy to the United States of America.'

'Ah yes, Captain Imlay.' His tone did not indicate a degree of warmth to their acquaintance. 'We met a few days ago when he came here in the – the *Delaware*, did you say? Your ship?' Nathan nodded. 'He brought with him two blacks who claimed to be followers of the former rebel leader, Toussaint Louverture – a man called Dubois and a woman called' – He glanced down at a paper on his desk – 'Adedike otherwise known as Sabine Delacour. Both were known to us. Do you know them?'

'We have met, yes. They were near neighbours on La Tortue.'

'And are you aware of the – arrangement – they proposed?'

Nathan shook his head.

'Really? So, Captain Imlay did not inform you of it?'

He spoke in a lazy drawl, as if it was a bore to phrase the question and he did not give a damn whether it was answered or not. Additionally, he pronounced certain words as if their absurdity amused him. Nathan was neither charmed nor deceived by this conceit.

'We had very little time together.'

'I wonder why that was, but we will come to that presently. To continue – they had hoped to discuss this proposal with the Governor-General, but as he was indisposed, they were obliged to talk to me. The proposal, as I am sure you know, was for a cessation of hostilities, during which Monsieur Louverture would return as Governor of the colony, and work would resume on the coffee and sugar plantations using free labour. The produce would be sold, at a favourable rate, to France. What do you think of that, *monsieur le capitaine?*'

'It is not for me to say. What did you think of it?'

'Oh, I had them arrested, of course.'

'On what charge, or is a charge not necessary?'

The general took the trouble to shrug. 'Treason? Armed rebellion? Mass murder? I would have had Imlay arrested too, but I was advised that he is an envoy of the American President and has what might be called diplomatic immunity. However, he was instructed to leave Saint-Domingue immediately and has, I believe, done so. You, I should point out, have no such immunity.'

'Why would I need it? Is it not enough that I am an American citizen and have not broken any laws – that I am aware of.'

'Is that so?' Rochambeau considered him thoughtfully. 'Where have you been these last few days?'

Here was the problem. It had occupied most of his time in the cage.

'I was sent to Port-au-Prince by Captain Imlay on official business.'

'In one of the several ships at your disposal – the *Falaise*.' Again, this was more of a statement than a question, but Nathan had prepared an answer.

'I set out from La Tortue in the *Falaise*, but I was dropped off with a companion in one of the ship's boats at Port-Paix . . .'

'That is a long way from Port-au-Prince.' The general glanced at one of his officers.

'Two hundred kilometres,' the officer supplied.

'I planned to continue my journey by horse,' Nathan informed him.

Rochambeau feigned astonishment. 'Good God – are you mad? Or do you think I am? The country is swarming with black savages who are killing every white man, woman and child they can lay their hands on. God knows what they do with horses. Eat them, I suppose.'

'We had arranged for a guide but unfortunately he was not there.' This was not coming out as well as it had in his head, and it had not been especially convincing there. He struggled on. 'But while we waited, we saw fires burning on Tortuga and went back to see if we could be of assistance.'

'What, in lighting them?'

'In defending Madame Leclerc.'

'I see. So, you were not aboard the *Falaise* when it attempted to land guns for the use of the rebels a short distance from Port-au-Prince?'

Nathan tried to look mystified. The general selected a document from the papers on his desk.

'This is a report from Admiral Latouche in Port-au-Prince to the Governor-General. It arrived late last night and, in his Excellency's absence, was brought to me.' He read: '"*Having received intelligence that an illegal arms shipment was to be landed at the mouth of the River Anse-a-Veaux on the Tiburon Peninsular, I despatched the vaisseau Guerriere of 84 guns with three frigates to intercept the shipment and apprehend the vessel involved which – according to our intelligence – was the Falaise, a former corvette of the French Republican Navy now in British hands and commanded by a serving officer of the British Navy with a mainly British crew*".'

Nathan tried to maintain the look of mystification, supplemented by one of shock, which was not entirely feigned.

'"*I regret to inform your Excellency that in the course of the operation the Guerriere suffered an accidental explosion of the magazine with the loss of all hands and in the confusion that followed, the Falaise unfortunately escaped, though without landing its cargo. A thorough search for survivors has been instituted along the coast of Tiburon and on the outlying islands but at present I am devastated to have to report that among those reported missing is Officer Cadet Jérôme Bonaparte*".'

He threw the report on his desk. 'The younger brother of the First Consul, in case you did not know. So, *Captain Turner*, what do you have to say to that?'

'Well, of course, I am – desolated – by the loss of life, but' – Nathan struggled – 'as to the involvement of the *Falaise*, why . . .'

'You were observed by Captain Bruski boarding the *Falaise* at Le Roche early on the morning of October the twenty-second. On the morning of

October, the twenty-fourth the *Falaise* was sighted off Tiburon. You are, by your own admission, a sea captain, but I do not believe your name is Turner, or that you are an American, and now I want the truth.'

'I have told you the truth . . .'

The general leaned forward. His voice was controlled but his fists were clenched on the desk and Nathan could see his arms trembling as if with the palsy. The man was in a cold, murderous fury. 'I have just heard that the younger brother of General Bonaparte has been killed in a battle with British gunrunners. In a few hours, when I can bring myself to it, I will have to send him a despatch to that effect. Can you even begin to imagine how I am feeling about this? Or to what lengths I am prepared to go to find and punish those responsible? Well, perhaps not, so I will tell you.'

He lent back in his chair, keeping his eyes on Nathan's face. 'A number of dogs have been imported from Cuba, a special breed trained to track down and kill escaped slaves seeking refuge in the forest. We had a similar task for them here, but they are not so effective when the slaves are armed. However, I have devised a new role for them. We had the first demonstration of it this evening. A convicted rebel was publicly executed by exposure to these animals. An animal retribution for men who act like animals. I hope it will prove to be an effective deterrent. Tomorrow evening, Captain, if you have not given me a full and frank confession, stating who you really are and what you are doing in Saint-Domingue, *in writing*, I shall repeat this performance with a greater number of dogs and not one, but three prisoners – Dubois, his female companion, and your black manservant whose name escapes me. And you will be there to witness it. Call the guard,' he instructed his aide, 'and have him put back in his cage.'

'And that will be the end of Officer Cadet Jérôme Bonaparte,' said Nathan. 'You will receive his head in a sack, and you may send it back to his brother, with your report.'

One of the officers sprang at him and punched him in the face, knocking him and the chair to the ground. He stood over him, swearing a stream of abuse, and drew back his boot, but the general was on his feet screaming.

'You will wait for my order, you peasant!'

The officer stood back a step. The general looked down at Nathan.

'You will be sorry you said that. After the dogs have finished with your friends, I will feed them your tongue and then let them have what's left.'

In fact, Nathan had spoken without thinking, but he was thinking now, and he had the beginnings of a plan in his mind.

'Not as sorry as you will be,' he said, 'when the First Consul hears that you had a chance to save his youngest brother and you spurned it.'

'What are you talking about?'

Nathan stood up and picked up the chair and sat on it. He had taken the blow on the other cheek, but not deliberately. He was in as murderous a rage as Rochambeau, in his own way, but he fought to contain it, and his voice was calm.

'You are right, I was on the *Falaise*. However, we were not landing arms to rebels, and had no intention of doing so. We were attacked without warning by a ship of the French Navy. We did not fire back. I have no idea what caused the explosion, but we saved all those we could. Fourteen of them in all, including Officer Cadet Bonaparte. We had dinner together only yesterday.'

'You are lying.' But he did not sound completely sure of it.

'Would you care to take the risk? He expressed great admiration for you, by the way. He thinks you should be in command here, and not General Leclerc. But then, he was drunk at the time.'

'What proof do you have of this?'

'Nothing that I have with me. He had a locket with a picture of his brother and his mother, and a letter from the First Consul, but I left them on the *Falaise*. I can remember the name of his servant, however, who was saved with him.' The purser had supplied a list in his usual efficient way, and it had struck in Nathan's mind. 'Clovis Brule. But I do not suppose you know the name of Jérôme Bonaparte's servant. A pity. It could have saved your life, certainly your career.'

'Where is he now?'

'Clovis? On the orlop deck of the *Falaise*, sharing his quarters with a cow.'

Rochambeau struggled to contain himself. 'The First Consul's brother.'

'Jérôme? In a safe place. Unless I return there by noon tomorrow. Then . . .' He shrugged. 'That rather depends on you.'

'You seriously think I am going to let you go – on the strength of this?'

'I do, as a matter of fact.'

They regarded each other for a moment in silence. They could have torn each other apart. Like dogs. But the general's voice, like Nathan's, was composed.

'Just – imagine for a moment that I would do as you propose – what would happen then?'

'I would exchange him, at a time and place of my arranging, for Monsieur Dubois, Madame Delatour, and my friend, George Banjo.'

'At a time and place of your arranging?'

'Yes. Not far from Le Cap. They will be escorted there by a small guard commanded by Captain Bruski. You will also deliver a letter from me to Madame Leclerc – and a note for General Bonaparte whom I had the honour of knowing in Paris – as you will discover if you ask the right people.' He stood up. 'I will require pen and paper and a quiet room to write in. Also, a sandwich and a glass of wine. In the meantime, please have my associate Mr Banjo sent to me with our belongings and a letter of safe conduct from yourself in case there is a problem with some of your animals. I will send word of where the exchange is to take place.'

'Sit down.'

Nathan raised a brow. He remained standing.

'You are not going anywhere, Captain. However, I will let you send your associate, and if you are able to produce Monsieur Bonaparte, alive and well, the exchange will take place as you propose. Otherwise . . . *les chiens attendront.*'

. . . the dogs will be waiting.

25

The Beach

It was a new moon and a clear sky. A light breeze from the south-west –
and the tide on the ebb. Better for getting out than coming in, but that
was what you wanted at a time like this.

They stood on the edge of the treeline, about 200 yards back from the
sea. Nathan could hear the soft break of the waves on the shore. There
was no surf which was a blessing. He looked up at a sky full of stars, but
it was not a time for stargazing. It was an open stretch of beach, visibly
broadening as the tide retreated. Over to his right was the mouth of a
river – the Grande Riviere du Nord, though it did not look so very grand
from Nathan's present vantage. There were a few fishermen's huts on the
riverside, their boats drawn up on the beach and their nets hung to dry,
but there was no sign of the men themselves. Over to the left the ground
rose steeply to the headland to the east of Le Cap. It was thickly wooded
and there were no houses. The trees came down right to the shore and
he supposed you could hide an army in them if you wished, but it would
have taken Rochambeau some time to organise an army, or even a troop
of horse, in the circumstances. Besides, Nathan was assured he would take
no chances with the life of Napoleon's brother. The only soldiers with
them were Bruski and eight of his Polish guard, as agreed with Rochambeau's aide-de-camp. He had not seen Rochambeau again and hoped he
never would.

He looked at Adedike and smiled reassuringly. As usual she did not look as if she needed reassurance. She looked faintly bored. Dubois was more agitated, gazing about him constantly as if for signs of treachery. Neither of them had been physically harmed, but Dubois was concerned about the rest of his family, especially the two children, who had remained on the *Delaware* when they went into Le Cap. Nathan had tried to set his mind at rest. Imlay would look after them, he said, until they could be reunited. In truth, he had no idea what Imlay would do, not after his clash with Rochambeau, or where he would go.

One of the guards called out something in Polish, pointing out to sea, and Nathan's heart lifted as he saw the *Falaise* – a ship, at any rate and at the right time and place – creeping up along the coast under a full press of sail. She overshot the landing point and continued to the end of the headland where she came about and approached on the starboard tack, close-hauled now as she fought the offshore breeze. Tully had the guns run out on both sides, and he was towing the ship's boats astern, as if for action. There were no other ships in sight, but there was an entire fleet in the Bay of Le Cap and at last some of them must be in a condition to fight. The first glimpse of a sail and Nathan had told Banjo they must run for the open sea, but that would mean leaving the hostages on the shore, and his past experience of Tully did not encourage him to think he would obey a command like that, even if it risked losing the ship.

He suggested they move forward, away from the trees, so they would be more visible from the sea. The tide had retreated since their arrival, leaving a wide stretch of wet sand for them to cross. They were about 200 yards away from the water's edge when Bruski halted them. A moment later, he saw a boat detach itself from the ship and row towards the shore. The most dangerous time now. He stopped himself from looking back towards the tree line and kept his eyes on the boat. On it came. He could hear the splash of the oars now, and the voice of the coxswain. There were two figures in the prow, one of whom was probably Banjo. The figure beside him might be Tully. But Tully should have stayed with the sloop. Who had he left in command – Keppler? The problem with Tully was that whatever rank he held in the King's navy he would always be a smuggler at heart, and a Guernsey smuggler, which was the worst kind for indiscipline and independence of mind, though the Cornish were pretty bad.

He was rambling in his head, more nervous than he had been in a while, even when he was being interrogated by Rochambeau.

He watched as the boat crew shipped their oars and the boat ground gently on the sand. Banjo and his companion were down in the shallows, and another man was making his way forward from the stern. It looked like it could be Jérôme Bonaparte, but in the darkness at this distance it was impossible to be sure and Bruski was not going to take any chances. He spoke to one of his men who left his musket with a comrade and advanced towards the boat. Nathan was very tense now. This was taking far too long. He watched the soldier confer with the figures on the shore and then come back at a stumbling trot. He called out to Bruski as he approached and though he spoke in Polish, Nathan caught the name Bonaparte. Bruski looked at Nathan.

'So, you can go.'

His manner was still stiff and formal, but Nathan stretched out a hand and after a moment, Bruski took it.

'Go well,' he said. 'If we ever meet again, I expect I will have to kill you.'

Nathan had known sweeter partings.

They began to walk towards the sea. A solitary figure was advancing towards them. After a few paces Nathan saw who it was, not that he had been in much doubt, and he obviously recognised Nathan for he raised a hand in salute and grinned. Nathan responded in kind. He had nothing against the lad, but then he remembered what he had said about Rochambeau and how they needed someone that ruthless in command. He was a Bonaparte, after all. They passed at a distance of about ten yards and continued walking in opposite directions. Nathan did not look back.

They were about fifty strides from the sea, and he could see their faces now in the moonlight – Tully and Banjo, as he had supposed. For one brief moment – that treacherous optimism again – he thought it was going to be all right. Then there was a sudden shout from the boat. One of the crew was pointing over to the right, towards the headland. Nathan looked in the same direction and saw that a group of horsemen had emerged from the trees at the far end of the beach. He did not wait for them to reveal their intent.

'Run!' he shouted, urging the others on ahead of him, though in truth they did not need much encouragement. But it was heavy going on the wet sand. Dubois stumbled and fell, and they had to help him up. Tully and Banjo were running towards them, but then they knelt, aiming their muskets. Nathan snatched a glance towards the headland. The horsemen had fanned out and were charging along the edge of the sea towards them. At least a score of them, regular French cavalry – *cuirassiers* – the moon-light gleaming on their breastplates. They were no more than a cable's length away and closing fast. Banjo fired, then Tully. Nathan stopped behind them waving the others on towards the boat. Some of the crew had jumped down into the water and were running towards them. Banjo fired again and Nathan realised they were using the Ferguson rifles. Tully was struggling with the trigger guard, trying to work the screw, and Nathan longed to snatch it from him, but he just stood there, uselessly, sword in hand. It was more like thirty than twenty riders, but the soft sand was slowing them down. One horse went over, bringing another with it, horse and rider, and now the men from the boat had reached them and were levelling their guns. All rifles. He supposed he must thank George Banjo for that and hoped it would be a thanks and not a curse. He remembered the armourer's morose comment: '*I wonder how long that screw would last in a proper ruckus.*' A man after his own miserable heart. But they were firing again and again. Nine shots a minute, Gabriel claimed. Nathan did not keep a count, but it was impressive. Half a dozen riders were down, and they were pulling away now to the higher ground. But then four or five of them broke to the left, heading to cut off Dubois and Adedike at the water's edge. Nathan ran towards them, but it was heavy going. He was still twenty yards away when there was a volley from the boat. Two of the troopers went down but there were two more and they were coming on, sabres drawn, splashing through the shallows at the water's edge. He saw Adedike pulling Dubois towards the far side of the launch. Then there was another fusillade at point blank range and another of the *cuirassiers* went down. The last of them decided he had had enough and wheeled his horse around and rode at Nathan instead.

Nathan took a moment to think about it, sword in hand. Fight or flight? But he had not been trained to fight cavalry on foot. He ran as fast as he could back towards the men on the shore. He saw Banjo turn towards him, the rifle held across his chest, working the trigger guard. He swore he could feel the horse's breath on his neck, he could hear it for sure. Then the rifle was at Banjo's shoulder and he fired. When Nathan reached him and looked back, the horse was on a different tack and the rider lying in the sand. He could not remember which of his own lives that was, but he must be well past the nine.

There were riderless horses everywhere, but at least a dozen men still in the saddle and they were firing back now with pistols or carbines and he saw two of his own men go down. He snatched up one of the rifles and knelt by the body scrabbling for powder and shot. Then suddenly Jérôme was there, running into the gap between the two sides, calling out the magic name of Bonaparte. *I am Jérôme Bonaparte and I order you to cease fire!* You had to hand it to him for nerve – he could not see Prince George doing that, or any of his brothers – but if he died now, they all would. Bruski and his men came running up and formed a square around him, in as much as eight infantrymen and an officer can form a square. Their bayonets were extended towards both parties.

Nathan told his own men to cease fire. They had lost one dead, shot through the head, another wounded in the arm, but he could walk as far as the boat. Dubois and Adedike were stowed in the stern, Tully took his place at the tiller and Nathan and Banjo shoved the launch off the beach and then scrambled aboard. Nathan was still struggling to find his oar when he heard Tully's command of 'Back water' and he gave up and sat for a moment catching his breath as they backed off from the shore.

'Starboard side hold water!'

As the launch swung round to face the open sea, Nathan gazed back towards the shambles they had made of the shore. The dark humps of the dead and wounded, Jan's guards moving among them, the riderless mounts, the survivors riding for the trees. He could not pick out either Bruski or Bonaparte, but he raised his hand in a salute that was both thanks and farewell.

There was no acknowledgement from the shore, but he supposed this little incident came close to levelling the score, so far as he and the Bonapartes were concerned.

He reached again for his oar as he heard Tully's final command: 'Together, row!'

26

The Fate of Até

Ship's log. Falaise. October 29th, 1802. Friday. Course NNW. Wind SWbS. Lat 22.12N Long 76.17W. Light breeze and good visibility with slight haze and swell as before. Studding sails set aloft and alow.

'*And God is in his Heaven and all is Right with the World,*' Nathan was tempted to add to the log as he gazed out from the quarterdeck of the *Falaise* upon a sparkling sea, a clear sky and a string of small islands, named on the chart as the Ragged Isles, emerging from the slight haze on his starboard bow. But while this might reflect his own mood, unusually, at this particular moment in time, it was not true of the world in general. Saint-Domingue had become a Hell on earth and was likely to remain so for some considerable length of time, he thought, and though he had not contributed personally to its distress, or at least not much, he had done precious little to make things any better. He consoled himself with the thought that he had at least been able to rescue Dubois and Adedike from the shambles, though they were very anxious for the fate of the rest of their family, especially the two children.

It was for this reason that Nathan had set his present course, up through the Old Bahamas Channel towards the British port of Nassau on the island of New Providence, for this was where Imlay had stopped on his way to Saint-Domingue and where he clearly had contacts. However, in his less sanguine moments, which were plentiful, Nathan knew that Imlay could be anywhere in the Caribbean – or anywhere at all. He might be halfway across the Atlantic by now on his way to England, to get his story in before Nathan did, and further prejudice the views of the Earl Saint Vincent.

Nathan was still confused about what had happened in the Gulf of Gonâve. Someone had betrayed them for sure, but it need not necessarily have been Imlay. Indeed, what possible reason might he have for doing so? He would lose his own ship and the munitions he had invested in, and to no purpose, or at least no purpose that Nathan could discern. Unless he was in the pay of the French, of course, in which case all bets were off. It would not be the first time. But it would be devious even by Imlay's conniving standards, and even self-defeating for his treachery would have been apparent to his superiors in Washington. Besides, he must have known for some time that the French bid to restore order to the colony was doomed, and that if he wished to make a trade deal, he would be a lot better off negotiating with the rebels.

But you could spend a lifetime puzzling over Imlay's motives and be none the wiser. Nathan tried to put him out of his mind and recapture his earlier content. He leaned back the better to contemplate the immense spread of canvas the *Falaise* had been able to spread. As the log recorded, they had been able to set stuns'ls on both fore and main, the wind being favourable for this rare indulgence – as rare, in fact, as the sense of well-being that had come over him. He wondered how the sloop would appear to any watchers from the islands off her starboard bow and the image of a swan came to mind, cruising serenely along a river with wing feathers fluffed out to achieve maximum effect. This was unusually whimsical of him, but there were several reasons for his uncommonly good mood. It was the first time he could remember that he had commanded a ship without having to answer to some remote but absolute authority, whether it was the Admiralty or the East India Company. He had made a number of decisions for himself and though he had recorded them in his journal, he had ensured there was no reference to them in the ship's log.

He had first put the Frenchmen ashore on the coast a few miles west of Le Cap and then the Africans on La Tortue, where Dubois had assured him they would be as safe as anywhere. Then he had decided on the trip to Nassau, though he was perfectly aware it could be a waste of time. If

Imlay had not landed his passengers on the island he would have to think again, though he had half made up his mind to land Dubois and Adedike there anyway, with sufficient funds to make their own enquiries, even if it meant a journey to Washington. It appeared that they had no desire to return to Saint-Domingue in the foreseeable future, Dessalines being almost as unpalatable to them as Rochambeau.

On a more personal note, Nathan had begun to forgive himself for his liaison with Pauline Bonaparte – a name he preferred, for obvious reasons, to Madame Leclerc. Though he was aware of the charge of hypocrisy, he had said many a silent prayer for the recovery of her husband from his present affliction, and her own future happiness.

That apart, he was inclined in his present mood to pass off what had happened on the island of Tortuga as an interlude, as out of character for him as the several months' idleness that accompanied it, a temporary sojourn in the Garden of Eden before the serpent struck. The line he had decided to take, should he be challenged on the issue, in this world or the next, was that two lonely people had been drawn together by force of circumstance and the strength of their own passionate natures (he had not before now conceded that he had a passionate nature, far from it in fact), and had been lulled into a treacherous hedonism by the seductive airs of the beautiful and mysterious island on which they had been stranded (with due acknowledgement to Shakespeare). Also, he reflected, he had been genuinely in love with the woman, and she with him. *Love as an ecstatic, overpowering force that supersedes all other values, loyalties and emotions.* Where had he heard that? His mother again, probably, referring to another Shakespearian play though he could not for the moment recall which one.

But he was wandering again. He must draw a line through the episode. Pauline Bonaparte. The end. But he missed her, and not just physically. He very much admired her spirit as well as her body. They had enjoyed a rare rapport. Though it was as well that it had come to an end when it did.

He was shaken from these philosophical reflections by the trill of the boatswain's pipe, reminding him that it was time for the midday issue of grog. And here was Kidd, shimmering up in his usual fashion to announce that his own superior version – which, whatever he might say to the contrary, differed only from that served to the rest of the crew in the addition of an egg-white and a small grating of nutmeg – was ready to be served in the stern cabin.

'Ask Monsieur Dubois and Madame Delatour if they would care to join me,' he instructed the steward. He caught Tully's eye and with a slight jerk of the head included him in the invitation.

'To Freedom,' he announced, thinking it was probably more appropriate to the present company than 'the King'.

But Dubois was frowning. He drank to the toast, but the frown remained.

'I wonder shall we ever see it?' he mused. 'Not in Saint-Domingue, I think, not in my day.'

Nathan regarded him with sympathy. It was rare for him to be with someone in a more negative mood than himself, but this appeared to be the present case.

'I know things are bad,' he remarked, 'but I do believe there are grounds for optimism.' Tully looked startled. 'The French are finished in Saint-Domingue. What we are seeing is the enraged savagery of the tiger when it knows it is fatally wounded.'

'Oh, I would not dispute that,' said Dubois, 'but I do not believe it will bring freedom. Not under Dessalines.'

Dubois had a poor opinion of the new rebel leader.

'I can understand his policy of tit-for-tat,' he said. 'Hanging a French prisoner for every one of ours they kill – at least it demonstrates that our lives matter as much as theirs – but I fear that when the war is won, he will turn on his own people.'

Dubois believed that Dessalines was personally inclined to tyranny and capable of great brutality. But you could say that of most rulers, Nathan thought. King George was more benign, but then he was not always sane.

'Did you discuss your proposals with him?' he asked.

'What proposals are these?'

'To work the plantations with free labour.'

Dubois smiled, though not with humour. 'I did not. Dessalines does not believe in free labour. And he would consider the notion of giving workers a share in the profits laughable.'

'And when he had stopped laughing, he would feed you to the crocodiles,' said Adedike.

'It is rather a radical proposal,' Tully pointed out mildly. 'Though feeding you to the crocodiles does seem excessive.'

'You do things differently in England?' Adedike was smiling but Nathan noted the edge to her tone and tried to catch Tully's eye.

'Yes, if only because there are no crocodiles, though there is always Botany Bay,' reflected Tully. 'However, perhaps it would be advisable to take one step at a time. Free labour is a big advance on slavery, surely.'

'Have you ever worked on a sugar plantation?' Adedike asked him.

Tully confessed he had not.

'Nor would you want to,' she said. 'That is why they brought slaves here in the first place.'

'All I am saying is that you can see why your proposals might be met with some reservations,' Tully persisted.

'And yet you were prepared to discuss them with the French,' Nathan put in, if only to change the subject. It had been drummed into him at an early age that there should be no discussion of politics, religion or sexual relations when food was on the table, or drink. The conversation often became boring, but it avoided duels. (He was privately rather puzzled by this ruling, for it was rare that he did not think a duel would be infinitely preferable to the conversation.)

Dubois sighed. 'Only at Imlay's urging, because he said they might consider it, if only to get out of the mess they are in.'

'How could he have known that?' Nathan frowned. 'He had only just returned to the colony – and then only to La Tortue.' He caught the look between his two guests. 'Or have I missed something?'

'Imlay had discussions with French officials in Nassau,' Dubois told him. 'That is when he decided to betray me to Rochambeau.'

'You think he betrayed you?'

'I know he did,' Dubois said quietly. 'Rochambeau as good as told me so. Imlay does not believe in free labour on Saint-Domingue, any more than Dessalines does.'

Nathan was still puzzled. 'I do not understand. Why would it bother him?'

'Because if it should prove a success, think of the example it would give to others. What an inspiration to the cause of abolition! And think how it would be regarded in the slave states of America. Or in Washington where Jefferson depends on their votes to stay in office.'

Nathan could follow the reasoning. He was not sure he agreed with the conclusion.

'So, you think when he took you into Le Cap . . .'

'He knew that Leclerc would have me arrested, and very likely deported to France to join Toussaint in whatever prison he is rotting. He may not have known that Leclerc was dying, and that Rochambeau had a different means of disposing of human life, but that is scarcely a point in his favour.'

'I find it hard to believe that Imlay would be so devious,' said Nathan. Did he? After all he knew of Imlay? 'At least – I do not think he would betray you personally.'

'He betrayed *you.*' It was the first time Adedike had spoken. 'Why not us?'

'I do not know that he betrayed me.' Nathan admitted cautiously.

'But *we* do.'

'Adedike . . .' Dubois glared at her fiercely.

'He deserves to know,' she retorted. 'Imlay has always planned to betray you,' she said to Nathan. 'Right from the start of this, before he went to England. He told us when he first came to Le Cap and met Toussaint, that the only way to save us from the French, and stop them from moving into North America, was to provoke another war between France and England. Everything he has done since then was to bring that about, mainly by convincing them that the English were supplying us with weapons and support – despite their agreement with Bonaparte.'

'Is that true?' Nathan turned on Dubois. He said nothing but the look on his face was enough.

Later, when he was alone, Nathan inspected the desk that had been Imlay's when the cabin had been divided between them. It was over by the quarter-gallery, in the light of the stern windows. He had considered it several times since they had left Saint-Domingue, but some lingering sense of honour had prevented him from investigating its contents.

Besides, he did not for a moment think that Imlay would have left anything of value there, or interest. The drawers were locked but he opened
them easily enough with the blade of a knife. There were some receipts,
some paper money in several different currencies and a lot of paperwork.
He sat down and went through the papers. It did not take him long to
find some things that were very interesting indeed. So interesting, in fact,
that he concluded they had been left there with the deliberate intention
of someone finding them, though probably not him.

The first was a legal document – a transfer of ownership of the sloop
Falaise – 'with all the equipment, stores and consumables on the attached
inventory' – from the North Atlantic Trading and Shipping Company to
Captain Nathan Peake of His Britannic Majesty's Navy. Signed Gilbert
Imlay, director general.

The second was a receipt made out to the same Captain N. Peake
for 1,000 Spanish M1752 muskets, 100,000 rounds of ammunition and
2,000 lbs of gunpowder. It bore the distinctive signature of Toussaint
Louverture – a long, elegant curve on the last e, and four dots.

The third was on the notepaper of the British Admiralty and addressed
to 'whomsoever it may concern', advising that Captain Nathan Peake
of the sloop *Falaise* was in the service of HM Government and, in the
familiar phrase, 'requesting and requiring' whatever assistance might be
necessary to aid him in the completion of his duties in the Caribbean. It
was dated 26 March 1802, and signed 'Saint-Vincent'.

There was an almost identical instruction to HM Dockyard in Nassau,
'requiring and requesting' prompt attention in the way of repairs, stores
and other equipment, the reckoning to be forwarded to the British Admiralty in Whitehall.

Nathan sat contemplating these documents for some time as the motes
of dust circled in the light of the stern windows and the reflections of the
water danced on the underside of the deck above his head. Then he sent
for Tully.

'This is presumably why the *Guerriere* did not blow us out of the water,'
he said when Tully had read them. 'They were after the evidence, and
here it is.'

Tully was philosophical.

'Well, you are now the proud owner of a ship of war,' he said. 'And a
quantity of munitions.'

'You think I can get away with that?'

'I think it would be hard for Captain Imlay to dispute it. Or to bring a case in an English court.'

This was true.

'But what am I going to do with her?'

'Sail her to England?'

Nathan thought about it but did not come up with a better idea. Besides, according to Imlay, the crew had signed on in this expectation. He understood now why he had secured an overwhelmingly English crew.

But there was something else he had to do first. He summoned the carpenter to his cabin.

'Mr Penn,' Nathan greeted him with a benevolent smile designed, but failing to put him entirely at his ease. 'I want you to remove our friend the Goddess of Strife and Folly.'

The carpenter's eyes wandered a little from the centre. 'Pardon me, sir.'

'Até, sir, the daughter of Zeus, the curse of mankind.'

The carpenter appeared less than enlightened.

'The ship's figurehead, Mr Penn, the mad-eyed creature that adorns, or not as the case may be, our prow.'

'When you say "remove", sir . . . ?'

'Cut her off, sir, raze her, dissever her, amputate her at the roots.'

'You are serious, sir?'

'Whenever am I not, Mr Penn?'

There had in fact been frequent occasions, and the crew very likely talked about them, but the carpenter was not the man to mention this.

'Get out your saw out, sir, and saw away. Use a sling from the bowsprit, or lean over from the heads, or get one of your lads to do it. I leave the details to you.'

'But what am I to do with her, sir, when I have removed her?'

'Drop her in the water, sir, and let her sink.' But then, as the carpenter backed towards the cabin door . . . 'Wait! Let me know when you are nearly there. No! Secure her with ropes and I will finish her off with an axe.' He raised his voice: 'Kidd there! Fetch me an axe!' And in a gentler voice to the carpenter: 'Thank you, Mr Penn, you may go.'

Despite his bemusement, the carpenter executed the job with his usual speed and precision. Nathan had the boatswain pipe the crew to quarters and announced what he was about to do and why. He did not want them to think he had gone mad. Then he took the axe procured by his steward and advanced forward. He looked down over the prow.

The goddess was leaning towards the sea at a slightly greater angle than before, with a length of messenger cable looped around her neck. The other end was attached to one of the knightheads. The axe, Nathan saw, was not practical; the rope was not sufficiently tense. He begged the loan of Mr Penn's saw. Mr Penn parted with it reluctantly. The cable parted soon after. There was a large splash and a half-hearted cheer as Até hit the water. Most of the crew, he thought, were rather more bemused than delighted. But a half-hearted cheer was better than none.

Nathan gave the saw back to the carpenter.

'Thank you, Mr Penn,' he said. 'A good day's business.'

They reached Nassau early in the morning of 1 November, All Saints' Day – which happened to be Toussaint Louverture's birthday, according to Dubois – and anchored off Paradise Island while Nathan considered his line of approach. There were several issues for him to consider, none of them as difficult as those he had encountered recently in Saint-Domingue, but still worthy of some careful thought.

One problem was that having cut her cable in the Gulf of Gonâve, the *Falaise* was now down to one anchor and liable to swing at her mooring, to the detriment of herself and other shipping in the crowded harbour. Another was Imlay's assertion that the *Falaise* had stopped at Nassau on her voyage out to Saint-Domingue. If this were true, and there was no particular reason to doubt it, then Imlay would have informed the authorities of his eventual destination. It was important that Nathan should come up with something consistent with this, whatever it was, all the more so as the orlop deck was still full of munitions and he did not wish to invite an inspection by His Majesty's Customs. Then there was the question of the Dubois family. If they had been dropped off at Nassau, then all well and good; if not, Dubois would have to pursue Imlay through the courts – on a charge, presumably, of kidnap. As the *Delaware* was an American vessel, it would probably have to be the American courts, but a formal complaint could be lodged with the U.S. consul here in Nassau.

The first thing, however, was to report to the harbourmaster. He told Tully he was going ashore in the gig.

'Back already?' the harbourmaster remarked. 'We do not seem to be able to get rid of you people.'

Nathan gathered that he meant Americans. Nassau was largely populated by loyalists who had fled the states after the Independence War. The harbourmaster – a retired naval lieutenant with a peg leg by the name of Havelock – was clearly one of them. He remembered the *Falaise* from her last visit.

'So, did you complete your business in Cap-Francais?' he enquired.

This was helpful. In fact, Nathan had already guessed that Imlay would have introduced himself as the U.S. envoy to Saint-Domingue and said that he was bound for Saint-Domingue. It made sense for him to do so and would account for his conversation with a British naval officer about the situation in the colony.

'I did,' said Nathan. 'We delivered Captain Imlay safely and are now on our way back to Boston.' He mentioned his problem with the second anchor.

'Well, you had better stay out in the Roads,' said the harbourmaster. 'Will you be here long?'

'Probably not,' said Nathan, 'but I have some enquiries to make in the town.'

He asked if a ship called the *Delaware* had stopped by in the last few days.

'Indeed,' said the lieutenant. He consulted his records. 'That would be Captain Lowell. Bound for Alexandria with despatches for the United States government.' He gave Nathan a look. 'You gentlemen are very active in these parts.'

There was a question in his tone.

'The French make a lot of work for us, I am afraid,' confided Nathan. 'I know Captain Lowell very well, of course, but tell me, did he drop off any passengers whilst he was here.'

'I believe he did. A family of blacks. Free people of colour, as he described them. A man, a woman and two children. Refugees, he said, from the troubles in Saint-Domingue.'

Nathan restrained himself from throwing his hat in the air. It had been a very long shot and it was gratifying to know he had pulled it off.

'Do you happen to know where they are lodged?' he enquired.

But Mr Havelock had no idea. He advised Nathan to enquire at Government House on Mount Fitzwilliam.

Two hours later, after a frustrating but eventually fruitful visit to the governor's residence, Nathan stood outside a rundown boarding house on the Strand. He was about to knock on the front door when two young children came hurtling around the corner of the building pursued by an elderly black man with a broom. Nathan moved to block their flight and addressed them in French.

'Maître et Mademoiselle Dubois, je suppose?' He nodded to the man with the broom to indicate that he would take care of this. 'So, what have you two been up to?'

They observed him guardedly. 'It was my sister,' said the boy. 'Nothing to do with me.'

The door opened and a woman appeared, looking fraught.

'*Qu'ont-ils fait maintenant?*' she demanded. *What have they done this time?*

When Nathan had delivered his news, he engaged a fiacre to convey the family to the harbour where he handed them over to the care of the boat crew. But before he left, he had one more call to make.

His Majesty's Dockyard at Nassau was not a grand establishment. The harbour was too shallow for ships of the line and since the peace with France it was unusual for even a sloop of war to stop by.

'I do not know what you are expecting of me,' said the superintendent, examining the note from the Earl Saint Vincent with a dubious air, as well he might. 'But we have very little in the way of stores or equipment and our repair facilities are extremely limited.' This was no more than Nathan had anticipated. It was the same story in most Royal Navy dockyards from Chatham to Kingston, Jamaica, but possibly truer of this one than others. 'What is it you require?'

Nathan told him.

'An anchor?' The superintendent frowned. 'That is an odd item to lose.'

Nathan refrained from asking him where he had been the last few years. It was obvious. He had been in New Providence.

'It was necessary to cut the cable,' he said, 'when a hurricane came upon us, unexpectedly.'

The superintendent, whose name was Mr Percy, observed him warily, as if he knew he was being made game of, but Nathan kept his expression perfectly bland.

Mr Percy exposed the document to further scrutiny but found nothing he might object to, or at least no words to express it. 'Well, I expect we can let you have a small fluke,' he said. 'If you pick it up yourself. Nothing else?'

'I do not suppose you have such a thing as a figurehead,' said Nathan, chancing his luck.

Mr Percy took a step back. 'And how did you contrive to lose that, young man? But no, do not tell me.'

'It is not essential, of course,' said Nathan, 'but I thought, as I was here . . .'

'Well, we do not have a great demand for figureheads,' said Mr Percy, 'but as it happens my predecessor made something of a collection of them, from ships that had been broken up.'

He led Nathan to a corner of the yard.

'Take your pick,' he invited him.

There were six of them – four female, one male, possibly Neptune, and one mythical beast, possibly a griffin. Nathan walked down the line and then walked back. He stopped beside one of the females.

'Do you know who this is?' he enquired.

'I do not,' said Mr Percy. 'Do you?'

'I was wondering if you knew what ship she came off.'

'I do not know that either and I do not suppose a record was kept. My predecessor only kept them, I think, for decoration. He was of a whimsical nature.'

Nathan looked at her again. She was quite young with dark hair, and wore a faded yellow shift, not quite exposing her breasts. There were no other distinguishing features, or clue to her identity, but though it was by no means an accurate likeness, there was something about her, particularly her sad, rather whimsical smile that reminded him of Pauline Bonaparte. In a certain mood.

He experienced a momentary doubt but no, it would be a gesture of respect, he thought, for a beautiful and remarkable woman.

'I'll take this one,' he said.

Epilogue

At eleven o'clock on the morning of 1 November 1802, as Captain Nathan Peake was pursuing his enquiries in Nassau, Madame Pauline Leclerc, née Bonaparte, was led from the room where her husband General Charles Victoire Leclerc, governor general of Saint-Domingue, had just died from yellow fever.

A week later the widow returned to France aboard the frigate *Swiftsure*, taking the embalmed corpse of her husband with her in a lead coffin. Under his head was a cushion of her hair which she had cut off in the extremes of her grief.

The blond Bonaparte was succeeded as supreme commander in Saint-Domingue by General Rochambeau, who continued with his experiment of using starving dogs and poison gas as a means of execution. Far from acting as a deterrent, however, it strengthened the resolve of the rebels and brought them many thousands of new recruits, including several hundred soldiers of the Polish Legion. On 18 November 1803, Rochambeau and his remaining forces were defeated by the rebel army at the Battle of Vertières in the hills above Le Cap. A few weeks later the last French forces left the colony which became an independent Republic under the name Haiti.

Toussaint Louverture did not live to witness the birth of the new nation. On his arrival in France he was imprisoned in the remote fortress prison of Fort de Joux in the Jura Mountains, where he died, probably of pneumonia, in April 1803.

The defeat in Saint-Domingue shattered Bonaparte's dream of a new French empire in North America. On Sunday, 10 April 1803, he instructed his finance minister Monsieur Marbois to offer the entire territory to the United States. The price agreed was fifteen million dollars – twice the annual federal budget at the time.

After signing the accession treaty, which became known as the Louisiana Purchase, the U.S. envoy Robert Livingston declared: 'This is the noblest work of our whole lives . . . From this day, the United States take their place among the powers of the first rank.'

He was right. At a stroke of the pen, it almost doubled the size of the new nation and led to the creation of fifteen new American states.

Bonaparte told his foreign minister Talleyrand: 'I know the price of what I abandon. I renounce it with the greatest regret; but to attempt obstinately to retain it would be folly.'

But he was reasonably satisfied with the deal that was struck. France controlled only a small fraction of the territory, which was almost entirely inhabited by native Americans, and it freed him to focus upon his next and most desired project – the invasion and conquest of Great Britain.

The Sea of Silence: Fact and Fiction

I usually like to know the difference between fact and fiction in a historical novel, so in the assumption that many readers feel the same way, I'll
try to help distinguish between the two, at least so far as this novel is
concerned.

Where to start? Perhaps chronologically with Gilbert Imlay, who plays
an ambiguous role throughout the Nathan Peake series, though mostly
as villain. He was a real-life character and most of what I have written
about his background is true – in so far as we know. He began his career
as an officer in the rebel army during the American War of Independence
and later became part of a select band of secret agents working for General Washington, a kind of pioneer CIA known as 'Washington's Boys'.
There is no evidence that he continued in this role under President Jefferson or that he was involved in the supply of guns to the Haitian rebels,
or the events leading to the Louisiana Purchase. However, it is interesting
that in the Paris Archives des Affaires Etrangeres, Louisiana et Florides,
1792–1803, there are two documents entitled 'Observations du Capitaine Imlay' and 'Memoire sur la Louisiane' relating Imlay's plans for the
French invasion and conquest of Spanish Louisiana and New Orleans.

The balloonist André-Jacques Garnerin is another historical character. He was the Official Aeronaut of France and the inventor of the fra-
meless parachute. His student Jeanne Geneviève Labrosse, who he later
married, was also a balloonist and the first woman to make a parachute

jump – from a height of 900 metres. They toured England in 1802 to demonstrate their skills, but it was probably not as early in the year as I have said.

Nelson's sojourn at Merton House with Emma Hamilton and her husband Sir William is true, of course – there has been plenty written about that already – and so is the story of Nelson's visit to the undertaker's. After the French flagship *L'Orient* blew up at the Battle of the Nile, one of Nelson's captains thought it would make a nice coffin for him, and Nelson became quite attached to it, having it upholstered at an undertakers in Lambs Conduit Street, though again this happened later than in the book, just before he died at Trafalgar.

The French expedition to Saint-Domingue and Bonaparte's plans to occupy a large part of North America are matters of historical record. I haven't changed any of the essential details, such as the number of ships and troops, or the campaign itself. There are contemporary accounts of atrocities on both sides. The use of poison gas as a form of execution by the French was first reported by Antoine Méral in his 1825 history of the expedition. A more common way of disposing of rebel prisoners was to simply take them out to sea and throw them overboard, which led to protests by a number of ship's officers. The use of dogs has been documented by Philippe Girard in his more recent paper: *War unleashed: The Use of War Dogs During the Haitian War of Independence*, published in *Napoleonica La Revue* Volume 15, Issue 3, 2012, pages 80 to 105. A long list of citations, references and eye-witness accounts can be found in an online article by the same author entitled *French Atrocities During the Haitian War of Independence*.

It is also a matter of historical record that British and American ships ran guns to the rebels, though there is no record of any government involvement.

Napoleon's youngest brother Jérôme was an officer cadet in the French navy and he did serve with the fleet sent to Saint-Domingue, though the episode where his ship is blown up is fiction. He left the colony in 1803 to travel to the United States, where he met and married an American woman, though the marriage was later annulled on the orders of Napoleon and he became the King of Westphalia. The Bonapartes led an active life.

Which brings me to Pauline. It's true that she was more or less dragooned into marriage by the family after what they considered to be her ill-advised engagement to Stanislaus Fréron who was twenty-five years older than she, but she seemed to have been reasonably content with their choice of General Leclerc. She accompanied him on the expedition to Saint-Domingue and played an active role in creating a menagerie and a botanical garden on the island, even with a war going on. However, the deteriorating military situation and the death of Leclerc prevented the project from being completed. There were plenty of rumours about her taking lovers among her husband's soldiers, but they may have been invented, or at least exaggerated by the British and the French royalists to discredit her – and the Bonapartes generally. She returned to France with her husband's body but was married again within a year to a Roman nobleman, Don Camillo Borghese, Prince of Sulmona and Rossano. It was not a happy marriage; he had a mistress and she may well have had lovers, but it is always difficult to know the truth of these things. She rather liked being the subject of scandal, and scandal was certainly attracted to her. I think it's worth mentioning that she was the only one of Napoleon's brothers and sisters to visit him in his exile on Elba and that she liquidated most of her assets to help finance a comeback. But that all ended at Waterloo.

On the subject of battles, a quick note on weaponry. I've used two weapons as game changers – the French naval guns known as *obusiers de vaisseau* and the British Ferguson rifle. I didn't make them up – they were real-life weapons – but for various reasons they were not favoured by the naval and military authorities of the time.

The *obusier* was the French answer to the British carronade – made by the Carron company in Scotland – which was a relatively lightweight but heavy calibre navy gun that could be devastating at short range. The *obusier* looked more like a mortar and was designed to fire an explosive shell. However, it was difficult to get the timing right and after a few accidents when the shells went off in the muzzle, or shortly after emerging from it, the French gave them up as a bad job. There were very few in action by 1802 and they were mostly used to fire a solid iron cannonball. In the war that was coming the French navy used a gun much more like the carronade.

The Ferguson rifle was the British answer to the American long rifle – which was to prove so effective in the Independence War. The long rifle – also known as the Kentucky or Pennsylvania rifle – was based on the German jaeger or hunting rifle and popularised in America by German gunsmiths who emigrated there in the eighteenth century. The long, rifled barrel made for great accuracy, but it took a long time to reload – one or at most two rounds a minute. This was because it was a muzzle loader and you had to force the bullet down the barrel using a ramrod, sometimes with a hammer. Difficult when the enemy was charging at you, though at short range it was not unknown for the rifleman to fire the ramrod, with effective results.

The British used the Brown Bess musket. This was notoriously inaccurate, but a British infantryman was trained to fire three or four shots a minute, and it was lethal when firing massed volleys at up to 300 yards range. It was also very effective with a bayonet. So, you tended to see the British win in a pitched battle when the armies were out in the open, as they usually were on European battlefields, and the Americans winning when they could pick the Redcoats off at long range from cover, and had time to reload. The terrain in North America lent itself to this form of conflict.

In 1776, just after the start of the American war, Major Patrick Ferguson patented his own design of a breech-loading flintlock rifle, which he claimed could fire up to ten rounds a minute. The guns were first used at the Battle of Brandywine, which the British won, but Major Ferguson was wounded and while he was recuperating, his experimental rifle unit was disbanded, without explanation. It is possible that the British high command thought the guns were too expensive and took too long to produce. Also, they tended to break down too easily in combat – the wooden stock tended to splinter close to the firing lock. But this could probably have been put right if the British had persisted with them. The surviving Fergusons have a horseshoe-shaped piece of iron under the lock, and modern reproductions seem to work well enough.

The French army had rifles, too, but Napoleon didn't like them because of the time spent in reloading and they were not used at all after 1807. Probably the most successful rifle during the Napoleonic Wars was the British Baker rifle produced from 1800 and used by specialised regiments such as the 95th Rifles – the regiment of Richard Sharpe. But despite the impression you might get from watching the TV series, the maximum rate of fire even by a highly trained rifleman was two or three rounds a minute and the barrels easily became fouled up by gunpowder.

On the whole, rifles did not become truly effective as combat weapons until the invention of the expanding Minié bullet which proved so decisive in the Crimean War and the War between the States.

And finally – the bells. I don't know if the bells rang when Le Cap burned. But they rang in my home city of Liverpool during the Blitz of May 1941, when the city was attacked by massed air raids. The raids were so intense that one night the whole of the city centre and the docks seemed to be on fire. The church of Saint Luke's was one of those hit by incendiaries and the hot air from the blaze rushed up the bell tower and moved the bells as effectively as any bellringer. So, the firefighters, who couldn't get near the place, were astonished to hear the bells ringing amidst the inferno for at least a minute before the fire burned through the wooden beams holding them and they crashed to the ground.

So, I reckoned that if this happened in Liverpool, it could happen in Haiti.

Seth Hunter, October 2020

Acknowledgements

When I was asked to write the first book in this series, *The Time of Terror*, I was more than a little reluctant because I was such a great admirer of Patrick O'Brian, and I knew I could never approach his level of genius. However, I was encouraged by my publishers, Martin Fletcher, at Headline in the UK, and Alex Skutt at McBooks in the United States, to at least have a go. Because they were such fans of O'Brian themselves, they acted as mentors, even as guardians of the genre, ensuring that I did the hard work necessary to avoid one of O'Brian's famous rebukes, even from beyond the grave (though I may not have succeeded entirely in this). So, this is to thank them for that, because whatever my continuing reservations, it has been a great adventure working on the series, doing the research, visiting many of the locations and working out some of the nautical detail on my own boat *Papagena* and on one of the square-riggers belonging to Square Sail off the coast of Cornwall. More particularly, I would like to thank George Jepson, who became editorial director of McBooks in 2019 and inspired me to write *The Sea of Silence*. Until then I had meant to end the series in 1800, where Patrick O'Brian began. George, too, is an ardent admirer of O'Brian and other writers in this genre and I feel his presence at my shoulder as I am writing, ensuring that I don't skip on the research or reveal a nautical ignorance for which Stephen Maturin was famed. So, in many ways, this has been a team effort that chiefly involves these three but also my agent Bill Hamilton at A M Heath whose enthusiastic response to my original proposal did far more than he may imagine to keep me slogging away at the words that lay ahead; the people at Rowman & Littlefield who are doing so much to keep this particular genre thriving, and Sathya Shree Kumar and her production team at Apex. For nautical advice my thanks to John Taylor, who crews a Cornish pilot gig and put me right on some of the detail for the night landing in Chapter 25, and finally to Geoffrey Huband, who painted the picture on the cover, a copy of which I had on the wall of my study to inspire me through the grim days of the Covid pandemic when I could not do the research or the writing on location, as I usually do. Even during the black dog days which every writer knows and the blank screen of the computer is like the evil eye of some ruthless tyrant, I had only to glance at that picture to recall the nautical adventures that first enthralled me as a schoolboy – Treasure Island in particular, but also the books of Melville and Marryat, Conrad, Forester and Alexander Kent – and to knuckle down to writing words that at least did not disgrace the promise of that cover.